The U.S. LEADERSHIP PROGRAM

NICHOLAS LICAUSI

INKS&
BINDINGS

Inks and Bindings
888-290-5218
www.inksandbindings.com
orders@inksandbindings.com

Contents

Dedication

This book is dedicated to my late wife, daughter, and son. My son and I deeply miss them, but we find comfort in knowing they continue guiding us while they are in heaven.

I strongly believe that excess deaths can be prevented, along with the other technological changes that are in the projects of this book, would help improve the world if we make better use of these technologies and make them more easily available. Furthermore, improved utilization of technology has the potential to enhance the quality of life for everyone. Although this book is a work of fiction, its ideas, if implemented, can significantly improve the world.

This book is part of a series that combines fiction with solutions to contemporary global issues. It presents a method for improving global health through the application of technology and demonstrates how technology can address other world problems as well. Hopefully, someone in a position of influence, particularly in the United States, will read this book and take action to initiate projects of this nature.

Foreword

After the loss of my daughter, I wrote a book called "*The Medical Project*" as a means of diverting my mind from the pain my wife and I were enduring. I am motivated to write this book due to the positive reception of my previous works, namely "*The Medical Project*" and "*Self-Help and Mental Health Path to Wellness,*" which inspired me to write this book. Additionally, the lack of progress in the medical industry in harnessing the available computing power, along with other global issues that could benefit from computer technology, compelled me to undertake these projects.

While the book is fictional, it contains numerous ideas that have the potential to address various problems prevalent in our society if implemented. Given the interest in adapting the first book into a movie, I decided that it would not be prudent to write a second and third book in anticipation of a potential series.

Now that I have retired from my positions as an engineer, programmer, manager, and executive in several large companies, I have decided to pursue writing. It allows me to explore ideas aimed at improving the world, promoting positive change. Given the fictional nature of this book, I can envision and bring to life the transformations I believe should occur.

When writing this book, just like in the first one, the ideas flowed effortlessly onto the paper. Additionally, throughout the process of writing all my books, it felt as if I were immersed in the scenes, watching a vivid movie unfold. I made a conscious effort to convey the content in plain English, ensuring accessibility for readers of all backgrounds.

Our hope is that someday, an individual or entity with financial resources, perhaps even the government, will undertake the development of a medical computer as described in these three books. This advanced medical computer would possess the capability to diagnose illnesses, identify optimal treatments, and halt the spread of viruses such as COVID-19. The most challenging aspect for us was the editing process, for which I sought assistance. Nevertheless, the journey of crafting all three books has been immensely enjoyable for me.

Meeting at the White House

I t was a cool, clear Monday morning in Washington, D.C. This marked John and Kate Colombo's return to the United States after eliminating the individual who sought to halt the Medical Project and was responsible for the deaths of its personnel worldwide.

Having just picked up their daughter, the Colombos were en route home when they received a call from Jim. Jim retained oversight of the Medical Project due to its broad agency coverage, its status as one of the President's special projects, and its global scope. Jim bore a striking resemblance to James Earl Jones and possessed a voice reminiscent of his.

Adept in navigating Washington politics, Jim had earned even greater admiration from his subordinates for successfully revitalizing the Medical Project. He provided comprehensive briefings to Congress, the Senate, and the President, elucidating the events in Brazil and ensuring their understanding of the demise of Sam Jacob, the individual responsible for the killings of project personnel and the attempted assassination of John and Kate.

Over time, John had visibly aged since the inception of the Medical Project. Because of all his near-death experiences on that project, he did have a few more gray hairs. He commanded attention with his notable height, approachability eccentricity and occasionally gruff demeanor. Athletic and strong, he maintained a slender and rangy appearance. The passage of time had transformed his hazel eyes and brown hair into a distinguished silver-gray.

1

Meanwhile, Kate possessed flowing black hair and expressive brown eyes, bearing a slight resemblance to Sandra Bullock. Both John and Kate, now in their late forties, share a profound connection. Their paths first crossed when Kate was in her final year of high school and John was beginning his freshman year of college. They married four years later.

Although everyone who encountered their daughter, Katelin, remarked on her resemblance to Kate, John and Kate themselves always thought she looked like John. Recently, she received a positive medical evaluation from the hospital treating her cancer, affirming her improved health.

They put Jim on speakerphone, and he informed them that the President wished to meet with John and Kate as soon as they returned to Washington. Kate mentioned to Jim that they had planned to go home and have dinner with Katelin, who was in the car with them. After some discussion, Jim convinced them to have dinner with the President.

They changed their car's course and headed towards the White House. Although John and Kate had visited the White House on multiple occasions, this was Katelin's first time, and they thought she would enjoy seeing the White House.

Upon their arrival at the White House, Jim greeted them at the gate. A staff member parked their car, and they all proceeded to meet the President at the door.

Kate smiled at the President and said, "This is a wonderful surprise. Thank you for inviting us to the White House."

As they walked alongside the President, he informed them, "There is something very important that Jim and I need to discuss with you and John. Katelin can have dinner with my daughter, who is home from college."

At that time, the President's daughter took Katelin's hand, and they went to a different area of the White House.

The four of them were escorted to a separate dining area by the butler. As they settled down to begin their meal, the President, while looking at John and Kate, commended them, saying, "You both did an excellent job in restarting the Medical Program. I continue to receive letters from leaders all over the world congratulating you both and the U.S. Government for reviving the program."

He further added, "Both Congress and the Senate were equally delighted. Jim and I believed this would be the right time to introduce something we have been thinking about, and it received unanimous approval. You both led this effort and risked your lives. The entire world is aware that the Medical Program was disrupted and that individuals working on the project were being killed. You successfully located and apprehended the mastermind behind the program's obstruction."

John then addressed the President and Jim in a serious tone, expressing his gratitude. He said, "Thank you both, because you know that we couldn't have achieved getting the program restarted without your support, as well as the support of several other people."

With a smile, the President responded, "I am just happy to have both of you working for us. I want to discuss a new program we want to start. It's not easy to get everyone to agree on any new program, but we managed to do so. We are calling it the 'U.S. Leadership Program.' With your consent, we would like to announce that both of you will be the inaugural U.S. Leaders in this program. A U.S. Leader is an individual who has achieved significant goals that are important to the U.S.A. and the world. They will receive a very high salary to prevent any potential recruitment from another company or government. We want them to be free from financial concerns."

The President added, "Also, there will be adequate funding and personnel to conduct thorough research to determine whether a program should be brought forward and started. They will report directly to the President, the leader of Congress, and the leader of the Senate. Every quarter, they will provide updates on ongoing programs as well as propose new ones. You will have the freedom to choose the next project you want to start and will continue to lead the Medical Project. While we will hope to announce more U.S. Leaders in the future, we would like to announce this program tomorrow, with both of you as the first U.S. Leaders. It required approval from Congress, the Senate, and the President to appoint you to these positions, which will remain in place until your retirement or until the Congress, Senate, and President decide to remove you otherwise."

"The projects you initiate and work on may extend across multiple presidential administrations around the world. Both of you have already been doing this work without the official title, which is why it was easy to get approval for your appointment. Do you accept the positions as the first two U.S. Leaders?" the President asked as he concluded his statement.

John and Kate exchanged glances and shared a smile. Then, they both turned to the President. Kate gestured towards John, indicating that he should tell the President their decision. They knew each other so well that they could almost read each other's minds. John smiled at the President and said, "We are both honored and accept the positions."

The President then instructed Jim, "Set everything up for an announcement tomorrow."

Turning to John and Kate, the President added, "I will assume that you want to see the Medical Project through to its completion, or at least until it is fully operational worldwide. Additionally, let me know what project you believe should be pursued next for the betterment of the world. While it took some time to get the Medical Project approved and launched, I understand that you have been researching a couple of projects. I anticipate that one of these projects will involve atmospheric changes, and you should obtain quicker approval for it. People will approach you, urging you to initiate their projects. However, we trust both of you to select projects that will truly improve the world rather than projects others wish to start, unless you deem them suitable for your office. Both of you possess multiple patents and are highly inventive. Many people may want you to adopt their projects, driven by the prospect of personal wealth. However, we trust your discernment, as you have a good eye for what the U.S.A. and the world need. You have already made us and the world proud with your successful initiation and completion of multiple projects."

Kate stepped forward towards the President and Jim. She inquired, "We have a strong working relationship with Jim, and he has connections within our government and other world governments that we lack. Will we still be able to collaborate with Jim on the day-to-day aspects of these projects?"

The President turned to Jim and asked, "Jim, will you be able to continue working with Kate and John as before and manage the tasks we have underway?"

Jim, delighted to work with Kate and John, smiled and replied, "It will be my pleasure and honor to work with them. We will ensure the success of this program, Mr. President."

The President smiled and addressed the three of them, saying, "The three of you are the best of the best. I will make the announcement tomorrow."

After finishing their meal, Katelin joined them, and they all headed towards the exit. Jim turned to John and Kate, suggesting, "Why don't we meet at your old offices in the West Wing tomorrow morning at around 10 a.m.? We can discuss the President's announcement and prepare for the press conference, which we will schedule for 1 p.m. A car will pick you and Kate up from your house at around 9 a.m."

John nodded and replied, "Sounds good, Jim. We'll see you tomorrow at 10."

After departing from the President's residence, their car was brought to them, and the three of them got in and headed home. On the way home, Kate and John provided Katelin with an update on their new positions but emphasized that she would need to keep it a secret until after the President's announcement the following day.

John and Kate held hands throughout the ride, gazing into each other's eyes, and simultaneously expressed, *"I love you."*

That night, John and Kate celebrated with Katelin before retiring early to bed, knowing that Tuesday would be a significant day ahead.

Announcing a New U.S. Leadership Position

J ohn woke up at 6 a.m. for his morning run. As he stirred, he tried to rouse Kate, saying, "Would you like to join me for a run? I'll be back around 7:30, and we can have breakfast with Katelin at around 8 a.m."

Kate groggily opened her eyes and replied, "I don't know how you manage this every day. I'll see you at breakfast by 8 a.m. I'll also have Katelin join us so we can discuss today's announcement. I believe she'll be heading to work today."

John completed his run while listening to a podcast. He typically enjoys listening to sports or podcasts during his runs. When he visits a non-English-speaking country, he endeavors to learn the local language. As he ages, he has shifted his podcast preferences to include topics such as maintaining good health and managing taxes.

After finishing his run, John showered and joined Kate and Katelyn at the breakfast table. With a smile, John inquired, "So, what are we having for breakfast?"

Katelin returned the smile and responded, "Mom prepared a selection of pancakes, eggs, bacon, and coffee." The breakfast was served in a country-style manner, with all the dishes placed in the center of the table for individuals to choose from.

John leaned in and replied, "I am trying to cut down on carbs, so

I'll just grab the scrambled eggs, bacon, and some coffee."

Kate wanted to discuss the upcoming announcement with John and the potential projects they will undertake. She looked at him and said, "I'm sure Jim and the President will ask us about our next project. The President mentioned one of them during dinner yesterday. Which projects do you think we should propose, and who should be part of our team?"

John responded, but he turned his attention to Katelin and emphasized, "The same rules we've always followed still apply. What we say at this table is confidential and cannot be repeated to anyone."

Katelin smiled and nodded, indicating her understanding of the situation.

John then focused on Kate and continued, "We've been working on a couple of projects independently, with the assistance of various companies and universities. Perhaps it's time to move forward with them. The first one that comes to mind is about the prevalent issue of climate change, or global warming. The second project concerns the mitigation of large storms, particularly hurricanes."

"Kate, you've had software experts at your university working on modeling the Earth and its actual conditions, while I've been focusing on modeling and preventing the destructive potential of large storms. I suggest we express our interest in pursuing both of these projects. Additionally, we must ensure that the Medical Project stays on track. Although we were successful in stopping the main individual trying to stop the project, it's likely that other people in smaller countries may attempt to obstruct its completion, potentially resulting in casualties. We need to prevent that at all costs," John said, suggesting ideas to Kate.

Kate looked at John and replied, "We're on the same wavelength. All three projects are at different stages of development and require additional personnel and testing to be finalized. We'll need to simulate storms in the lab and experiment with chemicals that could neutralize their intensity. Our current hypothesis is that hurricanes intensify as they absorb heat from the ocean, meaning that hotter oceans lead to more severe storms. We need to create software models, conduct lab experiments to validate our findings, and ultimately test our conclusions on an actual storm. I have already conducted extensive modeling of the Earth and global climate, but there is still a lot of work to be done. You have made progress in software modeling related to plant-based solutions for improving the climate, but that area will require the most effort."

John interjected, "Implementing the Climate Project may indeed take longer, but once we address the climate issues, there will likely be a reduction in the frequency of hurricanes. We have a device that can assist in addressing hot spots on Earth, but we must also direct our attention to the atmosphere. As we all know, the government has been deliberately altering the atmosphere for the past fourteen years through the use of chemtrails, which has had a significant impact on weather patterns."

He continued, "The current practice of dispersing chemicals from planes, such as alkaloid metals and barium salts, has been changing the atmosphere by chelating out soot and blocking light. However, in the process, it has also been removing regular oxygen and hydrogen from the atmosphere, resulting in the creation of atomic hydrogen and atomic oxygen. Atomic oxygen means the HOs are missing one electron from the oxygens and one electron from the hydrogens. Consequently, we have been left with polluted air containing isotopes of oxygen and hydrogen. Furthermore, the chemicals dropped by the planes in the clouds, combined with the compounds already present in the atmosphere, can break down volatile organic compounds due to the alkaline metals and barium salts. While altering the atmosphere in this manner does reduce smog and block radiation, it hinders the process of electrolysis necessary for producing real oxygen and hydrogen. Reintroducing the electrons that were chelated out is crucial to rectifying the current state of affairs on Earth's surface and within the lower ozone layers and atmosphere. Instead of solely focusing on the air itself, we should consider the importance of cultivating plant and animal life on the Earth's surface."

Kate added, "We won't be able to communicate this information to the press in such technical terms. We need to explain it in plain English, ensuring that they understand. Additionally, we must exercise caution in not disclosing our implementation strategy, especially to our U.S. competitors, as they may attempt to replicate our solutions and infringe upon our companies' patents."

John replied, "Indeed. Our first priority should be completing the Medical Project. After that, we can dedicate our efforts to the storm mitigation project, followed by addressing climate change. We do not need to disclose the specific details of how we plan to accomplish these goals. I will refrain from explaining how we intend to halt the storms to prevent other countries from copying our methods and violating our patents. We are currently testing various solutions, but so far, we have achieved success in storm mitigation using a combination of denatured alcohol, a special cooling agent, and other ingredients found in Palmolive dish soap mixed with epsom salt and diatomaceous earth. If these substances are sprayed from planes or exploded into the storm, they can help control its intensity while also benefiting the plants and animals inhabiting the Earth's surface."

Katelin looked at both of them and expressed her admiration, saying, "You are both amazing. I learn more sitting at this table than anywhere else. I'm so proud of both of you for tackling some of the most critical issues our planet faces. The only concern I have is the individuals who try to hinder your progress due to their own interests, particularly with The Medical Project."

Katelin held immense respect for her parents and cherished the special mother-daughter bond they shared. They shared interests and enjoyed spending time together, nurturing a friendship that went beyond their roles as mother and daughter. They had been inseparable since Katelin's birth.

John responded, "Thank you for reminding us about the challenges we faced with The Medical Project. Kate, we need to inform Jim that we require security not only for ourselves but also for Katelin.

Although I can't fathom who would oppose the efforts to mitigate storms and improve our planet, I'm certain we will encounter opposition or individuals attempting to steal our ideas and sell them to the highest bidder."

Kate added, "I believe Jim understands the security better than we do, which is why he is sending a car for us. In fact, we better get ready because the car will be here in 15 minutes. Katelin, are you going to work today?"

Katelin smiled and replied, "Yes, I will be going to work, and I'll be driving myself."

They all stood up, gathered the dishes that needed cleaning, and stored the leftovers in the refrigerator.

John heard someone at the door, so he went to check through the peephole and saw two cars. He informed Kate, "The car has arrived, and it looks like there are two cars outside."

John opened the door and asked the person in the first car about the presence of the second car. The driver explained that the second car was for security purposes.

Kate joined John at the door, carrying both of their attaché cases. She remarked, "It will be challenging to delve into the details of the other two projects without this information," pointing at the cases.

On their way to the White House, John explained to Kate the reason for the two cars. Upon their arrival, the cars dropped them off near the West Wing, where Jim was waiting.

Jim welcomed them and said, "I thought it would be wise to have additional security, similar to what we had during The Medical Project. We've received indications that some countries are still experiencing issues involving the deaths of individuals working on the project. Although it's not as bad as before, they believe they can handle it within their country. However, with the potential for new projects, I didn't want to take any chances, which is why we have extra security."

Kate looked at Jim with a smile and said, "That is why we like you, Jim. You have a keen sense of anticipation. John and I were actually going to discuss the security matter with you, but you beat us to the punch. What about Katelin? Do you think she'll need the extra security?"

Jim responded with a serious expression: "We didn't want to be too intrusive, but she will have people keeping a close eye on her. If anyone tries anything, they will intervene."

John tightly held Kate's hand, looked at Jim, and said, "Now that we don't have to worry about our family's security, we can fully focus on our work and concentrate on the projects. Great job, Jim!"

John and Kate were deeply in love. They were always seen holding hands, and people would comment on how they still held hands despite their age. Their love story began the moment they met. Sometimes Kate would tell John that she loved him even before they met because she overheard his laughter from a distance. She asked her friends about him, but they never introduced him to her, leading her to believe they wanted him for themselves. This was a story Kate often shared with John. In return, John would tell Kate that he knew she was the one from the moment they first met. It was a true love story.

Jim then guided them to the offices they had on The Medical Project and asked, "Will these offices be okay? I thought you might want to work on any issues the project is facing in other countries and also start working on any new projects here in your old offices."

Kate responded, "These offices will do. What do you think, John?"

John agreed, and then he briefed Jim on the progress and objectives of the two new projects. He provided an overview of where they currently stand and expressed their desired final outcomes.

Jim looked pleased and mentioned that he would brief the President for his upcoming press conference at 1 p.m. today. He then turned to John and Kate, saying, "Be prepared to speak about the projects you'll be working on, as the President will probably call you up to the podium."

John responded, "We look forward to seeing you around 12:30, so you can take us to the press conference and inform us of any last-minute changes."

Jim agreed and left to brief the President. Around 12:30, the

President and Jim arrived at Kate and John's office to accompany them to the press conference. John and Kate were pleasantly surprised, and John said, "Mr. President, thank you for coming to pick us up. We're ready to go with you."

The President replied, "This meeting is about you and the contributions you both have made to the country and what you'll be doing in the future."

The four of them walked together towards the press conference, and the West Wing staff applauded and followed them. As they entered the press conference room, everyone stood up and began applauding. The people truly loved John and Kate and for everything they had done for the world, which does not happen very frequently. Representatives from press outlets all over the world were present at the event.

The President went to the podium and also applauded John and Kate. He proceeded to recount the entire story of the Medical Project and emphasized that John and Kate would see it through to completion. He then introduced the formation of the U.S. Leadership Project, explaining that many large companies had similar programs to allow their most innovative leaders to come up with solutions for their organizations.

The President further expressed the need for a similar initiative in the U.S. Government so that outstanding individuals already working within the government could easily initiate and complete new projects. These projects would be too substantial for any single company but not beyond the capabilities of the government. The initiative would not compete with other companies but might subcontract some of the work out if necessary. He also announced that John and Kate would be the first two members of the U.S. Leadership team, with the possibility of adding more individuals in the future.

They would report to the President as well as to leaders in Congress and the Senate. All relevant parties had given their consent to John and Kate's appointment. Following this long announcement, the press rose to their feet and applauded. The President concluded by stating,

"I'd like John and Kate to describe the new project they'll be working on for the United States and the world."

John and Kate then approached the podium, with John signaling for Kate to speak first. "Thank you, Mr. President, Congress, and Senate, for entrusting us with this new endeavor," Kate began.

She continued, "Our primary focus will be to complete the Medical Project worldwide. As we near its conclusion, we will place particular emphasis on addressing substance abuse and schizophrenia. Schizophrenia has been a longstanding challenge for over a millennium, and we believe it is time to unveil a remedy. By analyzing the data collected in the Medical Project, we aim to identify patterns underlying the development of schizophrenia and assist others in finding a cure. Our attention will thus be directed towards mental health and substance abuse, including aiding individuals in overcoming illegal drug addiction by exploring the use of supplements and therapies.

"In addition to the critical need for a medical computer to contain this information and facilitate the development of treatments and cures for various diseases, John and I have two other major projects we are eager to commence. I will now invite John to discuss the project we have been focused on, followed by my description of another project we will work on."

John expressed his gratitude and proceeded to describe the project. "In our laboratory, we have meticulously devised and tested a project we call the Storm Project. We created simulated storms and experimented with different chemicals placed at the core to disrupt their intensity. Since most storms rely on heat to intensify, our objective is to cool them down. We are now prepared to conduct the live tests, which could potentially save millions of dollars. All the models we have run indicate the feasibility of conducting this test on an actual storm."

Around of applause filled the room as John concluded his presentation. He then added, "I would now like to invite Kate once again to share details about a project she has been diligently working on."

Kate approached the podium, expressing her gratitude once more, and proceeded to discuss her project. "In our laboratory, we have been developing a project called the World Climate Project, which aims to create a computer model of the global system. Through this model, we can identify hot spots and cold regions around the world. Additionally, we can introduce factors that can impact the climate, ultimately working towards its stabilization. While the Climate Project is not as advanced as the Storm Project, we are making significant progress. Once the Climate Project is complete, it may obviate the need for the Storm Project. However, since the Climate Project is a longer endeavor, we require an immediate solution to address severe storms."

Once Kate concluded her remarks, the audience rose to their feet in applause. As there were no questions, the President, Jim, John, and Kate exited the room and reconvened in John and Kate's office to discuss the next steps necessary to bring all the projects to fruition.

Following the discussion, John and Kate returned home to relax and enjoy each other's company intimately.

Planning Work on All Projects

J ohn and Kate rose at 6a.m., and Kate suggested, "I think I'll join you for your run today."

"Excellent," John responded. "Let me check outside the front door and inform them that we'll both be running."

John opened the door to find Bill Collins from The Medical Project, their collaborator, waiting there.

Seeing John, Bill greeted him, "Hi John, going for a run today?"

John smiled and replied, "Good to see you again, Bill. Yes, we're both going for a run. Will you be working with us on these projects?"

Bill, with a big smile, responded, "Yes, and I've actually been promoted since we all kept ourselves alive on the last project."

"Excellent! I'll let Kate know. We'll be heading out for a run in about half an hour," John said, expressing his delight with regards to Bill's good news.

"Could you do a street run so that we can follow you in the car?" Bill suggested.

"That will work. See you in half an hour then," John said, agreeing with Bill's suggestion.

John went to the bedroom where Kate was getting ready and shared the news: "Good news! Bill has been promoted as a result of our last project with him. He mentioned that he'll be following us in his car, so it looks like it'll be a street run."

Kate responded with a smile, saying, "A street run it is. I gave Bill an excellent recommendation when we completed the project. I'm glad they are reading the recommendations. He truly deserves the promotion."

"You're amazing, Kate! I informed Bill that we'll be out there in half an hour," John said, proud of what his wife has done for Bill.

After enjoying a quick cup of instant coffee. John and Kate poked their heads out the door and asked if anyone wanted coffee. They were informed that everyone had already had breakfast. With that, John and Kate exited their home, locked the door, and announced, "Okay, we're ready to go. Which car will follow us?"

Bill pointed to a car, so John and Kate approached the vehicle and informed the driver of the route they would be taking. They started their run. After approximately an hour, they returned to their house, approached Bill, and informed him that they would be ready to go to the office in about an hour, arriving at 10 a.m.

Upon reaching the office, they invited Bill to join them as they brainstormed who might be upset if the two new projects were completed. They also discussed the necessary security measures for all three projects.

In the West Wing, they proceeded to Jim's office, briefing him on their planned focus for the upcoming days. Their first step would be compiling a list of individuals needed to complete each project, as well as identifying possible people who would try to stop the projects. Jim agreed with their approach, and they scheduled a meeting at the end of the day to update him on what they would need.

Standing before a whiteboard, Bill, John, and Kate began discussing and documenting the names of people, governments, and companies opposed to the Climate Change Project and the Storm Project. In addition, they reviewed the progress of the Medical Project and determined the remaining tasks to bring it to completion.

Bill initiated the conversation, stating, "Any country that can control the weather can control the world. Therefore, we can expect to have many enemies or countries that want to partner with us."

Kate continued, "Creating hurricanes and other climate-affecting phenomena on a computer, as we are doing, is unprecedented. Our initial results from the computer models indicate that China and Russia are the countries that are creating the biggest problems concerning hot spots. Their lack of regulations and extensive manufacturing may make them resistant to change. As for the Storm Project, certain countries might be apprehensive about our ability to both stop and potentially create storms. While we are conducting experiments in labs and simulations, we have no intention of generating real storms. However, if they distrust us, they may attempt to impede our progress on the project."

John proposed, "We could transform this into a worldwide project and attempt to engage the countries identified by our models as having the most significant issues. We attempted a similar approach with companies during the Medical Project, but they were unwilling to join us."

Towards the end of the day, John and Kate completed their analysis and visited Jim's office to share their concerns and discuss the necessary personnel. John initiated the conversation about involving Russia and China in all the projects. However, Jim was hesitant, fearing the potential loss of the competitive advantage the United States held in software and hardware modeling.

"Jim, we won't provide them with the software programs responsible for the modeling. Instead, we will assist them in using the application. The object and source code will remain our proprietary information, but we can supply them with a user's manual to operate the application," Kate said, reassuring Jim.

Jim then inquired, "Do you have anyone whom you can trust from Russia and China that you have been working with? If we can keep politics aside and have technical experts work on this problem, much like how we handle the Medical Program, then it might be feasible. Doctors all over the world input and access information without understanding how the software programming makes everything function."

John replied, "We have connections with technical experts all over the world, and we don't need to share the software code with any of them. In fact, they probably prefer to function as users, just like in the Medical Project."

Jim chuckled and remarked, "So, what you and Kate are telling me is that the only option to these two projects would come from governments who don't trust us and believe we might create storms to destroy their territories, or manufacturers who fear that the software will expose them as the cause of global issues and lead to the shutdown of their factories worldwide. That's a substantial number of individuals and countries."

Kate, with a smile on her face, chimed in, "I guess we'll need to strengthen our security measures."

John, adopting a serious expression, added, "Let's discuss how we can announce the launch of these two projects. If we acknowledge their concerns and emphasize our commitment to collaborating with them to address any issues arising from the climate study, while also assuring them that we aim to stop hurricanes and cyclones rather than create them, it may help alleviate their concerns."

Jim responded to John, saying, "Our enemies won't believe us until we successfully stop a severe storm heading towards a country that we have problems with and manufacturers causing climate issues will remain a problem until we assist them. Let's achieve some successes as soon as possible."

Jim then shook hands with Kate and John, commending them, "This is why you are the best. You understand the problem and propose solutions. Let me discuss this with the Congress, Senate, and President, and obtain their approval. You two should reach out to the people all over the world, and inform them of our plans, and enroll them in the project. Once we secure commitments from countries at the outset, along with approvals from our government, we will set up a press conference."

John and Kate acknowledged the end of the meeting and left Jim's office, heading to their own office to begin contacting their network of global connections, gauging their interest in participating. Every country and person they called expressed their desire to be part of the Storm Project but sought assurances that storms would not be created and that a designated group would decide when to halt storms, as there are time and areas where storms are necessary.

Some prominent multinational manufacturing companies were against the climate project, fearing the potential shutdown of their facilities, and were prepared to resist its initiation. They could not understand what Kate and John were trying to tell them or did not believe what they were saying could be done.

John and Kate developed a computer model of the world, identifying hotspots resulting from manufacturing or other factors. They implemented measures such as vegetation and large devices to counteract these hotspots, followed by running additional computer models to ensure effective mitigation.

John and Kate returned to Jim's office to provide a comprehensive update. Jim shared the initial feedback from the U.S. Government and several major countries.

Jim remarked with a smile, "With the Leadership Project in place, obtaining approval for large projects like these is much easier. We have received approval to proceed with both projects and to complete the Medical Project. In discussions with the government leaders of Russia and China, they were concerned about being compelled to shut down manufacturing plants. They struggled to grasp the concept. However, our objective is not to shut anything down but rather to implement measures to prevent environmental damage caused by their manufacturing processes."

John, wearing a smile, chimed in, "So I guess this means we'll maintain security measures for some time until we can demonstrate some successes."

Jim concurred, stating, "Yes, we will continue the security, and I'll have the President make a brief announcement about the two new projects. Since we've obtained approval to commence, let's get started."

Kate then pointed to a sheet of paper on Jim's desk and added, "We've provided the list of people required for each project, along with the necessary equipment and office space. You can work on that while we focus on identifying the first storm and determining the initial climate issue to address. Let's plan to reconvene tomorrow morning at nine to outline our course of action for all the projects."

The Fourth Day

Getting Started on the Storm Project

J ohn and Kate woke up at 6 a.m., and John suggested going for a run before heading to work. This time, when he asked Kate to join him, she agreed. They completed a six-mile run with security following in a car. During their jog, John asked Kate, "Did you see the weather report last night? It looks like a hurricane is forming and might pass over Cuba before hitting Florida."

While still running, Kate replied, "Yes, we need to use the Storm Program and see if we can help Cuba and the U.S."

Upon returning to their home, they quickly got dressed, enjoyed a cup of coffee, and John opened the front door, noticing the security personnel. He addressed them, saying, "We aim to be at work by 9 a.m. today, so could we leave in half an hour?"

In half an hour, John and Kate were ready, and they went straight to the West Wing, making their way to Jim's office. As soon as John and Kate entered, Jim rose from his desk and greeted them, saying, "I guess you guys saw the weather report last night and want to use the Storm Program."

John, with a smile, replied, "You read our minds."

Jim then assumed a serious expression and said, "I have already called the Cuban Government and inquired whether it would be permissible for us to fly across the Cuban Island to put some chemicals in that storm to reduce its intensity. However, they informed me that any U.S. aircraft that crosses their airspace will be shot down."

Both John and Kate wore disappointed expressions and replied, "That is not good. Is there an aircraft south of Cuba that we can use? Or do we have a large cannon that can fire large payloads into the center of the storm?"

The next thing Jim did is one of the main reasons everyone admires him. He called the President and obtained permission to convene a meeting with all the generals in the armed forces, instructing them to gather in his office within the hour.

During the meeting, Jim raised a question to John and Kate, asking, "How many pounds of chemicals do we need to disperse in the eye of the hurricane?"

After a brief discussion, Kate responded, "We ran a model, and it indicated that we would require approximately 1,000 pounds of chemicals. By doing so, we would transform the hurricane into a mere storm with winds of around 30 miles per hour and rainfall of 2 inches."

The generals huddled for about fifteen minutes, after which the head of the Air Force spoke up, saying, "We don't have a single aircraft in the area that can carry 1,000 pounds. However, we can dispatch several planes toward the storm and launch several missiles containing the chemical. We have three jets available in Texas and two in Florida that can fly close to the storm, fire their missiles into it, and detonate them."

John interjected, "We need to act swiftly. We must expedite the process of loading the chemicals onto the missiles and ensure they are ready for deployment from the aircraft. Additionally, we need to transport the chemicals to Florida and Texas."

John and Kate each took around 500 pounds of the chemicals they had on hand and boarded separate jets. Kate flew to Texas, while John flew to Florida, where they met with the pilots who would be flying toward the storm. They collaborated with the engineers to load the chemicals into the missiles.

While overseeing the loading of missiles onto the stealth fighters,

John contacted Kate and said, "It looks like they want me to go with them to ensure the missile detonates in the eye of the hurricane."

With a hint of concern in her voice, Kate replied, "They asked me to do the same thing, and I told them I would do it."

John affirmed," I told them I would go with them as well."

Kate then voiced her concern, saying, "Let's make sure the pilots stay out of the Cuban airspace, although we may not have to worry too much since these are stealth fighters."

They performed all the calculations and aimed to time the missile launches simultaneously. They planned to fire their missiles when the storm was 100 miles south of Cuba, with one stealth fighter firing from the east and the other from the west. Without any delay, both fighters took off at approximately the same time.

The President, the leader of the Senate, and Congress were present with Jim in the war room in Washington. The first communication came from the stealth fighter that departed from Florida, piloted by John.

Urgently, John reported, "We have five missiles, each loaded with a hundred-pound of chemical, ready to be fired. We should be firing the missiles in 10 minutes. We managed to avoid any detection from the Cuban government."

Kate then joined the conversation, stating, "We are positioned west of the storm, also with five missiles, each carrying a hundred-pound of chemical, ready for launch. We have not been detected by the Cuban government either."

The President chimed in, saying, "My two favorite people. You have my permission to fire the missiles when you're ready. Once the missiles are launched, please vacate the area immediately, as Cuba will detect the missile launch and scramble their jets to pursue the ones responsible."

At that moment, John came back on the line and informed Kate, "I will initiate a countdown from ten, and then when I reach zero, fire all five missiles."

Within a minute, John started the countdown. At the conclusion of the countdown, all ten missiles were fired and exploded at the center of the storm. Instantaneously, the hurricane dissipated, completely vanishing. Everyone in Washington and aboard the stealth fighters let out a loud cheer. Just then, a voice came over the speaker, indicating that Cuban jets were taking off.

The stealth fighters immediately turned around, accelerated to supersonic speeds, and headed back to their bases. Simultaneously, F-15 fighter jets took off from Florida and Texas, rendezvousing with the returning stealth fighters. The U.S. fighters intercepted the Cuban jets as they approached the stealth fighters. The U.S. pilots instructed the Cuban fighters to immediately turn back, warning that they would be shot down if they entered U.S. airspace. The Cuban jets complied and returned to their base. And again, there was a loud cheer in Washington.

The President then returned to the line, commending, "Well done, team. You make me proud to be an American. This is a good day."

John then communicated with Kate, stating, "My pilot said he would drop me off in Washington, so I'll meet you at home."

Kate replied, "My stealth fighter pilot also informed me that she would drop me off in Washington. I'll meet you at the airport."

With a smile adorning his face, the President concluded, "Since all of you will be in Washington at the same time, you and the people in this war room are all welcome to the White House for dinner."

The pilots and their colleagues enthusiastically agreed to meet for dinner, prompting a resounding cheer. When the stealth fighters and F-15s landed almost at the same time, it was a beautiful sight. They parked side by side, and as they disembarked from the planes, everyone was dressed in their aviation attire. John hurried over to Kate, embracing her tightly and planting a tender kiss on her lips. "You always look beautiful, and I am so grateful we made it through this alive," he expressed with relief.

Kate smiled warmly and replied, "It's always a good day when everything works out as planned." Hand in hand, Kate and John strolled towards the helicopters, a customary gesture between them.

Subsequently, they were all escorted into two helicopters and flown to the White House. The President, Jim, the heads of the Senate and Congress, along with a contingent of the press, awaited their arrival and erupted in applause as they disembarked from the helicopters. The President commented to Jim, "Now, that is a remarkable sight to behold. People returning from a perilous yet successful mission—all dressed in Air Force outfits."

The President led everyone to the main dining room, where they enjoyed a splendid dinner. Upon concluding the meal, the President rose from his seat and addressed the gathering. "I received a call from the Cuban President, expressing gratitude to Jim and me for averting the storm. He stated that he would place more trust in us the next time a hurricane arises. Numerous nations witnessed the extraordinary event as news stations worldwide reported the sudden disappearance of a hurricane. We have been inundated with calls asking for further details on this extraordinary occurrence."

As the President had invited members of the press to the dinner, John directed his attention to the journalists present and recalled, "As you may recall, a few months ago, when Kate and I held a press conference upon assuming our roles as the first U.S. Leaders, we mentioned that we were working on two projects—the Storm Project and the Climate Project. We extensively modeled both projects, both in computer simulations and in laboratory experiments. We were ready to put the Storm Project to the test with an actual storm. Therefore, when an opportunity presented itself and the President granted approval, we decided to apply our laboratory findings to a real storm. Fortunately, everything unfolded according to plan."

Once again, applause filled the room for Kate and John, prompting a member of the press to inquire, "How will you test the Climate Project?"

Kate promptly responded, "We have already conducted tests in the U.S. for the Climate Project. Using computer software, we identified hotspots within the country, most notably around a manufacturing plant. Rather than shutting down the plant, we installed a revolutionary converter device capable of transforming the plant's harmful emissions into oxygen. This device, an innovative invention originating in the U.S., underwent successful testing at a company we had identified. Consequently, we provided additional funding to facilitate its mass production. When we ran the computer program again after the device's installation, the hotspot vanished. Our intentions are to replicate this approach all over the U.S. and potentially the world, with the consent of governments."

With everyone having finished their meals, the President stood up, wearing a smile on his face. He expressed his gratitude, saying, "I want to thank all the pilots, John and Kate, for making the initial test of the Storm Project a resounding success. Additionally, although we haven't discussed it tonight, the Medical Project is ahead of schedule, and all countries around the world are participating in it. Keep up the excellent work, team."

Everyone rose to their feet once more, offering another round of applause, and the dinner concluded. As their security detail escorted John and Kate home, they called their daughter Katelin and gave a detailed account of the day's activities.

Upon finishing their narrative, Katelin expressed profound pride in her parents, saying, "You guys are truly incredible. I can't believe what you went through today. I am so proud to have you as my parents."

John and Kate returned to their residence, where they shared a loving and intimate moment.

A Problem with the Medical Project

In the morning, John woke up at 6a.m. and asked Kate if she would join him for a run. Kate agreed, and John informed their security team that they would be going for a run, with security following in a car.

After their run, they both prepared for work, and their security detail drove them to the West Wing. Upon arriving at work, someone came running up to John and gave him some bad news. A doctor in Turkey had filed a complaint about the slow response time and difficulty in retrieving accurate information from the database. The doctor needed information on treating a patient with cervical cancer and wanted to identify the best hospitals for this type of treatment.

Upon learning about the issue, John immediately requested a meeting with Jeff, the database expert. John and Jeff had previously worked together in Brazil, so they were familiar with each other. Within minutes, Jeff joined John and Kate in the conference room. John, visibly upset, looked Jeff straight in the eye and expressed his dissatisfaction, saying, "We were aware that response time could be a significant problem with the Medical Project, and you assured us this would not happen. If doctors believe that it takes forever to input information or receive a response from the computer when they ask a question, then they will stop using the system."

Jeff felt remorseful but responded, "Turkey opted for cost-cutting measures and decided to use their older computers, which do not meet the minimum requirements for the Medical Project."

John, still frustrated, retorted, "If word gets out that the response time is poor with the Medical Application, doctors in Turkey and potentially worldwide will simply stop using the system without questioning why. You need to take whoever you need and get on a Zoom call with them to address and resolve the issue. If it cannot be resolved remotely, you and your team should fly to Turkey and rectify the problem. If they require a new system, install one and let them know that they can pay for it with the funds saved by using the medical system."

Recognizing John's authority and respecting his and Kate's concerns, Jeff promptly replied, "Okay, I will provide an update by the end of the day on whether the issue is resolved or if we need to travel to Turkey."

After the conference room emptied, Kate, wearing a concerned expression, asked John, "Is there anyone you truly respect and have confidence in?"

After a brief pause, John looked her directly in the eye and replied, "Yes."

There was a slight delay before he continued, "I respect and have confidence in you." Kate returned his gaze and simply smiled.

At the end of the day, Jeff returned to the conference room with John and Kate, wearing a worried expression. He informed them and said, "As we suspected, the Turkish government was using an outdated Russian computer that falls well below the minimum requirements. We offered to upgrade their computer system with deferred payment options, but if they choose not to upgrade, they must inform their people that they are no longer part of the program. They have decided to proceed with the upgrade, so we will need to fly to Turkey and assist in improving the response time of the existing system while transitioning to the new one."

Kate interjected, "That's a good plan, but we need to take additional steps. I believe we should send an urgent email to everyone, notifying them about this problem. If any organization fails to meet the minimum system requirements, then we will not install the medical system. We can also reiterate the minimum system specifications and provide information on how they can pay for the necessary upgrades if they require them, with support from the U.S."

"Great idea, Kate," John said, acknowledging his wife's brilliant suggestion.

The meeting ended, and everyone returned to their respective offices. John and Kate began planning for the following day and provided Jim with an update on the day's events. After the meeting, they headed home.

The Sixth Day

Day Off—Weekend with Katelin

J ohn and Kate woke up at 6 a.m. They wanted to go for a run before calling Katelin and inviting her to spend the weekend with them. Katelin was working on an important project at her company but informed her parents that she and her team would work on Saturday morning. However, she could take off Saturday afternoon and Sunday.

John and Kate were overjoyed at the opportunity to spend time with their daughter. John smiled at Kate after finishing the call with Katelin and said, "You don't realize how fortunate we are to be able to spend time with our daughter until we almost lose her to cancer."

Kate responded with a serious expression: "We are so blessed to have such a beautiful and kind daughter. She brings joy to our lives, and I genuinely believe she enjoys spending time with us as much as we do with her."

John then suggested, "Should we go to The Cheesecake Factory and then catch a movie?"

Kate smiled and replied, "I think that's something you would enjoy, but how about having lunch at The Cheesecake Factory and then doing some shopping at the mall?"

John replied, "Let's leave the decision to Katelin."

They both called Katelin and presented her with the two options. She responded, "Okay, I'll meet you both at The Cheesecake Factory at 1 p.m., and after that, we can go to the movie at 3 p.m. and do some shopping right after."

Kate and John exchanged smiles, and John remarked, "We're the luckiest parents in the world. She knows how to make both of us happy at the same time."

Kate affectionately said, "You're amazing, my daughter. You get to pick the movie."

Deciding they had time to spare, John and Kate went for a run. John notified the security team that they would be running on the street in about half an hour. and informed them of their plans for The Cheesecake Factory, movie, and shopping.

Half an hour later, John and Kate went to the street where the car that would be following them had parked. The car had one security guard along with the driver. John informed them of their running route, and then they commenced their run. There weren't many people or cars on the road.

Around the three-mile mark, they noticed a car approaching them head-on. John shouted to Kate and the security team, "We need to get out of their way!" Suddenly, he saw two individuals leaning out of the car's window, wielding machine guns, and firing at them. The security team pulled their car in front of John and Kate. The security guard returned fire, but both he and the driver sustained injuries. The car that attacked them continued past John and Kate, turning around to head back.

John said urgently, "Kate, get in the car and grab the security guard's machine gun. Lay him on the floor in the back seat. I'll get in the car, move the driver over, and lay him on the floor in front. Then I'll get us out of here."

The driver informed them that he had called for assistance, but it would take some time for help to arrive. John quickly got in the car and started driving directly toward the other vehicle. He instructed Kate, "Keep firing that machine gun. I'll try to force them off the road."

As they neared the other car, John swerved to avoid a collision but kept driving toward their home. Kate continued firing her machine gun as the pursuing car followed closely behind.

John turned down a dead-end street where their house was located and drove into the driveway. The other car followed closely behind, assuming they had caught their targets. As the attackers began exiting their car, several U.S. security guards emerged from the house, armed with machine guns. They quickly neutralized one of the assailants and yelled at the other, "Drop your weapon and lie face down, or you will be killed."

The security team then instructed John and Kate to enter the house. They assured them that additional security personnel were on their way and that an ambulance had been called for the injured guards. The remaining assailant would be taken in for questioning.

Once inside the house, John immediately picked up the phone and called Jim on his private line. He relayed the incident, saying, "Jim, there was an attempt on our lives, and two security guards were injured."

Jim responded with alarm, asking, "Are you and Kate okay?"

"We're fine, but we're concerned about who would want to kill us," John replied.

Jim explained, "We believe it was the Russians, or perhaps a small group within Russia. They are concerned that we are surpassing them in terms of innovation. We received a call from Cuba expressing gratitude for our assistance during the recent hurricane. The majority of Cubans now desire a return to democracy, realizing it's a better form of government that fosters new ideas. The Russians were also displeased when Turkey returned their computers and adopted our system, as their computers didn't meet the minimum requirements."

Kate interjected, "We will try to involve them more in what we're doing without revealing our secrets."

Jim concluded the conversation, saying, "I'll contact my counterpart in Russia and see if they can identify those responsible for these incidents in our country. I'll ask them to put an end to it. I'm sorry your weekend was disrupted. We'll see you on Monday, and hopefully I'll have some answers. In the meantime, I'll increase your security."

"Thanks for everything you do, Jim. We truly appreciate your help," John said, expressing his gratitude.

After ending the call, Kate and John used the speakerphone to talk to Katelin. Kate began, "You won't believe what just happened to us."

Katelin, adopting a serious tone, replied, "I don't care about what happened. We're still going to The Cheesecake Factory for lunch, then the movie, and then shopping."

John chimed in, "You're absolutely right, Katelin. We're going to do all that because we love you and we need to have some fun. We'll tell you all about it at lunch. We can't wait to see you."

Kate then informed the security team at the door about their plans and requested that they be ready to leave by 11:30 a.m. so they could meet their daughter for lunch at noon.

The security personnel looked at Kate in awe, finding it hard to believe that after everything they had been through, the family was determined to have a full afternoon of activities.

When they saw Katelin at the lunch spot, they greeted her with a warm hug and a kiss on the cheek, expressing, "We're so happy to see you." They sat down and had lunch, taking the opportunity to recount what had occurred during their run.

"So, what movie do you want to see?" Katelin asked her parents.

John quickly responded, "Top Gun! I like Tom Cruise, and it's a thrilling movie with plenty of action."

Katelin smiled and replied, "You may think Tom Cruise's movies have a lot of action, but both of you have experienced more action and thrills than any of his films."

John and Kate nodded in agreement and shared a laugh.

After the movie, they went shopping. Katelin and Kate enjoyed browsing at Anthropology and purchased several items of clothing, while John found solace in reading the books being sold.

Having spent a full day with Katelin, John and Kate returned home, reflecting on how fortunate they were to have such an exceptional daughter.

On their way home, John and Kate discussed their plans for Sunday. They both agreed to go for their run despite the incident this morning. This time, they opted to jog in a nearby park. They also considered attending church, viewing it as a meaningful activity for tomorrow.

Day Off—Exercise, Church, and Work

J ohn and Kate informed their security team yesterday that they planned to go for a run at a nearby park. They wanted to ensure that the security personnel were prepared and that they would not encounter the same problem they faced the previous day. Rising at around 6 a.m., both John and Kate were surprised to find Bill Collins, a trusted security personnel who had helped them in the past and was a West Point graduate, standing outside their front door.

John expressed his delight, saying, "Bill, it is so good to see you again. Will you be on this project permanently with us?"

Bill, wearing a broad smile, replied, "After hearing about what happened to both you and Kate yesterday, I requested to become a permanent member of your security team. We have doubled the security detail for you and Kate, and we have assigned security personnel to protect Katelin as well. So, I hear we'll be running in the park today. Will both you and Kate be running?"

"Yes, we'll be running together in the park today, in about half an hour. It's great to have you on the security team since you're familiar with our routine," John answered.

"A few of us will join you on the run, and we have positioned extra security who will be available if needed," Bill informed them.

"Great. Oh, did they tell you that we'll be going to church at around

35

10 a.m. after our run and shower? Then we'll be working from home," John added.

"We'll be ready. See you in half an hour," Bill confirmed.

John went inside the house and gave Kate the latest information that Bill had provided. After about half an hour, they were both ready for their run. Stepping out the door, they began their run, which lasted approximately an hour before they returned home. Kate then informed the security team that they intended to go to church at 9:30 a.m. After getting dressed, John and Kate headed to the church, leaving the house on time.

During the church service, they each prayed for the same intentions and added specific items based on the week's events. The first two things they prayed for were Katelin's health and happiness, followed by a request for forgiveness for any sins they had committed. The subsequent prayer differed slightly for John and Kate. John prayed for Kate's continued health and happiness, while Kate prayed for John's well-being.

They then offered prayers for all the people they had lost due to the projects they had initiated. To John and Kate, it felt like a war since they were losing many talented individuals due to their projects, which had the potential to bring about significant change in the world. However, some wealthy people were resistant to change, even if it meant improving the lives of people all over the world. When they initiated the Medical Project, there were wealthy individuals within the medical community who didn't want to change the existing system and resorted to killing people just to stop the project. They were driven by the fear of losing substantial profits, even if the new system would have been better for all the people around the world. Presently, small groups of people seem perturbed by the United States' technological advancements as they struggle to keep pace.

John and Kate had gained global recognition, and the companies they collaborated with had developed innovations that had the potential to improve the world. Their Storm Project aimed to prevent storms and save lives, while the Climate Project focused on purifying the air and addressing climate issues.

These groundbreaking inventions were possible due to the nature of the U.S. government, where people or companies could become wealthy through their inventions. This fostered an environment where everyone was searching for the next big idea that could make them rich. However, such systems were not prevalent in other countries.

Both projects had the potential to influence countries like Cuba and Turkey, prompting them to re-evaluate their governments and align themselves more closely with the U.S. than Russia. Consequently, some people in Russia might attempt to hinder these projects and steal U.S. secrets. Additionally, there could be individuals within the U.S. who were motivated to steal these secrets to sell them and make a profit.

John, Kate, and their boss, Jim, were fully aware of these risks. Their astute leadership skills allowed them to strategize and devise plans that would ensure their success. This was why John and Kate were chosen to lead important projects both within the U.S. and worldwide.

After the church service concluded, the security team accompanied John and Kate back home. They decide to work from home on Sunday, preparing a plan to present to Jim on Monday.

Once at home, John and Kate began discussing who in Russia would want to stop the three projects and the reasons behind their actions. It didn't make sense to them since Russia was already facing bad press due to the war in Ukraine. Why would they seek negative attention by attempting to halt projects that could benefit the world?

They concluded that it couldn't be the Russian President but rather someone was against him and hoped to replace him. Consequently, they started contemplating the actions they would need to take to create a win-win situation for both the U.S. and the Russian president.

As it was getting late, they aimed to get at least seven hours of sleep, so they made love and went to bed.

Back to Work in the West Wing

A s soon as John and Kate arrived at the West Wing, they went directly to Jim's office to speak with him. They asked if they could have an hour of his time to strategize on the next steps for all three projects. Jim was in his office with his new executive assistant, Valerie. She had a bachelor's degree and was known for her intelligence and strong work ethic.

Jim called in his secretary and requested that she clear his calendar for the morning, unless it involved the President or one of the Congress or Senate leaders. "Let whoever was on my calendar know that we can meet after 5 p.m. today," Jim instructed.

He held John and Kate in high regard and never wanted to delay hearing their thoughts. They were highly skilled at accomplishing tasks and devising winning strategies. They were truly the best at making things happen. Jim then introduced Valerie to them, saying, "First, let me introduce you to my new executive assistant, Valerie."

This was Jim's first executive assistant since he lost his previous one to murder. John, Jim, and Kate had apprehended the murderer, who was killed in a battle. Jim said to John and Kate, "I seriously want both of you to consider getting an executive assistant. As you know, I always have one to ensure they understand how the government works and to prepare them for the next important project. I need each of you to start training the next John and Kate."

Kate then turned to Valerie and said, "After this meeting, if you have time, let's have some coffee together."

Valerie smiled and replied, "That would be great. I've heard so much about you and John. It would be an honor."

Kate then informed Jim of the discussion she had with John on Sunday. She said, "Jim, I believe John and I need to go to Russia and meet with their president. We must collaborate with Russia on the Storm Project to eliminate the numerous storms in the countries they are supporting. Russia can take the lead, and we will provide them with a solution to eliminate the storms using their rockets. We will ensure that it appears as if Russia is leading the effort. Additionally, for the Climate Project, we will use our computer to identify their hotspots and deploy the device we invented to eliminate harmful gases."

Kate added, "The rocket solution and the gas elimination device that we will give to them will be locked in a way that prevents the act of theft. However, we will allow them to rent the equipment. Furthermore, we will assist them in assembling a medical computer that meets the minimum requirements for The Medical Project to prevent a recurrence of what happened in Turkey. As part of these arrangements, they need to find the person or company in Russia that attempted to kill us and hold them accountable for it. Also, for these items we will provide them, they must adhere to the two conditions we require from them: first, they must withdraw from Ukraine; and second, they must put a stop to any attempts to impede our projects."

Jim responded, "This is why you guys are our leaders. This will work. The timing is perfect because Ukraine now has drones that are starting to knock out Russian forces and Russia may be more open to ending this war. The only modification I would suggest is that only one of you should go. I cannot afford to lose the both of you in this dangerous mission. "

John and Kate exchanged glances, smiled, and flipped a coin. The coin landed in John's palm, showing the heads, and then he declared, "I will be the one going. Kate will stay behind and make sure the projects stay on track."

It was around noon, and Kate turned to Valerie, saying, "How about we go to lunch? I know of a small diner near the West Wing that serves everything."

Valerie smiled, looked at Jim, and asked, "Is it okay if I take my lunch now?"

Jim smiled back and replied, "Absolutely. This will be the best training you'll ever get. Have a great lunch!"

While Kate and Valerie went to lunch, Jim and John began making plans for John's upcoming meetings in Russia and also discussed the necessary security arrangements he would need for the trip.

As they walk toward Kate's suggested diner, Valerie initiates a conversation with her, saying, "I know a lot about you and John because Jim talks about you all the time. He appreciates that he can assign any project to both of you and it gets done. He also mentions that you both have strong connections and have invented many things, holding numerous patents. He admires your delegation skills."

Kate nodded and said, "John and I learned a long time ago that if we choose the best and brightest people to work on a project with us, we can delegate many tasks to them. Sometimes, we have to remind our team members that we want them to make decisions. Just the other day, one of my subordinates informed me that a subcontracting company had an idea on how to improve the climate system, but it required an initial investment of $50,000 to build a prototype. I asked if it was a good idea, and they confirmed it was. I then inquired if they knew where to secure the funding, and they said they did. So, I told them it was their decision to make, and I expected them to make it happen."

She added, "John and I need to focus on more significant decisions, such as identifying those who are attempting to hinder our projects and kill us. We also need to complete ongoing projects and determine what our next ventures should be. If we have to deal with decisions that our subordinates should handle, it won't be for us or for them."

"Now that you know a bit about John and me, tell me a little about yourself," Kate said, encouraging Valerie to share anything about herself.

As they arrived at the diner and took their seats, Valerie replied with a smile, "I had heard many positive things about Jim and had the opportunity to speak with people who previously or currently work for him. Everyone speaks highly of him. When I had a chance to transition from my previous job, I asked my boss if there was an opportunity to work for Jim. Jim and I have had a few conversations in the past."

Valerie added, "I was conducting a competitive analysis, and Jim wanted a pitch on what we were doing in an area compared to the Russians and Chinese. After presenting my findings, he suggested that I give him a call if I ever wanted to discuss future opportunities. I knew he was looking for an executive assistant, so I approached my boss and then contacted Jim. Jim mentioned that he would be filling the position soon and asked if I was interested."

Kate responded with a smile on her face, "You must be exceptional because if you excel in this role with Jim, you'll have many options for your next job."

They placed their orders, enjoyed their meal, and returned to work. Upon their return, they noticed Jim and John on the phone with a Russian interpreter, indicating that they were arranging John's meetings in Russia.

Having just concluded the call with Russia, Jim turned to Kate and Valerie with a serious expression, holding a list of names. He said, "Kate and Valerie, John and I need to speak with both of you. Valerie, I need you to confirm all these meetings and make the necessary arrangements for my jet, hotel, and dinner reservations for John. I need you to do all this because some of these meetings haven't been confirmed yet. The Russian President wants John to meet with everyone on this list before their meeting. He believes that any one of these individuals might be the ones trying to kill both of you, or it could be someone from our side."

Jim added, "The Russian president mentioned that they would discuss Ukraine when John arrives in Russia. He was genuinely interested in collaborating with us on the Medical Project, Storm Project, and Climate Project. He expressed his enthusiasm for all three initiatives.

I can tell he's trying to find a way out of Ukraine but wants to secure a victory if he does."

This time, Jim turned to Kate and John. He said, "Kate, you and John need to investigate who might be assisting Russia in the U.S. or if someone is framing Russia for attempting to kill you. John, I would like you to catch a flight to Russia tonight."

Looking directly at Jim, John replied, "I need to leave now to pack and prepare. Will you make sure all the transportation and security are in place for the trip?"

Kate embraced John and said, "Don't take any chances. I plan to interrogate the person we captured—the one who tried to kill us—as soon as you leave this office. I'll call you once your plane safely lands in the Russian airport and share what I found out."

Jim nodded and added, "Have a safe trip, John. We'll be in touch."

The Ninth Day

Kate's Questioning and John's Meeting in Russia

K
ate went down to the police station and asked if it was okay for her to question the prisoner. They had already received a call from the White House, notifying them of Kate's intention to question the prisoner.

The prisoner was held in a separate room. Kate entered the room accompanied by her security team and introduced herself, saying, "My name is Kate Colombo, and you attempted to kill both John and me. I have a few questions for you. What is your name?"

The prisoner replied, "My name is Dimitri Ivanov, and I am a U.S. citizen."

Kate then sternly stated, "You have injured several people, and one person is in critical condition. If you do not cooperate with us, you will either face the death penalty or many years in prison."

Dimitri, wearing a serious expression, responded, "I really know nothing."

Kate locked eyes with him and asserted, "If you answer all our questions truthfully, we will assess whether you possess valuable information to assist us. We will also consider if we can provide any assistance to you."

Dimitri winced in pain as he replied, "I was told that if I spoke to anyone about what we did, my family here and in Russia would be killed."

Kate stood up, walked closer to Dmitri, and reassured him, "We will ensure that no one discovers you are cooperating with us. Your family will be protected."

Dimitri realized he was cornered and had no options but to reveal everything he knew. He reluctantly said, "If you place me and my family in witness protection and prevent the people I work for from knowing what I've told you, I will talk."

Kate conferred with the others in the room and then announced, "We agree to your terms, but if you cannot give us information about the people who hired you, you will be sent to jail."

Dimitri looked upset, slumping back in his chair, and began recounting his story, "I was born in the U.S., but my parents were sent as spies to the U.S. about fifty years ago during the Cold War between Russia and the U.S. They both died in a car accident, though I believe it wasn't an accident but rather a result of something they did wrong. I was in college when they died, and they left me a trust fund to live on. After completing college, I got married and had two children. Jim Seamore, a friend of my parents, contacted me. He threatened to kill my wife, children, and family in Russia if I didn't attempt to kill you and John. I considered going to the FBI, but I didn't know whom I could trust. So, me and the other guy that was killed in the car accident took the job to save our families."

Kate felt sorry for Dimitri and did not know whether to believe his story or not. With a skeptical voice, Kate responded, "Dimitri, we need to verify the truthfulness of your account. We also need to locate Jim Seamore and gather information from him."

Kate throwed several questions to Dmitri: "Where can we find him? Does he know the mission he had for you failed? How were you supposed to report back to him once the mission was completed? What does your family think you are doing?"

Dimitri hastily answered Kate's questions, "Jim lives in a house next to my parents' old house. They were close friends and used to have dinner together every Sunday. We were supposed to call him today, in about two hours, with the mission's results. Our plan was to meet at his house. My family thinks I am playing golf and then having dinner with some guys I am playing golf with."

Kate then said to Dimitri and the whole team, "We will report to the press that two people died when they were trying to kill John and me. We will then pick up your wife and kids and put all of you in the witness protection program. We will give Jim a chance to report back to the people who hired him, so they will not suspect you. I want you guys to put a tap on Jim's phone and track his movements for two days to see how deep this goes. Then we will apprehend him once we have all the information we need from him."

Then she looked directly at Dimitri and said, "Do you think this is a good plan and will it work?"

Dimitri, with a look of appreciation, said, "Yes, it will work, and thank you."

As soon as Kate left the room, she got Jim on the phone and conference-called John, who recently landed at an airport in Russia. On a conference call and told them the whole story. Jim then said on the call, "Great job, Kate. It does not change any of our plans. John, you still need to investigate from that end to see if their country started this whole thing. Kate, you need to work it from a U.S. perspective to see if it is similar to what happened in the Medical Project, which started here in our own country."

Kate then returned to the room where the questioning was taking place to ensure everyone was following through with the plan.

John's plane had just landed, and he was on his way to his first meeting in Russia. It was with one of Russia's top officials. The person had an office similar to John's boss, Jim, who was the Chief of Staff to the president, so he would know all the projects going on in Russia. John had some security people with him, and Jim had arranged for the U.S. Ambassador to Russia pick him up at the airport.

The ambassador had been briefed on what happened to John

and Kate but still had a few questions for John on how he wanted the meeting to go with Andrei Nikitin, who was the chief of staff to the president of Russia. While the Ambassador's limo was taking them to the meeting, he informed John and asked, "Andrei does speak English. What do you hope to achieve in this meeting?"

John was familiar with the ambassador well since they had attended the same college and taken several classes together. Joe Campo, the ambassador, had continued his education, earned a law degree, and then worked on the President's campaign, which led to his ambassadorship to Russia.

It was challenging for John to answer Joe's question, but he leaned closer to him, looked him in the eye, and said, "The perfect answer to your question is for Andrei to tell me who tried to kill Kate and me, as well as their motive. However, we know he may not answer that question either because he really doesn't know the answer or because his country might be involved, and he can't disclose it. Therefore, I will need to ask him some questions to see if he knows something and if he is telling us the truth."

Joe Campo asked, "Do you need me to do anything?" He then added, "I know Andrei well since we have attended some meetings together. When I talk with him, he seems to be straightforward. I have always known him telling the truth, but if he wants to get rid of you or see you fail, he also shoots straight. He usually has meetings with me at his home, so we will go to where he lives and works most of the time."

John quickly responded and said with a low tone so only Joe could hear him, "We have captured one of the people who tried to kill Kate and me. I would like Andrei to believe he is dead so we can protect his family here and in the U.S. Also, we know Jim Seamore in the U.S. hired him to kill us, and Kate has her eye on him to see if he can lead us to someone."

"You and Kate have not changed from our college days and now on our work collaboration on some projects. No one should get on your bad side because they will regret it in the end. You are both the smartest people I know, and I am sure glad you are on our side. Both of you really deserve the recognition the President gave you by being the first U.S. Leaders," Joe Campo said with a smile on his face.

At that moment, the limo was pulling into Andrei's office parking lot, so John had to be brief and just said, "Thanks, Joe. Now let's talk with this guy. You can chime in anytime."

The security guards, John, and Joe all got out of the car. Joe led the way since he was familiar with the area. As they approached the door, it opened. John acted surprised, and Joe said to John, "This always happens. From this point forward, you can assume everything is being watched and recorded. I was surprised also when I first came here and the doors opened."

Just as the doors opened, a rather tall Russian guard appeared and said, "Mr. Ambassador, you and Mr. John Colombo can come in. Please have your guards stay out here or in your limo."

Joe then turned to his guards and said, "We will be safe. Why don't both of you wait in the limo, and we will be out right after our meeting with Andrei."

At that moment, the guards turned around and went to the limo. John and Joe went through the door, which was then closed behind them. Then a loud voice came from inside the house, saying, "Hello, Mr. Ambassador and John, welcome to my home. Let's go in here to the dining area, and we can have something to drink and some snacks."

"Andrei, I was going to introduce you to John, but it seems like you know him well," Joe Campo said to Andrei, smiling.

Andrei smiled and said, "Yes, everyone around the world knows John Colombo and his wife Kate."

John always felt uneasy when he received a compliment like that, so with half a smile, he said, "Thank you, Mr. Mikitin, or would it be okay if I called you Andrei?"

Andrei smiled and said, "If I can call you John, then you can call me Andrei, but we will still call Joe Mr. Ambassador."

John then got a serious look on his face and said, "The reason I came here is to talk about a recent attempt on Kate's and my life. The two people who tried to kill us were killed, but we believe the person who ordered the hit was Jim Seamore."

After John said this, he looked very close at Andrei's face to see his reaction, but there was no reaction. Andrei then said, "Mr. Ambassador, you know me, and you know I would do nothing like this. I like the people in the U.S., and I want us to have a good relationship. If anyone would bring this up in a meeting I was in, then I would vote no to killing anyone in the U.S."

John then said, "I did not say that you had anything to do with trying to kill Kate or myself, but do you know anyone in Russia that would try to do this?"

Andrei then said, "The only time your name was brought up was when we discussed what happened in Turkey and them removing our computer over yours, and again when you stopped the storm in Cuba, and Cuba rethinking their relationship with the U.S. I thought that was the reason for this meeting."

Joe Campo then said, "Do you think that there could have been a person in that meeting that would take it upon themselves to do something like trying to kill John and Kate without telling you or the President?"

Andrei then looked at them and said, "Our government is like yours. We have people in a different party who may try to take things into their own hands and do something stupid. It would be the last time they did this, and I promise you I will dig into it more."

John then spoke up and said, "If you promise to look into this on your end, we will also look into it on our end and will share our results with you so you can take action."

Andrei, with a serious look, then said, "It's a deal." He reached across the table and shook hands with Joe and John.

John then said with a serious look on his face, "Now we can talk about the original purpose of this meeting, which is the sharing of the three project solutions the U.S. has: the Medical Project, the Storm

Project, and the Climate Project. We can share the Medical Project by allowing everyone in Russia to use it, just like everyone in the U.S. Since we are in Phase One, this will allow all doctors to have visibility of cures for all diseases, and we are now starting a study which we will involve your country."

He added, "Both the U.S. and Russia have many people with mental illness. We will be looking for a pattern on what causes schizophrenia. We believe all people who developed schizophrenia were doing the same things which caused it to happen. We need to figure out what that is so we can advise our people. The theory based on initial results shows that people were using drugs like marijuana, have a genetic predisposition, and could have been depressed. So, we will have doctors all over the world inputting what people were doing before they developed schizophrenia. We promise to give Russia full access to the Medical Project and also involve you in any studies we conduct.

"We will also supply you with the chemicals we use to stop storms. You only have to point out the storm you want to stop, and we will stop it initially for you. And then later on, you will be able to stop it once we give you the solution to put in your rockets to fire into the storm. As for the Climate Project, we can identify hotspots in Russia and provide you with the devices that eliminate them from being warm. In return, you will leave Ukraine, and the Ukraine president will apologize for how they have treated the Russians living there. This will then give the invasion a purpose and make it look like a win-win agreement. If you agree to all this, then we can get started."

Andrei looked satisfied with the agreement but then said with some hesitation, "If it were just up to me, then I would say yes, but you need to give me a couple of day to get agreement from everyone in Russia. It will also give you time to find out who tried to kill you and Kate."

"Okay, I will spend a few more days in Russia, just in case you want to meet again. Now, since we are sitting here at the dining room table, can we eat and drink?" John said, inviting Andrei and Joe to feast the food in the table.

Andrei laughed and then said, "Okay, my friends, get ready for the best vodka and the best snacks in the world."

Several people came in from another room carrying wine, vodka, and trays of food. Everyone was happy after a very successful meeting and shared interesting stories about past projects.

On the way to the limo, Joe turned to John and said, "I have something interesting to tell you when we get into the limo."

John couldn't wait to get into the limo, and when they were seated, Joe leaned over to John. With a whispering voice that only John could hear, Joe said, "I know you do not know this, but when Andrei heard you talk about the study you were going to start on schizophrenia, his eyes lit up with interest. The reason why is because his brother, his son, and his nephew are all schizophrenic. Of all other things you mentioned in that meeting, that is the one that will drive him to get agreement on your proposal."

John had a tear in his eye and said, "I didn't know, but I will make sure we get that study started immediately. This is an illness that really affects not only the person with the illness but also the whole family, as you can see by Andrei's reaction. Usually, a person with schizophrenia is in and out of hospitals their whole life and also in jail, and some even kill themselves. We need to find a cure for schizophrenia, and it has been in the world for over a thousand years. I need to brief Jim and Kate on the meeting. Can we give them a call from the limo?"

Joe Campo picked up the phone in the limo and asked his secretary to get Jim and Kate on the line, and when they had them, they called back. It was getting dark, and Joe was taking John to his hotel. A few minutes later, the limo phone rang. Jim and Kate were on the line, and Joe handed the phone over to John. John gave them a complete rundown of the meeting.

After John gave them an update, Jim gave some orders to the team and said, "John and Mr. Ambassador, you both did an excellent job. John, you need to stay there until Andrei has a chance to talk with his leaders. He may also find the person who tried to kill you and Kate.

Mr. Ambassador, you need to make sure that John stays safe while he is there. Whoever is trying to kill him may try to kill him again. We will also double the security on Kate. I suggest he stays with you at the embassy. Kate, put pressure on your team here to see if Jim Seamore leads you to his boss. If by tomorrow we do not know his boss, I suggest he be picked up and questioned before someone tries to kill him."

After that call, everyone began doing what Jim suggested.

Second Meeting with Andrei and Kate's Information

K ate contemplated the previous day's call with John, eager to gather the results of her team's wiretapping and surveillance on Jim Seamore. Upon waking up, she immediately emailed her team to convene in the West Wing conference room at 11 a.m. for a comprehensive review of their findings. Recognizing the importance of supporting John's endeavors in Russia, Kate had scheduled a 9:30 a.m. meeting with the Medical Project team to discuss the schizophrenia study.

Aware of John's need for up-to-date and valuable information, Kate always ensured she provided him with the best support, just as he had her back in all matters. This mutual support made their bond enjoyable and endeared Kate to John's friends and colleagues. Likewise, John's friends held him in high regard due to his unwavering commitment to Kate's well-being.

Before leaving for work at 8:30 a.m., Kate informed her security personnel and invited them for some coffee, toast, and cakes. Although they had already eaten breakfast, they agreed to join her for coffee. With increased security measures in place, two personnel remained at the house while two accompanied her to work. All four securities sat with Kate at the dining room table, and one of them expressed their respect to Kate: "We are really honored to be a part of your team. What you and John are doing is so important to the U.S. and the world."

Kate smiled and replied, "John and I are honored to lead these projects at the request of the President. I wish we could focus solely on the work instead of dealing with individuals trying to obstruct our projects and harm us. I truly appreciate all of you being part of the security team."

After the brief exchange, they all got into the limo except for the two security personnel who stayed at the house. Upon arriving at the West Wing, Kate went straight to her office and then to the conference room, where the medical team awaited her. As she entered the room, everyone stood up, shook her hand, and greeted her. Since John and Kate had personally chosen each member of the team, they were well acquainted and shared a friendly rapport. The secretary had arranged for coffee and donuts, and Kate got herself a cup of coffee and took a seat.

Kate began the meeting by updating everyone on John's mission in Russia and the significance of the schizophrenia study without disclosing personal details about Andrei. Standing by the white board, she began, "When John had his first meeting in Russia, it became apparent that Russia was interested in collaborating closely on the Medical Project, particularly with regards to certain studies on schizophrenia."

Dr. Joe Andrews, the psychiatrist who was responsible for the schizophrenia study, stood up to provide a status update. He stated, "The Medical Computer Project has been established and is operational, with input from several countries. We have asked questions regarding the activities of individuals prior to their schizophrenia diagnosis, and we are beginning to discern patterns. However, we still require additional data to validate our theory."

Kate then responded, "Excellent! I want you to prepare for travel to Russia and assist them in recruiting individuals for the study from their country. I will provide more details at 5 p.m. today. But in the meantime, please focus on gathering more data from around the world."

Continuing the discussion, Kate said, "I need to know who will be responsible for determining the next deployment locations for the Storm and Climate Projects. We need to prioritize the deployment in

Russia without compromising our secrets."

A person in an Army uniform stood up and stated, "I am Major Henry Jones, responsible for the Cuba storm deployment. I have also been tasked with deploying the Climate Project across the U.S."

Kate then said, "Major, you or one of your subordinates need to be ready to inform me about the deployment locations in Russia or Russian-held countries like Cuba. Also, please have that information ready for me by 5 p.m. today here, as you may need to accompany Dr. Andrews on a plane to Russia."

As the meeting concluded, another group of people gathered outside the conference room. Kate invited them in, and after everyone was seated, she began the meeting by saying, "As you all know, John is currently in Russia, and attempts have been made on both of our lives. You have been monitoring Jim Seamore so we can find out where he is getting his orders. I need that information now so that I can relay it to John, allowing him to discuss it with the Russians tomorrow."

One person from the group stood up and introduced himself, saying, "My name is Frank Gasbe, and I am with the FBI. We have been tapping Jim Seamore's phones and monitoring his activities. We have discovered that he has been communicating with someone in Russia named Sergey Ivanof. They instructed him to return to Russia as his cover is blown, and he has made a plane reservation for tomorrow at 11 a.m."

Kate responded, "Excellent work, Frank. I will be discussing this with John after this meeting, and we will decide whether to detain Jim Seamore or allow him to return to Russia. Please meet with me at 5 p.m. today in this conference room."

Following the meeting, Kate went into Jim's office for a lunch meeting scheduled for noon. They had a conference call with John and the Ambassador, who were having dinner, and had a 2 p.m. meeting the next day in Moscow with Andrei.

Kate updated everyone on her meetings, and when she finished, John said, "During our meeting with Andrei at 2 p.m., I will give him an opportunity to mention the name Sergey Ivanof and see if he is genuinely willing to help us. If he doesn't bring it up, I will provide him with the name."

Jim responded with a positive tone and said, "That sounds like the right approach. If he discloses the name, find out if he wants to take action against Jim Seamore or if we should handle it. Regarding the partnership with the Storm and Climate Projects, it will depend on his honesty in the first matter and his withdrawal from Ukraine. Since there have been drone attacks on Russia by Ukraine then I believe Russia will be looking for an opportunity to get out of the Ukraine.

I will update the President on all this, and it seems like we'll have an early morning meeting at 8 a.m. here in the West Wing. Call us at 4 p.m. to provide an update on your meeting with Andrei, and we'll determine our next steps regarding Jim Seamore and the Climate and Storm Projects."

Jim and Kate then strategized on the Climate and Storm Projects if they were to form a partnership with Russia. Kate wanted to end the meeting to call John before he went to bed, and once the meeting ended, she went straight to her office and called John on his cell phone. Before John could say anything, Kate said, "I want you to be very careful. I don't want to lose my one and only."

John replied lovingly, "Have you been listening to that song again by Brooks and Dunn, 'Neon Moon'?"

With a tear in her eye, Kate replied, "You won't believe this, but when I was listening to the radio, that song just started playing on a loop, and I couldn't figure out why the radio station would keep playing it. After about the tenth time, I realized it was on loop from my playlist. I didn't touch anything, so I don't know why it just came on."

John, with a tear in his eye, responded, "I don't want to lose my one and only either, so please be careful. I remember getting that CD. It was when Katelin took us to a Brooks and Dunn concert. Whenever I hear any of their songs, it brings me joy because it reminds me of that happy time. No matter where we are, we'll always have each other.

Right now, I'm in Moscow, and you're in DC, but we'll be alright as long as our dreams come in and out of a neon moon."

Kate then tearfully said, "You remember the words. I love you."

John replied, "I love you more. Talk to you tomorrow."

The next day, John and the Ambassador woke up late and decided to have a late breakfast before their meeting with Andrei. When they arrived at Andrei's house, someone opened the door before they could knock. They were welcomed inside, and Andrei greeted them, saying, "Happy to see you, my friends. I believe I have good news for you. Why don't we go to the dining room area and discuss?"

John and Joe, following their prior agreement with Jim and Kate, allowed Andrei to take the lead and see what he had to say. They smiled, and Joe Campo said, "We're always delighted to receive good news. Thank you for seeing us again."

Once seated, Andrei wore a serious expression and looked at both of them before saying, "The person in our government who ordered Jim Seamore to kill you and your wife is Sergey Ivanof. He works for an agency similar to the CIA. When we contacted his boss, they decided to take action against him. Jim Seamore was not punished as he was simply obeying orders, but he has been asked to return to Russia, where he will face consequences. We cannot tolerate members of our government taking matters into their own hands.

Sergey stated that he believed you and your wife embarrassed Russia, but we made it clear that if we were to eliminate anyone who outperformed us, we would not be the country we aspire to be. Sergey agreed and understands why he is being punished. Please don't ask how they will be punished, but rest assured, they will face consequences. We will not make any public announcements about this incident as it would be a source of embarrassment, and we hope your government will do the same. This will remain between us and our presidents."

Joe Campo, with a serious expression, responded, "We appreciate your honesty and will relay your request to keep this matter confidential to our President. We will do our best to make this happen."

John then spoke up, saying, "Thank you for being honest with us. If we can find a way for Russia to withdraw from Ukraine, we would like to partner with you on the Medical, Storm, and Climate projects."

Andrei smiled and replied, "I have more good news for you. If the Ukraine President issues a statement expressing improved treatment of Russians in his country and offers an apology to our President for forcing us to intervene, we will withdraw from Ukraine. This is a war that is an embarrassment to us. This will give us a good reason to stop the war. Additionally, we would like John to make an announcement outlining our collaboration on these three projects."

John, with a smile, said, "Andrei, if it is okay with you, I would like to make this type of announcement."

Clearing his throat, John continued, "As everyone knows, we aim to have every country join the Medical Project. We have asked Russia to partner with us in conducting initial studies, starting with schizophrenia. Our goal is to identify patterns and determine the causes of schizophrenia in certain individuals. Within one year, our best doctors from both countries will review all the data and provide recommendations. Furthermore, we will partner with Russia to gather stories from around the world and put an end to this terrible illness. Additionally, we will work together to put together a plan for the deployment of the Climate Project."

Andrei, smiled and said, "I wouldn't change a word. Now, let's see if we can turn all this into reality."

They shook hands, and Andrei suggested, "Okay, let's have something to drink and eat."

As soon as he said that, food and drinks were promptly served, and they all enjoyed their meal. Andrei, John, and the Ambassador knew they had a lot of work ahead of them, so they tried to quickly wrap up their meeting to begin the implementation process. John also knew he had a scheduled call with Jim and Kate at 3 p.m. Moscow time.

Upon returning to the Embassy, John and Joe connected with Jim and Kate on a conference call. Joe Campo began by reiterating what had been said at the start of the meeting: "Jim and Kate, we have good news. However, there is an information that must remain confidential between us and the presidents."

Jim assured them, "It's just the two of us, and we're in a secure room."

John began the news, saying, "Andrei provided us with the name of the person who was attempting to kill Kate and me. It matches the name you gave us: Sergey Ivanof. Russia will push for consequences against him and Jim Seamore. They are embarrassed and apologetic about what transpired, and they wish to keep it from the public. So, tomorrow, let Jim Seamore board the plane to Russia."

He added, "They will also agree to withdraw from Ukraine if the Ukrainian President apologizes for the mistreatment of Russians in his country. He needs to contact Andrei and come to an agreement with him. It seemed reasonable to us. When I return, I will draft an agreement with Andrei to ensure everyone on our end is in agreement. I believe working with Russia will benefit our projects."

Jim, expressing satisfaction, replied, "You all did great, and everything turned out exactly as we hoped. I will brief the President, and I'm sure he will be pleased. Great Job! Have a safe trip home, John. Until we are certain that the individuals involved have been dealt with, we will maintain the same level of security."

Knowing John's arrival time that afternoon, Kate called Katelin, and they both met him at the airport with security.

The Eleventh Day

Kate, John, and Katelin Together

W hen John arrived, Kate and Katelin met him at the baggage area. They both came up to him, wrapped their arms around him, and said, "We missed you so much. Thank God, you made it back to the U.S."

John responded, "You both hold a special place in my heart and in my life. Thank you so much for meeting me at the airport."

It was reminiscent of their time dancing at one of the nightclubs at Disney World. They were in a circle, holding hands, and spinning. John recalled the moment they were waiting for their bags and said to both of them, "This reminds me of the time we were at Disney World and we all got on the dance floor to dance. Katelin asked me what I was doing, and I said dancing. Then she showed me the right way to do it."

They all laughed but continued to hold hands. Kate said, "You remember the nicest things—the three of us dancing together, and now the three of us holding hands at the airport. That is why we love you."

John then saw his luggage, and the security guards had already retrieved theirs. The guards were in conversation with Kate's security personnel. One of them approached John and said, "It was a great trip. Kate's U.S. security guards will take over from here."

The guards who had accompanied John on the trip went in a different direction, and Kate, Katelin, and John followed the U.S. security guards to the limo.

As they got into the limo, John asked, "Will this be a pizza party night? Katelin, will you be able to spend the night at our house?"

"Yes, Daddy. I heard your trip and Mom's meetings were a success, so we thought we should celebrate. We will have pizza and some dessert," Katelin said, smiling.

On the way home, as usual, they talked more about Katelin's job and how things were going for her. Both John and Kate loved hearing about everything Katelin was doing and if she had made any new friends. When they reached the house, two security guards were waiting for them, allowing them to enter immediately. John ordered pizza for everyone, along with deserts. When it arrived, they all ate at the dining room table in the house. During dinner, John and Kate informed the guards of their plans for tomorrow. John wanted to fit in a morning run, and they both aimed to be in their offices by 9 a.m.

Afterward, John opened a couple of his suitcases, revealing the gifts he had brought home for Katelin and Kate. He loved making them happy and knew exactly what to buy to bring smiles to their faces. Unable to shop in Russia due to safety concerns, he had requested an early drop-off at the airport in Russia to do some duty-free shopping.

Knowing their shared appreciation for Chanel and Louis Vuitton, he purchased a Louis Vuitton pink bumbag for Katelin and a pair of Chanel pants with Chanel emblems glued all over for Kate. They were expensive, but seeing his girls happy made it worthwhile.

Kate, wearing a broad smile, remarked, "You know what we like. When did you find the time to shop?"

John, equally beaming, replied, "I made the time. I was thinking about what I wanted to get both of you the whole time I was in Russia."

Since the day he met Kate, John hasn't changed. He was always trying to make her happy and never failed to hold her hand wherever they went. She was the love of his life.

He also enjoyed watching Katelin and Kate together. From the day Katelin was born, Kate knew she had a lifelong friend. When Katelin was just a little girl, all Kate had to do was look at her, and if Katelin thought Kate was mad at her, she would cry or her face would turn red.

Kate was so proud when Katelin went to the same college as her. It would make Kate's day if a professor asked Katelin if she was Kate's daughter. Katelin was a good daughter. Kate made John promise he would never spank Katelin, even if she misbehaved, and he never did. She had turned out perfectly.

Commitments Promised and Made

John woke up early to complete his run and arrange a meeting, intending to honor the commitments he and Kate made to the Russians. When John woke up, he had the idea of convincing Kate to run with him and then have breakfast at a nearby diner. The alarm went off around 6 a.m., and John quickly got up while Kate lazily opened her eyes. Seeing that she was awake, John proposed, "Kate, I just thought of a good idea. Why don't we run about 2 miles to the diner, have some coffee and breakfast, and then run back home and get ready for work?"

Kate smiled and replied, "I'm in. We have a big day today, and we need to strategize on how we are going to make everything we committed to happen. Let security know, and let's go."

John informed security of their plans, and they made the necessary arrangements to ensure their safety. Kate and John got dressed in their running clothes and left through the front door. The security guard at the door pointed out the car that would be following them to the diner.

John and Kate started running at a slow pace to avoid sweating too much before reaching the diner. During the run, John turned to Kate and said, "Remember when we used to make this run every day when Katelin was in middle school? We would sit at a table, and they all had jukeboxes with all kinds of music. Most of the time, we would listen to old Willie Nelson songs."

Smiling while running, Kate replied, "Why do you think I said yes to this crazy run we are doing today? Great memories!"

They were approaching the diner after completing the two-mile run, and John said to Kate, "Well, the diner is still there. Let's see if they changed the tunes in the jukebox." They slowed down as they neared the diner, and the security guards were already inside.

John and Kate walked in, and as usual for that early hour, there was only one other person sitting at a table. The security personnel were already seated at a table near the door, providing a complete view of the restaurant. When John and Kate entered, they nodded at the guards. The owner of the diner approached them and said, "We are so happy to see you back again. Let me take you to the table you always used to sit at when you came here every morning."

John and Kate were surprised because they had never met the owner, but they followed him to the table they always occupied during breakfast. Kate pointed to a picture from the local newspaper and exclaimed, "Will you look at this!" It was a picture of them with the caption, "These two famous people used to eat here every morning."

John laughed and said, "You know you've made it big when the local diner does this. I guess this means a big tip."

Kate inserted a quarter in the jukebox and played John Denver's "Take Me Home, Country Roads" and Brooks and Dunn's "Neon Moon." She chose the first song because they both loved West Virginia, and the second song because they never wanted to feel the pain of lost love. They had made many good friends and wanted to keep making more.

They then held hands across the table and looked into each other's eyes. Their love for each other had grown stronger since they got married with no money. John always shared the story his grandfather told him: "When my grandfather was at his 70s, he told me that his brother died young, and he was still alive. I asked him why that happened, and he said, 'I married for love, and my brother married for money.'" John knew that when he met Kate, they both got married for love, as they had no money. They couldn't have married for money since they had student loans, were on food stamps, and were just trying to finish college.

After breakfast and a couple more songs, Kate and John left a generous tip and headed out for their two-mile run back home. They showered, got dressed, and entered the limo to the West Wing for their 9 a.m. meeting. Kate had set up the meeting with the same team from John's time in Moscow. The purpose of the meeting was to provide everyone with an update on what happened in Moscow, the commitments that were made, and the actions needed to honor those commitments. Also, they had a meeting scheduled with the FBI to discuss Jim Seamore.

As Kate and John entered the conference room, everyone stood up, shook their hands, and greeted them. This wasn't typical for all meetings, but the team that John and Kate had assembled was close-knit and understood the risks involved. They want to show their appreciation. Kate initiated the meeting by saying, "Well, as everyone can see, John made it back from Russia in one piece. Everything we wanted to accomplish in Russia has been achieved. They made a commitment to leave Ukraine as soon as the Ukrainian President grants them amnesty. After their departure, we will announce our partnership on the three projects, but we won't disclose any proprietary information."

Dr. Sam Andrews raised his hand and asked, "When should we start making contact with the people in Russia? We want to expand the number of participants in the schizophrenia study. We have several countries involved now, and we are starting to observe a pattern that reveals what people were doing before being diagnosed with schizophrenia. Including Russia in the study may either prove or disprove our theory."

John and Kate looked at each other, both nodding in agreement. John replied, "As a gesture of good faith, indicating Russia's intention to exit the Ukraine, I will provide you with the name of the person in Russia who will serve as your point of contact for the schizophrenia study. You can share the data we have and discuss the data we need to validate our theory on the cure for schizophrenia."

John knew Andrei had a particular interest in the schizophrenia study, as several members of his family had the condition. This gesture would demonstrate good faith in partnering with Russia and trusting their commitment to leave Ukraine. However, they would not announce the partnership at this time.

Major Henry Jones raised his hand and inquired, "What about the deployment of climate gear and possible upcoming storm locations? Do I have a contact in Russia to work with?"

Kate, referring to John for confirmation, responded, "I believe it's permissible to make contact with this person and inform them about the criteria for deploying the Storm and Climate gear. However, actual deployment should only occur once Russia has withdrawn from Ukraine."

With the meeting concluded, John and Kate had to provide Jim with an update and learn from him whether the President had contacted Ukraine to discuss Russia's terms.

John and Kate proceeded to Jim's office across the hall. Jim was in a meeting with his executive assistant, Valerie, but upon seeing John and Kate, he invited them in and said, "Come in and have a seat. We just finished a call with the President. He spoke with the President of Ukraine, who agreed to make the announcement as requested by the Russian President. However, due to the ongoing bombings in Ukraine, we need to be the first to deploy the Climate Project. We want to showcase its deployment while the Ukrainian President discusses how he will treat the Russians in Ukraine better. Our air quality has been severely impacted by the Russian bombings, and we require climate gear deployed throughout Ukraine."

John interjected, "Timing is everything. First, we need Russia to cease the bombings and initiate its withdrawal from Ukraine to ensure the safety of our people. We also need to ensure Russia agrees to the deployment of climate gear in Ukraine before the Ukrainian President makes the announcement of their departure. Ideally, the Ukrainian president should also acknowledge the joint deployment of climate gear by the U.S. and Russia."

Jim summarized the meeting by saying, "Alright, I'll have our President contact the other two presidents to secure their agreement on the announcements and deployment. John and Kate, we will need both of you to arrange a conference call with the Ambassador and Andrei to obtain the contact names in Russia who will be working with Dr. Andrews and Major Henry Jones. Valerie, please set up that call for them ASAP."

John and Kate had another meeting in their conference room with the FBI. They swiftly left Jim's office and headed to the conference room, where Frank Gasbe awaited them. He greeted them with a smile and said, "This will be a short meeting. Jim Seamore boarded the plane to Russia as planned."

John and Kate felt relieved and expressed their approval, saying, "Good job! It's a commitment we made in Russia. He will face consequences there, and the Russians were embarrassed by the incident and want no mention of it. Thank you, Frank."

The meeting with the FBI was brief, and the only task remaining for John and Kate was the conference call with Andrei and the Ambassador, which Valerie scheduled for 9 a.m. on Saturday, U.S. time, taking into account the time difference with Russia.

The Thirteenth Day

A Call with Andrei and the Ambassador

Since this was the only meeting that John and Kate had on Saturday, they decided to make the call from their home. When John and Kate joined the call, they noticed that Andrei and the Ambassador were in the same room at the U.S. Embassy in Russia.

Valerie, who set everything up, wanted to ensure everyone was connected. She then mentioned that she would be leaving the call but advised them to reach out to her if they encountered any problems. She promptly hung up.

John initiated the conversation by saying, "Sorry to have this call on Saturday, but we thought it was important enough to try and settle things since lives are at stake."

Andrei responded with a happy tone, "Thank you for setting everything up. I figured since you always come to my place for meetings, I would come to the U.S. Embassy this time. My president was pleased with the speech made by the Ukrainian president, so he has already begun withdrawing troops. He wants to deliver a speech about the withdrawal, the U.S.-Russia partnership on the three projects, and the deployment of the Climate Project throughout Ukraine. He would like John, Kate, and the Ambassador to stand by his side during the speech."

Joe Campo, the Ambassador, adopting a serious tone, spoke up and said, "We would be honored to stand by your president during his speech. However, before we accept, we will need a copy of his speech and approval from our government."

Andrei quickly replied, "A copy of his speech is in this envelope, and he plans on making the speech on Tuesday. I will be standing by his side as well. He just wants to bring some recognition to the people who made this happen."

Kate and John couldn't help but smile and shed a tear of joy. Kate said, "Let's hope the Ambassador can secure all the necessary approvals so that we can stand by his side during his speech. Once the speech is delivered, we can begin the deployment of the Climate equipment, identify a storm to neutralize, and address any tasks required to bring Russia up to speed on the Medical Project. We have a researcher in the U.S. working on the schizophrenia study, and he is ready to draw some conclusions that could prove our theory based on a small sample. So far, the theory suggests that drug use, the environment, depression, and genetics contribute to the onset of schizophrenia. Who should we have Dr. Joe Andrews, who is leading the study, call in Russia to get started there and draw our final conclusions?"

Andrei quickly responded, "Please have him call me. I am very interested in this study for personal reasons. You may already know this, but my son, nephew, and brother all have mental health issues, and we need to look into what the thousands of people in the study were doing before they developed schizophrenia so we can identify any patterns and warn people about what they should avoid doing. I don't know how schizophrenia skipped me, considering most males in my family have it. I consider myself lucky. I will get you the names of the Climate and Storm leaders in Russia."

John then said with a sympathetic tone, "I am so sorry, Andrei. This illness has been around for over a thousand years, and it is time we find a cure. We also have Major Henry Jones leading the deployment of the Climate and Storm projects. Let us know who they should be working with in Russia. Although the first deployment of the Climate Project will be in Ukraine, it would be good for Russia to lead that effort."

"I agree, but I need to verify and get approval from the person or persons who will head up those two items. I will get back to you on Monday," Andrei said with a sense of urgency.

The Ambassador, eager to conclude the meeting, stood up and said, "I can see why our presidents chose you three to lead the most crucial projects in our countries. It has been an honor to work with the smartest and most honest people in the world. Our countries are incredibly fortunate to have you as leaders."

Immediately after the call, John and Kate dialed Jim on his private line to inform him of the meeting's outcome. Jim responded, "I will inform the President of the call's details. I'm confident he will be pleased and will allow both of you to go to Russia once we have reviewed the speech. I will have Valerie make travel arrangements for you on one of our jets, along with providing security and a limo. For the time being, I want to maintain tight security, and I suggest you both stay at the U.S. Embassy in Russia. I found out that Alexsel Ivanof, the person who wanted you killed, has been executed in Russia. It was kept quiet."

He added, "He was heavily invested in the medical and insurance industries. He was undoubtedly working on his own, but he utilized Russian resources to target you both. Once the Medical Project was completed, he would have lost a substantial amount of money since he wanted to maintain the current state of the medical industry. He would also have suffered losses in the insurance sector due to reduced insurance purchases resulting from fewer storms."

Kate, expressing her gratitude, replied, "Thank you, Jim. We will await Valerie's call concerning our trip."

They then made an attempt to call Katelin, but her answering service greeted them instead. They left a message expressing their desire to meet with her the following day. With a full day ahead, they retired early to bed.

The Fourteenth Day

A Free Day with Katelin

As soon as John and Kate woke up, they called Katelin. "Did you get our message? We want to spend the day with you. Can you come over for breakfast, or do you want to meet at the mall for breakfast and take in a movie?" Kate asked her daughter.

"The second one. We will meet at The Cheesecake Factory in one hour for breakfast and then go from there to a movie and do some shopping," Katelin responded from the other line.

Kate quickly agreed and said, "Deal, see you in an hour."

John rolled over with a big smile on his face, and Kate wasn't sure if it was because they made love last night or because of what he heard. He said, "It must be nice for both of you to make decisions without asking me. What freedom you both have. I remember having that freedom before we got married."

"We have been married a long time, and we both know each other well. You are not only my husband but also my best friend. I know one of your favorite days would be breakfast at The Cheesecake Factory and a movie," Kate said with a smile on her face.

John, still smiling, said, "That's why I love you so much. You are so beautiful that you take my breath away. You are also the smartest person I know, and you are someone who always has my back. You are the total package. You know we married for love because neither of us had any money. We just loved and trusted each other. I will be ready in fifteen minutes and will let security know of our plans."

That brought a tear to Kate's eyes, and she said, "I love you too!"

Both of them greatly admired each other and cherished their freedom. However, they worried about how long it would last. They had originally moved into a gated community because they were concerned about some of the people John was working with. It provided them with a safe area that looked really nice. Whenever they entered through their community gates, it felt like stepping into Disney World. However, after the President's announcement, they began to lose some of that freedom when they went out to eat or shop. People started recognizing them, but that recognition faded over time. Now, with the new announcement in Russia, even though it was an honor, they knew they would lose even more freedom, which worried them a lot.

When they arrived at the mall, Katelin was not there. Kate decided to do some shopping, while John put their names down for a table and went out into the mall, observing the bustling crowd. In the distance, John caught sight of a beautiful lady dressed in white jeans and a white shirt. He took just a quick glance, as Kate had trained him well not to stare at other women. He then entered the restaurant and took a seat, waiting for their names to be called.

A few minutes later, John heard his name and was led to a booth. He ordered a diet coke for himself and coffee for Kate and Katelin, knowing how much they needed their morning coffee. As John perused the menu, he suddenly looked up and noticed a pair of white jeans. He looked all the way up and saw Kate and Katelin. He felt a twinge of embarrassment because he had never before regarded his daughter as pretty, but she was, just like his wife.

The next day, John recounted the story to his wife and assured her that he couldn't see her face from that distance, but he knew it was her when they reached the table. Kate simply laughed and said, "I knew our daughter was beautiful from the day she was born, but as she grew into a teenager, I noticed boys and men would look at her more than once as she walked by."

"I guess that's why they asked her to do some modeling when she was in high school," John commented.

Kate laughed again and said, "That's why you're a lucky guy. You have a beautiful wife and a beautiful daughter, and they're both intelligent as well." John simply shook his head and smiled.

Later that night, they got a call from Valerie, who instructed them to pack their bags. The plane would depart for Russia at 10 a.m., and a limo would pick them up at 9 a.m. They wouldn't need tickets as it would be one of their own planes, but they were advised to bring their passports. Upon arrival in Moscow, an Embassy car would transport them to the U.S. Embassy in Russia, where they would stay.

After the call, Kate called Katelin to let her know about their plans and assure her not to worry if she needed to reach them. She informed Katelin that she and her dad would be standing next to the President of Russia when he made an announcement. While she couldn't provide any details, she speculated that it would likely be covered in the news and they should be back on Wednesday. She advised Katelin to contact the U.S. Embassy in Russia or Jim at the West Wing in case of an emergency.

Katelin jokingly responded, "See, I knew you guys were famous! I'll see you on Wednesday."

After hanging up, Kate turned to John and said, "We are so lucky to have such a beautiful daughter in our lives. I think I'll join you for a run tomorrow. Wake me up at 6 a.m."

John pondered for a moment, gazing at a picture of his wife and daughter, and then expressed his thoughts aloud: "I am so lucky to have these two beautiful people in my life."

Kate leaned over, gave him a kiss, and they made love.

Preparation for the Meeting in Russia

The alarm went off at 6 a.m., and they both woke up and put on their running gear. John always enjoyed seeing Kate in her running gear. She had a beautiful figure and looked great. He looked at her and said, "You look beautiful. Are you ready to do this?"

"Put your eyes back in your head. I can't believe you're saying that to me with no makeup on and in my running outfit. You must really be in love. Let's get this over with, and then we have to sit on a plane for over ten hours," Kate said while smiling.

They both left the house, and a car was waiting for them to follow along as they ran through the streets near their home. After finishing their run, they showered, packed their belongings, and stepped outside to enter the limo that would take them to the jet heading to Moscow.

During the trip, they didn't have much to do except stand next to the President of Russia while he gave a speech. When they boarded the plane and settled into their seats, Kate looked John straight in the eye and said, "I know we don't have much to do on this trip, but I would like to push the agenda and ensure that all the Russia and U.S. personnel working on the three projects have been communicating. We need to emphasize the importance of the mental health study, specifically adding all the Russian individuals with mental health issues to the medical computer database. We should also collect data on their activities prior to developing schizophrenia to identify any patterns and potentially find a cure for these diseases around the world. Additionally, I would like to identify at least one climate deployment and one storm we can address. It's crucial that the Russian and U.S. deployment teams are in communication."

John looked at Kate with a serious expression and said, "I guess we are not going to sleep or relax on this flight."

He immediately picked up the satellite phone to call their boss, Jim. When Jim picked up the call, John said over the line, "We need to have Valerie arrange conference calls with our team leaders for the Medical Study on Schizophrenia and the deployment of Storm and Climate Projects on the U.S. and Russia efforts. She has the list of those people, and we would like to be updated on the progress of each team as soon as we land."

"Will do. You guys are the best. It's important to ensure we're making progress on what we committed to Andrei, the Ambassador, and the President. We will arrange the calls once you arrive at the embassy. It might be a late night for the both of you. Try to get some rest on the plane," Jim replied with assurance and concern to John and Kate.

During the flight, John and Kate discussed the expected results of the upcoming calls with their teams. Though they managed to sleep for a couple of hours, John and Kate typically didn't require more than seven hours of sleep per day, and they had most of that the previous night.

After landing, a U.S. Embassy limo and security vehicles were waiting for them. When they arrived at the Embassy, Joe Campo, the Ambassador, was waiting outside to greet them. He said, "I already met John when he was here, and now I want to say it is an honor to meet you, Kate. Both of you are the best leaders in the world, and Andrei and I are honored to work with you on these projects. We heard about the conference calls you set up. Would it be possible for Andrei and me to join the calls? Andrei thought it would be helpful to have a Russian representative present in case any issues arise on their side."

Kate replied, "Excellent idea. The first call will begin in one hour, focusing on the Medical Project's schizophrenia study, followed by the other two calls. Each call will last an hour."

"Okay, show us to our room so we can change clothes, freshen up, and get ready for the first call," John added.

John and Kate both dressed in more formal clothing since they were on a video conference call with the Russian and American leaders for each of the projects. They walked into the conference room about fifteen minutes before the first call on the Medical Project study on mental health and substance abuse.

It was evident that both Andrei and Joe seemed excited, and an IT staff was in the room, preparing to connect the leaders from Russia and the U.S. The IT staff turned to everyone and announced, "Everyone is on the line, and we are ready to begin."

John initiated the meeting by confirming if everyone could either speak English or had their translator on. He also requested each person to introduce themselves and reviewed the meeting's purpose, which was to update Russia on the progress of the Medical Project and the schizophrenia study.

John then requested that the Russian leaders provide an update on the status of the project's computers in Russia. The Russians were able to comply, and John subsequently asked the U.S. leader to provide an update on the overall progress of the Medical Project around the world and the schizophrenia study.

The U.S. leader responded, "The leader in Russia and I have been in contact and are aware of our status as of a few days ago. I will now bring everyone up to speed on our current position. The Medical Project computers have been installed in every country in the world and have started collecting information on schizophrenia. We have just begun collecting this information in Russia as well. The study of schizophrenia is starting to reveal patterns in the early stages of the disorder. However, we are refraining from drawing any conclusions at this point, as we are awaiting input from Russia and other countries."

Kate then interjected and asked, "Does it appear that our theory regarding the correlation between marijuana or other drugs and a family history of schizophrenia is the main cause of the disorder in individuals?"

The U.S. leader promptly responded to Kate's inquiry, stating, "Based on the responses we have received so far—over a hundred thousand in total—they are confirming our theory, along with identifying some other contributing factors. This is why Russia's input is crucial to our study. As they have just begun compiling their data, we anticipate including it in the study within the next two weeks."

"Is that true? Will we have our input into that study in two weeks?" Andrei asked, directing the question to the Russian leader.

The Russian leader answered, "We expect to provide 90% of our findings within two weeks. However, there are a few cities that have been delayed due to insufficient funding for computer upgrades."

"Please provide me with the names of these cities and the individuals who communicated this information to you. Let them know that I will be contacting them directly," Andrei said with authority.

John expressed his gratitude to everyone for their participation in the call and scheduled another meeting in two weeks to review the results of the schizophrenia study. Subsequently, the call concluded, leaving everyone visibly pleased, especially Andrei, who has been striving to uncover the root causes of schizophrenia and find a resolution.

The next call regarding the Storm Project was scheduled to start in ten minutes. The IT personnel began connecting all the participants and then turned to Kate, signaling that everyone was on the call. Kate initiated the meeting by stating, "I have been informed that everyone is present for the Storm Project call, so let's get started. Could the U.S. Leader provide us with an update on the storms we are currently tracking and preparing to address? Additionally, I would like to know the progress of the Storm Project collaboration with Russia."

The U.S. Leader quickly began his update by saying, "We are tracking another storm leaving Africa, which is projected to hit the Bahamas and the U.S. in five to six days. It is currently the only storm we are monitoring that has the potential to reach hurricane status.

Regarding the collaboration with our Russian counterpart, they have not spotted any storms they wish to stop. However, we have provided them with our storm-stopping liquid under the agreement that they will not attempt to replicate it. If they find a storm, they will call us, and we will work with them as to the best way to stop it. If they encounter a storm they want to address, they will notify us, and we will work together to determine the best course of action. If the storm we are tracking appears to be heading toward Cuba, we will coordinate efforts with Russia to stop it."

Andrei then turned to the Russian Storm Leader and asked, "Do we require any further assistance from the U.S.? Also, how would you assess our relationship with the U.S. in the context of the ongoing Storm Project?"

"We have an excellent working relationship with the U.S. team. We hold weekly meetings, but if the need arises, we are open to convening more frequently. Currently, there are no storms we need to stop, but we are closely monitoring the one leaving the African coast now," the Russian Storm Leader responded.

Expressing his gratitude, John addressed everyone on the call: "Thank you, everyone. This was a productive meeting. We have another call scheduled in ten minutes, so let's conclude this one."

As the IT staff began connecting the participants for the Climate Project call, he turned to Kate and said, "The Russian leader will not be on the call, but his associate will be sitting in for him."

Andrei motioned to Kate, indicating that he would like to start the meeting. Kate agreed, and Andrei started by saying, in a firm tone, "Welcome, everyone, to the Climate Project meeting. I must express my disappointment that the Climate Project leader is not in attendance. I request the person representing him in this meeting to explain his absence."

"We apologize for our Climate Project leader's absence. During the attempt on your life, Andrei, there was also an attack on our leader. He managed to defend himself but sustained serious injuries and is currently hospitalized. Although he wanted to join this call, the doctors prohibited it. We have captured the person responsible, and they are questioning him now." The nervous representative said.

Joe Campo spoke softly: "Do you think it would be a good idea for all of us to visit him at the hospital to offer our well wishes?"

"Please arrange that meeting. Also, can you provide us with an update on the status of the Climate Project?" Andrei said, instructing the representative of the Climate Project Leader.

The nervous representative replied, "After our leader was hospitalized, we halted the weekly meetings with the U.S. team. However, when he learned about the pause, he became upset, believing it played into the hands of those seeking to delay the Climate Project. Consequently, we have resumed the meetings and are actively identifying suitable locations for installing the Climate devices."

John, with a hint of annoyance in his voice, turned to Andrei and suggested, "I strongly recommend meeting with this individual. Consider having all your leaders present during tomorrow's announcement by your president. Once this call concludes, I will inform the U.S. team to enhance security measures for all our leaders involved in these three projects worldwide."

Kate, aiming to shift the meeting's tone, asked for a global update on the Climate Project from the U.S. leader.

"Our meetings have been productive, and we are deeply sorry for the challenges faced by our Climate Project colleagues in Russia. We will redouble our efforts to ensure that we do not lose any time. Regarding the global status, nearly every country has reached out to us, expressing interest in utilizing the Climate Device. We have provided them with cost estimates for manufacturing the device and invoiced them accordingly. Our intention is not to generate profit but rather to cover our expenses. All countries have acknowledged and agreed to this arrangement, and demand for the devices is outpacing our productive capacity. Russia is a priority, so once they identify the required locations, we will expedite the delivery. We have already installed devices in prominent hotspots within the U.S. and will continue to install more as new areas emerge," the U.S. Climate leader said, sounding nervous.

As the hour for the Climate Project call came to an end, the Ambassador spoke urgently, "Thank you all for the updates. Looking around this table, it seems we are satisfied with the progress despite the challenges. We need to prepare for the President of Russia's speech tomorrow, so let's adjourn this meeting."

John stood up from the table and added, "Please discuss any necessary changes to be made to the President's speech. I need to make some urgent calls to the U.S. to ensure heightened security measures are in place for all our project leaders involved in these three initiatives worldwide."

Andrei and Joe exchanged glances and agreed to take a thirty-minute break before reconvening in the conference room. John and Kate contacted Jim and Valerie, providing them with an update on the preceding meeting and emphasizing the need for heightened security for all project leaders involved in the three initiatives around the world.

After reconvening in thirty minutes, they agreed to acknowledge the Russian Leaders of the three projects and explore the possibility of the hospitalized leader attending or watching the announcement on Russian TV. They also announced the partnership between Russia and the U.S. in the three projects, along with the deployment of Climate devices throughout Ukraine and Russia's withdrawal from Ukraine following the Ukrainian President's speech.

The new speech had received approval from both the U.S. and Ukrainian presidents. With everything set for the next day, they adjourned the meeting at the embassy. Andrei departed for his office, while John and Kate, exhausted, retired to their respective rooms. The ambassador remained concerned about security for the following day's event and ordered extra security for the Embassy and the ride to the venue where the speech was being made.

John and Kate were too tired to do anything else but return to their room. They decided to call Katelin to check on her. Kate managed to reach her daughter's phone and jokingly said, "Hello, Katelin, this is your mother calling from the Russian Embassy in Moscow. How are you doing today?"

"Hello, Mother. Did you and Dad get into trouble again, and they shipped you off to Russia?" Katelin jokingly asked while laughing.

With the phone on speaker, John joined in the laughter, finding joy in the playful interaction between Kate and Katelin. He even relished their occasional arguments. Their mother-daughter relationship was remarkable, and John appreciated witnessing such warmth and connection. He wished to see that kind of bond between mothers and daughters everywhere—it was truly special.

When Kate finished her conversation with Katelin, she handed the phone to John, who remarked, "We have one more significant meeting tomorrow, and then we should be coming home. Every time we have one of these meetings, we lose a little bit of our freedom."

John's statement stemmed from his awareness that he and Kate would soon gain international recognition, making it increasingly difficult for them to enjoy simple outings like going to The Cheesecake Factory or watching a movie without the need for heightened security.

Understanding his sentiment, Katelin replied in a somber tone, "I am so proud of you and Mom. The work you both do truly makes a difference and contributes to making the world a better place. I love you both."

As John expressed his gratitude and bid farewell to Katelin on the phone, a tear welled up in his eye. Glancing at Kate, he noticed a tear in her eye as well. He said, "We are incredibly fortunate to have such a beautiful daughter in our lives. I am so grateful for every moment I have with her."

Kate, with a tearful gaze, looked at John and responded, "She is the love of my life, and so are you. You better put your head in my lap and stop working because we never know how much time we have together. It seems there are many people opposed to these three projects. However, the good news is that there are more individuals who support them and stand to benefit from their outcomes. As usual, those who oppose progress are motivated by their financial interests, disregarding the positive impact these projects could have on people worldwide. Okay, let's go to bed. We have a big day ahead tomorrow."

A Big Day in Russia and the U.S. President's Call

K ate and John both woke up at 6 a.m. and decided to take a run around the Embassy compound. They got dressed in their running clothes and went to the front door to ask if they could run inside the Embassy. The guard pointed them to an area where they could run safely.

After their run, they approached the secretary at the front desk and asked about breakfast. She informed them that the Ambassador wanted them to join him at 8 a.m. in the cafeteria. They had about half an hour to get ready, so they quickly showered together, got dressed, and went down to the cafeteria.

Joe Campo was already sitting at a table, waiting for them. He asked, "I think you both have Top Secret clearance, correct?"

John and Kate nodded in confirmation. They had held that clearance since they started working for the government.

Joe continued, "Excellent. I get briefed every morning at breakfast, and it would be good for you to hear this since you'll be around until tomorrow." He motioned for the security personnel to join them, indicating that John and Kate could listen to the briefing.

One of the security personnel introduced himself to John and Kate and instructed them not to tell anyone about his briefing. Once John and Kate agreed, the security personnel began speaking while they were served breakfast.

During the briefing, John and Kate learned that two attempts had been made on their lives. One was stopped by Russian security, and the other by U.S. security. The next attempt was planned for when they left the Embassy on their way to the Russian President's speech.

These attempts were intended to embarrass the Russian president. Both Andrei and Joe were aware of the location and timing of the planned attack, and they were making arrangements to apprehend those involved. The Ambassador, John, and Kate would be traveling in a different car, taking a different route to the speech venue, which was the Presidential Palace. The car with the decoys John, Kate, and Joe would leave at 11:30 a.m. for the 1 p.m. speech, while the real car would depart through a secret exit at 11:45 a.m.

After breakfast, they were provided with bulletproof vests and escorted back to their rooms to get ready, as it was already 10 a.m. Upon returning to their room, they found a message instructing them to call Jim, their boss, who was in the U.S. President's office. They immediately picked up the phone, put it on speaker, and dialed the President's number. A lady on the other line recognized the number and informed them to hold for the President and Jim.

The President came on the line and reassured them, saying, "You two are the best of the best, and Jim, myself, and the President of Russia are not going to let anything happen to you. Just like we did during the Medical Project when we caught that terrible American attempting to put your lives in danger, we will do it again and capture that terrible Russian. I apologize for putting your lives at risk again, but soon it will end, and we can begin making the world a better place."

The President added, "Don't worry about Katelin. We invited her to come here for our call with you and also watch TV with us later. She is safe, and we plan to put more security on her just in case."

Katelin then came on the line and encouraged her parents, saying, "Do good today; I really admire both of you. You are the best!"

Both John and Kate had tears in their eyes as they responded,

"Thank you all for everything you are doing. We will be okay. We have the Russians and Americans working together to keep us safe."

After the call ended, John and Kate looked at each other, tears still in their eyes, and almost simultaneously said, "Imagine how Katelin must feel being in the President's office. WOW!"

John, Kate, and the Ambassador expressed their well-wishes to the occupants of the decoy limo. Everyone in the decoy limo was armed and traveling in a bulletproof car with Marines and Russian soldiers for security. Russian security personnel dressed as civilians had already surrounded the intended ambush location.

The decoy limo left at 11:30 a.m. as planned, and at around 11:40 a.m., gunfire and explosions erupted midway between the Embassy and the Palace. Two security cars—one in front and the other behind them—accompanied the real limo carrying John, Kate, and the Ambassador as it left through a different exit at 11:45 a.m.

John noticed that the limo driver was on the phone when they left the Embassy, which struck him as unusual. He whispered to the Ambassador, "Do you know this driver?" The Ambassador shook his head in response.

In a loud voice, John requested, "Please stop the car."

When the driver refused to comply and accelerated, John, seated directly behind him, kicked the back of the driver's seat with all his strength, causing the driver's head to hit the steering wheel and break his nose. At that point, the driver stopped the car and fled on foot. The Marines in the car ahead chased after him and apprehended him.

Seizing the opportunity, John took the driver's seat and said to the Ambassador, "I am going to drive straight to the security car. I think we should all get into the security car and have our armed security personnel join us."

With that decision made, John started driving the security car and inquired, "Does anyone know the quickest route to the Palace?"

The Marines pointed straight ahead, and John drove straight in that direction, followed closely by the limo and the other security car.

As they approached the Palace, another car collided with the limo, and its occupants began firing their guns. John called for backup, and upon seeing several cars from the Palace rushing toward them, he drove straight to the Palace garage. They all exited the car, and the Ambassador looked at John, saying, "Thank you! You saved all our lives."

Kate chimed in, "He has a habit of doing that."

At that moment, the palace guards arrived and escorted them to the President's office. The President wore a grave expression as he addressed the Ambassador, John, and Kate, saying, "I am so sorry this is happening in my country. We have captured many individuals, and they have provided us with information about their leader. We will soon put an end to this problem."

They traveled to the room where the Russian President would deliver his speech with Andrei, security personnel, the heads of the three projects, including the injured leader, John, Kate, and the U.S. Ambassador. Upon entering, the Russian president noticed one of his ministerial aides looking very surprised. He walked directly towards him, accompanied by imposing security guards, and stated, "You look very surprised, Volkov. I wanted to see the look on your face—the face of someone who didn't expect certain people to be here. Guards, please take Volkov in for questioning; we believe he is responsible for all the attempts on the lives of these U.S. and Russian people."

Everyone applauded the Russian President's actions, and he declared, "Okay, let's get this started."

The IT staff in charge of the TV broadcast announced, "We will begin in ten minutes."

When the IT staff organized the positioning of everyone in the room and he attempted to remove the chair occupied by Volkov, the President requested that it be left empty. He intended to make a point about capturing the individual responsible for the assassination attempts against everyone involved in the three projects.

The President of Russia delivered an outstanding speech, receiving applause from all attendees, particularly when he announced the partnership with the U.S., their exit from Ukraine, and the captivity of the person attempting to sabotage the U.S.-Russia partnership. He also received great applause when he acknowledged the work done by Andrei, John, Kate, and the U.S. Ambassador in making all this happen.

After the short meeting concluded, John, Kate, and the Ambassador returned to the Embassy. Upon arrival, the Ambassador's wife ran outside, hugged and kissed her husband, and then turned to John, saying, "Thank you so much for saving my husband's life."

The entire incident had been recorded and televised. She proceeded to give John a kiss on the cheek and a big hug, and she did the same for Kate.

Inside the Embassy, the secretary urgently informed them, "There is an important call waiting for you in the conference room."

John, Kate, and the Ambassador made their way to the conference room, where a screen displayed the President's conference room, featuring the President, Vice President, and the heads of Congress and Senate. The President spoke up with great pride, saying, "Congratulations to all three of you! You have made all Americans proud. We saw the footage of the assassination attempt on your lives and your subsequent triumph, as well as the Russian President's speech commending your efforts in bringing peace to the region. Outstanding job!"

In response, everyone in the President's conference room stood up and applauded, joined by the onlookers gathered by the doorway in the Embassy. It was a momentous day that the Ambassador, Kate, and John would cherish forever.

Taking the floor, John stood up and proudly remarked, "Receiving compliments like this is both humbling and remarkable. It's an acknowledgement we will always cherish. Thank you all for recognizing our work."

Kate added, "We have a few more meetings in Russia to ensure the progress of the three projects, and then we will be heading home tomorrow. The Ambassador has arranged for a helicopter to transport us to the airport, and we will have our plane take us home. We plan to return to work on Thursday or Friday."

Their boss, Jim, who was present in the room, said firmly, "We do not want to see either of you until Monday morning. You both deserve a few days of rest. You have earned it."

Kate and John Relaxing with Katelin

J ohn and Kate had been home for a couple of days and were both working from home for most of the week, despite Jim's suggestion to take some time off. They were both hardworking individuals who had been employed since their teenage years. It was Sunday, and they wanted to spend time with Katelin, so they made plans to meet her at The Cheesecake Factory and then catch a movie at the mall, with some shopping in between.

Arriving before Katelin, they started looking at old movies of their daughter from when she was still a baby and some from their dating days. When Katelin arrived, they said, "We put something together for you."

"I know what you guys are doing," Katelin said, acknowledging the efforts her parents made for her.

Kate simply smiled and said, "Enjoy the moment." It was striking how much Kate and Katelin resembled each other when they were young.

John admired both of them and expressed his love, saying, "You guys are great. I love seeing both of you together. I feel incredibly lucky to have both of you."

Katelin responded with a smile, saying, "You sure are!"

Just then, their names were called, and they were shown to their booth. Kate and Katelin sat together on one side, while John sat on the other side, enjoying the view and being able to talk face-to-face with both of them.

Starting the conversation, Katelin said, "You guys are really something. Your pictures have been on TV—day and night, during and after your trip to Russia. How are you both doing?"

"We are both fine now that we're sitting down with you. We're excited about getting back to work and completing these three projects. You should understand how we feel because, when we lived with you in Tokyo, you were on the cover of a magazine and your face was in subway station advertisements. And just before you completed high school in Tokyo and were supposed to go back to the U.S., you even had a television advertisement," Kate quickly responded.

Wanting to change the subject, as she knew her parents didn't like discussing their successes, Katelin remarked, "I'm glad they caught the person in Russia who was trying to stop the projects."

John, recalling the danger they had faced in Russia, added, "If we can complete these three projects worldwide, it would benefit everyone. But I must ask both of you to be extremely careful, no matter where you are. I've asked Jim to increase our security and the security of people working on these projects worldwide. We have our best people working on these projects, and we need to keep them safe."

He continued, "If I were to lose both of you for any reason, it would bring loneliness knocking at my door when the sun went down in my part of town. I informed Jim of our whereabouts today, and I noticed he placed two securities at a table between us and the door."

Everyone in the restaurant recognized Kate and John, and the manager came over to their table, offering them a complimentary meal. When John and Kate agreed, they left a tip as generous as the cost of the meal. As they were preparing to leave, John said to Kate and Katelin, "I know which movie I want to see—it's all about Seal Team 6."

Katelin replied, "I like that one too, and I think our security detail will enjoy it as well."

They all headed upstairs to the movie house, and while John was in line, he asked a couple of guys if they were with a SEAL team, considering it was the first movie of the day and the young men waiting to get in appeared to be very fit. After getting a positive response from the men, John felt assured that he would enjoy the movie. He informed Kate, Katelin, and the guards who they would be watching the movie with today. Once the movie ended, John drove everyone home, with one of the guard's cars in front of them and another behind.

When they reached the house, Kate looked at Katelin and said, "Katelin, can you stay with us tonight? We need to get to work first thing in the morning, and so do you. It would be easier for the guards, and you've left some of your work clothes at our house."

Katelin replied with a smile, "You know, I always like to spend time with you guys. I'll stay with you tonight, but the rest of the week, I'll have to stay at my apartment."

Kate happily responded with a thumbs-up, saying, "Deal!"

Both Kate and John knew the next day would be significant, so they went to bed early to ensure they could wake up early and go for a run. They made arrangements with their security team for the morning run and for Katelin to get to work.

Resuming Work After the Russia Trip

The alarm went off around 5:30 a.m., waking Kate. By 6 a.m., everyone in the house was ready to go out running. Even Katelin joined them that day. They returned home by 7:30 a.m. and were in their limos, heading to work by 8:30 a.m.

During the ride to work, Kate expressed her concerns to John, saying, "I really don't like all this security, especially having someone with Katelin all the time. We caught the guy in Russia who tried to have us killed. Why do you think we still need all this security?"

"We should be okay, but it's better to be safe. I'm sure that's what Jim is thinking," John replied.

When the limo pulled up to the West Wing, several people were waiting at the entrance. As Kate and John got out of the car, they were greeted with applause and cheers. Feeling a little embarrassed, they waved and went straight to Jim's office. Jim, with a smile on his face, sat behind his desk with Valerie sitting across from him and said, "Welcome back to the West Wing. Are you ready to get back to work?"

"What's with all the hoopla?" Kate asked.

Jim responded with a smile: "You are both heroes. The U.S. is now in a leadership position, and countries around the world, even our competitors, want to partner with us. The countries that oppose our success will try to stop us. You two have harnessed the power of the free market and are leading most companies to produce something the world needs. It's capitalism at its finest. Through the Medical Project, the Storm Project, and the Climate Project, the world sees the U.S. as the leader, and you both are making it happen. People around the world appreciate the way capitalism works and want to be on our side. Our competitors also want what we have, so they'll ask to be our partners. And there are others who oppose change because they can't stand to lose money. They will try to eliminate both of you and sabotage the projects. That's why I've increased security. Any large company or government leader has significant security measures, and it's no different for you, Katelin, and me."

John, visibly relieved, said to Jim and Valerie, "You read our minds. We were wondering why you increased security. Now we understand."

"Alright, guys, we need to get these three projects going. Valerie, have you set up the calls I requested?" Kate interjected.

Valerie quickly replied, "Yes, I have. Your first call with our leaders is scheduled in about fifteen minutes."

Both John and Kate smiled and then left Jim's office, heading to their conference room to prepare for the call.

When John and Kat left the room, Jim turned to Valerie and asked, "Do you think it's time for you to move on to your next job, which would be assisting John and Kate?"

Valerie looked Jim straight in the eye and said, "I know my current role is only temporary until we find my next opportunity. I believe the best job for both of us would be to work for John and Kate. Do you think they would want me?"

Jim laughed and said, "They have already requested you. So, if you want the job, it's yours. As I mentioned when you started working for me, you would have exposure to all the jobs in the West Wing and get to choose your next position. I believe John and Kate are exceptional people to work for, and they are spearheading the most critical projects in the U.S. and the world. As soon as you help me find a replacement for your current role, I'll let you go and join John and Kate. I'll contact them later today and set up a transition plan for you. Right now, get with HR and get me a list of candidates we can both interview for your current job."

When Valerie went to HR office, they laughed and said they had already started looking for her replacement as soon as Jim hired her. They found a person who had just received her Master's degree from MIT. She was an African-American lady who was doing well in all her projects and would be an excellent fit for Jim. Valerie told them to set up interviews with all the appropriate people, including her and Jim as interviewers. The HR person then asked, "When do you plan on leaving, and where will you go?"

"I will leave as soon as we find a replacement, and I can train her. Also, the plan would be for me to go work for John and Kate," Valerie responded, informing them of Jim's plan.

Valerie left HR and went directly to Jim's office to inform him of the meeting. Jim said, "Great. Let John and Kate know the plan, and you can begin the transition to them as soon as we accept the new candidate."

Valerie went to John and Kate's conference room before the calls started and informed them of the plan. John and Kate were smiling and said, "I hope you have understanding boyfriends because you are going to be working long days and many weekends."

"I only have one boyfriend, and he works in the West Wing. He was hoping I would get this job and supports me completely," Valerie said with a smile.

Kate smiled back and responded, "Smart man!"

The phone then rang, and the zoom call for The Medical Project was about to begin. Kate said, "John and Kate are here. We were just ending a meeting with Valerie."

Turning to Valerie, Kate asked, "Do you want to sit in on the calls?"

Valerie responded, "I would, but I need to transition out of Jim's area with the new person."

"We understand. Do a good transition, and let's get started here as soon as possible," John said.

Kate then started the call by asking the Medical Project team, "Give John and me an update on how the Russian and schizophrenia studies are going, and also how the deployment of the Medical Computer installations is going around the world."

The Medical Project Leader responded, "Every country has at least one Medical Computer installation, and that is usually the most challenging part since it requires a lot of training. Each country is now installing them in all their major cities, and those installations will continue for several years."

"At our next meeting, I would like to see a scorecard with every country listed and the number of Medical Computers installed. Small countries will naturally have fewer installations than larger countries, so we will need to show the total number installed and then a percentage relative to their population. We should reward each country for their efforts and have them speak at the next meeting to share what they are doing to lead in installations," John said.

The Medical Project Leader responded, "That is a great idea. Now, let me update you on the schizophrenia study and what is happening in Russia. The theory linking schizophrenia to drugs and the interplay of genetics with perceptions is consistent, but we are waiting for the Russians to get their Medical Computers installed so we can analyze their data and prevent misguided perceptions about schizophrenia related to drugs and genetic factors, both in the U.S.A., Russia, and other countries."

"I want an announcement about our theory and any results from the study in the U.S.A. and Russia. Complete the work, and when they are done, I want a meeting set up with John, myself, you, and the Russian team to plan how we can make a joint announcement as partners," Kate said with a stern voice.

John reinforced Kate's statement by saying, "It's crucial that we make this announcement together with Russia as a team. We cannot have any leaks to the press, and anyone found responsible for leaking will be fired."

"I understand, and I will make it clear to the team so that everyone is aware," the Medical Project Leader said with a positive tone.

Kate responded, "Thank you. This is very important for our relationship with Russia and the U.S. going forward on many fronts. Now, let's hear from the Storm Project Leader. I would like to know where the next storm is that we need to address."

The Storm Project Leader displayed a weather map showing storms worldwide and said, "We have been monitoring two storms closely. As you can see, there is a typhoon that appears to be heading towards Taiwan and/or Japan. Then there's the storm we discussed a week ago that may hit some islands in the Caribbean and Cuba."

John spoke up urgently and said, "Okay, team, this is very important. You have a relationship with the Storm Team in Russia. Work closely with them to determine how we can collaborate and put an end to the storm that may hit Cuba. Regarding the typhoon in Asia, we will have Jim contact China and see if they would like to partner with us in addressing the storm. If they decline, we will handle it ourselves. Don't take any action on the Asian storm until you hear from us, but keep us informed of its progress."

Kate added, "Alright, it seems like these two projects are progressing well. Let's now hear from the Climate Project Leader."

The Climate Project Leader spoke with a positive tone, saying, "Since the announcement in Russia about deploying the Climate Project devices throughout Ukraine, we have received requests to deploy these devices globally. As you know, we are working with a U.S.-based company that invented the device and is profiting from its sales. They hold the patent and want to prevent theft."

"That's capitalism at its finest. This is why the U.S. leads in many inventions. We need to ensure we protect the company's invention and make it clear to other countries that they must pay for the devices through monthly or yearly payments or by purchasing them outright. However, they cannot reverse-engineer them. I suggest we encourage the company to establish additional manufacturing locations within the U.S., which would help lower costs and maintain our competitive pricing even if others had access to the technology," John said, commenting about the Climate Project Leader's update.

The Climate Leader responded, "I will relay our discussion to the company and provide their response at the next meeting. We currently have sufficient production to meet demand, but it is steadily growing."

"Excellent. Pretty soon we will have the cleanest planet in the universe," Kate said with enthusiasm.

John's tone turned negative as he said, "Team, as you all know, we have encountered problems in Russia where individuals attempted to disrupt our projects or undermine our countries. Fortunately, their efforts backfired. However, I need to know if there have been any assassinations or assassination attempts targeting our project members."

Each of the leaders spoke up, stating that two people were killed and several were injured in Hong Kong and Tokyo.

John responded, "Thank you for those updates. I will inform Jim that we need to enhance security measures for our personnel in our home country and abroad. Kate and I will also need to make plans to visit those countries."

Kate added, "Okay, team, keep up the good work. Let's plan on meeting again next week." After the meeting, John and Kate went to Jim's office to provide him with an update.

Upon hearing the updates, Jim responded with an annoyed tone, "I will also inform the President, and he will contact China and Japan to inform them of your visit and the deaths of our leaders in their respective countries."

Planning Trips to Tokyo and Hong Kong

John and Kate woke up early to go for their runs, now covering a mile-long route to a nearby diner. They would then sit at a table with a jukebox playing country music and enjoy breakfast before running back home. The couple cherished their time together. Today, they were accompanied by security personnel who would have breakfast at another table in the diner.

While sitting at the diner, John turned to Kate and said, "I still remember the first time I saw you; I fell in love with you instantly. You've been the only girl on my mind since we met. Do you remember when we first met?"

"Yes, I remember it was at a football game. You took me and my three girlfriends to the game. While you knew two of my friends, we officially met when you picked me up. Little did you know, my girlfriends were keeping you all to themselves and purposely not introducing us. I recall walking by some basketball courts with one of my friends when I heard you laugh. I became interested at that moment, but my friends, afraid I might win your attention, withheld introductions," Kate replied, recollecting her memories back then.

The conversation soon shifted to work, and John said, "Kate, I think it's important for both of us to visit Hong Kong and Tokyo. We have lived in Tokyo for three years, and we're familiar with Hong

Kong as well."

Kate responded, "If Jim allows both of us to go, then I want to go with you. I wish we could take Katelin, but she's been unwell due to excessive work. I've always known Katelin is special, and a few things have really impressed me. One of them was when she wanted to be on a rifle team at the American School in Japan (ASIJ). Also, I remembered seeing her and her teammates dancing on the basketball court during game breaks," Kate said as she reminisced about Katelin's school activities back in Japan.

John raised his hand, wanting to share his thoughts. He said, "What really impressed me was that she would do fantastic things and let us know about them. We didn't have to tell her what to do. I recalled the time you mentioned that Katelin was doing some modeling in Japan. I didn't think much of it until I stumbled upon her picture on the front cover of a magazine in a small Japanese town. And later, I saw her picture on a big poster in the subway. With Katelin, all we have to do is sit back and watch as she accomplishes one amazing thing after another."

"Enough about Katelin. We love her more than anything. Let's focus on our next trip. I believe we should meet with Jim and explain that both of us need to go to ensure the projects are on track. We also need to find out who is attempting to sabotage these projects by targeting and killing people," Kate said, interrupting their discussion about Katelin.

John agreed, saying, "I agree that both of us need to be present in both countries. We must ensure we have adequate security measures in place for ourselves and for the people in Japan and China. Shall we run home now and get ready for work?"

During their runs and especially at the diner, they felt an immense closeness. They would arrive at the diner when it was still dark, and by the time they left, the sun would have risen. Though they didn't visit the diner every day, it was important to sit together and discuss problems and possible solutions. They always sat facing each other, ensuring they could maintain eye contact. Their love for each other was evident.

Upon returning home, they informed the security personnel, who had followed them to the diner, that they would be out in approximately forty-five minutes before heading to work.

John and Kate went to separate bathrooms to shower, knowing that showering together would definitely make them late for work. After forty-five minutes, they were in the limo, accompanied by a security car in front and behind, on their way to the office. Upon reaching their workplace, they both entered Jim's office as planned and conveyed their discussion from the diner.

Jim smiled and said, "Valerie and I anticipated that you would bring up these points, so we have already started making arrangements. She managed to listen in on most of the calls."

"I knew we made the right decision by bringing her on board. We were thinking of leaving on Wednesday morning and arriving two hours later in Tokyo so that we could be at work on Thursday morning. Then, on Saturday, we will depart for Hong Kong and fly back on either Thursday or Friday," Kate said, smiling back at Jim.

Jim responded, saying, "I will handle all the travel and security arrangements. Since you both know the people in those countries as well as I do, why don't you take charge of setting up the meetings with the relevant individuals? The President and I will make the necessary calls to the Prime Minister of Japan and the President in China to arrange those meetings with the project leaders."

John, Kate, and Valerie returned to their conference room to begin making all the necessary trip arrangements. Their plan was to leave for the airport at around 10 a.m., fly with security in Business Class on a regular airline, and be met at Tokyo's airport by the U.S. Ambassador and their security team.

John and Kate left work at 5 p.m. to allow themselves some time to rest and prepare for the flight to Tokyo.

The Twentieth Day

From Breakfast with Katelin to Tokyo NRT Airport Arrival

They both woke up at 6 a.m. and decided to go to the diner for breakfast. They put on their running clothes and informed security that they would be running to the diner, having breakfast, and running back home. Their flight was scheduled for 11 a.m., so they had plenty of time. They sat and talked for about two hours, listening to music and discussing important matters. When they say they are solving world problems, they are truly engaged in finding solutions.

Katelin wanted to surprise them, so she had security notify her when they arrived at the diner. Around 7 a.m., Katelin walked into the diner and said, "Imagine seeing you two here having breakfast. Do you mind if I join you?"

Both Kate and John laughed and were pleasantly surprised. Kate replied, "Of course you can join us. This reminds me of the time we were in Tokyo, eating dinner at the same restaurant we always went to, and you walked by in your long coat because it was cold outside. We spotted each other, and you sat down and joined us for dinner. Now we're going to Tokyo, and you've surprised us again."

"Thank you for making our day. Today was a day we weren't looking forward to because of the twelve-hour flight. I want to express my gratitude, even in situations when I am upset. Like the time I slipped

100

on some pee the dog left on the floor, wearing my three-piece suit. I was lying there in pee, feeling upset and ready to give you a punishment. But you were just sitting on the couch with one of your girlfriends, laughing at the situation. Your laughter made me laugh too, sitting there in pee, and I forgot all about the punishment. Katelin, you and your mom have a way of lightening up my mood. I am a lucky guy," John said while smiling at his daughter.

Tears welled up in Katelin and Kate's eyes as they gave John a big hug. Katelin then said, "You guys are going to one of Mom's favorite cities, and you're not taking me. I don't mean Tokyo, even though both of you tried to convince me to stay there after I graduated high school. I mean Hong Kong, where mom and I loved to go shopping. I remember Stanley Market, where we got so many good deals."

Kate responded, "If we thought we could do some shopping, we would definitely bring you along. But we'll be quite busy during our stay."

John added, "I hope that many years from now, when both of you are in heaven, there will be shopping up there. Now, we have to leave so we can get to the airport two hours before our flight. We'll be using regular airlines this time—no Air Force jets."

"I'll say my goodbyes here but want a call when you arrive so I know you're okay. Please don't take any chances and be very careful," Katelin said, wishing her parents a safe trip.

They all stood up and shared a three-way hug. John paid the bill while Katelin and Kate talked, and then they all left. John and Kate ran back home, while Katelin drove her car to work, with security following them.

When Kate and John arrived home, they noticed Bill waiting at the door with his suitcases. Bill asked the couple, "Guess who will be your security in Tokyo?"

John replied, "I feel safe knowing you'll be with us on the trip."

John and Kate went into the house with Bill, who stayed downstairs in the den while Kate and John showered and got ready for the trip. They hurried, knowing they had to be at the airport by 9 a.m. By 5 p.m., they were downstairs and ready to go. They rushed out to the waiting limo, which took them to the airport. The three of them went through security and boarded the plane, which departed at 7 p.m. They all tried to get some sleep, as they knew they would arrive in Tokyo around 8 a.m. local time on Thursday.

Upon arrival, Bill informed Kate and John, "I have my luggage and will go outside these big sliding doors. Take these two walkie-talkies and wait for my signal before you come out. I want to make sure the Embassy car and security are here before you come out."

John and Kate gave it a thumbs up and started looking for their luggage. After finding their last piece of luggage, they awaited Bill's call. As soon as he gave the okay signal, they went through the sliding glass doors and saw Bill waiting with the Embassy security.

As they walked, Kate glanced at John and said, "Do you remember the first time we arrived here? They had geisha girls meet us and take us to the buses that would transport us to the hotel."

"Yes, we've certainly moved up in the world. Now we have an embassy car," John responded.

They both chuckled, and it was cut short when Bill introduced them to the security team: "The U.S. Ambassador wanted to meet both of you, so he and his wife will be riding with you. You'll be staying at the U.S. Embassy during your time in Tokyo."

John looked at Kate and jokingly said, "What did I tell you?" He then turned to Bill and added, "It was just a private joke."

The Embassy car was spacious, with a security car in front and behind. Bill got into the front vehicle, while John and Kate entered the Embassy car. John expressed his gratitude, saying, "Thank you both for coming to the airport. As you know, we lived in Tokyo for about three years several years ago, and it's great to be back."

The U.S. Ambassador responded, "Please, you can call me Jim, and this is my wife, Caroline. You are both well-known around the world, and it's an honor to meet you. We want to ensure your safety while you're here, but there are people who may want to disrupt Japan or oppose changes, so we need to be careful. We have about an hour-long ride from Narita Airport to the Embassy. Perhaps you can update us on the three projects during the journey."

Kate began discussing the climate project, explaining, "There are a few hotspots in Japan that they want to focus on for the Climate Leader initiative here. We also need an update on the status of the Medical Project deployment in Japan. I don't believe there are any storms in the area, but we'll ensure we are prepared if any arise."

"We have all the meetings set up at the Embassy with the Japanese leaders you requested. If you don't mind, we were hoping to add one event to your agenda. Japan is very concerned about the rockets being fired by North Korea. The North Koreans don't want to meet with the Japanese officials directly, but they would like to discuss the three projects with both of you. Do you think it's possible to arrange a meeting with the President of North Korea?" the U.S. Ambassador asked intriguingly.

John and Kate exchanged glances, and both seemed amenable to the idea. John replied, "Let's do it. We'll be here until Sunday, and then we'll travel to Hong Kong for meetings next week. My suggestion would be to see if we can leave China and go to North Korea towards the end of the week. It would be ideal to have both the North and South Korean presidents present at that meeting. Have your contact set it up, but keep Jim back home in the loop about what you're doing."

The U.S. Ambassador and his wife smiled, and he said, "That's why you guys are the best. You can make things happen. Thank you for coming. We've arranged a small brunch and get-together for you. Everyone is eager to meet you both."

John and Kate, feeling slightly embarrassed by the compliments, smiled and changed the subject. It is precisely the reason why everyone likes them.

Upon arriving at the Embassy, many staff members were waiting outside, cheering and applauding as John and Kate stepped out of the car. John and Kate lowered their heads in appreciation and followed the U.S. Ambassador into the Embassy.

Once inside, the U.S. Ambassador apologized and said, "Sorry for all the commotion, but they are so happy to see both of you in person. Your first meeting will be with the Prime Minister, with some of his leaders and your U.S. leaders joining remotely. It will start in two hours, and then after that meeting, we will have dinner with the attendees and some of the Embassy staff."

"Is there a place within the Embassy grounds where Kate and I can go for a run or exercise before the meeting?" John asked.

Bill, who was still with them, replied, "I found a place on the Embassy grounds where you can run, John, and there's a gym where both of you can exercise. Tomorrow morning, we can also run outside the Embassy if you'd like. I've made the necessary arrangements."

"Well, it seems your security is on top of things. I'll see you and Kate in a couple of hours," the U.S. Ambassador said, praising Bill's advance thinking.

Kate added, "That's why we like Bill."

A staff member then approached John, Kate, and Bill to show them their rooms. Bill turned to Kate and John before they went into their rooms and said, "Me and a couple of other people will run with you today around the Embassy grounds. Should we meet in about a half hour outside your room?"

John and Kate gave a thumbs up and quickly entered their room to prepare for their run. They always enjoyed running after a long flight to wake up their senses and adjust to the local time zone.

The Twenty-First Day

Embassy Grounds Run, Brunch, and Dinner Meetings

J ohn and Kate were shown to their room at the Embassy. They quickly changed into their running clothes and met Bill outside their rooms. Together, they went downstairs to a small running path within the Embassy grounds. Bill explained, "Since we are in the middle of Tokyo, there isn't much land to run on here. However, tomorrow we can run outside in the morning."

Kate responded, "For now, let's just get in an hour-long run, then return for a shower and prepare for our first meeting. I believe these meetings will serve as an introduction between our leaders and Japan's leaders, ensuring effective communication and updating each other on the project's status."

John and Kate knew that preparing for status updates would motivate everyone to get their work done. In Japan, particularly, nobody wanted to be embarrassed or fall behind on any project. These meetings pushed them to make progress on all three projects.

As John and Kate entered the conference room, they noticed the Ambassador had prepared bento boxes full of food for everyone, along with some green tea. The three U.S. project leaders joined via Zoom, while the Prime Minister and his three leaders were present in the room. The Medical and Climate projects were already being deployed and were on schedule. As there were no storms at the moment, the Storm

105

Project had not been tested, but the team was prepared for immediate action in case of a storm.

While analyzing the data from the Medical Project, Kate and John noticed that the Japanese people were in excellent shape. Their diet, consisting of mostly fish, vegetables, and smaller portions of meat, contributed to their lower rates of illness compared to the U.S. and other countries.

When the discussion turned to the Climate Project, the Japanese expressed concern about not receiving enough devices to deploy in their hotspots. Kate spoke up, addressing the U.S. Climate Leader, saying, "I thought we were actively seeking additional manufacturing companies to ensure this situation wouldn't happen."

"We have three new manufacturing companies that are currently ramping up production. We should be able to meet all demands," the U.S. Climate Leader said.

John, Kate, the Ambassador, and the Prime Minister were pleased with this answer. John spoke up, saying, "We are extremely pleased with the progress. It's evident that all the leaders are meeting weekly, and significant progress is being made. If any problems arise that you can't solve on your own, remember that you can always contact us. Let's conclude this meeting and continue the good work."

After the meeting, John, Kate, and the Ambassador asked the Prime Minister to stay in the conference room to discuss the North Korea situation and the meeting they had requested. The Prime Minister gladly obliged and said with a smile, "We are delighted that they are genuinely interested in what you have to offer. They recognize the value of all three projects and wish to collaborate with you to improve their country in these areas. They have expressed trust in both of you and specifically requested to meet with you. This may be due to the meetings you had in Russia and the upcoming meetings in China."

"China and North Korea see these three projects as global initiatives that every country wants to implement. They also recognize the significance of these projects for their own countries and the world.

They are willing to cease any actions that are causing concern if they can gain access to these three projects," the Ambassador said, adding to what the Prime Minister has said.

John chimed in, "Before partnering with them on the three projects, we will present two conditions for their agreement. First, we need to understand what steps Taiwan must take to prevent an invasion by China. Second, we must determine what North Korea requires in order to halt missile launches. We are willing to collaborate with them on the three projects as we have with you, but we need to know their additional expectations."

The Prime Minister looked at the Ambassador with a smile, privately remarking, "If these two individuals can make this happen, it would be a miracle. Their approach and logical thinking are right on target."

Speaking loudly enough for everyone to hear, the Prime Minister continued, "It is a pleasure to meet both of you. I understand why the U.S. President initiated the leadership program and appointed you as the first U.S. Leaders."

Kate responded with a smile, saying, "Thank you, but we haven't achieved anything yet. We will do our very best to make it all happen. Your team is doing an outstanding job right now. Let's continue this success in Japan."

The Prime Minister recognized that the meeting had concluded. The Ambassador, John, and Kate all stood up after him. As a gesture of appreciation for everything they had done and would continue to do, the Prime Minister bowed deeply to Kate and then to John. In response, Kate, John, and the Ambassador nodded their heads in appreciation of his compliments.

John and Kate made their way back to their room and called their boss, Jim, to provide him with an update on the meeting. Jim assured them that he would brief the President as well as the leaders of the Congress and Senate. He encouraged them to proceed with the scheduled meetings and wished them luck.

Aware that they had a dinner engagement with the Embassy staff,

Kate looked at John after the meeting, aware of the respect he held for her. With a tear in her eye, she said, "With all the things we have going on, the one beautiful certainty in life is our love for each other."

Moved by Kate's words, John also had a tear in his eye and embraced her tightly, saying, "Okay, we have one more important meeting to attend today. You are the love of my life, and you know it."

John and Kate opened the door, finding a butler waiting to escort them to the main dining room. As they entered, everyone in the room erupted in cheers and applause. The attendees recognized Kate and John's ability to accomplish great things around the world, but they also witnessed the love they shared, which endeared them even more.

John and Kate smiled as they greeted each person, shaking their hands and expressing gratitude for the sacrifices they were making by being away from their homes and the important work they were doing on the three projects.

The dinner went well. Knowing they wanted to wake up early the next day for a run before their meetings, John and Kate went straight to bed. They set the alarm for 6 a.m., intending to call Katelin around 5 p.m. her time and then go for their run outside the Embassy.

The Twenty-Second Day

Calls from Katelin and Jim and an Outdoor Run Beyond the Embassy

The alarm went off at 6 a.m., and both Kate and John decided to go for a run and give Katelin a call. John dialed Katelin's cell phone, just in case she wasn't at work or home. As expected, he reached her at work since it was only 5 p.m. on Thursday. Recognizing her voice, he greeted her with, "Good afternoon, young lady."

John always enjoyed making fun of Katelin and trying to catch her off guard, but he never succeeded. Katelin had a playful relationship with her father. Whenever John made a mistake, like slipping, falling down on his rear, or dropping a plate on the floor, she would burst into laughter. So, whenever something similar happened to John, he would jokingly ask himself, *"Are you watching, Katelin?"*

John had a lengthy conversation with Katelin about her work, and then Kate said, "Give me the phone." Kate and her daughter would discuss the men Katelin had met or how her dating life was going. After about fifteen minutes, John pointed to his watch, indicating it was time to end the call so they could talk to Jim.

Kate finished talking with Katelin and noticed John was already dressed for the run. She handed him the phone so he could call Jim while she prepared her running clothes.

John managed to reach Jim in his office and said, "Hey, Jim. Just calling to make sure you're up to date on things. We have you on speaker, so Kate can hear you too. By the way, have you found a new Executive Assistant? Can Valerie work for us full-time?"

Jim chuckled and replied, "Valerie and I are still interviewing candidates for her position, but she is indeed working for you full-time. She's putting in some extra hours since she currently has two jobs, but she's happy and hasn't complained. That's why you wanted her on the team, and I had her on mine."

Jim continued, "As for the second topic, I've been briefed on the situation with China and North Korea and the plan you have for the meetings with their presidents. I have my fingers crossed. Is there anything you want me or the President to do before your meeting?"

After a brief pause on the phone, Kate and John exchanged glances, and John pointed at Kate, indicating that she should speak with Jim. Kate leaned closer to the phone and said, "We hadn't discussed having the President and yourself make calls before our meeting with them, but maybe it would be a good idea. They saw what happened in Russia, and if they really want to partner with us on these three issues, it might be worthwhile for you guys to reach out to them. We can ensure that China won't invade Taiwan and that North Korea will cease firing missiles towards Tokyo. Our assumption is that North Korea needs some assurances that no one will invade them, and China wants Taiwan to open up more for trade with them."

Jim remained silent for a few seconds and then, in a serious tone, said, "That's why you two are the best. I will talk with the President and see if he agrees to make the call before your visits. We can plant the idea that closing those deals is crucial in addition to partnering on the three projects. They trust both of you since they initiated the talks with you and are eager to collaborate."

"We have some people waiting for us, and I know you want to focus on finding a new Executive Assistant, so we better hang up," John said, interjecting in a playful tone.

Before hanging up, Jim added, "I know you called me so early in the morning in your time because the people waiting for you are probably your security team joining you for the run. You don't fool me."

Jim laughed and continued, "Listen, I want both of you to be careful and take care of yourselves."

John and Kate stood up, exchanging smiles and a long hug. Kate remarked, "The one beautiful thing we have in life is the love between you and me. Now it looks like we'll have to include Jim, too. He really likes us and would do anything to support us."

John looked at Kate once again, this time at arm's length, and said, "You and I are both dressed for a run. Let's get Bill and go. I want to pass by the place where we used to live and also the Prince's and Emperor's Palaces."

As they opened the door, Bill sat in a chair next to another guard, waiting for them. Bill expressed his reservations about the run. saying, "I'm having second thoughts about this run. The embassy security informed me that a group opposing the current government in Japan has acquired short-range rockets."

"We are currently deciding on our running route, but we believe that if they were going to fire rockets, they would target our Embassy rather than us. We think we'll be safe running outside," John said, reassuring Bill, while Kate nodded in agreement with John.

Bill agreed and asked about their running route. He motioned for five Japanese and five American security personnel to gather around.

Kate remarked, "I see you came prepared today."

Bill replied, "We'll have five guards in front of us and five behind us. It's early, so there should be little traffic, and only runners will be out at this hour."

"Our plan is to run by the Akasaka Twin Towers, right down the block and across the street from the Embassy. Kate and I used to work there. Then we'll run uphill to Aoyama Ichome, where we used to live. Afterward, we'll run around the stadium, where there are many soccer and baseball games. Finally, we'll head downhill to the Prince's Palace and then on to the Emperor's Palace before returning to either here or the Okura Hotel for breakfast," John said, detailing to Bill their planned running route.

Bill and all the guards were amazed by John's familiarity with the area and agreed that it should be safe at this early hour.

They began their run, and when they reached Aoyama Ichome, they passed by the place where John and Kate had lived during their time in Tokyo. They noticed a police car had pulled over another vehicle, and the trunk was open, revealing rockets ready to be fired.

One of the guards caught up to Bill, John, and Kate and informed them, "They were preparing to fire the rockets at the Prince's Palace because initially, they thought that's where you and Kate would be staying. Many important guests stay there when they're in Tokyo. However, the Embassy building is much stronger and could withstand a rocket strike, so we decided to move you there instead."

When they finished their run and returned to the Embassy, they decided to shower before breakfast since they were all sweaty. As they entered the Embassy, a guard informed them that the Ambassador and his wife would like to join them for breakfast.

Kate turned to Bill and John with a smile on her face and said, "I guess we know where we'll be having breakfast, and it won't be the Okura Hotel up the block from the Embassy."

During their time living in Tokyo on weekends, John and Kate used to have breakfast at a different hotel, and they were aware that the Okura Hotel, just a few steps up the block from the Embassy, offered an excellent buffet.

John smiled and replied, "We've eaten there several times, but we've never had breakfast at the U.S. Embassy." They all shook their heads and laughed before heading to their rooms to shower.

John and Kate quickly showered and got dressed. When they opened the door, someone was there to escort them to have breakfast with the Ambassador and his wife. John and Kate didn't have any scheduled meetings, but they knew that after their discussion with Jim about

China's stance on invading Taiwan and North Korea's missiles, Jim would soon set up some meetings. As they entered the breakfast area, they noticed that the Prime Minister had also been invited, accompanied by some of his reports. The Ambassador's was not around, indicating that this would be a working meeting. In Japan, it was customary not to bring wives to official meetings, and the Ambassador understood that Kate was viewed differently due to her involvement in various groundbreaking projects.

The Ambassador spoke up first, saying, "Kate and John, let me apologize for the surprise meeting. You thought we were going to have a quiet breakfast, but it's your President's fault. He has been making calls to leaders all over Asia. He liked the plan we discussed the other day and has added some items to the agenda. We are also planning a Zoom call with the presidents of South Korea and Taiwan in about an hour."

The Prime Minister chimed in, "I would also like to apologize to Kate and John. There was an attempted attack on their lives this morning, but we managed to catch the individuals before they could do any harm. Typically, we accommodate important guests at the Prince's Palace, and those individuals had rockets ready to fire as soon as they spotted you. Fortunately, we had switched your accommodations to the Embassy, which left them disappointed. The missiles you saw in one of the cars' trunks during your run were theirs. There were three cars in total, and we apprehended the individuals riding the cornered vehicles. They are currently under questioning. We know the identity of their boss, but until we capture him, we need you to remain inside the Embassy for your safety. He sought to embarrass both me and Japan, but he will soon pay the price of his misguided deeds."

John and Kate expressed their gratitude by bowing their heads and thanking the Ambassador and Prime Minister. John then addressed them, saying, "Our original plan was to depart from Tokyo tomorrow, meet with the Chinese President on Monday, fly to North Korea on Wednesday, and return home on Friday."

The Ambassador assured them, "That should still work. The

President believes that both you and Kate have gained the trust of many individuals. He sees both of you performing the duties of the Secretary of State. After the President's discussion with the two presidents, he believes that they are genuinely concerned about potential invasions or trade disruptions. He is considering forming an Asian trade agreement, similar to NATO, for all countries in Asia. This would facilitate trade and ensure that if someone were to invade North Korea, they would be at war with all the member countries. It would also promote trade between Taiwan and China, which is currently limited. This will bring these two countries closer, not only in the trading industry. On top of all that, you would involve them as partners in the three projects. We have our first call scheduled with Taiwan in ten minutes, followed by a call with South Korea in an hour."

While the assistant at the Embassy arranged the calls to get Taiwan on the line, they all enjoyed some coffee and breakfast. Upon reaching the Taiwan leaders and proposing the plan, Taiwan agreed to the proposed Asia Trade Agreement (ATA) as well as South Korea. They leave the task of persuading other Asian countries to Jim and the President.

After the calls, John remarked, "Well, now all we have to do is get North Korea and China to agree."

John and Kate spent the rest of the day strategizing on how to convince China and North Korea to support their plans. They ended up skipping lunch but had dinner together at the Embassy. John and Kate expressed their gratitude once again to the Prime Minister and Ambassador for all their help. They retired to their room and made love, intending to wake up early the next day for some exercise before departing for the airport and heading to Hong Kong.

From Tokyo to Beijing—Travel and Meetings

J ohn and Kate woke up early to get some exercise before heading to the airport. They ran around the Embassy grounds and then prepared to leave for Narita (NRT) Airport. When they used to live in Tokyo, it was a two-hour bus ride from their hotel. Due to the extra security required, an Embassy car with two security cars, each with armed guards, would be taking them to NRT. Upon returning to their room after exercising, they received a call from Jim, and they needed to call him back.

John picked up the phone and dialed Jim's office. When they got him on the phone, John said, "We got your message to call you. I have Kate on the speakerphone here with me."

Jim quickly responded and said, "I know you are getting ready to go to the airport, but there has been a change of plan. The President of China wants to meet you in his office in Beijing. He would like to make a joint announcement with both of you when the agreement is reached. I haven't seen what he is going to say, but my guess is that he wants to work on it with both of you. Valerie has made all the necessary changes. Right now, you will be scheduled to fly to Beijing in one of our planes and stay at the U.S. Embassy in China. The same plane will then take you to Pyongyang, North Korea, where you will meet with the North Korean President. We are thinking that you will spend most

115

of your time in China and then fly early in the morning on Wednesday to Pyongyang, spend the whole day with the North Korean President, and fly out Wednesday night. But before any joint announcements are made, we need to review them first. Our President made that clear to the other presidents. Does this plan seem okay with both of you?"

Kate quickly responded and said, "Well, it looks like we are keeping Valerie busy. Did you get a new Executive Assistant? The plan seems okay to us. I understand the reason for flying in and out of North Korea on the same day. You are worried about security. If North Korea needs us to stay longer, we will let you know and ensure proper security measures are in place."

Jim jokingly said, "Her name is Susie, and her first day is on Monday. Valerie is keeping her very busy. You and John can decide on the agenda for the meetings. We are all very proud of everything you are doing. We are just trying to keep both of you safe. We will talk after your meetings in China. Please stay safe and don't make any changes to the plan. Safe travels!"

"Thanks for all you do. We will be in touch soon," John said, ending their phone call with Jim.

John and Kate finished dressing and packing, then headed down to the limo that would take them to their plane. They joked about how well they were being treated and decided to call Katelin once they got in the limo to let her know their plans, just in case of an emergency. As they made their way to the door, the Ambassador and his wife were there. The Ambassador said, "It was truly an honor to meet both of you. The things you are doing may change the way the U.S. interacts with the rest of the world. You are also doing things with those three projects that will make the world a better place."

John and Kate were not good at accepting compliments, but Kate was a little better than John, so she said to the Ambassador, "Thank you for those kind words. You also did a great job getting everything set up so we could be successful in Japan. You helped us put the plan together for China and North Korea."

Kate turned to the Ambassador's wife and said, "I lived here several years ago, and I know how difficult it is for women to be in this country. John and I really appreciate everything both of you have done to make our stay wonderful. We look forward to seeing you both again sometime. Thank you both for all you do."

They both left and went to the limo. Kate dialed Katelin's home number. Katelin answered the incoming call and said, "Hello, this is Katelin."

"Hello Katelin, this is Mom and Dad. How are you doing tonight?" Kate asked, checking on her daughter from time to time despite their busy schedule.

Katelin briefly giggled in response and said, "You know, the same old stuff: meeting with ambassadors, prime ministers, and presidents. It gets boring after a while. So, Mom, did you and Dad do any shopping while you were there?"

"We were at the Embassy most of the time. We got out once, but there were some people trying to kill us, so we spent most of the time in the Embassy. We also found out that we wouldn't get to Stanley Market in Hong Kong. We are going directly to Beijing," Kate said, a bit disappointed.

Katelin started laughing and said, "You guys are doing important stuff. I'll try to do the shopping for all of us."

"We love you, honey. Please be careful and do what your security tells you," John said in a sincere tone.

"I will be careful, Dad. You guys should be careful too. I'll see you when you get back," Katelin said in response to her dad's sincere concern for her.

The call ended, and both Kate and John looked at each other, thinking how lucky they were to have such a great daughter.

John then said to Kate with a disappointed look, "You know, I always thought that Katelin got all that funny stuff and spontaneous different ways of looking at things from you. I remembered back when we were dating: I would be thinking of going to the library, while you would suggest that we read books and work out problems on the beach instead. Even after school, you would be the one suggesting going to a Paul McCartney or Toby Keith concert. You are the funny, spontaneous person, and I'm just an engineer."

Kate laughed and said, "You finally figured that out. I married the guy who was the engineer. As I said before, the one beautiful thing there is in life is the love between you and me. You married the right person, and I married the right person. That's why we have such a great daughter. She got a little bit of both of us."

They were just arriving at the airport in their limo, but Kate reached across while they were seated and gave John a big hug. They both got out of the limo and went to the private hangar that had their plane. Someone was there to check their passports, and they boarded a plane similar to Air Force One, only a little smaller.

The pilot greeted them before boarding and said, "It is an honor to be flying both of you on this mission. If you need rest, there is a bedroom. If you need to work, there is an office with satellite phones and computers. But for now, please take your seats for takeoff. Food and beverage service will be available after takeoff. We will arrive at 5 p.m., and a private car will take us to the Embassy. We will fly to Beijing now and then, on Wednesday, fly in and out of Pyongyang, North Korea. From there, we will fly to Washington, D.C. Just so you know, we will all be staying at the U.S. Embassy in Beijing, so if there are any changes, please let us know so we can adjust our flight plans."

"Thank you for the update. We will inform you of any changes," John said.

John and Kate held each other's hands and took their seats. Kate then said with a smile on her face, "This beats flying commercial."

On the plane ride, they did some work, watched TV, and relaxed. The plane arrived promptly at 5 p.m. They both noticed it was gray outside. There were two limos waiting to take everyone to the Embassy.

When they arrived, the U.S. Ambassador and his wife were there to greet them. The Ambassador said, "Welcome to our home and your home away from home. Everyone wants to meet you. Tomorrow, we are scheduled to meet with the President of China in his office; however, he would like you to dine tonight with his second-in-command and a person he greatly respects, the Secretary General. Does all that seem okay with both of you?"

John responded with a serious look and said, "You know the players and also the topics of interest to them, along with the protocol we should follow, so you will have to take the lead on the meetings. In the dinner meeting today, is it alright if Kate comes?"

The Ambassador, looking at Kate and then at his wife, said, "It is okay for Kate to be in the meeting because both of you were involved in building the three projects. My wife will not come since the Secretary General is not bringing his wife. Also, everyone in the meeting can make a point on any topic, but no yelling or putting someone down, even if their point is way off the mark. Since the meeting starts in an hour, you should follow my wife's lead up to your room, get some rest, and then we will see you in the meeting."

The Ambassador's wife was showing them up to their room. She leaned over to Kate and said, "If you can break out of any of these meetings, let me know, and we can do some shopping and sightseeing."

Kate smiled and responded quickly, saying, "As soon as I get the agenda for all the meetings, I will see when I can meet up with you. I would like that a lot. I will call you."

The Ambassador's wife just smiled and gave her a thumbs up. They had just reached their room, and the Ambassador's wife opened the door. She gave John and Kate the room's key. "Don't forget dinner is in about forty-five minutes," the Ambassador's wife said, reminding them about dinner time before she left.

Both John and Kate showered, unpacked, and put on some dinner clothes. As they left the room and opened the door, someone was there to show them to the dining room. When they arrived, they noticed the Secretary General and the Ambassador were sitting at the table with a glass of wine. As they entered the room, both of them stood up, and the Ambassador introduced everyone.

John smiled and said, "Thank you for inviting us to your country. Kate and I have only been to Hong Kong and have not seen any other part of China. I hope to get in a little sightseeing before we leave."

The Secretary General motioned to the Ambassador and said, "Why don't you offer them some wine, and we will talk a little before dinner?"

The Ambassador motioned to the server, and they asked John and Kate what they wanted. They requested drinks the same as what everyone else had. When everyone had their drinks, the Secretary General said, "We are very interested in the Medical Project. As you know, we have started deploying it all over China. Our doctors and patients love it. It has already saved many lives. We also want to get into some of the studies you are doing so we can get ahead of some of these diseases. Also, COVID would never have spread if we had the Medical Computers deployed and people were using them. Everyone thinks it started in China, but if we had these Medical Computers deployed around the world and people were using the Medical Computer Application, then there would be no debate on where it started. We would know, and we would have stopped it before it spread."

Kate quickly responded and said, "I can tell you I understand the results of the Medical Project and how it works."

The Secretary General paused for a moment, and suddenly a tear escaped from his eye. He then said, "I understand because it saved my wife from colon cancer, which was detected early here in China. They wanted to have it removed, but she would have to wear a bag her whole life. The Medical Computer allowed us to find the best surgeon. He was called 'Dr. C' in Jacksonville, Florida's Mayo Clinic, and he was able to remove the cancer before it spread, and she did not have to wear a bag her whole life."

Now everyone had tears in their eyes. Kate responded by saying, "Thank you for that story. It made our day. We can get you working with our leaders on the Medical Project, so you can get in on all the early studies being done."

The Secretary General then said, "I want to thank you both for coming up with the Medical Project. You outlined all the problems you had in getting it deployed around the world in a book called 'The Medical Project'. It is an honor to meet you both. My wife wants to meet both of you someday, and we will take you up on that offer to get involved in the early studies. Also, we are now interested in the Climate and Storm Projects. We would like to partner with you on those projects, similar to what you did in Russia."

He added, "As you know, our sky is gray, and based on what I have researched, you have come up with a device that can change that, along with some other tools. Once the climate is fixed, there will be a lesser need for the storm tool, but for now, we are also interested in that tool. We saw what you did off the coast of Cuba, and that was amazing. Our presidents have talked, and I understand you would like something from us before we can partner on these projects."

John then said in a very serious tone, "You understand what Kate and I have been working on very well. We believe partners should not be worried about each other's security and must have trust. That is why Kate and I are proposing we form an Asia Trade Agreement (ATA). This would allow trade between you and Taiwan or any other country to happen easier than ever before, and it would also allow Taiwan and North Korea to not be afraid that someone is going to invade them."

A tear welled up in the Secretary General's eye, and his voice trembled as he spoke: "If anyone else were proposing this to China, I would have some mistrust. But I know you both understand the depths of my despair when they informed my wife and me that she would endure a lifetime with a bag. It was the Medical Computer, your invention, that led us to the exceptional doctor who saved her life. I owe both of you a debt of gratitude beyond measure. I trust you implicitly, which is why I will wholeheartedly recommend our participation in the ATA. And in return, we will join forces on your three projects.

On Sunday, I will have a meeting with the President at 9 a.m. Once our discussion concludes, I will draft a speech for him to deliver on

Monday. If you find it suitable, we will stand united behind him during his speech. Let us convene at 8 a.m. on Monday to finalize the details. If all goes well, we can make the announcement to the world at 9 a.m.

Oh, and I have one other request. My wife is waiting in our limo outside. Would you allow her to join us for dinner?"

The Ambassador immediately spoke up, his voice choked with emotion: "Absolutely, she should join us. I will extend the invitation to my wife as well."

They sealed their agreement with firm handshakes, and the wives were graciously invited to join them for dinner. As the Secretary General's wife arrived, she hurried over to Kate, enveloping her in a warm embrace, and then repeated the gesture with John. Her eyes shimmered with tears of gratitude as she uttered, "Lately, all my husband can talk about is how the Medical Project, with its far-reaching implementation in China, has not only saved my life but countless others as well. It is an honor to meet you both, and I was so happy when I found out about this meeting. I pray everything has fallen into place. I suppose I'll find out tomorrow."

The Ambassador brought the dinner and meeting to a close, his voice filled with sincerity: "Having Kate and John here with us is an absolute honor. Secretary General, your presence and that of your wife have made this a day we will all remember for the rest of our lives. Thank you everyone for the most remarkable dinner and meeting of my life."

One by one, they bid their farewells, leaving the Secretary General to prepare for his crucial discussion with the President of China, where he would endeavor to secure their support for the ATA.

Upon returning to their rooms, Kate and John eagerly briefed Jim on the phone call, who, in turn, shared it with the President. Delighted by the outcome, the President requested a copy of the President of China's speech in advance, allowing him to inform our partners in Asia as well the esteemed leaders of Congress and the Senate.

Aware that tomorrow held great significance, John and Kate sought an early night's rest. They meticulously prepared their attire for the upcoming meetings, ensuring each garment was impeccably pressed. Anticipating a morning jog, they informed the guards of their plans, expressing their desire to explore the streets of Beijing. With a wake-up call set for 5:30 a.m., they hoped to commence their run at 6 a.m., long before the city's bustling traffic took hold.

As they settled into bed, a swell of profound joy enveloped John and Kate. Tears of elation streamed down their faces, for they had witnessed firsthand the immense impact of their ideas and inventions, touching lives across the globe.

The Twenty-Fourth Day

A Big Breakfast and Dinner Meeting

J ohn and Kate awoke promptly at 5:30 a.m., as they had planned. By 6 a.m., they were prepared for their morning run outside the Embassy. Six security officers were present with them—two in front, two behind, and one on either side—for their protection.

Their run proceeded without incident until they were about three miles in, preparing to turn around and return to the Embassy. A group of men standing near a building on the wide sidewalk caught their attention. As they hastened to pass the group, they heard a series of loud pops. Initially, everyone presumed it was gunfire, but upon closer inspection, it turned out the men were merely setting off firecrackers. Shaking their heads at the misunderstanding, John, Kate, and their security team quickened their pace, making it back to the Embassy by 7 a.m.

That morning, John and Kate had planned to enjoy a leisurely breakfast with the Ambassador and his wife at around 8:30 a.m. After a quick shower and a change into casual clothes, they were escorted to the dining room. To their surprise, the entire Embassy staff was present, rising to their feet and applauding as they entered. John and Kate, taken aback by the unexpected display, nonetheless appreciated the show of support.

Upon entering the room, they noticed a large screen had been set

124

up. The Ambassador took the floor and revealed that others would be joining them for breakfast as the President, his wife, Valerie, Jim, and the leaders of Congress and the Senate appeared onscreen, gathered in the President's dining room. This was news to most of the Embassy staff, and the room was filled with surprised faces.

The President, sporting a broad grin, addressed the room, and said, "I hope you don't mind if we join you."

He proceeded to praise John and Kate for their successful meeting with the Secretary General the day before, expressing confidence in the success of their ongoing endeavors. Following his remarks, the Washington, D.C., dining room erupted into applause and cheers.

John and Kate were asked to share their experiences from the meeting, and their account of their encounter with the Secretary General's wife moved many to tears. The President concluded the virtual gathering by commending John and Kate for their consistent success in the tasks they undertook.

This was met with more applause, which left John and Kate overwhelmed with gratitude. Kate took a moment to express her appreciation but also emphasized the importance of the team effort that had contributed to their success. She pointed out that the Ambassador's role in organizing the meetings and setting expectations had been crucial, and the President's and Jim's calls with various heads of state had been instrumental in obtaining agreement on the ATA.

After the meeting ended amidst applause and cheers, John and Kate returned to their room to start preparations for their next meeting in North Korea. The exciting news that the President of China had approved the ATA served to highlight their day. The Secretary General announced his intent to invite the leaders working on the three projects to the announcement ceremony and the subsequent meeting at the Presidential Palace.

With the need for coordination of a call involving all the relevant parties, John and Kate contacted Valerie to set up a Zoom call, adjusting for the different time zones. After this busy day, they enjoyed a pleasant dinner with the Ambassador and his wife, who shared the good news that the speech had been well received by the President's aides.

Exhausted but satisfied with the day's accomplishments, John and Kate set their alarm for 5:30 a.m., informed security of their intent to exercise in the gym the next morning, and headed straight to bed.

The Twenty-Fifth Day

The President of China's Big Announcement and John and Kate's Brief Vacation

J ohn and Kate woke up at 5:30 a.m. as planned, ready to run on the treadmills in the Embassy. They quickly changed into their running attire, opened the door, and were greeted by a guard who would escort them to the gym. Aware of their tight schedule, they knew their workout would be cut short, allowing them to leave for the Presidential Palace at 7 a.m., where they had a meeting scheduled before the 8 a.m. speech.

Standing on the same stage as the President of China was an incredible honor for John and Kate. However, they also recognized that as their recognition grew, they would inevitably sacrifice some of their freedoms, and not everyone would be pleased with their actions. Nevertheless, they firmly believed that the work they were doing would benefit people worldwide, making the personal risks worthwhile.

During their exercise routine, the Ambassador entered the gym and informed them that the President—along with leaders from the Congress and Senate—had approved the speech the President of China would be delivering. This confirmation solidified their participation in the event and reassured them of the support they had received. Additionally, Valerie had arranged meetings with the three project leaders from the U.S. and also from China, immediately following the President of China's speech. They were also aware that the President of China's speech would be broadcast worldwide. As a precautionary measure, they were scheduled to fly to North Korea on Tuesday afternoon in case any additional meetings were required.

John and Kate completed their workout while talking to the Ambassador, who extended an invitation to join him for breakfast and dinner after all the excitement. They showered, dressed, and headed down to the dining room, where they shared a quiet breakfast with the Ambassador and his wife. By 7 a.m., they were ready to depart and headed straight for the Palace. Upon their arrival, they were greeted by the Secretary General. "Well, I guess this is all going to happen. Was everyone okay with the speech? Were there any recommended changes?" the Secretary General asked.

"There were no necessary changes to the speech, and thank you for making all of this possible," Kate said in response to the Secretary General's questions.

Smiling, the Secretary General declared, "I am proud to have worked with all of you. The President wishes to speak with both of you and the Ambassador before delivering his speech. We must proceed quickly to his office."

The Ambassador's wife remained in the car, knowing she would be part of the audience during the speech.

Entering the President of China's office, they were met with a beaming smile. The President of China then said, "Maybe this would be the first of many partnerships between the U.S. and China. My Secretary General was pleased with the meeting, and so am I. I'm not sure if he told you this, but the Medical Project has already been implemented throughout China, and recently, my doctors suggested that I switch to alkaline water and follow a ketogenic diet based on the nutritional tips provided by the project. It looks like one of the three projects has already helped me. I have discussed these ideas with the President of North Korea, who was also considering the same changes."

John and Kate exchanged smiles and said, "We did the same thing when we read about its potential to prevent cancer and heart disease. In fact, the President of the United States expressed his interest in highlighting these findings in the Medical Computer. As for the speech, everyone thought it was fantastic, and we are honored to share the stage with you."

The President of China looked directly at John and Kate, and then he said, "I rarely say this, but both of you are highly regarded here in China. Your projects have helped many people, and I am proud to stand alongside both of you."

John and Kate, not accustomed to such compliments, simply smiled and thanked him. They were then led to a large auditorium, where they joined the three Project Leaders from China on the stage.

The President of China stepped forward and delivered his speech. He discussed how the partnership between China and the ATA would strengthen relations with Taiwan and the rest of Asia. He also emphasized the collaboration between the U.S. and China on the three projects: the Medical Project, the Storm Project, and the Climate Project. The President of China then introduced the three Project Leaders and mentioned that they would be meeting after the speech. He then called John and Kate to the stage, resulting in applause from the audience. The President of China turned to them and said, "I told you they loved you here."

After the speech concluded with great applause and cheers, they left and proceeded to a conference room.

The President of China informed everyone, "I have another meeting to attend, but the Secretary General will take over for me. He will ensure everything stays on track, and I will intervene if necessary. Let's hope everything goes smoothly."

John and Kate took over the meeting, gathering updates from all the leaders and scheduling weekly meetings to ensure the implementation stayed on track. After about two hours, the meeting concluded.

The Secretary General turned to the Ambassador, John, and Kate.

He then said, "I have increased security for the three Project Leaders, and while you are here, I will enhance security for both of you. There are always people who would like to embarrass our President, so we need to ensure your safety."

The Ambassador intended to surprise John and Kate, but he had to share his plans with everyone: "Since we had the rest of the day free, we'll treat John and Kate as tourists, taking them to a Chinese restaurant and the Great Wall."

The Secretary General added, "Excellent. Our security team will lead the way. Let them have some fun."

John and Kate were pleasantly surprised and expressed their gratitude. Kate smiled and said, "You are both so nice to do this. Rest assured that when the Secretary General someday visits Washington, D.C., we will do the same thing and extend our hospitality to him."

They shook hands, and together with the Ambassador, they all entered the limo. Two Chinese security cars led the way, and two followed behind. The Ambassador's wife seemed surprised, and the Ambassador explained to the driver and his wife, "You know the surprise we had for John and Kate? Well, it's no longer a surprise. We're all going to have lunch and visit the Great Wall of China. It will be a quick stop for lunch."

The limo driver informed the security team about their destination, and the five cars proceeded. After leaving the city, they arrived at a large Chinese restaurant, where they noticed two buses parked outside. Everyone exited the limo while the security guards surrounded them, and they walked into the restaurant. The restaurant was bustling with activity, and as John and Kate entered, they heard chatter, pointing, and then a loud cheer and applause. Understanding it was for them, they smiled, waved, and proceeded to an empty round table accompanied by the Ambassador, his wife, and their security team.

Kate asked, "How did they hear the speech?"

"Look at the round sticker on their shirts. They all came from cruising ships, and they are on a tour to see the Great Wall. They stopped here for lunch, like us. Ships usually have CNN and Fox broadcasting, so they must have seen the speech before leaving the ship," John said while observing the people cheering on them.

Everyone at the table smiled. The Ambassador, sitting next to another round table with people from the tour, asked, "Did you see the speech?"

The people at the nearby table, beaming with smiles, spoke loudly so John and Kate could hear: "You two are amazing, and you make us all proud to be Americans. The food here is excellent; you'll enjoy it."

The lunch proceeded splendidly, with occasional interruptions from people stopping by at John and Kate's table just to say hello. Once they finished eating, the Ambassador's wife turned to Kate and said, "Thank you both again for visiting China. Now, Kate and I will do some shopping at the gift shop before we continue to the Great Wall."

Kate expressed her gratitude and immediately joined the Ambassador's wife, accompanied by half of the security guards. John and the Ambassador stayed at the table, enjoying some tea that accompanied the meal. When Kate and the Ambassador's wife finished shopping, they returned to the table, and together with the security team, they made their way back to the limo.

About an hour later, they arrived at the Great Wall, where a gift shop awaited them. They entered, and Kate purchased various items while John got one sweatshirt with the history of the Great Wall on it, which he knew he would be wearing on his runs.

Then they embark the climb up the Great Wall. After reaching halfway, they decided it was sufficient and took a bunch of pictures. They then descended into the limo and headed back to the Embassy. Upon their arrival, the Chinese security team returned to the Palace.

Later that evening, John and Kate had a late dinner with the Ambassador and his wife. During the meal, Kate brought up an idea and said, "John and I think it would be best to travel to North Korea and stay overnight in Pyongyang at the Paekhwawon State Guest House. The President of China had recommended that facility to us as it often hosts heads of state and foreign dignitaries.

He told us that the facility appears to provide an optimal place to ensure security and privacy. Madelenine Albright, prime ministers, and South Korean leaders had previously stayed there."

"It would be impolite to fly in and out on the same day. Tuesday is a free day, so we should plan to fly out tomorrow afternoon and spend Tuesday night in Pyongyang. This way, we'll be well-rested for our meeting with the President of North Korea on Wednesday. We can still fly home on Wednesday night. Could you ask your secretary to make these arrangements? She should coordinate with Valerie, our assistant in the U.S.," Kate said, proposing a collaboration with the Ambassador on their secretaries.

The Ambassador quickly agreed, stating, "As much as we enjoy your company and would love for you to stay here, I believe you're right. We'll adjust your plans and arrange for your trip to North Korea tomorrow."

John and Kate thanked them for the support and the successful meetings. It was already 10 p.m., so everyone retired to their rooms. John and Kate decided not to set an alarm that night, relishing the joy of waking up without the need for a schedule. However, just as they were about to get into bed, the phone rang. It was Jim and the U.S. President calling. John answered the call, and Jim said, "Good evening, you two. Didn't you really think you could go to bed without talking to us? We just wanted to express our satisfaction with your outstanding work and let you know that everyone here and in Taiwan is thrilled. Great job!"

John chuckled and replied, "Well, if you have cameras, you would have seen that we just stepped into our room when your call came in. We were planning to give you a call and discuss a change of plans."

With that, John and Kate briefed both Jim and the U.S. President on their revised intentions. Both Jim and the U.S. President readily agreed and immediately set Valerie in motion to implement the necessary adjustments. Valerie also informed the Ambassador of her actions, ensuring that no duplication of effort would occur. With the conversations concluded, they all hung up, and finally, John and Kate were able to retreat to their shared bed, relieved to bring an end to an exceedingly eventful day filled with discussions with the two presidents.

John and Kate's Big Surprise and Dinner in North Korea

J ohn was the first to awaken, and it was around 9 a.m. He headed straight for the bathroom and got dressed to exercise. As he made his way out to the door, Kate noticed him and commented, "I guess no one wanted to wake us up. Are you going to the gym?"

John smiled and replied, "I didn't want to wake you because I thought today would be a day when we could wake up without any interruptions. And yes, I'm off to the gym."

Kate returned his smile and said, "I'll meet you at the gym."

With that, John smiled back and left the room, bound for the gym. Since Kate was now awake, she decided to prepare for exercise as well and joined John approximately fifteen minutes later.

As John and Kate were engaged in their workout, the Ambassador and his wife entered the room. The Ambassador quipped, "Don't you two ever take a break?"

Kate responded, saying, "We just got here."

While Kate and John continued their exercises, the Ambassador mentioned, "You have an excellent Executive Assistant. She collaborated with the local team to arrange the trip exactly as we discussed. You'll be departing in a couple of hours, flying to North Korea, and staying at the Paekhwawon State Guest House in Pyongyang. The President of North Korea will join you there for dinner. Additionally, they thought it would be beneficial to invite the President of South Korea to this meeting, who has stayed at the guest house before. It's turning out even better than we anticipated. You might want to consider giving Valerie a raise."

John and Kate exchanged knowing smiles, their thoughts aligning with the notion of involvement from Jim, the U.S. President, and possibly even the President of China.

Glancing at the Ambassador, John remarked, "Well, we're certainly glad we squeezed this workout in, as things are bound to get busy in North Korea."

"You better wrap up this workout because a few individuals want to have breakfast and dinner with you again to bid you farewell and wish you a safe trip," the Ambassador said with a grinned.

After concluding their workout, John and Kate returned to their room, pondering what awaited them at breakfast. They showered, dressed, and packed while they talk about the Ambassador's mention of several people wishing to bid them farewell. When they opened the door, they found someone ready to transport their luggage to the limo, and another person led them to the dining room. This time, they noticed the two large screens, and the Ambassador said that someone from the U.S. would be joining them for breakfast and dinner. However, their surprise knew no bounds when they saw the President of China and his Secretary General seated at the table.

Rising from his seat, the Ambassador announced with an enormous grin, "I wouldn't spring a surprise like this on just anyone, but John and Kate can handle anything. They excel under pressure, as we're about to reveal. Allow me to introduce the Secretary General and the President of China to our Embassy and to this meeting. Furthermore, let me introduce the President of the United States, along with the leaders of Congress and the Senate, to this assembly. Lastly, allow me to introduce the presidents of South and North Korea."

Their faces appeared on the screen, and the President of North Korea spoke, saying, "John and Kate, we await your presence here at the Paekthwawon State Guest House in Pyongyang. Hurry and join us so that we may commence this meeting."

Kate and John were left awestruck, exchanging smiles of amazement. Kate remarked, "Someone definitely deserves a raise for organizing all this at the last minute. I don't think either of us has ever been in the same room with four presidents and so many high-ranking officials."

The President of China then chimed in, saying, "Arranging our schedules to meet with both of you was not a problem. We always have something to learn from the two of you. What makes it even more pleasant is that you both remain oblivious to your own importance. You possess ideas that can change the world."

With a proud expression, the President of the United States added, "People admire both of you because you make things happen. The ATA is a joint effort, but it was your proposal that set it in motion. For that, among other reasons, we will be awarding both of you the Presidential Medal of Freedom, the nation's highest civilian honor. Since it says 'Presidential,' you can assume it comes from all the presidents on this call, as we have all discussed it and believe you both deserve it."

Following the speech, everyone stood and applauded. Kate and John beamed with pride, expressing their gratitude to everyone present. Amidst conversations, people took a few bites of breakfast or dinner. The Ambassador was about to conclude the meeting when the President of South Korea spoke up, wearing a slight smile, and jokingly said, "There are two presidents waiting for two people at the Paekthwawon State Guest House, so we can start this meeting."

Laughter filled the room, and Kate and John stood, waving to everyone, before making their way to the limo.

They arrived at the Paekthwawon State Guest House around 4 p.m. and were escorted to their room. After swiftly changing out of their travel clothes, they opened the door to proceed to the meeting, only to find someone waiting to take them to the meeting room. Inside the meeting room, the presidents of North and South Korea stood with glasses of wine while eating some snacks. John and Kate entered, and the President of North Korea extended a greeting, saying, "Welcome to North Korea. What kind of wine would you like?"

John replied, "We'll have the same as both of you. Could you share your thoughts on the Asia Trade Agreement (ATA)? Let us know if there are any changes you'd like to make. Also, have you selected the three leaders from your countries who will work with the U.S. leaders on those three projects?"

In a serious tone, the President of North Korea responded, "We have agreed upon the ATA, so no changes are necessary. Regarding the three leaders in North Korea, we have chosen them, and we have scheduled a meeting with a person named Valerie after this gathering. The three North Korean leaders are waiting outside this room."

"I brought my three leaders with me as well, and they too are awaiting the commencement of the meeting. As for the ATA, I see no need for any changes," the President of South Korea said, following the President of North Korea's update.

John, turning his gaze towards the President of North Korea, added, "When we put this agreement together, we had you in mind. You have the freedom to test weapons, but missile deployments throughout Asia must cease. You should have no fear of any invasion of North Korea, for if that were to occur, everyone who signed the agreement would rally against the aggressor."

The President of South Korea interjected, "That's precisely why all the smaller countries agreed to sign the ATA. We always harbored that fear. We feel safer now, and trading with all the signatory nations have become significantly easier. We genuinely thank both of you for making it all happen."

Kate chimed in, "Asia will be more stable, and once the three projects are implemented, the air will be cleaner, and people will be healthier. Should we bring in the three leaders from each country to provide updates on the projects?"

Upon hearing Kate's suggestions, the two presidents rose and walked towards the door to invite their respective leaders in. Meanwhile, an aide in the room initiated a Zoom call with the three U.S. leaders. When the U.S. leaders appeared on the screen, Kate and John thanked them for attending the meeting ahead of schedule. Each project leader provided a status update and committed to weekly meetings to ensure swift progress. As the meeting drew to a close, the presidents, John and Kate, expressed their satisfaction and agreed to meet monthly to address problems and find solutions. Given the late hour in North Korea, the presidents arranged to meet John and Kate for breakfast at 10 a.m. before everyone departed for their respective destinations.

Curious about their morning exercise, John and Kate asked the President of North Korea where they could exercise in the morning. The President of North Korea informed them that they could either use the gym or run within the compound, but urged them to stay inside the perimeter. John and Kate informed the security team that they intended to jog around the outdoor track and then use the sauna. Setting their alarm for 6 a.m., knowing it was a travel day, they aimed to fit in some exercise before their long flight back home.

The Twenty-Seventh Day

John and Kate's Change of Plans from Flying Back Home

J ohn and Kate awoke promptly at 6 a.m. as the alarm rang, feeling a sense of déjà vu. They had repeated this routine several times during their trip, but this time was different—they were heading home after a successful trip, carrying a couple of prestigious metals that brought them immense joy. They informed their security personnel that they intended to go for an outdoor run within the compound. Accompanied by two security guards, they embarked on a one-hour jog before realizing it was time to prepare for breakfast with the two presidents.

After a quick shower, they dressed in haste, knowing they had an important meeting ahead. As they entered the breakfast room, they noticed that the two presidents were already engaged in conversation while sipping their coffee. Taking their seats across from them, John and Kate joined the discussion while they savored their own cups of coffee.

Both presidents wore mischievous grins on their faces, as if concealing a secret. The President of South Korea, aware that his statement would catch Kate and John off guard, looked at them and said, "Do you know what we decided this morning? We have yet to announce the ATA to our people. Although the press may have already leaked the information, we believe it's important to make the announcement together with both of you in South Korea."

Kate and John exchanged surprised glances but quickly realized that these two presidents had a knack for delivering unexpected yet clever ideas. With a smile, John looked at Kate, who nodded in agreement, and he replied, "You guys are something else. We had planned to return home today, but we think it's a fantastic idea. Having both of you on stage in South Korea to announce the ATA is a great idea, and if you want us there, we'll adjust our plans accordingly."

Everyone stood up, exchanged handshakes, and then resumed their seats to finish breakfast. John and Kate reflected on how their breakfasts had been during this trip. They made arrangements to fly to Seoul that day and schedule the announcement for Thursday at 10 a.m. local time, which would be 9 p.m. Wednesday in Washington time. They agreed to have dinner in Seoul at 7 p.m., where they could exchange speeches and discuss any necessary modifications.

As soon as breakfast concluded, Kate approached the pilot to inform him of the change in plans, while John contacted Jim to share the updates. Jim enthusiastically approved of the idea and relayed the information to the U.S. President and other leaders.

Valerie organized accommodations for John and Kate at the U.S. Embassy in South Korea and arranged for their airport pickup. Meanwhile, the President of North Korea made arrangements to stay at the President of South Korea's compound. They all departed for the airport together, traveling in a limousine with security personnel both in front and behind them.

The trip to Seoul was uneventful, and upon arrival, John and Kate were greeted and transported to the U.S. Embassy in South Korea, where they prepared for dinner. At 7 p.m., they arrived at the dining venue, finding the two presidents standing and already enjoying a rice-fermented drink, the unofficial national beverage with about half the alcohol content of vodka. The President of South Korea asked John and Kate what they would like to drink, and they opted for the same beverage as the presidents. The President of North Korea exchanged a knowing glance with the President of South Korea, and with a grin, he said, "We have one more surprise for both of you. During tomorrow's ATA announcement, we've invited the presidents of China and Taiwan to join us on camera via Zoom, and you will stand between them."

Kate exclaimed, "WOW! You two sure have been busy. Are the papers in your hands copies of your speeches? Could we have a copy?"

The President of South Korea, smiling, responded, "Certainly! Both of you are the driving force behind all this. Here is a copy of each of our speeches."

Both presidents of North and South Korea handed John and Kate copies of their speeches. The President of North Korea interjected, "We made extra copies for you. We have already reviewed and approved them for each other. Let us know during breakfast at 8 a.m. if you have any revisions."

John and Kate expressed their gratitude for the speeches, and everyone settled down to enjoy a delightful dinner. Kate was pleasantly surprised when the South Korean chef—seemingly aware of her vegetarian preference—presented a stunning display of vegetable dishes resembling a waterfall. The sight was so tempting that John found himself momentarily wishing he, too, followed a vegetarian diet. The evening continued with entertainment, featuring Korean songs and captivating dancers. It was a memorable occasion for all. When Kate and John retired to their room, they promptly sent copies of both speeches to Jim, who assured them he would provide any necessary revisions before 7 p.m. his time, just in time for their breakfast meeting.

John and Kate decided to wake up at 5 a.m. in the morning as they planned to hit the gym before returning to their room to confer with Jim in preparation for their meeting with the two presidents.

John and Kate's Excitement— From Attending Significant Speeches to Homebound Flight

J ohn and Kate woke up at 5 a.m. when the alarm went off. They swiftly got dressed and headed to the gym, squeezing in a solid two hours of exercise. By 7 a.m., they were back in their room, where they noticed a message from Jim confirming that the speeches were good to go. Having already read and appreciated the speeches, John and Kate expressed their willingness to stand alongside the two presidents during their delivery.

During the speeches of the presidents of North and South Korea, thunderous applause erupted from the audience. They announced the successful implementation of the ATA and outlined future endeavors to be undertaken by their respective leaders, as well as John and Kate. China and Taiwan—also represented by a large video—were acknowledged for their contributions to the ATA.

The speeches captivated the audience, transforming what was once a hotspot into a desirable spot for everyone, whether for a visit or to live. After the speeches, the North Korean President, along with John and Kate, traveled together in the same limousine to the airport. During the ride, they engaged in meaningful discussions, all agreeing that returning home would be great.

When John and Kate's plane landed later that day due to the time zone difference, a helicopter was waiting to transport them to the White House. The heightened security measures were taken to ensure their safety, as Jim was unwilling to take any chances. The President, members of Congress, and Senate Leaders, as well as Jim, Valerie, and Natalie, Jim's new assistant, all extended warm welcomes to John and Kate as they arrived. The group escorted them to the dining room for a lunch meeting.

John and Kate remained vigilant, given the unexpected events that had unfolded during recent meals. Acknowledging their concerns, the U.S. President promptly addressed the issue of airport security. He said, "We have received reports indicating a strong interest in obtaining the details of the three projects and replicating them. That's why we've enhanced security measures, so please be careful."

Kate looked at Jim and the President and responded, "We appreciate the increased security, and we will remain vigilant. We must protect all the hard work invested in developing these three projects. If they hold value for other governments, certain individuals may see an opportunity to profit by selling the secrets of the three projects."

As the meeting concluded, Jim took Kate and John off to the side. "You've been traveling and away from home for a while. Why don't you take an extra-long weekend? We can discuss the status of the three projects on Monday."

John smiled at Jim and replied, "Thank you, Jim. We could use a couple of days to relax and maybe treat Katelin to a nice meal."

Jim looked at them both and said, "A limo and additional security will be taking you home. You will also have security stationed at your home."

Farewells and congratulations were exchanged as they bid farewell to John and Kate. They noticed a security car leading their limousine. Kate called Katelin and said, "Hello, Katelin. We've returned home. Can we pick you up from work?"

With a disappointed tone, Katelin responded, "I wish I could leave now, but I have a few more hours of work. Can I pick up a couple of pizzas and bring them to your house around 7 p.m.? We can have a pizza party, and I'll spend the night at your place."

"Great! We'll see you at 7 p.m. Oh, the limo has arrived at the house. See you later!" Kate said so with delight.

John and Kate were about to step out of the limousine, but a guard halted them, instructing them to remain inside until the house was checked. John observed that these were a new set of guards; Bill was not with them. Once the guards deemed the house safe, they motioned for John and Kate to enter the house. The couple entered with two guards following them as they carried their luggage. Meanwhile, two guards were stationed outside.

John informed the guards inside the house that he and Kate would be going upstairs to shower and prepare for Katelin's arrival at 7 p.m. After about an hour, they heard the doorbell ring and went downstairs to greet Katelin. To their surprise, they noticed only one guard at the door, but there were five other men inside the house. The three remaining guards were all dead. One of the men had Katelin in a headlock, a gun menacingly pointed at her.

John and Kate were shocked. It appeared that one of the guards had a silencer on his gun and had killed the other three guards, allowing five other men to enter the house. John's face filled with panic as he asked, "What do you want? You can have anything!"

The guard replied, "We want the secret plans for the three projects. Give them to us, or we will kill your daughter and wife."

Thinking quickly, John responded, "The plans are in a safe in another room."

The man holding Katelin in a headlock with a gun pressed against her head warned, "Don't try anything, or we will kill them both."

John led one of the guards into his bedroom and opened the safe. While the guard's attention was diverted towards Katelin and Kate, John discreetly retrieved a revolver from the safe, concealed it in his pants, and covered it with his shirt worn outside his pants. Realizing that the intruders wouldn't leave any witnesses alive, having seen their faces, John carefully handed over some papers, saying, "These are the confidential plans for the three projects."

The guard pointed his gun at John, took the papers, and declared, "Alright, let's go back into the room with your wife and daughter."

Upon returning to the room, the guard raised the papers triumphantly, announcing, "I've got the papers on the three projects!"

John, raising his voice, pleaded, "Please don't hurt my family!"

In response, both Katelin and Kate instantly dropped to the floor. This was a rehearsed plan that the Columbos had practiced. As soon as John uttered the words *"Please don't hurt my family,"* they knew they would drop to the floor. Capitalizing on the distraction, John swiftly shot the three men in the room, killing them instantly. As he fired, he commanded everyone to leave his house. However, three more assailants remained somewhere outside.

John turned Kate and Katelin and instructed, "Go to the safe room, take these plans, and call Bill."

Bill was a trusted guard. The safe room in their house featured a metal door, cameras, and a phone with TVs to monitor the entire house. Once locked, no one could breach that room. John chose to stay behind to ensure nobody followed them, as he was already engaged in a gun battle with the remaining three men.

The three men attempted to rush John, who aimed his gun at the door to the house. John managed to shoot one of them, but two more emerged from a car parked in the driveway, leaving four men still a threat. Two of them wielded machine guns while three of their assailants kept firing at John, and the fourth tried to find a clear shot through a window at him. John swiftly spotted him and dropped to the ground, shooting him. Just then, the sound of sirens grew closer, and a group of men arrived to rescue John. Amidst the exchange of gunfire, the remaining assailant eventually surrendered.

Seeing Bill at the door, John expressed his gratitude. "Thank you, Bill. I thought we were in serious trouble until I saw you."

Kate and Katelin rushed into the room, embracing John, and then said, "Thank God you are not hurt!"

Bill, wearing a smile, remarked, "These guys should have known better than to mess with the Columbos."

"Thanks for coming to our rescue!" Kate said, smiling as she hugged Bill.

Curious about their successful escape, Bill asked, "How did you manage to turn the tables on trained killers like them?"

With a smile, John shared with Bill their plan: "It was the move you taught me back in Rio, in case someone had me pinned and you needed me to create an opportunity for you to shoot them."

Bill laughed and commended, "So, you taught it to your family. Very good!"

John then asked Bill, "Why do you think the guard decided to betray us?"

Bill suggested, "Money. The word is out that those three projects are worth millions of dollars. I don't know that security person, but we will conduct a thorough investigation to uncover why he turned against us."

"Well, I better call Jim and let him know what happened. You should reach out to your boss as well," John said, realizing the importance of informing their colleagues.

Katelin asked, "Daddy, when did you learn to shoot like that?"

John replied, "You can do extraordinary things when your family is threatened. I love you and your mom. You two are the most important things in my life. Can you ask your boss if you can take tomorrow and Monday off, so we can have a long weekend together?"

Katelin smiled and responded, "Since all the network trucks are outside, I don't think he will mind me taking Friday and Monday off. But I'll give him a call first thing in the morning."

John picked up the phone and dialed Jim's number, saying, "Hi, Jim. I assume you've seen what happened at my house. I know you'll be investigating how this could have occurred in the coming days. Kate,

Katelin, and I would like to take some time off and go to the lodge where the Medical Project began. We'll stay there for a vacation and return to work on Tuesday, if that's okay with you."

Jim swiftly responded, "Since this guard was one of our own, we will get to the bottom of this. Taking a vacation after what just happened sounds like a good idea. I trust Bill Collins, and I'll ask him to arrange for security personnel he trusts to accompany you to Cheat River Lodge. We'll have a limo pick you up tomorrow, and two helicopters will transport you there. Does that sound alright to you and Kate?"

John, appreciative of the support, replied, "Thank you so much, Jim. It means a lot. We'll see you on Tuesday, but if you need us for any reason, you know where to find us."

Jim concluded, "Thank you, John. We've got a lot of bad guys today."

Having overheard the conversation, Bill and Kate entered the room. Bill assured them: "I'll take care of arranging everything—the limo, helicopters, security, and hotel reservations. I'll also inform Valerie and Natalie, so if anyone needs to contact you, they'll know how to reach you."

"Although we told Jim we'd be on vacation, he knows us well enough to expect that we'll be working on this case. So bring whatever and whoever you need for brainstorming with us on Friday. We'll be on vacation, but we'll also be working," Kate said in a serious tone.

Bill shook his head and left the room to make the necessary arrangements. John, Kate, and Katelin shared a meaningful look and embraced each other tightly. Katelin broke the silence, expressing relief: "Thank God we're all safe. Let's get some rest; we have a big day tomorrow. I'll call my boss tonight to let him know our whereabouts and to confirm the extended weekend."

They retired to their respective bedrooms, but before doing so, John suggested they indulge in a jar of sangria he had prepared. John always cuts various fruits and puts them in a mason jar. where he adds red sangria wine. The drink would help them relax and hopefully ensure a peaceful night's sleep before their eventful day of travel.

Lodge Bound—John, Kate, and Katelin's Travel and Strategic Discussions

Johnand Kate woke up to the sound of a knock on their bedroom door. It was Katelin who shouted from behind the door, "My boss saw everything on TV and was waiting for my call. He said he was about to call me and give me a couple of days off. So, I don't have to be at work until Tuesday. Let's get going!"

Kate yelled back, "Okay, we're up. Let's get ready to travel. Pack up and try to leave within the hour."

Everyone quickly got up and dressed. John poked his head out the door and instructed the security personnel to be ready to leave in about an hour. He informed Kate that he planned to go running in West Virginia at the lodge.

As Kate was getting dressed, she would often remind John to keep his eyes to himself. John was always amazed by Kate's beauty and received compliments from others whenever they went out together. He loved making her happy by buying her clothes and things she liked. In contrast, John was more laid-back, content in sweatpants and a T-shirt. Despite their differences, they complement each other well. Katelin was a mix of both, appreciating beautiful things while also enjoying the comfort of sweats.

Kate was aware of Katelin's beauty, as she would often catch guys giving her daughter a second look. During their time in Japan, Katelin even did some modeling and appeared on magazine covers and billboards.

John felt fortunate to have such beautiful and smart women in his life who loved him. They were a total package.

After an hour, they were all ready and out the door. Bill had arranged for additional security to accompany them to the helicopters, while two guards stayed behind at the house to ensure its safety from intruders or listening devices.

The helicopter ride from Washington to the lodge on the Cheat River took about an hour. Kate and John enjoyed the scenic trip, whether by car or helicopter, as they marveled at the beautiful mountains and lush forests.

While flying over the mountains, John reminisced with Kate, "Do you remember when we drove through these mountains in thick fog? I had to open my door while driving to follow the road's center line so we wouldn't fall off the edge."

Kate smiled and replied, "We had some good guardian angels looking out for us back then, and even more so now."

Katelin enjoyed listening to her parents' stories from before she was born, and she cherished those moments. Suddenly, she caught a glimpse of the lodge, nestled among mountains on three sides with the Cheat River on the other. Excitedly, she called out to her parents, "There it is! It looks beautiful!"

Once the helicopters landed, Bill instructed everyone to remain seated until the security guards in the other helicopter checked the surroundings and registered them at the hotel. They needed to sweep the rooms for any listening devices or planted bombs. They patiently waited in the helicopter for about thirty minutes before Bill guided them to their room. Bill informed John and Kate: "There will be a guard stationed outside your room 24/7, with additional security monitoring the grounds to make sure there are no problems. When do you want to go for a run, John? And will anyone join us?"

John looked at Kate and Katelin, both shaking their heads in response. Kate then said, "We'll be having lunch and spending some time at the gift shop. After that, I'll be working at that table."

John turned to Bill and said, "Okay, Bill, it looks like it's just you and me on this run."

Kate spoke with a serious tone: "Bill, will you be able to join John and me after the run at our usual table? We need to discuss the security guard who tried to kill us and find out who might have hired him. Katelin, since you were also involved in the incident, you're welcome to join us. But if you have other plans, let us know."

"I want to be involved in the security discussion. I'll join you, and thank you for inviting me," Katelin quickly said.

John then informed Bill that he would meet him in the lobby in approximately thirty minutes to start their run. He told Kate that he would meet her a couple of hours later at their usual working table in the hotel.

One security guard accompanied Bill and John as they went to change into their running clothes. Another guard remained downstairs with Kate and Katelin as they went for lunch. When Bill and John came downstairs to start their run, John suggested, "I want to go outside and see if I can spot Katelin and Kate at their lunch table. I'll wave to them to let them know we're starting our run."

Bill tilted his head and asked, "Why are we going to do that?"

John smiled and explained, "It's something I usually do to bring a smile to Kate's face."

Understanding the depth of their love, Bill didn't question it further. He knew they would do anything to make each other happy.

John and Bill stepped outside and searched for the lunch table where Kate and Katelin were seated. When John found it, he enthusiastically waved until they noticed and waved back, both smiling.

With their exchange done, John and Bill started their run along the Cheat River. After about an hour, they returned to the hotel and went up to their rooms to shower and change into comfortable clothes. Finally, they met Kate and Katelin at their usual working table in the hotel.

While wearing a smile, Kate initiated the conversation: "Please sit down, guys. I want to discuss something with you and see if you agree. We've already promised Russia and China a partnership, allowing them to use and deploy the three projects. While they may not possess the data in the patents, their governments have full access. So, I don't believe China or Russia was behind the attacks. Besides, Russia has already demonstrated its actions against those who try to kill people in other countries."

Kate continued, "The individuals targeting us are after the secrets behind the three projects. Killing us is just a means to acquire those secrets and reproduce them for the highest bidder. Their motive would be to incite a war by placing blame on another nation."

John chimed in, showcasing his talent for brainstorming: "We need to consider companies or individuals who would do anything to get the secrets behind the three projects, as we've agreed to partner with Russia and China to stop wars. They could also be people aiming to embarrass our President and our country. If it's someone within the U.S. government, they may have an easier time influencing a security person to break the law."

He looked toward Katelin and said, "Katelin, remember the same rules apply to this conversation. You cannot tell anyone about our discussion."

John then turned to Bill and said, "Bill, you need to be cautious and only trust those above you. They should be made aware of our thoughts. Kate and I will call for a break after this meeting, so you can start thinking about potential suspects. Jim might be on the same page as us, and if not, he would be the best person to uncover the culprit, given his knowledge of people's allegiances."

Kate added with a serious tone, "Until we identify and stop the person responsible, we need to be extremely careful. I think we're safe for now, as twenty-four hours ago, nobody knew we would be here. Bill, please ensure our safety."

That day, they decided to have dinner at the hotel. Bill didn't want to take any chances by going to an off-site restaurant at night, and John and Kate wanted to continue working.

Afterward, Kate and John gave Jim a call to inform him of their work progress at the lodge. Jim had conducted some financial investigations into the security guard who tried to kill John and Kate. Jim agreed with John and Kate's analysis, stating, "It appears your analysis is correct. Someone from the U.S. deposited money into the security guard's account. He had significant financial difficulties, and we are still searching for the person responsible. We will find out who caused this problem."

John quickly responded, expressing gratitude, saying, "We appreciate all your efforts. We'll remain vigilant, and Bill and his team will keep us safe. Keep us updated on any findings, and we'll do the same. Goodbye for now."

After ending the call, John, Kate, and Katelin headed to the lodge restaurant to meet Bill for dinner. A guard informed them that Bill had just left for the restaurant.

As they spotted Bill, he stood up and announced, "I have news about why the security guard acted as he did. Our team discovered several emails exchanged between him and a CIA agent. The agent had contacts outside the U.S. willing to pay a substantial sum for details on the three projects. Furthermore, the CIA agent was friends with the guard, and they were conspiring to uncover potential buyers for the project details. Their communications revolved around embarrassing our government."

John interjected, "It seems Jim has been coordinating with your team, but I'll drop him a message regarding the CIA agent."

After discussing the revelations, they proceeded to order their dinners and enjoyed their meal together. Once they finished, they returned to their rooms without setting alarms—intending to wake up without disruption—and then engage in exercise and relaxation.

The Thirtieth Day

John Wakes Up to Answer a Call from Jim

At 8 a.m., the ringing phone abruptly woke up John and Kate. Rubbing the sleep from their eyes, they groggily picked up the call. Jim's voice greeted them, apologizing for calling them early in the morning, but he quickly dived into the reason for his call.

"We have uncovered the low-level CIA employee responsible for hiring the Security Guard to assassinate both of you," Jim said.

He explained further: "This disgruntled employee was deeply dissatisfied with the government's handling of affairs and sought to emulate what happened in Russia, intending to embarrass our government and President. He amassed a considerable fortune through wise investments and used his resources to find a corrupt security guard who would carry out the killings and steal classified information for sale to unsavory individuals. Fortunately, we apprehended him. I wanted to inform you so you can update Bill, but more importantly, we need to intensify security measures to ensure the safety of your family until we can be certain they are out of harm's way."

John and Kate expressed their gratitude to Jim for the information and assured him they would see him in person on Tuesday. After bidding farewell, John went to the door where Bill, the guard on duty, was stationed. He shared the good news with Bill and informed him of his plan to convince Kate and Katelin to join him for a morning run, agreeing to meet Bill in the lobby in about an hour.

With some persuasion, John managed to convince Kate and Katelin to join him for a leisurely jog that morning. They met Bill in the lobby as planned, embarking on their run along the picturesque Cheat River. The breathtaking scenery combined with the pleasant company made it a truly enjoyable experience.

As they neared the end of their run, they spotted an Air Force helicopter descending along the Cheat River, gradually slowing down upon seeing John, Kate, Katelin, and Bill running on the path. It was a stunning sight, and they all halted their run to wave at the helicopter. Recognizing one of the Project Leaders who had been entrusted with overseeing the three projects while they were on vacation, they pointed in the direction of the lodge, picking up their pace to reach the lodge by the time the helicopter landed.

Many guests at the lodge had witnessed the helicopter's arrival and gathered on the porch as John, Kate, Katelin, and Bill made their way toward it. The Project Leader emerged from the helicopter and explained, "Apologies for interrupting your vacation, but we have an emergency. I discussed it with Jim, and he believed it was best for me to meet with both of you in person. He mentioned he had just spoken with you, so we knew you would be either at the lodge or out running."

John and Kate exchanged glances and simultaneously exclaimed, "Jim really knows us."

Then, turning their attention to the Project Leader named Nate Smith, they asked him to tell them what the emergency was all about.

The Project Leader wore a serious expression as he addressed John and Kate and said, "I apologize once again for disturbing your vacation, but Jim informed me that you both were the only people capable of solving this problem."

He continued, "The leader of China expressed their intention to withdraw from the ATA. They have lost trust in other parties and specifically requested to speak with both of you."

Kate inquired, "Did the Chinese leader leave a contact number and specify when we should call?"

"Valerie has made the necessary arrangements pending your approval. It might require another trip to Asia," Nate said, swiftly replying.

John interjected, "Wait for us at that conference table. There's a phone there. Set up a call with Valerie in about an hour. We'll freshen up and join you to discuss the next steps.

John, Kate, and Katelin each went to their rooms to shower and get dressed before reconvening downstairs. John and Kate proceeded to the conference table while Katelin went to the gift shop.

Nate informed them, "Everything has been set up, and Valerie will call this number in ten minutes."

Kate, Nate, and John discussed all the possible issues that could have arisen with the ATA. They realized that if Jim had instructed Nate to fly there, the situation must be very serious. They speculated that China might not be receiving all the desired benefits from the ATA, prompting someone to sabotage the agreement. They knew that without China's participation, there would be no agreement at all. At the designated time, Valerie called, and since there was no one else in the room, John put the phone on speaker.

Kate picked up the phone and activated the speaker, addressing Valerie, "Okay, we're all here, Valerie. What information do you have concerning China?"

Valerie replied, "Please hold on; I want to conference Jim and Natalie into the call."

After a moment, Valerie continued, "The reason for this call is that China wants to withdraw from the ATA. Jim, do you have any insight into why they want to leave?"

Jim joined the conversation with a serious tone: "When I spoke with the leader of China, he mentioned that they were considering leaving the ATA because Taiwan refused to engage in trade with them. China is eager to collaborate on the three projects we have been working on."

John interjected, "Jim, you need to have the U.S. President call the President of Taiwan and explain to him why it would be beneficial for them to manufacture chips for China, just as they do for us. We should also explore what China can offer Taiwan that would be more cost-effective than doing it themselves, like China does for us with clothing manufacturing. Valerie, can you set up a call with China after our President has spoken with Taiwan? Jim, once you receive the results of their conversation, I will call China. Valerie, please coordinate all the calls and try to schedule the call with China today for two or three days from now, allowing us time to address the issue and demonstrate our commitment to resolving it."

Jim spoke up at the end of the call and said, "We apologize for interrupting your vacation once again. It is evident that the people in China and Russia have placed their trust in the Colombos and recognize the positive impact we are making in the world. It fills us with pride to be Americans. I fully agree with everything John has proposed, so let's make it happen."

After the call, John invited Nate to stay with them until Monday. He explained that they could use the time to work and were planning to depart on Monday afternoon. Kate instructed everyone to prepare for an early dinner or late lunch, assigning Bill the task of arranging everything at the lodge hotel, including security measures.

With a couple of hours to relax, the group gathered for dinner at the lodge hotel diner. John and Kate arrived first and found family-style tables set up, accommodating several people with shared food in the center. They chose a table with ample available seats, hoping to reserve them for Bill and Nate. Seated at the table were a man and his daughter—clearly from West Virginia—with coal mine residue on the man's skin. The young woman appeared to be his daughter.

Approaching the table, John and Kate asked if they could join them and explained that a few others might join as well. The man and the young woman welcomed them, and he introduced the young lady with him as his sister. As they sat down, Kate recognized the man from a few years ago, when his daughter had passed away. Both the man and his sister wore sorrowful expressions. After introductions were exchanged,

John and Kate noticed that the man and his sister were nearly finished with their meal.

The man recognized John and Kate and remarked, "I see you both made it back to West Virginia and didn't wait ten years as we discussed a couple of years ago."

John and Kate explained that they were currently on vacation. Curiosity piqued, and John asked them why they were at the lodge. The man struggled to discuss the reason, and his sister chimed in, "My brother's wife, his partner for over sixty years, passed away a few days ago. We came here to attend her funeral; she wished to be buried next to her daughter."

Kate expressed sympathy, saying, "The bond between a mother and daughter is incredibly strong. My daughter is my best friend, and she sees me as both her mom and best friend."

Nodding, the man held back tears and shared, "My wife and our daughter had a close relationship. Even though they didn't live in the same house, they spoke nearly every day and went shopping together. Our daughter has respect for me as her dad, but her mother loved her more than anything from the day she was born until the day she passed away. When our daughter died, my wife made sure we purchased two grave sites next to hers, with the agreement that whoever died first would be laid to rest beside our daughter. I insisted that she be next to our daughter, regardless of the circumstances. Well, she died first, so I ensured she was buried next to our daughter. Now, the two most beautiful people in my life are gone, and I need to keep going. My sister, friends, and family help me through, as do a few hobbies. But when the sun sets in my part of town, loneliness sets in."

Both John and Kate welled up with tears, realizing how close they had come to experiencing such loss themselves with Katelin's cancer and the attempt on their family's lives.

As the man started to rise from his seat, he looked John directly in the eyes and said, "Sir, I hope you realize how fortunate you are. I can tell you have a wife that loves you, and that is something truly invaluable. Please cherish what you have because nothing surpasses it. And if you have a daughter, then you are truly blessed."

John stood up, shook the man's hand, and replied, "Thank you for sharing your story with us. You are truly a good person, and we are deeply sorry for everything you are going through."

Returning to the table, John embraced Kate, and both left with heavy hearts.

A few minutes later, Bill and Nate arrived, taking their seats at the table. They noticed John and Kate's somber expressions and the tears in their eyes. Concerned, Bill asked them, "Are you both okay? You seem quite saddened."

With teary eyes, Kate replied, "A person who was sitting here just shared a story that made us appreciate even more what we have, considering the significant losses he has suffered."

Nate chimed in solemnly, "I understand. This is why people working for both of you genuinely enjoy it. You have been through so much and possess a profound understanding of people, along with a genuine compassion for them."

John and Kate exchanged glances and held hands, deeply moved by Nate's words. John then turned to Nate and expressed gratitude, saying, "Thank you for saying that, Nate. Now, let's change the topic to China. When we speak with them, I want to convey positive news about our progress on the three projects. Could you please update us on each project's status or future plans in China?"

Nate directed his attention to John and Kate, providing an update: "We have already begun deploying climate devices all over China and have eliminated over a hundred hotspots without the need to shut down factories. There is a cyclone heading towards Taiwan, and we are considering utilizing the Storm Project to mitigate its impact. If we don't intervene, it will hit Taiwan on Wednesday. We are still in the process of deploying the Medical Computer throughout China, but we have already saved the lives of over a thousand people, including two individuals related to the President or his wife."

John responded with a smile: "That's excellent progress, and it's clear why the President of China wants to engage with us and trust us. Let's get Jim on the phone immediately."

John promptly dialed Jim's private line, knowing he would answer for them. Putting Jim on speakerphone, John addressed him: "Hi Jim, I have Kate, Nate, and Bill here with me. I believe we will be ready for the call with China, but we need our President to speak with the President of Taiwan and provide us with the results of their conversation. Make sure the President understands the importance of convincing Taiwan to open up trade with China, as it could be a good deal for them. Additionally, we need to schedule a call on Tuesday before the storm hits Taiwan, so both China and the U.S. can work together to prevent its impact. Please have Natalie arrange the call with the President of China for Tuesday morning, if possible, but it must be before Wednesday."

After dinner, John and Kate retired to their room, finding solace in each other's arms. They set a wake-up call for 7 a.m. to allow time for an early morning run before breakfast and the 10 a.m. mass.

John and Bill's Morning Run, Church Attendance, and Handling Various Matters

J ohn attempted to persuade Kate and Katelin to join him for a morning run, but they declined, leaving him to run with Bill instead. During their jog, Bill and John engaged in a conversation about the corrupt security guard and the CIA agent who had managed to save enough money to set up an attack on John, Kate, and Katelin.

After their run, John returned to his room to find Kate still in bed, assuming Katelin was still asleep in the adjoining room with the closed door. He woke Kate up and asked, "Time to get up. What do you want to do for breakfast?"

Opening her eyes, Kate responded, "Check on Katelin and see if she wants to go down for breakfast and then go to church."

John opened the connecting door and discovered a breakfast table rolling into Katelin's room. She had ordered room service.

Katelin, dressed and in bed watching TV, explained, "I was getting hungry and peeked into your room. I saw that Mom was asleep, so I didn't want to wake her. I decided to order room service, and I figured you were out running."

John smiled and turned to Kate, sharing, "You won't believe it. She ordered room service. I hope she doesn't get too spoiled with all these luxuries like helicopter rides, breakfast in bed, and round-the-clock security. Kate, do you want to go downstairs for breakfast and then head to church? I'll inform Bill about our plans, and we can meet him in an hour."

"That sounds like a good plan," Kate agreed.

She continued, "Let Bill know and ask if he wants to join us. It would be great if Katelin could come along too. She can have another cup of coffee before we head to church."

Katelin yelled loudly to ensure her mom and dad in the next room heard her: "OK, I'll join both of you for breakfast and church!"

The three of them had breakfast together, and then Bill located a nearby church a couple of miles away. They all got into two cars and drove to the church. John always prayed for God to forgive his sins, followed by requests for health, happiness, wisdom, and wealth. He also asked for God's protection from any external or internal harm and requested the same blessings for his wife and daughter. Lastly, John prayed for their deceased family and friends to be sent to heaven and reunite because he knew that they were kind and deserved to be there. Kate shared similar prayers. They always felt uplifted after attending church.

Feeling good after the service, John and Kate decided to go shopping in town before having lunch at a restaurant. Katelin insisted on tagging along with Kate since she knew her mother always ended up buying her something nice. They all had excellent taste in clothes and jewelry, and John enjoyed seeing Kate happy.

They walked down the street with two guards in front and two behind them as they looked in stores, smiling and holding hands. This was a customary practice for them, and Katelin walked beside Kate, equally happy.

After shopping for a couple of hours, they were ready for lunch and stopped at a local diner on the street. John and Kate noticed an advertisement for a banana split deal, couldn't resists buying one, and got another one for free. They convinced Katelin and Bill to get the same deal. The four security guards stood nearby and ordered sandwiches and drinks.

Once they finished lunch, everyone headed back to the lodge. John and Kate wanted to work on a project downstairs in the Hemingway area, overlooking the Cheat River. However, Kate needed to retrieve some materials from their room, so John and Bill talked for a while.

Curious about Bill's team, John asked, "How is your team doing? We've been through a lot together. Some security guards sacrificed their lives protecting my family, and one of your team members tried to betray us and steal our secrets. It's been a challenging journey for all of us."

Bill responded in a serious tone, "They are a resilient bunch and are really proud to be on this team because we are doing so much for the U.S. and the world. I believe it may be a good idea, maybe tonight, to have dinner with them and really tell them what you tell and show me all the time about how much you appreciate everything I do."

Kate arrived back at the table just as that conversation was beginning. When Bill finished speaking, she said, "I think that is a good idea. Bill, you set up the dinner. You pick the time and place, and try to find a round table so we can all talk together. Katelin will join us."

As Bill went off to get things set up for dinner, John and Kate began to discuss the next steps for the three projects.

Kate started out by saying, "It appears that the three projects are visible around the world. People have seen the value of the Medical Project and have also witnessed a storm disappear that was about to hit Cuba. I believe now would be the time to plan our around-the-world trip, visiting the countries that hate us the most and then the rest of them. If it's not possible to meet face-to-face, we should at least engage with the top people in those countries' governments."

John quickly responded with excitement: "There are conferences all over the world that top leaders plan to attend, including our President. Let's get Jim and the President to figure out the best way to help other countries utilize these three projects. They did an excellent job in getting all the world signed up to use the Medical Project."

John and Kate talked for a few more hours, delving into the

problems of the world. And yet, they were truly solving those problems. As dinner time approached, Bill hadn't gotten back to them with the plan, so both of them, along with a couple of security guards who were watching them, walked out of the lodge and headed toward the Cheat River. They walked hand in hand, thanking God that they were together, with Katelin joining them unexpectedly.

John and Kate turned around and were surprised to see Katelin behind them. "I saw you guys out here holding hands," Katelin said.

She continued, "It reminded me of the time in Tokyo when I was walking by the restaurant and looked in the window. The two of you were having dinner, so I decided to join you, and it turned out to be a memorable moment for all of us. I think this is one of those moments too. I was sitting by my window reading the book called 'Self Help and Mental Health: A Tough Path to Wellness' by Nicholas Licausi when I saw you both out here holding hands. I stopped reading this excellent book and ran out here to be with you."

The three of them stood there, holding hands and reminiscing about times gone by. Katelin excitedly mentioned the time when they were all here and they walked down the path, spotting a waterfall gently cascading down the mountain into the Cheat River. She reminisced about their failed attempt to climb up the mountain alongside the waterfall with her dad, as it became too dangerous."

Kate responded, her voice stern, "Yeah, I remember standing down by the Cheat River while you two crazy risk-takers climbed up the mountain. Please don't remind me about it. By the way, Katelin, we're going to have dinner with our security guards tonight. Bill is setting it up, and he's coming towards us right now with the time and place."

"Hi Bill, do you have everything set up for tonight?" Kate asked.

Bill quickly responded with a disappointed look: "I hope you're all okay with my choice of restaurant. It will be at a bar that has a room off to the side with a round table in it, so we'll be by ourselves, but it will be in a bar."

Kate laughed and said, "We're having dinner with a bunch of security guards and pilots. It will be fun."

Bill responded with a smile: "Okay, we're all set. We'll meet in the lobby in one hour."

Kate, Katelin, and John turned around and headed to their rooms to get ready for dinner. When they met downstairs in the lobby, it was a large group. There were four pilots, about six security guards, and John, Kate, and Katelin. They all got into two large limos and drove for about thirty minutes to the restaurant.

The restaurant was called Nick's Place. It was a delightful establishment with a bar, attracting a mix of old and young people. The servers were mostly students, a fact that John appreciated. He believed that he could be served by the next great engineer or doctor—students working their way through college, considering the proximity to a university. John and Kate had both worked their way through college: John worked in kitchens, cleaning, and painting dorms; Kate worked as a secretary at the Medical Center. John believed that his work experience, along with his good grade point average, had contributed to his success as an engineer. Both he and Kate were adept at working with people and getting the job done. They enjoyed working with individuals from all walks of life and took pleasure in recognizing those who showed promise.

John often reminisced about one university student he had brought in for the summer, along with five other students, to work on various projects. Most of them were seniors, each representing a different university. After assigning an important project, John noticed that one student seemed to complete any task within one or two days, while others took weeks. He had tried to hire him after graduation, but the student had aspirations of starting his own company. John never saw him again after the last conversation, but he was certain that the student would turn out to be the next Bill Gates or Steve Jobs.

During dinner, both John and Kate engaged in heartfelt conversations with the security guards and pilots. They acknowledged that many guards had sacrificed their lives for John, Katelin, and Kate to be here, implementing the ATA or working on projects that would benefit the world. They prayed for the safety of everyone in the room and expressed their gratitude to the individuals who put their lives on the line daily.

They reassured them, emphasizing the importance of focusing on the good people rather than dwelling on the bad. John and Kate also affirmed that they were willing to put their lives on the line for everyone present; they remembered how John saved Bill's life before. The room erupted in cheers and applause multiple times as Kate and John spoke. Some individuals even shed tears of appreciation. John and Kate had always possessed the ability to connect with others, which is why they consistently received top ratings in opinion surveys across the U.S. government and all over the world. People knew they had their backs, and they reciprocated that support for the Colombo family.

On the way back in the limo with Katelin and Bill, Bill said, "You guys are great. I've never seen the team so happy to be on a team."

With tears of joy, Katelin added, "I am so proud of you guys."

"We are so lucky to have such good friends. They know they can count on us, and we know we can count on them. We have accomplished a great deal, and we still have a few more things to do with these projects. Let's keep our focus on making everything happen as we planned," John said, his eyes also moistening.

There was a lot of discussion on the way back to the lodge, and they decided to fly back the next day since they had an important call with China scheduled for Tuesday. They planned to go for a run at 7 a.m., have breakfast, and then fly back to Washington, D.C. They informed Jim that they would fly directly to the White House around noon to discuss the next steps with China and address any other issues that needed attention. They asked Bill to make all the necessary security arrangements and coordinate with the pilots. They also informed Jim that they would arrive at the White House at noon the next day.

Everyone had a good night's sleep, although some drinking had taken place, except for the limo drivers and a few security guards. John and Kate set their alarm for 7 a.m., while Katelin requested not to be awakened until breakfast.

John, Kate, and Bill's Morning Run, Lunch with the President, and Coordinated Attack Planning

John and Kate woke up at 7 a.m. as the alarm went off. They both dressed in their running outfits, and as they were getting ready, Kate noticed that John kept on staring at her, and she said, "Okay, put your eyes back in your head. We told Bill we would meet him at around 7 a.m. for our run."

John smiled and replied, "You know I love you more every day. Whether you're in your best Air Force flying outfit or your running outfit, you still take my breath away."

"I love you too. Let's get this run over with. We have a big couple of days ahead," Kate said as she smiled back.

John and Kate went downstairs and found Bill waiting for them. Together, they embarked on their last run for the trip down the beautiful trail by the Cheat River. It was a breathtaking run, and they stopped at the three-mile mark to admire the mountains and Cheat River. They took a moment to reflect on their fortune and the stunning view.

However, their peaceful morning came to an end when they noticed Nate standing on the lodge's outside porch. They knew there was something they needed to attend to, and their relaxing morning turned into a busy one. Nate wore a worried expression as he informed them: "Jim just called and plans to have lunch with the President and some reporters when you land."

Realizing that they would be meeting with the President and the press, John and Kate knew they needed to dress more formally. They relayed the information to Nate and instructed him, Katelin, and Bill to pack and be ready to leave within an hour. Bill was tasked with notifying the pilots and the security team to prepare for departure, aiming to arrive at the White House around noon. They also instructed everyone to gather in the lobby in an hour.

Bill efficiently checked everyone out of the hotel and waited for Kate, Katelin, and John in the lobby. Once assembled, they split into two helicopters: Kate, John, Katelin, Nate, and Bill in one; the rest in the other. Moments later, the helicopters took off, leaving onlookers on the lodge porch captivated by the sight of the Air Force helicopters soaring down the Cheat River. Everyone enjoyed the beautiful view of the mountain and river.

As they approached the White House, they marveled at the grandeur of the buildings that held such significance. Several members of the press, the President, Valerie, Natalie, and the leaders of Congress and the Senate welcomed them upon their arrival. Stepping out of the helicopter, John, Kate, Nate, and Katelin knew they were about to participate in a significant meeting.

The President welcomed everyone and invited them to the main dining room. Since the press was also invited, they understood that nothing top-secret would be discussed. Therefore, Katelin was included in the lunch gathering. The President clarified, "Since we are working with other countries on the ATA, everything we discuss here is off the record. If anyone cannot comply, they do not have to join us."

As they walked toward the dining room, the President apologized to Kate and John, saying, "It seems like I am always interrupting your vacations. You are so important to the success of the United States and around the world. Jim and I debate this every time, but we always agree that we need to interrupt your vacation."

Kate responded, half-jokingly, "That's okay. We don't mind. It's nice to be wanted."

The President then said, "Why don't we all have a seat, enjoy some lunch, and take any questions? This lunch meeting was originally intended to be private—exclusively for the heads of the Congress and Senate, Jim, Kate, John, and I. However, due to the high number of inquiries, they decided to invite all of you to ensure a clear understanding of the situation. Since we are still in the negotiation process, we want all of this to remain confidential until all negotiations are concluded before writing about the ATA."

The first question came from a prominent news station, and it was rather unexpected: "When do John and/or Kate plan to run for President?"

Both John and Kate stood up, exchanging a knowing glance. John nodded to Kate, indicating that she should respond. Kate stood confidently and answered, "As leaders in the Leaders Project, we believe we can be more valuable to the U.S. and the world where we are right now. Governments engage with us because they value our accomplishments and trust us. Believe me, the President, Congress, and Senate made the right decision by establishing the Leaders Project. We can make a significant impact in our current roles, so we have no plans to pursue any other positions. We are happy where we are, and we are grateful for the support of our government."

Another reporter from a major network posed the next question: "What is happening with the ATA? Is it going to happen, or will it be dissolved?"

John and Kate stood up again, and this time, Kate gestured to John to take the lead in responding. John took the opportunity and explained, "As you've seen from the live televised speeches involving China, Taiwan, North and South Korea, and other Asian countries, we have an ATA in place. However, as we proceed with the implementation of the ATA, there are still unresolved matters that require further agreement. That's what we are currently working on."

The same reporter remarked, "That's a good answer that shouldn't upset anyone. Why can't we print that?"

Kate swiftly replied, "If anything is written about this topic, it can be misinterpreted or modified by someone else. It's best not to provide additional commentary at this time and allow the countries to work through each issue independently, without media interference. The ATA will undoubtedly materialize because all counties involved have agreed and desired its success. We should refrain from saying anything beyond what has been televised and officially stated by the countries. Everyone here is doing everything possible to ensure the ATA remains intact."

The President rose and asked, "Are there any more questions?"

After a brief pause and with no further inquiries, he declared, "Okay, let's have lunch. And let's all thank John and Kate for a job well done."

Applause and cheers erupted, and John and Kate acknowledged the love and appreciation from everyone with a nod and a smile.

Following lunch, the President, Jim, Valerie, Natalie, John, and Kate convened in the President's office. The President informed them, "I discussed trade with Taiwan, and they have reached an agreement with China. Taiwan subsequently contacted me. Therefore, when you speak with China tomorrow, it should go smoothly. Jim, when is the scheduled call with the President of China for John and Kate?"

Jim looked at Valerie, who responded, "I apologize, but due to an approaching storm heading toward Taiwan, we need to have the call at 8 p.m. today, which will be 8 a.m. on Tuesday their time."

Kate promptly interjected, "Well, team, it looks like we're in for a long day. We'll conduct the call here. Jim, Valerie, and Natalie will have to stay with John and me. We'll make the call from our office. If we need to deliver storm materials to China or utilize our Air Force, Jim, you'll need to make the necessary arrangements. I believe we left some rockets with storm material in China, but we need to ensure they are ready. We'll also consult our storm team."

The President approved the plan, and John, Kate, and Jim headed to their offices. They brewed copious amounts of coffee and prepared for the 8 p.m. call. Valerie and Natalie were able to get John and Kate connected with the President of China. John greeted the president of China: "Hello, this is John and Kate Colombo. We appreciate you taking this call so early. We believe it's essential that we have this discussion."

The President of China responded through his interpreter: "It's a pleasure to speak with both of you again. You've already done so much to maintain the stability of the ATA. I received a call from the President of Taiwan, and we have reached a trade agreement that benefits both parties. Additionally, I've received reports from my team and other individuals indicating how our Medical, Storm, and Climate projects have directly helped them, especially the Medical Project. Thank you for making all of this possible. As far as we are concerned, the ATA is working as planned."

"Kate and I are delighted to hear that. If there are any future concerns, please contact us directly as you did this time, and we will promptly address the issues," John said cheerfully.

Shifting gears, John brought up another topic: "We understand that a cyclone is heading toward Taiwan. Has your team calculated whether you have enough storm materials to stop it?"

The President of China disclosed, with his interpreter translating his Mandarin to English: "It is a larger-than-usual cyclone, and we will require 10,000 lbs. of storm materials, but we currently only have 5,000 lbs."

"With your permission, Mr. President, we can dispatch one of our fighters with the additional 5,000 lbs. of storm materials. We can coordinate the firing to ensure that all 10,000 lbs. explode at the same time. We will also have the same plane transport an extra 10,000 lbs. to replenish your supply. Also, I will obtain Taiwan's approval to fly missiles near their country," John said, proposing a plan.

With his interpreter's translations, the President of China expressed satisfaction, saying, "You and Kate think of everything. I am pleased with the plan. Let's make it happen. The head of China's Air Force will coordinate everything on our end. I will send you his contact details so that your representative can collaborate with him on the cyclone attack. This will be the first coordinated attack between China and the U.S. I like it."

"I like it too. I will ensure the number reaches the appropriate person, and we will warn Taiwan about our plan. We will schedule the attack for tomorrow, around noon, and let the pilots coordinate when they will fire their rockets," John said.

Kate met with Jim to inform him of the plan, and he promptly called the U.S. President to seek approval for the attack. Both the U.S. President and Jim gave their consent. As Kate was explaining everything to Jim, John burst into the room with the contact information of the pilot flying the plane from China. With this crucial detail, they arranged a call with the American pilot, who could communicate effectively in English. Together, they meticulously calculated the timing and coordinates for firing the rockets, ensuring they knew precisely when and where the explosions would occur. The attack was scheduled for the following day around noon, when the storm's outer ring would be within a hundred miles of Taiwan.

After thoroughly reviewing all the calculations, John and Kate headed home to rest before the momentous day ahead. They also coordinated with both pilots, confirming a time for further discussion before their departure.

Everyone's Excitement as the Cyclone Disappears

John and Kate went for a brief morning run before heading to the operations/command room at the White House. Their objective was to oversee and monitor the proceedings. Upon arrival, they found Jim, Natalie, Valerie, and an Air Force General already present. Some members of the press had been invited and were starting to arrive, along with the President, who entered shortly after Kate and John.

Kate connected with the U.S. pilot over the phone and inquired if everyone is ready for takeoff. To her surprise, it was the same person who had accompanied her on the mission in Cuba. Kate remarked, "It's great to be working together again. Are you prepared to take off?"

Turning towards the group, Kate declared, "She is the finest pilot I have ever encountered. When we needed to swiftly exit Cuban airspace after we fired our missiles, she skillfully guided us out of there."

Then Kate spoke with the pilot in China, who confirmed his readiness on the call. John then came on the line, meticulously going through the calculations with both pilots. Everything was in place.

The jet departed from California, while the jet from China took off from their homeland. The communication between the two jets was audible, just as it had been during the Cuban mission. Rockets were launched from both planes, resulting in the detonation and disappearance of the cyclone. People from the U.S., China, Taiwan, and around the world erupted in cheers upon witnessing the cyclone vanish. It was not only due to the coordinated attack but also because it seemed like a miraculous event. A cyclone that could have caused millions of dollars in damages and claimed numerous lives has been averted. John and Kate were once again hailed as heroes and respected around the world.

Amidst jubilation in both the Chinese and American command rooms, John returned to the line and announced, "We have 10,000 lbs. of storm liquid for China. Where would you want it delivered?"

A voice that sounded like the President of China's interpreter came on the line and replied, "Hello, this is a message from the President of China: we have accomplished something great today. It's a promising start for the ATA. Instruct your pilot to follow my pilot to an airport near the Palace. We will celebrate this great achievement with both the pilots and the members of my command room. Although I wish Kate, John, and your command room could join us, I'm sure your President will do the same."

Without delay, the President of the United States joined the line and expressed gratitude, saying, "Thank you, Mr. President, for your kind words and for taking care of our pilot. John and Kate, today is a momentous day for the storm project, which you both started. We will be celebrating alongside you, the members of your command room, and everyone else involved. Once the planes have landed, everyone, please join us in our dining area."

John then came on the line and added, "It seems both jets are close to landing."

The two planes touched down on adjacent runways, a sight captured by the cameras and televised. They parked side by side, with the U.S. pilot securing her plane to prevent any unauthorized access to sensitive information. The pilots shook hands and proceeded to a waiting limo that would take them to the Palace.

In the U.S. command room, everyone followed the President to the main dining area. As they took their seats, the President rose and raised his glass, proposing a toast to Kate and John. He declared, "Today marks a remarkable achievement for the United States, China, Taiwan, and the rest of the world. Everyone has done an exceptional job. Let's celebrate this great moment!"

The room erupted with applause, cheers, and a sense of pride in being American. The President also applauded and then turned to John and Kate, remarking, "What will be the next great projects we can expect from both of you?"

John and Kate exchanged a smile with the President, the leaders of the Senate, and the Congress. John responded with a low voice: "We'll be discussing that with you tomorrow, as we have some exciting plans in store."

The President and the leaders of the Congress and Senate smiled broadly, and the President leaned over to his secretary, saying, "Make room in our calendars for them if they want to see us."

Kate leaned over to Valerie and Natalie, whispering, "See if you can schedule a meeting for us tomorrow at 2 p.m."

While the President continued to address the diners with a smile, he remarked, "I'm not sure if all of you can hear the discussions taking place up here, but we were already looking forward to the next significant project. That's what makes these two individuals so exceptional—they are always looking ahead, seeking ways to improve not just the U.S. but the entire world. That's why they have earned the trust and respect of their people and leaders worldwide."

Once again, everyone in the room rose to their feet, applauding and showing their appreciation. Despite the extensive discussions taking place, no one could ascertain what the next major projects would be. Kate and John were determined to reveal their plans first to the President and the leaders of the Congress and Senate so they could obtain the necessary permissions to move forward.

John, Kate, Valerie, Natalie, and Jim returned to the conference room near their offices. They needed to strategize and prepare for the 2 p.m. meeting the following day.

Kate stood up and walked to the front of the room, announcing, "John and I had intended to wait before announcing these new projects. However, considering the President's near inquiry about our next endeavors, we believe now is the time to unveil them and bring them to fruition."

Jim promptly responded, "I agree! We must secure all the required funding and expedite the deployment of these projects because they will save lives. Valerie and Natalie, please ensure that you arrange the necessary meetings prior to the 2 p.m. meeting and identify the individuals you would like to have in attendance."

John and Kate instructed them to initiate the various meetings needed prior to the President's meeting. The meetings would commence at 9 a.m. and conclude by 1 p.m., allowing for any changes before presenting them to the President and heads of the Congress and Senate.

Everyone except Valerie and Natalie departed for their homes, as they were occupied with organizing the meetings.

During the limo ride home, John and Kate discussed their desired course for the 2 p.m. meeting. Bill was also present, so they informed him that they wanted to go for a run tomorrow at 7 a.m. for an hour before heading for work at 9 a.m.

The Thirty-Fourth Day

The Next Big Projects

J ohn and Kate woke up at 6 a.m. when the alarm went off and got ready for their run. They decided to call Katelin since it had been a couple of days since they last talked. As Kate dressed in her running outfit, she noticed John looking at her again, so she reminded him that they had a lot to do. They needed to exercise and then get to work.

John smiled and hurried to the door to inform Bill that they would be ready to run in about fifteen minutes. He asked Bill if he wanted any coffee, but Bill declined. Bill prepared the car to follow them during their run, and they set off as planned.

This time, John and Kate decided to run two miles to a diner where they could enjoy breakfast while listening to music on the jukebox. They also planned to discuss their upcoming meetings. Bill found a table near the entrance, allowing him to keep an eye on everything while enjoying his breakfast. After about an hour, they ran back home, showered, got dressed, and entered the limo to make it to their 9 a.m. meeting.

While in the limo, they decided to call Katelin. They put her on speakerphone, and Kate spoke first: "Sorry we did not have a chance to call you earlier. but I wanted to touch base with you and see if you were okay."

Katelin jokingly replied, "Yes, I know you've been busy. It's all over the press. You've been stopping cyclones, talking with presidents, and

177

taking on new projects. You guys are amazing, and I'm so proud to call you my parents. I can say I knew you both before you were famous."

John then chimed in, saying, "I remember when you were famous too, on the front cover of magazines and billboards in Tokyo during your modeling days. I guess fame runs in the family. Oh, can you meet us for lunch at noon at the little restaurant called Deanne's Place close to the White House? We'll make the reservations."

"Of course, I'll meet you for lunch. All I have to do is tell my boss who I'm having lunch with, and he'll say yes. I assume it'll be at Deanne's Place since we always go there to celebrate something," Katelin said in a playful manner.

They all shared a laugh and ended the call as they arrived at the West Wing, where they had their 9 a.m. meeting. They expressed their love for each other before hanging up.

John and Kate passed through security and got to the conference room at 9 a.m. The key people from the medical team were already seated, and a few others, whom only John and Kate knew, had also been invited to the meeting. Valerie had arranged for people in the medical industry from all over the world to join the meeting via Zoom.

John began the meeting, stating, "I believe we are ready to implement the next phase of the Medical Project. We have a couple of new members joining the development team whom I'd like to introduce: Sam, the President of Devices Company, and Judy, the President of Life Company."

He continued, "One of the crucial aspects of the Medical Project, which we were not ready to introduce until now, is the detection of illnesses in the body before they become severe or incurable. Sam's and Judy's companies will manufacture wearable devices that can detect any changes in the body, such as chemical imbalances or potential health issues. The data collected by these devices will be fed into the medical computer, which will analyze it based on the individual's medical history and notify them if there is a problem or a potential problem.

"I will give you a couple of examples. Let's say your medical history indicates that, due to your genetic makeup, you should avoid smoking pot or taking drugs, which you shouldn't be doing anyway. If the device detects drugs in your system, an alarm will sound on your device, warning you to stop because it could increase the risk of developing schizophrenia. Another example would be if you were working in your yard, where deer ticks are present, and you got bitten. The device would detect changes in your heart rate and blood composition, alerting you before the infection spreads throughout your body. This early warning would enable you to take medication to kill the infection and restore everything to normal.

"There are numerous examples, but let me share one more. Most people are unaware that there are parasites in the brain that wrap around small blood vessels. If these parasites die for some reason, it could lead to dementia because they serve a purpose in the brain. When these parasites migrate from the brain to the bloodstream, early detection in the blood could offer an opportunity to prevent the dementia from worsening or starting.

"Allow me to provide an example of how these devices can help cure various illnesses. Currently, doctors ask questions about a person's activities before the onset of schizophrenia to identify patterns and provide warnings to others. With the new devices, all relevant information will be transmitted to a computer, which can analyze the patterns that individuals followed before falling ill and warn people not to engage in those same patterns."

"These devices will be able to detect illnesses before you even notice any symptoms. They will also guide you on where to seek treatment," John said, assuring everyone in the meeting.

"Kate and I would like each of you to collaborate with Sam and Judy to integrate this into the Medical Project and make it accessible worldwide within a year. We will seek funding from the President, Congress, and Senate to support its global implementation. We have some initial estimates, but we expect your final figures within a week. Kate and I will now leave you to exchange information and arrange the necessary meetings to accomplish this. We will convene in this conference room every month for updates. Kate and I need to prepare for the next meeting, but you have this room for another thirty minutes before the next session begins," John said, concluding the first meeting of the day on time.

Kate and John exited the room, updating Jim so that he could brief the President before the 2 p.m. meeting. Afterward, John and Kate prepared for the Climate meeting scheduled to begin in thirty minutes.

People from the Climate Group began entering the conference room for the 10 a.m. meeting. Natalie managed to connect everyone via Zoom worldwide, allowing the meeting to start at 10 a.m.

Kate and John arrived exactly on time. Kate started the meeting, saying, "I know everyone has been discussing the Storm Project, but we need to advance the Climate Project to effectively control and improve our climate. Additionally, we must eliminate chemtrails and ensure clean air for breathing. We have successfully addressed factory pollution in hotspot areas through the installation of our devices, resulting in clean air in those regions."

She continued, "Allow me to introduce Sam and Judy. They are the Presidents of two companies: Devices and Life. Together, they have developed devices that will be deployed worldwide, no more than one mile apart, to detect any form of pollution. However, we need permission from every country to proceed with this initiative, which, once implemented, will enable us to detect and eliminate pollution. Data will be sent to a central computer, which will monitor and eradicate any pollution. A similar device will be placed in the sky to detect and eliminate airborne pollutants. Rest assured, this device will not interfere with air traffic, as it will be positioned above or below the usual flight paths.

"John and I would appreciate your estimates for implementing this project within the week. We will convene every month for updates, and I expect it to be completed within a year. If a serious issue arises, please reach out to John or to me immediately, rather than waiting for the monthly status meeting."

With no questions raised, the meeting adjourned. John and Kate briefed Jim for the 2 p.m. meeting.

As noon approached, Kate turned to Valerie and Natalie. "How about joining Katelin, John, and me at Deanne's Place, a diner close to the White House? We'll leave in a few minutes at 11:30 a.m.," Kate asked, inviting the two secretaries for lunch.

Both Valerie and Natalie informed Jim and accompanied John and Kate, along with security personnel, to Deanne's Place. Kate frequently included John in such outings, outnumbering him with women. Today, it would be four women to one man. John always enjoyed observing the interaction between Kate and Katelin; he could do that all day. It reminded him of Luke from Gilmore Girls, an old show that had gone off the air but still aired reruns. Kate has loved Katelin since the day she was born; she is not only her daughter but also her best friend. John found joy in watching their bond, which was likely why he appreciated the Gilmore Girls.

The two secretaries, accompanied by John and Kate, held hands while two security guards walked ahead and two trailed behind, escorting them to Deanne's Place. Katelin had arrived earlier and was seated at a large round table. Valerie had called ahead to make the arrangements. Upon John and Kate's arrival, the owner rushed up to them, expressing gratitude: "Thank you for coming. I remember when both of you were not as famous, and you visited during both sad and happy moments. Your daughter is sitting over there, and she's so nice, reminding me of my own daughter."

Kate inquired, "Where is your daughter?"

With a sorrowful expression, the owner replied, "She is in heaven now, looking down on us and undoubtedly happy that you are here with your daughter. Yes, she was beautiful, like your daughter, and very intelligent. Both of you would have adored her."

John shook the owner's hand, and Kate gave him a hug before they proceeded to the table. John remarked, "I knew there was a special reason why I love this place. The owner was kind enough to share that story with us."

Approaching Katelin, John and Kate enveloped their daughter in a warm embrace. Katelin gazed at her parents with a questioning look. In unison, John and Kate expressed, "We love our daughter."

As they settled at the table, the security guards occupied a nearby table with a clear view of the entire restaurant. Katelin provided everyone with an update on her well-being since the other individuals at the table were already aware of the events transpiring at the White House. It was refreshing to hear a different narrative.

They all perused the menu, and for some reason, Kate turned to the back portion of the inside cover and discovered a photograph of the owner's daughter. Observing the picture, she silently remarked on the young woman's remarkable beauty, thinking she could have been a model. Kate then noticed a story chronicling Deanne's short life, which ended at the age of thirty.

Kate's eyes welled up with tears as she read the account. The story mirrored Katelin's journey. Deanne attended an exceptional high school, modeled during her teenage years, pursued a college education, graduating within four years, and managed to work while in school. She eventually secured a position at a prominent company, got married, and subsequently battled cancer until her passing.

While reading the story, Kate looked at Katelin and contemplated how closely their paths aligned. Overwhelmed with emotion, she rose from her seat, walked around the table, and embraced Katelin tightly. In a soft whisper, Kate expressed their gratitude for Katelin overcoming her cancer before. John, understanding the moment, also stood and joined them in a heartfelt embrace. When the owner approached, concerned about their well-being, both Kate and John surprised him with a hug and expressed their condolences upon reading Deanne's story.

Tears filled the eyes of the entire table, but within minutes, they composed themselves and prepared to order. Kate, John, and Katelin all chose the Deanne Special, a dish comprising potatoes and eggs, which happened to be Katelin's favorite. John used to prepare it for her.

When it was time to settle the bill, John insisted on covering everyone's lunch expenses. The owner offered to take care of it, but John and Kate insisted on paying.

Since John and Kate were now famous, the owner requested a photograph of them to hang in his restaurant. Delighted with the request, they agreed. John, curious, asked the owner, "How did your daughter come to be named Deanne?"

Smiling, the owner replied, "I didn't know until my wife and I were dating that her middle name was Deanne. When our daughter was born, we were considering other names, but her mother suggested my wife's middle name, and we both thought it was an excellent idea."

After enjoying some dessert and coffee, everyone returned to work. On the way back, John and Kate approached Valerie and Natalie, requesting that they arrange another meeting with the Device and Life Presidents, as well as the leaders of the Medical Project. They wanted to ensure that a specific aspect of the Medical Project was implemented correctly, as they had doubts after the initial meeting about whether its importance was fully understood. The meeting was set up an hour after they got back from lunch.

John and Kate took a short break after lunch but noticed that several people were already seated in the conference room, eager to begin the meeting. Deciding not to keep them waiting, they entered the conference room and commenced the discussion.

Kate started out the meeting by sharing the story of Deanne, emphasizing that her death could have been prevented if the Medical Project had been operational. Not many people in the room or around the world were aware of Deanne's story, but this was one of the reasons why John and Kate were admired by many: they had a talent for storytelling that helped people understand why certain aspects of the Medical Project needed to be implemented and why data had to be gathered in specific ways.

During lunch, John and Kate discussed the need to convey this message effectively. With a serious expression, Kate addressed the group both present in the room and connected via phone, saying, "The new devices are crucial because they will immediately gather a person's medical history as soon as they fall ill. This information will help us identify patterns that can be used to educate others on what to avoid or what diseases they may be susceptible to. We want the medical computer to provide individuals with relevant information as soon as they input their medical history. Although it would be ideal for a doctor to enter the information, anyone should be able to do it as well."

Kate continued, "As soon as a person enters their medical history and puts on the devices, the computer should evaluate the data and provide them with specific recommendations or changes they need to make. Let me give you a couple of examples. Some scientists believe that all of us have cancer cells, but a robust immune system can eliminate them. I would like the devices to detect the presence of cancer cells and assess the person's immune system. If the immune system is weak, the computer should inform the individual about the necessary actions they need to take, such as taking specific medication, consuming alkaline water, or increasing exercise. It should even provide them with the exact number of miles they need to walk every day or recommend specific dietary choices and medications.

"If a person's family history indicates a predisposition to schizophrenia, and the device detects drugs in their system, they must be advised to stop smoking pot or taking drugs. Similarly, if it runs in the family but the person is not taking drugs, the medical computer should inform them not to engage in such activities."

Pausing for a moment, Kate then asked, "Does everyone understand that we want the Medical Computer to utilize both the history provided by doctors or individuals and the information gathered from the devices to provide immediate guidance to the one accessing the information?"

She added, "John and I realized as soon as we read about Deanne's story during lunch, that if we had the Medical Computer, we could have prevented her death. She was a beautiful and intelligent person, and her family wouldn't have had to endure such pain."

Interrupting Kate, John stood up and added, "Let me give you another example of why we need these devices and the Medical Computer immediately. If the devices detect an increase in heart rate and elevated body temperature among several people in the same area, we wouldn't need someone to confirm or deny the presence of a virus. The computer would recognize the pattern and issue a warning, and governments would have agreed in advance to isolate that area until a team confirms it is safe to leave. The spread of diseases like COVID or AIDS would never have reached a global scale. We possess the technology and computational power that could have saved millions of lives and trillions of dollars. Let's expedite the implementation of these initiatives. The world needs them to address the illnesses we face today and any future pandemics that may arise."

Jim noticed that John and Kate were once again engrossed in their new projects, and he didn't want them to burn out. So, he suggested that since they had everything going on for both the old and new projects, they should work from home on Thursday and Friday and return refreshed on Monday.

Both John and Kate agreed that it was a wise suggestion. They asked Valerie to schedule a series of meetings for Monday to obtain project updates, and since it was already 8 p.m., they decided to head home.

On the way home, they called Katelin and invited her to join them for dinner the next day, as they would be working from home. Katelin happily agreed, and they arranged to meet at their favorite spot in the mall—The Cheesecake Factory—at 6 p.m.

Dinner and Some Excitement

J ohn and Kate accomplished a significant amount of work on Thursday while working from home, but they were eagerly anticipating their dinner with Katelin. Spending time with their daughter was always a joy for them. They arrived at The Cheesecake Factory around 5:30 p.m., accompanied by two male security guards. The server led them to their table, and as they walked, he mentioned having seen their interviews. He appreciated their fairness and justice, understanding why their opinions held value for nations. Once seated, John and Kate exchanged glances, and John remarked, "That was genuinely kind of her to say. We should be proud that people perceive us that way."

Kate agreed, and she ordered Sangria for both of them. She reminisced, "This reminds me of the time we were in Barcelona. They would seat us at a table like this, surrounded by windows except for the space where they delivered the food. We would drink our Sangria and watch people pass by as we ate and drank. The only difference now is that there's one security guard outside and another one inside, keeping an eye on us."

John smiled, held her hand, and said, "I love you more with each passing day."

Returning the smile, Kate replied, "I love you more, John. I wonder what's keeping Katelin? She's already fifteen minutes late. I think I'll go to the ladies' room. I'll be right back."

The security guard tried to maintain his vigilance over John and Kate. As Kate entered the ladies' room, she noticed two larger women. One of them held a gun and issued a chilling threat: "You will follow us out to our car without a word, or we'll kill you. Our accomplice in the restaurant will kill John and your daughter."

Kate knew that her daughter wasn't there yet, so she knew that there was likely no one in the restaurant who could harm John, given the presence of two guards. These two women were much bigger than her, so she knew she had to find a way to overpower them. She quickly assessed the surroundings, noticing two stalls. The woman with the gun stood behind the other woman. Kate determined that she couldn't allow herself to be taken to a secondary location; otherwise, everything would be over. Thinking swiftly, she pivoted and grabbed the lid of the toilet cover, slamming it onto the woman standing between her and the one with the gun. In the chaos, a gunshot rang out, and the bullet struck the woman who had served as a barrier.

Seizing the opportunity, Kate used the heavy lid to strike the hand of the woman with the gun, causing it to discharge and fall to the floor. She then delivered a forceful blow to the woman's head, causing her to collapse. Acting swiftly, Kate rushed to the door, shouting John's name. He and the security guard came running. When John reached the ladies' room, he found both women who had attempted to assault Kate lying on the floor. The security guard promptly called the police, who transported the assailants to the hospital and then the police station for questioning.

John embraced Kate, remarking, "I guess they've learned not to mess with you."

Kate trembled slightly but held John close, and she saw Katelin entering the restaurant. Katelin noticed the police's presence inside and saw her parents hugging. Katelin playfully commented, "I can't leave you two alone for a minute without getting into trouble."

They all laughed at Katelin's infectious smile, lightening everyone's mood. The owner approached their table and announced, "If you all would like something to eat, dinner is on us, The Cheesecake Factory."

Kate responded, "This is our second favorite place to eat and drink. Let's start with some more Sangria and order dinner."

They settled at their table and discussed how the incident occurred. Kate and John realized they hadn't informed anyone of their whereabouts until they were already in the limo. Katelin mentioned informing her boss about her plans approximately an hour before leaving work, speculating whether he had any involvement. John and Kate promptly called Jim for an update, while the security guards informed their supervisor. Security was heightened, and the government dispatched personnel to the detention facility to press federal charges and initiate an investigation.

John, Kate, and Katelin enjoyed a pleasant dinner, persuading Katelin to stay with them until they could uncover the reasons behind the incident. Throughout dinner and the ride back home, Katelin continually praised her parents' strength. Kate and John decided to visit the location where the two women were being held for questioning the following morning, hoping to provide assistance during the interrogation.

Since it was already past midnight, security deemed it best to inform everyone that they should meet at the police station around 10 a.m. on Friday for the questioning. Everyone agreed, and the necessary arrangements were made. The two women were placed under special surveillance to ensure their safety at the hospital and police station.

The Thirty-Sixth Day

Kate's Fight for Survival or Certain Death

J im called them first thing in the morning at their home and stated that he intended to set an example for anyone attempting to harm government officials. He wanted people to think twice before engaging in such acts. Since it was early, John, Kate, and Katelin decided to go for a run up toward the diner and have breakfast, and then run back home to prepare for their visit to the location where the two women were being held for questioning.

As John opened the door, he noticed Bill and some of the security guards outside. He informed Bill that the three of them were heading to the diner and then to the questioning session with the two ladies who assaulted Kate. Bill and two security guards followed Kate, Katelin, and John to the diner, where they all had breakfast. Afterward, the Colombos returned home, followed by the security guards in a car. Within an hour, they were ready to proceed to the police station.

Upon arrival, they discovered that the two ladies already had a lawyer. Kate wished to speak with them since she was the intended target of their attack. Before entering the room, she asked Katelin for her boss's name, knowing he was the one aware of their whereabouts. Katelin named her boss, Josh Kaplan, and she remembered asking his permission to meet her parents for lunch and informing him of their meeting location.

The police granted Kate permission to enter the room with the two ladies and their attorney on the condition that she bring the District Attorney (DA) with her to negotiate a deal. The DA, resembling Bridget Moynahan in *"Blue Bloods,"* was named Jane Meadows. Kate and the DA had a discussion beforehand to strategize and align their goals.

Upon entering the room, Kate inquired, "I would like to know who hired you to kidnap and assault me. Right now, you are facing many years in jail. We can reduce that sentence if you provide me with a name." Kate thought she would take a chance and gauge their reaction by mentioning Josh Kaplan. She continued, "If you want to take the full penalty for this and let Josh Kaplan off the hook, that is okay with us. However, If you testify and tell us who paid you, he will serve twenty years, while you will only serve two years. Otherwise, you will both face a twenty-year sentence."

After consulting with their attorney, one of the two ladies responded, "We will tell you who paid us if you let us off with no jail time."

In response, the DA proposed a counteroffer, stating, "If you answer all our questions honestly, help us put the person who paid you behind bars with your testimony, and cooperate fully, we will reduce your sentence to one year. However, this offer is time-sensitive and will be off the table if you don't accept it immediately."

The attorney and the two ladies discussed the offer and agreed to the deal. One of the ladies, who was in a wheel chair due to a gunshot wound in her back, also had a big bandage around her head from Kate's earlier attack. The other lady had her hand in a sling and a big bandage on her head from the confrontation as well.

Although Kate had emerged victorious in the restroom, she remained deeply upset, imagining what could have happened if Katelin had entered instead of her. With a stern look, Kate demanded, "I want to know who paid you, how much you were paid, what you were supposed to do, and why you decided to do what you did."

The woman who had held the gun spoke up first, saying, "If we had known it would be this difficult, we would have asked him to double the payment. It was Josh Kaplan who paid us. He gave each of us $1 million and an additional million dollars for each of the two men waiting in the men's room, in case John went in first. The plan was to capture any one of the three of you and force the other two to hand over the plans for the three projects. No one was supposed to get hurt. Josh wanted the plans and secrets for the projects. We don't know where Josh is going to get the rest of the money. He gave us $10,000 each and promised the remainder upon receiving the plans. We decided to do it solely for the money."

Kate then inquired, "Who were those two men who were supposed to target John? Where can we find them?"

"We don't know who they are or where you can find them. Ask Josh when you see him," the other lady said.

The DA reminded them, "Everything discussed in this room must stay confidential. If any information is leaked, the deal will be off, and you will face a twenty-year sentence in prison."

Exiting the room, Kate and the DA joined Bill, John, and Katelin in a separate room where they had been listening to the questioning. John, Bill, and Katelin couldn't help but laugh when they entered the room. John apologized, saying, "I'm sorry for the laugher, but seeing those ladies with all those bandages and Kate looking fantastic, we couldn't hold back."

Then, addressing the DA, John asked, "How will we find the two men and discover the source of Josh's money?"

The DA turned to Bill and the Colombos, saying, "We will tap Josh's phones and his call history. We'll also have him followed by our men. He may be aware that we are onto him, so the three of you will need to stay in a secure location until we catch the two men. However, we'll keep Josh in the dark for now while monitoring his actions. Bill, do you have a place where the three of them can stay?"

Bill glanced at Katelin and replied, "Can you send a text message to Josh saying you had an emergency and will need to take the remainder of the day off? We want to keep him worried until we gather more information. The safest place for all of you this weekend will be Kate and John's home. On Monday, you can either work from home or join us in the West Wing."

The DA agreed, saying, "That's a good plan. By Monday, we will have gathered all the necessary information about Josh Kaplan, and we will charge him with multiple crimes. For now, we will let him hang himself while we investigate further."

Katelin's voice trembled, and a tear welled up in her eye. "I can't believe Josh would do something like this," she said, her voice filled with disbelief.

Shaking her head, the DA chimed in, "People will do crazy things for money. Josh made the wrong decision, and he will pay for it along with anyone involved. Right now, we'll leave him out there so he can hang himself and anyone he is working with. I want to see just how far this conspiracy goes. Furthermore, these two women and their attorney understand that any contact with outsiders will nullify the deal. So, we'll keep Josh in the dark for now."

During the limo ride home, John observed Katelin engaged in conversation with her mother. Their bond was strong, and it was evident that Katelin looked up to her mom and the DA as powerful women. With her beauty, intelligence, and practicality, Katelin seemed poised to follow in their footsteps. John recognized that Katelin had gleaned invaluable lessons from this experience.

Upon arriving home, Jim reached out with a phone call. He reassured them that their security had been significantly bolstered and encouraged them to find some relaxation over the weekend. He scheduled a meeting for Monday to discuss the progress of the three projects, with Valerie and Natalie taking charge of organizing the day's agenda. The meetings were set to commence at 10 a.m. sharp.

DA and Kate Uncover More Facts

J ohn decided he would go for a run. Kate and Katelin had already informed him that they had enough exercise over the past few days and would skip the Saturday run, so he shouldn't wake them up.

John informed Bill that he would be running alone, with two cars and guards following him. The remaining four guards stayed at the house with Kate and Katelin. When John returned, he found Kate and Katelin on the phone with the DA. Katelin had received a text message from Josh asking about the emergency.

The DA and Kate believed it was best to keep Josh in the dark, so they instructed Katelin to respond with a message saying, "Nothing too serious. I should be in on Monday."

The DA and Kate started to appreciate each other's thinking and wanted to strategize the next steps. The DA already had several phone and text messages that could potentially put Josh in jail for a long time, but they wanted to gather more information to see if there were higher-level individuals providing Josh with money.

Kate, the DA, and Katelin agreed to meet for lunch at the Columbos' house. Although it was intended to be an all-girls lunch, John and Bill, having just returned from their run, were invited on the condition that John would take care of the preparations. John agreed and went to Costco to purchase rolled-up sandwiches, shrimp, desserts, and ingredients for

Sangria, which he prepared in mason jars with a lot of fruit.

When the DA arrived, she was surprised to see John serving but went along with it and sat down at a clear glass table near the kitchen. The three ladies began conversing while John observed from a distance. Kate noticed his eagerness to join the conversation and told him, "John, you don't have to stand at a distance waiting to serve us. We'll be fine for a while. We have all the food and drink we need. Why don't you join us? There's an extra seat here at the table."

With a smile on his face, John quickly moved to the table. Kate could tell he wanted to be a part of the conversation. Just as John was about to speak, Katelin preempted him and said, "I know, Daddy. 'Everything we discuss at this table stays at this table. We shouldn't tell anyone else.'"

Everyone smiled, and then the DA spoke up: "Josh was in communication with the two ladies and two other men, whom the police are currently apprehending. He used to work in the DA's office and has a law degree. We discovered that he was involved in drug use, so we had to let him go when we found some missing drugs. Although we couldn't prove he took them, we didn't pursue the case because it would require retrials for about thirty cases he was involved in. We weren't sure if he had tampered with evidence or planted any. It doesn't seem like he was working with anyone else besides these four individuals. He used his own money to pay them $10,000 each initially and promised to pay the rest when he sold the stolen secrets on the open market. Before we arrest and charge him, I wanted to get your input. The charges would likely result in 20–30 years of prison time, meaning he would probably die in prison. If you all agree, we'll proceed with his arrest and charges."

Everyone agreed, and the DA gave the order to apprehend Josh. Approximately 10 minutes later, the DA received a call on her mobile phone. Suspecting it was about Josh, she put it on speakerphone so that everyone could hear the news simultaneously. Just as the detectives were about to arrest him, Josh took out a gun and shot himself. They felt a twinge of sadness upon hearing the news but knew justice had been served.

The DA announced, "Since we made a deal with the ladies and they provided us with all the information they knew, we'll honor the one-year prison term, but we will put them on probation for an extended period to keep an eye on them. We'll impose the maximum sentence on the two men and extend their probation once they're released as well."

As the DA was leaving, she remarked, "I can see why everyone holds you in high regard. It was an honor to work with you on this case. I'll coordinate with your office to ensure the appropriate publicity, so no one would dare attempt something like this again."

John, Kate, and Katelin all smiled and shook the DA's hand. As Kate held her hand, she pulled her closer and said, "Would you mind if I called your office sometime this week? We have a significant position in our office that we've been trying to fill, and you may be the perfect person for it."

"Sure, it would be an honor. I look forward to your call," the DA said, smiling back at Kate.

As soon as the DA left, Katelin retreated to her room to contemplate her work situation. Meanwhile, John and Kate put Jim on speakerphone to update him on the whole situation and seek his permission to create a new position within the Leadership Project, aimed at preventing further attempts to steal their secrets.

They informed Jim that they would arrive early at the West Wing to discuss the new position and potential candidates. They acknowledged that this was not a new problem they had to solve. Many companies faced similar challenges in safeguarding important information and patents, although they weren't subject to assassination attempts or kidnappings targeting their presidents. Companies typically had security measures in place, yet attempts on a president's life were relatively rare.

They also recognized the risk of embarrassing the President or the government, but they believed it was a problem that could be addressed. They agreed to convene at the West Wing at 9 a.m. on Monday to discuss the new position, as they had other meetings scheduled to begin at 10 a.m.

The Thirty-Eighth Day

Exercise, Church Service, and the DA's New Role

J ohn woke up at 6 a.m. and asked Katelin and Kate if they wanted to join him for a run, but they declined, citing yesterday's unpleasantness. John felt the need to put in some extra effort, so he decided to extend his routine to about 2.5 hours, incorporating sauna, hot yoga, and swimming. He didn't return home until 9 a.m. When he arrived home, Kate scolded him, expressing how she had missed him all morning. They agreed to attend the 10 a.m. Mass together.

The church service was exceptional, offering them a sense of relaxation through prayer and song. They sought forgiveness for their sins and prayed for good health, happiness, wisdom, and wealth, while also asking for protection from any internal or external harm. Thus far, they believed that God had been answering their prayers.

After Mass, Kate and John invited the DA to their house for Sangria and lunch. She arrived around 11 a.m., and they all sat down to discuss the potential role she could have if she joined John and Kate's team.

Kate began by explaining, "We envision your role to involve describing what has been accomplished and what lies ahead. Your first task will be to prosecute the two ladies in a high-profile federal trial, making it clear that attacking a government official will not be tolerated."

She continued, "We also want you to communicate that the Medical, Storm, and Climate projects will be shared with our partners and friends around the world. These projects cannot be stolen or taken away; rather, they will be used globally to create a better world."

With a stern expression, John interjected, "Your responsibility will be to prosecute those who break the law and assist governments in prosecuting those who engage in unlawful activities related to these three projects. You will also be responsible for promoting worldwide awareness of the benefits of these projects and how other nations can partner with us to advance them."

"I like it! I accept the job," the DA said and smiled.

Kate added, "Since it's a new position, we don't have a salary, but it will be twice what you were previously earning, considering that you'll be taking on two roles."

The DA smiled back and shook their hands in agreement. Kate then suggested, "Why don't you come to the West Wing on Monday after lunch, so we can make this official?"

New Careers for Katelin and the DA and the Three Projects

The President of Katelin's company called her at home at 8 a.m. and requested her presence in his office at 10 a.m. He apologized for Josh and offered Katelin a promotion and salary increase to take over his position. She accepted the offer over the phone and informed her parents. A limo with security was waiting to take her to work.

Kate and John decided to run to the diner for breakfast to discuss their plans for the day. Afterward, they ran back home, prepared for work, and were driven to the West Wing in a limo. They spotted Jim in his office, and Kate said, "Jim, if you have a few minutes, we need to brief you on some upcoming changes."

Jim gestured for them to enter and instructed his secretary to hold all calls and ask Natalie to join them.

Kate explained, "We are going to hire the DA, who has been assisting us in prosecuting the two ladies and helping us locate the person funding them. I believe we told you about the whole situation over the phone. We need someone with a legal background who can support us and the federal prosecutors in ensuring these individuals and others are imprisoned. Also, she is intelligent and can help us construct a narrative that discourages attempts on our lives or theft of the three projects' secrets. With her onboard, John and I can focus more on completing the projects and initiating new ones."

"If she can accomplish all that, then hire her immediately," Jim said, smiling.

John enthusiastically added, "Great! We asked her to come in around lunchtime. Valerie will assist her with the onboarding process, and she can start today or tomorrow. You'll recognize her when she arrives; she is tall and bears a resemblance to Bridget Moynahan. Her name is Jane Meadows. We'll bring her up to speed in our conference room, so stop by if you get a chance."

Jim smiled in agreement and said, "It's good to have you both safe and back in the West Wing. I look forward to meeting our new team member."

Soon, it was time for their first meeting. Valerie had gathered all the leaders of the Medical Project in the conference room, with others participating remotely. John and Kate entered the room and commenced the meeting by requesting updates from the various countries and the U.S. leader. The smaller countries were not connected to the call, but their representatives provided status reports.

John and Kate paid particular attention to response times, as the data volume was substantial. However, Jeff, the leader of the database team, had done an excellent job designing a system that efficiently managed the data. They were also interested in ongoing studies to identify patterns leading to illnesses.

Andrei from Russia shared that they had gathered sufficient information on certain mental illnesses, enabling them to advise people on measures to reduce the occurrence of schizophrenia. He credited the medical computer and the collaborative efforts of their global partners for their progress.

John informed everyone on the call about the attempt on Kate's life and emphasized the need for constant vigilance. He also introduced Jane Meadows, the new hire, and suggested that each country consider appointing a similar liaison in their respective regions. The participants either volunteered themselves or nominated someone temporarily. This meant that Jane, the DA, already had a network of contacts worldwide.

The Climate Group was already assembling outside the conference room, prompting John and Kate to conclude the meeting so Valerie could commence networking with individuals worldwide. Some larger countries remained on the line, as they had a similar structure to the U.S., where a single person oversaw all three projects while individual group leaders were also present.

Kate initiated the meeting by introducing the new addition from the DA's office and explaining the reason for her inclusion and the responsibilities she would assume. She suggested that the attendees consider incorporating a similar role in their respective countries. Kate also collected the contact information of her counterparts, even if they were temporary placeholders until suitable individuals were identified.

She then urged everyone to begin tracking their progress to evaluate the effectiveness of the new devices. Kate emphasized that the goal was not to completely eliminate CO_2, or carbon dioxide, as plants rely on it for survival and convert it to oxygen, much like the devices deployed in hotspot areas worldwide.

Russia provided a brief update on the deployment of devices in Ukraine and how they were aiding in air purification. The leader in the U.S. seemed to be ahead of everyone else in the climate-related efforts due to their early initiation of the projects.

After a few more updates, the participants of the Storm meeting gathered outside the door, indicating the end of the session. They agreed to reconvene in one month, following the same schedule as the Medical Project meeting.

The Storm team entered the room with a sense of satisfaction, as their achievements were highly visible worldwide and they had received numerous commendations. John began the meeting by celebrating their successes and expressing gratitude to the team. He then informed them that the U.S. Storm Team was exploring alternative methods of storm prevention, as launching jets and firing rockets into storms proved to be costly. He mentioned that they had been waiting until the last moment to intervene, just before the storm reached land.

John explained that the team had conducted storm modeling and proposed another approach: using a ship filled with the storm solution to penetrate the center of the storm and disperse it using fire hoses. If that method failed, they would resort to launching rockets. Currently, they have deployed ships carrying the solution to areas where storms typically form to test their theory. They have their eye on one storm right now off the coast of Africa, heading west. If the storm developed into a hurricane, they planned to test their new approach.

As the Storm meeting drew to a close, John and Kate noticed Jane Meadows, the newly appointed member, entering the room. They motioned for her to join the meeting and introduced her to everyone, requesting their contact information as they had done in previous gatherings. Each person provided the name of their designated interface.

The Storm meeting concluded after acquiring all the necessary interface names for Jane. Kate handed Jane a list of names from the other meeting and said, "These individuals indirectly report to you from around the world. We will refer to your department as the Strategy Department, and you will oversee the tasks we previously discussed as well as those written on this paper. Valerie will guide you, introduce you to everyone, and assist with the necessary procedures. Let her or us know if you need anything. Once your processing is complete, we can reconvene in this conference room later today."

After Jane, the DA, now the head of the newly established Strategy Department, finished her processing and Valerie informed Kate and John, they proceeded to the conference room. Kate arrived first and noticed Jane's badge, remarking, "I see you have your badge and have completed processing. How did everything go? What would you like to focus on first?"

As John entered the room, Jane responded, "Yes, I am now an official member of the team. My initial focus will be on the federal prosecution of the two men and two women involved. I want it to receive significant visibility to deter others from taking similar actions.

I will also highlight what happened to Josh, Katelin's boss. I knew him before he got involved with drugs, and it's disheartening to witness the impact they had on him."

Jane continued, "I will contact all the people indirectly reporting to me around the world, ensuring they understand and communicate the consequences of targeting government officials. Please include me in future status meetings so I can stay informed about the three projects. Valerie provided me with a briefing on the recent meeting."

Noting that Jane had a computer and an office, John remarked, "I will send you a set of files to get you up to speed on the projects. Given your Top-Secret clearance, please handle them with care. I see your office is in close proximity to ours."

He then turned to Valerie and commented, "Great work, Valerie. Please ensure that Jane is invited to all our meetings."

John returned his gaze back to Jane and continued, "Jane, I understand you will be occupied with prosecuting the four individuals. Just attend the ones you can, and we will inform you of any essential ones."

Turning back to Valerie once again, John instructed, "Valerie, let's meet with Jane once a week to discuss her progress, and she must attend the weekly status meetings for the three projects."

Valerie nods in agreement, and John follows up with a question for her: "Valerie, did you arrange a dinner with Katelin at Deanne's Place?"

He then turned to Jane and invited her. "Jane, if you're available, it would be great to have dinner with two individuals who have assumed new roles. Valerie, please join us as well."

Jane expressed her willingness to join, and Valerie confirmed that the dinner would take place in an hour. Kate smiled and said, "Great!"

Approximately thirty minutes later, Kate and John boarded the limo and headed to Deanne's Place. Valerie and Jane followed in their respective cars. When they all arrived, they discovered Katelin seated at a round table that Valerie had reserved, perplexed by the extra chairs. Upon spotting Valerie and Jane, she lit up with joy.

When Kate caught Katelin's attention, she asked, "So, tell us about your new job. Was there much discussion about Josh's suicide?"

"I met with the President of my company this morning, and he and everyone else apologized for Josh's actions. They also offered me Josh's position as a promotion with a salary increase. I'm enjoying the job, and I have a great team supporting me. So, I'm a happy person," Katelin said with excitement.

Jane, Valerie, and Kate all smiled, but John interjected with a serious tone, "A promotion and an increased salary mean you'll have to work harder. Be prepared to put in extra hours."

"Why did I know you were going to say that, Dad? I love you!" Katelin said with a smile.

John smiled warmly and replied, "We all love you too! I know you well, and I'm confident you'll immerse yourself in your new role. I believe you'll excel, but while dedicating yourself to work, remember to prioritize your health. I've seen many talented individuals become so consumed by work that they neglect their well-being. Your mom and I still want to meet with you at least once a week to keep an eye on you."

Expressing her affection to her parents, Katelin responded, "That's why I love you guys. You understand me better than I understand myself, and I will always listen to you."

Katelin then turned to Jane and said, "So, Jane, how was your first day at work? I noticed you now have a West Wing badge. Are you going to keep my mom and dad safe?"

Jane quickly removed her badge from her blouse and said, "Thank you for letting me know I still had my badge on. We have devised a plan to deter anyone attempting to harm a government employee. They will face severe consequences. Also, there's no reason for anyone to steal anything from the three projects since they will soon be available for everyone's use. I will do my best to ensure their safety."

Katelin smiled appreciatively and suggested, "Thank you. I'm thrilled you joined the team. Shall we order? I need to get back to work early. I don't want to set a bad example on my first day in the new job."

Everyone enjoyed a delightful lunch and returned to their work. Jane scheduled a meeting with Kate and John for 9 a.m. the next morning to discuss necessary changes and share her findings about her global team.

Jane's Brilliant Ideas and John's Urgent Trip to Ukraine

K ate and John arrived at work promptly at 9 a.m. and proceeded to the conference room, where Jane awaited them, accompanied by Valerie. Jane had prepared some charts and wore a serious expression on her face as she began, "I apologize for delivering this news during my first week of work, but it cannot be postponed. During my conversation with Andrei in Russia, we discussed my position and the counterpart for Russia. He informed me that he would be taking on the role, but he also mentioned encountering significant difficulties with the deployment of Climate devices due to Ukraine's refusal to allow us access."

She continued, "Our Russian soldiers are handling the deployment, but if neither of you personally oversees it, they will be left in a polluted atmosphere. I attempted to engage with the Ukrainian President, but he directed me to his appointed representative for the Climate Project. It appears we need to find a replacement for him since he lost friends in the war with Russia and refuses to collaborate with them."

Jane emphasized, "One of you needs to go to Ukraine, accompanied by Andrei and the Ukrainian President. Together, you must convey that the war is over and that Russia aims to assist in repairing the atmosphere to prevent further loss of life."

Following their usual procedure for dangerous missions, John took out a coin and flipped it, asking Kate to call it. Kate lost the toss, so John smiled and stated, "I will be going to the Ukraine tomorrow. Valerie, I want you and Jane to arrange all the meetings and speeches so that when we finish, the Russians and Ukrainians will be deploying the Climate devices together. Either the Ukrainian Climate Representative will work with us or we'll have a replacement coordinate the deployment. Kate, you and Valerie will need the project leaders to bring her up to speed on all three projects while I'm traveling to Ukraine. I may have to utilize the Air Force to get there since commercial airlines might not be flying into Ukraine. Valerie, you'll need to coordinate with Natalie and Jim to make the necessary arrangements."

After the meeting, Kate and John called Katelin to inform her about the upcoming mission and the following day's plans. Katelin agreed to stay with her mother while her dad was away. Jane then entered the Columbos' office as Kate briefed him on the projects. She appeared somewhat downcast and expressed, "Once people in the countries get to know me, I'll be able to handle these issues myself. Right now, they trust both of you, believing that only you can solve their problems."

Kate responded with a smile: "John and I discussed this after the meeting, and we prefer our team members solve these types of problems without always involving us. Otherwise, we won't be able to address future challenges. Therefore, we decided that you should accompany John on this trip so you can meet the President of Ukraine and Andrei, who is the right-hand man to the President of Russia. We apologize for the short notice, but we believe it's the best course of action for you and us. You know the schedule since you helped set it up. Just inform everyone that you'll be joining this trip."

Jane smiled and said, "This is why you are exceptional leaders. I already see that I made the right decision to work for both of you. The limo picking up John in the morning will swing by my place first to pick me up. We'll fly to Kyiv in the morning, make the necessary speeches with the Ukrainian President and Andrei, commence the deployment of Climate devices with Ukrainian and Russian Climate

Leaders, as well as the Ukrainian and Russian troops, and then fly back that night since Kyiv is still somewhat dangerous. Kate, we'll be back in Washington, D.C., tomorrow morning."

That night, Kate and John made love and discussed the idea of moving to a gated community closer to the West Wing that had a gym.

John entrusted Katelin and Kate with the task of choosing the place and showing him their decision upon his return. Kate informed John that Katelin had been scouting locations and showed him a few options that they could review together later. Aware of the demanding day that awaited them, Kate and John retired to bed early.

Jane and John's Trip to Ukraine

I
t was a ten-hour flight to Kyiv, Ukraine, and they arrived in the morning as planned. The Ukrainian President and the Ukrainian Climate Leader met them at the airport while they were both waiting in the limo. He shook their hands and introduced them to Jane.

The limo drove down the runway towards another plane, a Russian aircraft. Andrei stepped out of the plane with his Climate Leader and approached the limo. John exited the vehicle, shook Andrei's hand and the hand of the Russian Climate Leader, and introduced everyone in the limo to Andrei and his counterpart.

Their destination was the Television Station in Kyiv, where they would deliver speeches on the deployment of the Climate devices. Before leaving their respective countries, Jane had arranged for an exchange of speeches to avoid any surprises. John could see that everyone appreciated Jane's efforts, and she was already gaining the trust of the leaders because she was so smart. Additionally, she possessed both beauty and height, catching everyone's attention.

Upon their arrival at the Television Station in Kyiv, the President of Ukraine took the stage first, emphasizing the significance of deploying the Climate devices. His Climate leader explained how the devices would help cleanse the air. Then, John addressed the audience, explaining how the Russian President had collaborated with the U.S. to repair the damage caused. Jane followed, emphasizing the importance of Russian and Ukrainian soldiers working together to ensure a swift deployment, thus guaranteeing breathable air. Finally, Andrei explained the deployment process and encouraged the people to assist the soldiers on both sides, speeding up the work.

As the speeches concluded, the sound of cheering echoed throughout Ukraine. Chants of "John and Kate" could even be heard, as everyone recognized the two as the inventors of the Climate devices and the reasons behind the cessation of war. This victory belonged to everyone on stage, as their intended message had been understood and accepted.

The President of Ukraine invited everyone to a lunch that turned out to be a delightful event. Eager to reach Washington, D.C., in the morning to meet Kate and Katelin, John wished to depart early. The President of Ukraine graciously gave everyone a thoughtful gift, and John asked for two, one for his daughter and one for his wife, but the President smiled and offered him three.

After enjoying lunch, John and Jane bid their farewells and headed to the airport. On the way, John expressed his gratitude to Jane for her hard work and dedication, acknowledging the success they had achieved. He remarked, "I suppose we'll keep the Ukrainian Climate leader around for a while, considering his contribution to our success."

Jane responded once again, expressing her genuine honor in working with John and Kate. She now anticipated recognition wherever she went, knowing that accepting this job with them had indeed transformed her entire life. Glancing at her phone, Jane noticed countless messages from friends expressing how moved they were by the event.

Both John and Jane attempted to rest on the flight back, but the excitement of the day made it difficult. The Air Force plane was abuzz with conversations, turning the journey into a long day and night.

The Forty-Second Day

John's Unforgettable Haircut and Shave, and The Discovery of a New Home

O n the way home, Kate looked at John and said, "You look terrible. We found this great new place, but you need a haircut and a shave."

Kate asked the limo driver to stop at an old barber shop on the way to the place she wanted to show John. The barber shop had a spinning barber pole outside and some vintage barber chairs. When they entered, Katelin told the barber, "My dad needs a haircut and a shave."

John would never forget that haircut and shave. After a long and tiring trip, being with the two most important people in his life, who knew exactly how to make him happy, was a priceless moment. At that instant, he knew that if these two ladies went to heaven, it would undoubtedly become an even better place, if that is possible, because they were so giving. The two ladies just sat there watching John relax, which gave them joy.

He could tell that Kate and Katelin enjoyed his haircut and shave as much as he did. They sat there, pointing and smiling, watching him relax after the exhausting trip. When it was all done, they expressed their satisfaction, thanked the barber, and gave him a generous tip. It was a memory John would never forget. John cherished countless wonderful memories with them, as they would do anything to bring him joy. Making him happy brought them immense delight. They always had his back, and he had theirs.

Their next stop was to check out a new house in a gated community. Security personnel, who had been following the limo, were pleased to see the additional security provided by the community. Kate and Katelin knew John enjoyed the sauna and working out, and the development boasted a fantastic gym.

John knew Kate wanted a new house that she could decorate. Kate had a talent for making things beautiful, so they decided to buy it. Everyone was thrilled, but they now had to focus on the three world-changing projects and move into their new home simultaneously.

They exchanged smiles, knowing they would make everything happen. But for now, they planned to have a good dinner at Deanne's Place and get some rest, ready to resume work the next day.

When they arrived at Deanne's Place, the owner warmly greeted them and led them to a secluded table for three in the corner. John sat across from Kate and Katelin, gazing at them and saying, "I'm the luckiest guy in the world. Sitting across from two of the kindest and most beautiful people fills my heart with gratitude. Thank you for making today yet another fantastic day for me. You both always take care of me and have my back. You knew I would be tired after today's trip, so you arranged for a shave and haircut. It made me feel like a new person,"

John continued, recalling a past memory: "I still remember when we were in Hong Kong, and you both noticed my bad haircut. You immediately stopped your shopping and dragged me back to the barber shop because they had given me a Chinese cut with pointed sideburns. You two always looked out for me."

As they settled at the table, John, Kate, and Katelin ordered their drinks and asked the waiter to return in a few minutes to take their food order. John turned to Kate, a smile playing on his lips, and shared some exciting news: "Jane is going to give you a big compliment tomorrow.

On the way home, she expressed her genuine appreciation for you offering her the job. She truly loves working for us."

Kate's chair faced the door, and she noticed someone entering. Waving towards them, she said to John, "I think she's coming to tell me right now. Jane, Valerie, and Natalie just arrived, and they're heading towards our table."

John quickly turned around, waving as the approaching group drew near. Katelin faced them and suggested, "We haven't ordered yet, so why don't you join us for dinner?"

Kate smiled and pointed to a table behind them, saying, "We can all move to that table."

The owner accommodated the group and relocated them to the new table. Jane expressed her gratitude, acknowledging the efforts of Kate and Katelin: "I wanted to treat these ladies to lunch because they played significant roles in the success of our meetings. Kate, I thanked John for offering me the job, and now I want to thank you. I've been receiving calls from everyone I know, expressing their happiness for me and thanking me for what we're doing."

John's smile widened as he responded, "Tonight's dinner is on the government. I'll cover Katelin's expenses, and everyone else is taken care of."

Kate then shifted the conversation, her tone becoming more serious: "Jane, we understand that you're enjoying your new job, but now I'm curious to know how Katelin feels about her new role. What did the president of your company discuss, and what will your new job entail?"

Katelin's face lit up with a big smile as she enthusiastically shared her experience. "It exceeds my expectations. It felt like a double promotion. The president expressed his dissatisfaction with Josh for several reasons, and since his superior failed to address the issue, he was also unhappy with her. Instead of demoting her, he decided to place her in a position that better aligned with her skills and offered me her job. I'll be reporting directly to the president, and based on my new responsibilities, I anticipate being quite busy."

Kate's voice took on a stern, motherly tone as she expressed her concerns: "We are incredibly proud of you. But, as your dad mentioned, your health is the most important thing. We've seen this happen—taking on bigger roles and more demanding jobs without prioritizing your well-being. That's why you opted for the job reporting to Josh, as it was less demanding. However, now that the company recognizes your value, they keep assigning you larger responsibilities, and it's crucial for you to take care of your health."

Katelin promptly reassured them: "When Daddy expressed his concern, I scheduled monthly meetings with my primary care physician, regardless of whether I needed them or not. We'll discuss any health issues. The first meeting is this week, and I'll undergo a complete physical examination."

John smiled warmly and replied, "That's why we love you more each day. You listen to us and follow through on our discussions, and I truly appreciate that."

With their orders placed, they enjoyed a lengthy dinner meeting. Even though it was past midnight when they finally arrived home, they made a decision to be at work by 9 a.m., considering their packed schedule. Valerie informed them that their first meeting was scheduled for 9 a.m., with subsequent meetings every hour until 5 p.m. Since the Columbos only had one limo and it was running late, Katelin decided to spend the night at her parents' house and arranged for her security and limo to pick her up at 8 a.m. from there.

Deliberating Next Steps with Everyone

J ohn woke up at 6 a.m. and invited Kate and Katelin to go for a run with him, but they declined. He informed Bill that he would be running alone. After completing his run, John prepared for work at 8 a.m. with Kate.

Arriving at the West Wing slightly before their 9 a.m. meeting, John and Kate found themselves alone in the conference room. Jane entered exactly at 9 a.m. and announced, "I am your first meeting for the day. I wanted to update you on the prosecutions of the individuals involved: the two women who attempted to kill Kate and the two men who posed a threat to John if he had used the rest room. I have invited Valerie and Natalie to join our meetings, with Natalie providing briefings to Jim and Valerie taking the minutes of the meetings, as well as scheduling follow-up meetings."

Valerie and Natalie entered and took their seats as Jane continued: "Regarding the two women, we had promised them a one-year prison sentence. However, they will now serve that year in the toughest prison available, followed by five years of parole. This way, we can keep a close watch on them. I made it clear to them that any violations during those five years would result in their return to prison. Also, they will issue a statement to the press, expressing remorse for their actions and acknowledging their mistake, cautioning others against following a similar path. They will also disclose that their instigator, Josh, who subsequently committed suicide, coerced them. They will express gratitude for the deal we made in exchange for their cooperation in identifying their boss, Josh.

"As for the two men, they had nothing of value to offer in exchange. Consequently, they will receive the maximum sentence for attempted murder. However, we have reduced it to ten years on the condition that they also make a statement to the press. I will ensure that people are informed about the actions both of you have taken and emphasize the gravity of committing crimes against government employees. By the time they complete their sentence and parole, they will be very old. I will also communicate with other governments, underscoring that such crimes against government employees can potentially lead to war. This will help countries understand the severity and encourage vigilance in their own territories to prevent harm to government employees. I wanted to give you a heads-up since you may face press inquiries regarding these assassination attempts.

"I have been meeting with officials from various countries responsible for strategy and prosecution. There is an idea proposed by the Storm leaders in the U.S. and China regarding the next step in the Storm project. They wanted me to present it to you. The U.S. Storm leader will discuss this in detail during their meeting as well.

"In our discussions with Russia and China, we explored the possibility of a partnership, and this is a good example of collaboration. The two Storm leaders brainstormed and suggested using a remote-guided barge equipped with the Storm solution. This barge can be released into the center of a storm remotely. They believe it would result in significant cost savings on jet fuel and rockets. We have a cyclone approaching Tokyo in two days, and they propose testing this approach on that storm."

John and Kate leaned in close, whispering to each other so only they could hear. Then, John gestured towards Kate and said, "This is why we hired you, Jane. First, you shared your idea on the prosecutions, and then the barge concept."

"We'll agree on the barge idea, but before that, we need to conduct a quick modeling experiment in the lab. We need to determine if the solution should be shot up into the storm or dispersed at the storm's center in some way. John's team can handle the lab modeling within the next couple of hours so that we can ensure the remote on the barge will release the solution correctly," Kate explained.

She continued, "Another important point is involving Russia in this change, as we have a partnership with China and Russia. We need the leaders to agree that this is a good strategy, and then we can announce that China, Russia, and the U.S. are jointly working on the Storm Project. In the announcement, we must inform everyone that we will be implementing this solution for the storm set to hit Tokyo. We want the barge ready to go to the storm's center one day before it reaches Tokyo. In case the solution doesn't work, we should have China and U.S. jets ready to intervene and stop the storm conventionally."

The meeting ended fifteen minutes later, giving Jane time to prepare the Storm team for their arrival at noon. The subsequent meeting involved the Medical Leader and their team, including Medical leaders from around the world. Natalie facilitated the call while the U.S. leaders were physically present in the room.

The U.S. Medical Leader began by presenting a chart displaying the global usage of the Medical Computer for data entry and retrieval. "Based on the data in the Medical Computer, we and most doctors are beginning to observe patterns. By identifying and addressing these patterns, we can prevent certain illnesses. We are prepared to make an announcement to the world," the U.S. Leader stated.

He continued, "The announcement regarding illnesses would convey the following message: 'You could be at risk of this illness if you engage in these activities and have a family member with the same illness. While we can't force people to change their behavior, we can provide them with factual information to help them make their own decisions. Some countries are eager to make this type of announcement immediately, while others prefer gathering more information."

As the U.S. Leader spoke, Kate and John huddled together once more. This time, Kate pointed to John to voice their shared thoughts. Then John said, "Considering the urgency of the situation, we should all agree on this type of announcement. Even if we don't have all the information and some fail to see the risks, we can still prevent some illnesses. The wording of all the announcements should be consistent, while the recommended actions may vary. We are still gathering data on these illnesses and their causes. Therefore, we want to provide you with preliminary information so you can decide on the appropriate course of action for yourself and your family."

John added, "Out of the hundred thousand people who contracted this illness, we identified a pattern of engaging in five to ten specific behaviors, along with having a family member with the same illness. Please take the action you deem appropriate, and we will continue updating you on this illness. I want to get the data out there as soon as we believe we may have a pattern, so we can begin to shed light on these illnesses as soon as possible. If we hold back on an announcement and someone contracts the illness, they will be very upset because we did not provide them with the information sooner.

"Keep in mind that if any of you make this type of announcement, it will spread worldwide. Therefore, we need to agree now that a minimum sample size of ten thousand is required to draw conclusions. Additionally, we should make these press announcements together in every country around the world. This is very important, so if anyone disagrees with the wording or the minimum sample size, we should discuss it. I noticed that someone suggested in an email that the minimum number before we can identify patterns should be twenty thousand. Are there any proposed changes?"

John waited for about five minutes and then said, "Natalie has sent the work to everyone. Once we have twenty thousand people who exhibit the same pattern and have contracted this illness, we will hold off on further updates to the Medical Project. Considering the current situation with COVID and AIDS, if over a hundred people turn up with the same virus within a hundred-mile radius, we will send a group of doctors to that location and restrict travel out of that area until we can identify the virus and find a cure. Once we establish the right parameters and wording to be used, we should be able to let the computer do its thing. It will identify patterns, and once it identifies twenty-thousand people with this pattern, the computer will inform us of the resulting illness. But for now, we need to have these weekly meetings with all the medical team leaders from around the world. Together, we can decide what messages to give the press and deliver to the world. The Medical Leadership Team should meet every week, and Kate, Jane, and I will attend at least once a month, unless you need us more frequently. We have another meeting scheduled to start in ten minutes. We have accomplished a great deal today."

Natalie began connecting everyone for the Climate meeting. Kate initiated the meeting by asking the U.S. Leader if they had been holding their weekly meetings and inquiring about any issues reported by the countries. The U.S. Leader expressed disappointment and replied, "Our main problem is that our manufacturer in the U.S. cannot produce the Climate Devices fast enough."

"I see you invited the U.S. manufacturer to this meeting," Kate remarked.

She turned to the lady representing the company and asked, "Is there a way we can allow other countries to manufacture the product under your guidance without revealing the secret of how the device works?"

The Lady responded positively, saying, "Yes, we can achieve this by supplying the parts, and they can assemble them in their own manufacturing facilities and distribute the devices within their countries. Their governments will still have to pay us for the parts, but it would save us a great deal of time in manufacturing and shipping."

Kate expressed her appreciation and said to the countries, "This is excellent! I want each country to inform the U.S. Leader of the number of manufacturing plants they will require. Our current manufacturer will collaborate with other manufacturers worldwide to set up these facilities."

The China Climate Leader then spoke up, saying, "The plants we previously used for manufacturing warships and other materials will be repurposed to produce Climate devices. The previously uninhabitable land in China, due to the poor atmosphere, will increase by more than fifty percent, providing ample space and resources for our own people. There will be no need for further expansion."

The Russian Climate Leader shared a similar sentiment. Jane commented, "This is an unexpected positive result from the Climate Project. When the time is right, I would like to share this news with the world. I will work with each country to ensure we have agreed upon a press release before disseminating any information. This is good news that everyone will want to hear."

Kate had another question and directed it to the U.S. Climate Leader: "Do you have the results for the U.S. that show how the deployment of Climate devices on land and in the sky has eliminated our hot spots and improved air quality?"

The U.S. Leader promptly replied, "We no longer have any hotspots in the U.S., and the concentration of harmful particles in the air has decreased by fifty percent. We are observing similar results around the world where we have a sufficient number of Climate devices deployed."

John could no longer contain his frustration and interjected with a hint of anger, "You are all Climate Leaders in your countries and report indirectly to the U.S. Leader. We expect the U.S. Leader and each of you to address such problems. You don't need to involve Kate and me. We have given you the authority to make these decisions. Once the manufacturer informed us of their solution, you should have implemented manufacturing in other countries, especially since we are operating at full capacity in the U.S."

Everyone nodded in agreement, and a faint applause could be heard from those participating remotely. Kate concluded the meeting on a positive note, saying, "As Jane mentioned, we have a truly positive story to share about the Climate Project. Let the world know we are repurposing plants previously used for war materials to produce Climate devices. When deployed, these devices will provide countries with more habitable land for their people and agricultural growth. It will also generate employment opportunities worldwide. All of you should collaborate with Jane so we can spread this good news to the world. Okay, we have another meeting about to start. Great job! Keep up with your weekly meetings, and we will see you at least once a month. If you need us sooner, we are here."

Before the next meeting began, as Natalie connected all the Storm Leaders, Jane remarked, "I know both of you can see this as well as I can. The Climate Project's story, as well as the Medical Project's story, is something that people would want to hear. It's truly exceptional!"

John and Kate smiled, and John gestured for Kate to express their sentiments. Kate, with a smile on her face, stated, "As we mentioned before, we trust that you will do the right thing. Prepare the story and present it to the presidents. But before you do that, share it with Jim and ensure he shows it to our President. He will decide how it should be presented and by whom."

Jane responded with a smile and nod. Natalie informed everyone that the Storm Project meeting was about to begin, and the U.S. Storm Leader and his team were present, with participants dialing in from around the world.

John initiated the meeting by saying, "You all know what I am going to ask. How did the barge idea perform in the lab simulation and off the coast of Tokyo?"

The Storm Leader replied with a smile, "I have only good news. I brought the person who conducted the simulation, and the President of the Company that manufactures the Storm solution, and the remote guidance for the barge."

He added, "First, John, I want to acknowledge that simulating everything in the lab, as you suggested, was crucial. We needed to spray the solution instead of relying solely on the storm to disperse it. That's why the rocket launch from the plane worked so well. It effectively sprayed the solution everywhere, just like we needed to do with the barge. I must also commend the Tokyo team for their assistance in positioning the barge about a hundred miles off the coast, right in the center of the storm. This allowed us to test the barge's efficacy, and even if it failed, we still had time to deploy our planes and neutralize the storm. Russia, China, and Japan were all part of this collaborative effort to halt the storm, as you requested. We have it all recorded. It was a beautiful sight to witness. The barge entered the storm under remote control, disappeared into it, and about thirty minutes later, all we could see was the barge calmly floating in the ocean, with no sign of the storm. We have this all on film and ready to release it."

Jane then remarked, "I will release this information to the press. The story should highlight the partnership and include the recorded footage. I will need to consult with my colleagues in Japan, Russia, and China to make sure we are in agreement regarding what we will convey to the press. I will also inform Jim of our plans, so he can brief the President."

Kate, sporting a smile, exclaimed, "Good job, team! We now have another method for taming storms."

That marked the end of the day's meetings, which had extended until around 7 p.m. John and Kate stopped by Jim's office to inquire if he had been briefed on the meetings. He confirmed that he had and raised one concern—safety. Jim stated, "Right now, both of you are more popular than the President, and you see the level of security that surrounds our President. Moreover, when you initiate global changes, it's inevitable that you may unintentionally harm someone, and they might have friends who would want to retaliate. Although I haven't heard anything specific, I am concerned. Don't be surprised if we enhance your security."

John and Kate proceeded to their limousine, and true to Jim's word, their security measures had been doubled. They eagerly looked forward to Saturday, as it marked the end of a full week of meetings. On their way home, they called Katelin and invited her to join them for lunch at The Cheesecake Factory in the mall at 11:30 a.m. She accepted but jokingly requested that they use the bathroom at home rather than at the restaurant. They all shared a laugh and headed straight home, not setting the alarm for the next morning to ensure they received ample sleep.

The Forty-Fourth Day

Time with Katelin

T hat morning, when John and Kate woke up, they couldn't stop thinking about what Jim had said when they left his office. They deliberated on the possibility of someone trying to harm them or Katelin, but ultimately decided not to upend their lives based on an unknown threat. They opted to go for a run together through the park, informing the security team to ensure their safety.

The run was invigorating, with picturesque views and enjoyable company. Upon returning home, they prepared for lunch with Katelin, and by 11 a.m., they were on their way to the mall. Suddenly, four security cars surround—two on either side, one in front, and another at the back.

One of the security guards next to the driver of the limo informed them, "We have a situation. We're heading to the hospital. Your daughter was airlifted there after her limo was hit by another car. The driver tried to flee, but they apprehended him. Unfortunately, your daughter Katelin sustained severe injuries from a bullet fired by the occupants of the car that crashed into hers."

Kate and John were devastated, urging the driver to rush to the hospital quickly. Upon arrival, they were directed to the surgery waiting room while the doctors removed the bullet lodged in Katelin's chest. Embracing one another, they prayed for their daughter's recovery.

After the surgery, a young doctor approached them, wrapping his arms around both John and Kate. He reassured them that Katelin would be okay, as the surgery went well without any complications. She would need around two weeks of rest and recovery before returning to her normal activities.

John and Kate showered the doctor with gratitude, unable to hold back their tears of relief. The doctor informed them that Katelin would spend some time in the recovery room before being transferred to a regular hospital room. He assured them of his continuous vigilance in overseeing her complete recovery.

As soon as Katelin woke up in the recovery room, both John and Kate held her hands, gazing at her with worry. With a playful tone, she jokingly remarked, "Okay, no more Cheesecake Factory for a while."

Laughter filled the room, although Katelin winced in pain and said, "Don't make me laugh. It hurts too much when I laugh."

At that moment, the young doctor entered and advised them, "We need to let Katelin rest. I suggest that the both of you go home and get some rest as well. I will stay here and make sure Katelin's fine."

Kate and Katelin exchanged a glance and whispered to each other; their voices barely audible. They wondered if the doctor was married and expressed their admiration for him. John noticed their conversation and understood their thoughts. He reassured them, saying, "I think Katelin will be fine. Jim has assigned a couple of security guards to watch over her."

As he escorted Kate out of the hospital, a tinge of anger in his voice, John suggested, "We should go to the police station and interrogate the guy. I called Jane, and she has already used her contacts to put him in a private area so we will be able to question him. He already has a lawyer."

With a police escort that had lights and sirens, the limo driver took them quickly to the police station quickly. Upon arrival, they were led to the location where the prisoner was held. Jane met them there, her voice as stern as when she said, "I believe you're familiar with this man. His name is Joe Jacob, brother of Sam Jacob, the individual involved in 'The Medical Project' killings who ended up getting killed."

John and Kate shook their heads, indicating they didn't know Joe.

John clarified, "We knew Sam but were unaware of anyone in his family."

Jane continued, "Sam and Joe's father, Mike Jacob, took over the company after Sam's death and has been running it with Joe. We recently discovered that Mike has cancer and only has a couple of days left to live. I believe they seek vengeance for Sam's death."

She added, "We don't require any more information from Joe. He knows he will spend the rest of his life in prison. I'm unsure if you wish to speak with Mike, but he is currently in a hospital a few miles from here. He has only a few hours to live."

John then expressed his gratitude, saying, "Thank you, Jane. You've done the right thing by obtaining evidence against this man, so we don't need to talk with him. However, I do want to speak with Mike. Kate, would you like to accompany me?"

In a sympathetic voice, Kate replied, "No, John, you go talk to Mike. I'll go to the hospital and see Katelin. I think I'll bring her some cheesecake."

John made his way to the hospital and arranged for a bishop from the church to meet him there. Upon entering Mike Jacob's room, he noticed Mike's displeasure at his presence and heard him say, "Hello, Colombo. I'm surprised to see you."

John looked at Mike and saw him still angry over Sam's death and his other son's imprisonment. In a compassionate tone, John said, "I'm sorry for all you've gone through—losing a son and having your other son in trouble. I understand the pain, as we almost lost our daughter to cancer. Do you want someone to talk to?"

Mike, still deeply upset, retorted, "Get out of here, John! You think I want to talk to you?"

John clarified, "No, not me. But the bishop."

At that moment, the bishop opened the door and walked in, saying, "Hello, Mike. Do you want to talk?"

Mike gestured for the bishop to enter, and John left the room.

The Forty-Fifth Day

Kate, Katelin, and the Doctor

John and Kate thought it would be important to attend church and offer prayers for Katelin's quick recovery. John decided to shorten his exercise routine to ensure they wouldn't be late. They wanted to attend the 10 a.m. mass and spend the rest of the day with Katelin.

After church, they planned to have brunch at The Cheesecake Factory and pick up some breakfast for Katelin—her favorite Belgian Waffles and eggs combo. Arriving at the hospital, they found Katelin conversing with the young doctor just as she received her hospital breakfast. Upon entering the room, the doctor quipped, "Sneaking in some food, huh? Katelin really needs to eat the hospital food, but if she finishes that, I'll allow a few bites of The Cheesecake Factory food you brought."

Katelin laughed, and her beautiful smile made everyone in the room join in. Jokingly, she said, "So you went to The Cheesecake Factory without anyone trying to kill you in the restroom or hitting your car on the way? I told you not to make me laugh—it hurts!"

The doctor then approached Katelin, lifting the sheet to check her stitches, and spoke in a serious tone, "A couple of inches to the right, and the bullet would have hit her heart. Katelin, I want you to stay in bed for a few more days and try to remain calm."

After the doctor left, Kate jokingly remarked, "If he wants her to stay calm, he should find an uglier doctor."

Kate and Katelin shared laughter, while John managed only a slight smile. Katelin interjected, "Stop already; it hurts!"

Kate then asked, "Do you know if he's married?"

With a smile on her face, Katelin replied, "He's not married, and he already wants to take me out for lunch or dinner. I can choose the place."

Kate, wearing a bigger smile, said, "Alright, that's my daughter."

John shook his head, expressing a mix of amusement and exasperation, and commented, "I don't know what it is between you two."

He understood that Kate and Katelin had a unique mother-daughter bond since Katelin's birth. Kate knew she had a lifelong friend and companion in her daughter, and by the time Katelin turned seven, their inseparability was evident. Kate would often ask Katelin to skip school so they could spend time together, but Katelin would insist on attending, emphasizing the importance of not falling behind.

John enjoyed observing their close relationship, as they rarely disagreed and seemed to always be on the same page. He remembered a time when Kate called him, describing an argument she had with Katelin in Tokyo, only to receive an apologetic call from Katelin two subway stops later. Their mother-daughter bond was truly exceptional. While Katelin respected her dad and would do anything for him, John knew the mother-daughter bond was unique.

Kate and Katelin lay in bed together, while John made sure proper security measures were in place, despite his belief that there wouldn't be another attempt on Katelin's life. In the hallway, the young doctor approached John and introduced himself: "Hello, I didn't introduce myself formally. My name is Jim Asher, and I've been a surgeon at this hospital for two years. I happened to be on call when your daughter came in with a bullet wound and bruises from a car accident. I wanted to let you know and make sure you're okay with me asking her out on a date when she gets better."

John responded with a serious tone: "I trust my daughter's judgment, and if she says yes, then I'm okay with it. She's my only daughter, so when you're on a date, you need to ensure her safety, and I don't want her to be hurt in any way."

The doctor could tell John was being serious and simply replied, "Yes, sir!"

Just then, John's phone rang, and he excused himself to take the call. "Hello, Jim. You probably heard what happened. Katelin is doing fine. I expect we'll be out of the hospital sometime this week. I want to thank you for doubling the security. It likely saved Katelin's life. The security guards took down the perpetrator before he could fire a second shot."

Jim responded, "John, I want you and Kate to take as much time off as you need. Jane and the team can handle things for a while."

John quickly replied, "Kate and I discussed it, and we think we can work from home for a week, then return to the office the following Monday. We've already informed Valerie to keep all our meetings, but we'll be joining remotely from home."

With an appreciative tone, Jim said, "You two are remarkable. You always anticipate my every move. My wife and I will pray for Katelin's speedy recovery. I worry about you and Kate because I know how focused you both can get. If you find yourselves skipping dinner or working late into the night, take a moment to talk with each other and Katelin. Consider going out for dinner or attending a show to take your mind off things."

John responded appreciatively, "Thank you, Jim, for your prayers and advice. That's why people admire you as a person and a boss."

When John returned to the room, Kate was starting to get out of Katelin's bed and motioned for John to keep quiet. Katelin was sound asleep, and the doctor assured John and Kate that he would keep an eye on her while they went home to rest. Exhausted, they headed straight home. With security present everywhere, they felt safe and quickly took showers before going to bed early, watching TV from the comfort of their bed.

From a Run to the Diner to Katelin's Hospital Discharge

W hen John woke up, his mind was preoccupied with what Jim had told him. Both of them experienced a profound shock when their daughter nearly lost her life. It occurred to John that he and Kate should incorporate more exercise into their routine. Since Kate was still asleep, he gently roused her and suggested, "Why don't we go for an extra-long run? It would be good for our overall health."

"You're right," Kate agreed, rubbing her eyes.

"Let's run up to the diner, listen to some music, gaze into each other's eyes, solve a few problems, and then make our way back home," Kate said.

John smiled, pleased with the idea. "Sounds like fun. I'll inform our security team about our plans. Once we're done, I'll let them know we're heading to the hospital. I'll also give Valerie a call and ask her to contact us on our cell if she needs anything."

When they arrived at the diner, the owner welcomed them, as he had seen the news reports about Katelin's ordeal in the newspaper and on television. Leading them to their regular table, the owner promptly placed their order, knowing what they liked from previous visits. He inquired about Katelin and mentioned that he had said a prayer for her.

Kate's eyes welled up with tears as the owner finished speaking.

"Your prayers worked because she's doing well. She should be discharged from the hospital in a few days. Thank you for praying; your prayers have truly made a difference," Kate said.

One of the reasons everyone adored John and Kate was that, despite having conversed with numerous presidents, they genuinely enjoyed engaging with friends and people who had served them. Their down-to-earth nature was evident to ordinary individuals on a daily basis.

Upon leaving the diner, the owner insisted they didn't pay, but John and Kate insisted on settling the bill and left a generous tip. Another reason why many people admired them was because of this. They understood that the owner and the staff needed the money more than they did and consistently paid their bills.

As John and Kate walked hand in hand out of the diner, some of their security guards joined them for the run back home. Once they reached their house, they headed to the bathroom to freshen up, took a shower, and dressed before making their way to visit Katelin at the hospital.

Upon arriving, they proceeded directly to Katelin's room. She was overjoyed to see them and exclaimed, "What happened? You didn't bring me any breakfast from The Cheesecake Factory?"

The three of them smiled, and Kate replied, "Today, we ran to the diner and talked about you. We want you to get well soon. We miss you."

Just then, the young doctor entered the room and witnessed the scene—John, Kate, and Katelin holding hands while they were engaged in a conversation. The doctor shared some excellent news with them, saying, "I have some wonderful news for all of you. I examined Katelin today, and she's progressing so well that I'm authorizing her to go home with you today. However, she must remain in bed or use a wheelchair. She can only take short walks from the bed to the bathroom. I'll make a few house calls this week to ensure her recovery is going smoothly."

The Columbos beamed with joy, and Kate expressed her gratitude, saying, "Thank you, Doctor, for saving my daughter's life and for her swift recovery. When you visit us, please schedule it during dinner time.

We'd like to discuss some other plans we have in mind."

"It would be my pleasure to discuss your plans. You both have done so much already," the doctor promptly said, expressing his honor at the invitation.

John and Kate began packing Katelin's belongings, and within an hour, a nurse wheeled her out of the hospital. As they made their way down the corridor, a line of people spontaneously burst into applause, eager to shake their hands. The impact of their actions resonated with everyone.

Back at home, John and Kate set up two beds in the den to ensure they could be close to Katelin throughout her stay. They were elated that she was recovering well and wanted to remain by her side.

That evening, they retired to bed early, making plans to arrange a call with Jane the following day at 10 a.m. to discuss future projects.

The Forty-Seventh Day

Working from Home and the Doctor's Visit

J ohn and Kate woke up multiple times during the night to check on Katelin, ensuring she was okay. Around 7 a.m., John got up and dressed in his running outfit. Katelin, seeing him awake, smiled and jokingly said, "I don't think I'll go running with you today."

John chuckled and shook his head. Kate woke up and climbed into Katelin's bed, wanting to make sure she was alright and available if Katelin needed anything. They had a close bond.

After John finished his run, he prepared for the scheduled phone meeting with Jane and Kate. Kate asked, "Is the team prepared to discuss the next project? Will we be talking to Jane about initiating it?"

With a serious expression, John replied, "We've thoroughly simulated everything in the lab, and we're ready to move forward to the next step, which involves finding a company to construct the real thing."

John had a degree in Aerospace Engineering and had always dreamed of space travel. However, fuel limitations and lengthy interplanetary travel times posed challenges. Since high school, John has been fascinated by rockets. In fact, he and his friend had built their first rocket to earn extra credit. The rocket he planned to build now would require no fuel and would surpass any other rocket in terms of speed and range.

Once John and Kate were dressed, they heard a knock at the door, followed by the doorbell. Katelin called out from her bed, "Is someone

233

going to get the door, or should I get up and answer it?"

John and Kate assured her they would handle it and headed towards the door. Kate opened it to find two security guards and the young doctor. Kate instructed John to take the doctor to the living room while she went to the den to see Katelin. Back in the den, Kate told Katelin about the doctor's visit. They hurriedly made both beds, fixed Katelin's hair, helped her into her bathrobe, and placed her in a wheelchair.

John guided the doctor to the living room and offered him some coffee. When Katelin wheeled herself into the living room, she looked toward the young doctor and remarked, "We didn't expect you so soon."

She then turned to her dad and asked, "Can mom and I have some of that coffee?" John nodded in response.

The doctor observed Katelin and said, "Just by looking at you, I can tell you're doing well. I don't usually make house calls, but since your house was on my way to work, I wanted to ensure you were okay. Let me examine the wound and your bruises."

John and Kate left the room and went into the den while the doctor assessed Katelin. After about thirty minutes, the doctor wheeled Katelin into the den and said, "She is healing perfectly, and I believe she won't need the wheelchair in about a week. For now, it's best to keep her in a wheelchair or bed as a precaution. I like how everything is arranged here, allowing you to keep an eye on her in case she needs anything. If you don't mind, I'll make a few more visits to ensure her recovery progresses smoothly."

Everyone smiled and shook hands. John escorted the doctor to the door. When he returned to the den, he found Kate and Katelin giggling. John knew they were talking about the doctor, so with a stern look, he reminded Kate, "We have a call in about ten minutes. We should head to our office."

He then turned to his daughter and asked, "Katelin, would you like more coffee before we take this call?"

Katelin smiled and replied, "Don't worry about me. I can wheel myself into the kitchen and get my own coffee. You guys go on the call and continue saving the world."

It was a lighthearted comment, but it held some truth given the nature of their discussion.

John and Kate entered their home office, and the phone rang. It was Valerie calling from the conference room in the West Wing, accompanied by Jane. Jane sat beside Valerie and asked, "How is Katelin doing? We heard you wanted to discuss a future project. I also wanted to provide you with an update on the three ongoing projects."

Kate shared the recent report from the doctor, delivering good news about Katelin's progress. Jane also provided positive updates on the three projects and mentioned an approaching storm off the African coast. Russia and the U.S. were considering using a barge, similar to what they had done in Asia, to mitigate its impact.

With a serious tone, John took over the conversation, saying, "If we don't handle this next project properly, it could potentially lead to another war. The utilization of this new technology will catapult the U.S. far ahead of any other nation. Therefore, it's crucial that we ensure no one feels threatened. The key is to involve other countries without divulging the technological secrets."

Jane and Valerie were on the edge of their seats, and Valerie remarked, "I noticed that Jim is in his office, and based on his calendar, he has an hour available."

John and Kate exchanged nods, and Kate said, "Yes, please get him and Natalie invited to this meeting, just in case we need to arrange a meeting with the President, Congress, and Senate."

Since it was a Zoom call, everyone took their seats, and John spoke in a serious tone, saying, "Jim, we apologize for interrupting your day, but we believe it's crucial that you hear about this new project directly from Kate and me."

Kate continued with a serious tone: "If the other projects were not on track or had encountered significant issues, we wouldn't introduce this now. However, we are confident that our team can handle the four projects."

John took over again, intensifying his tone: "I've been working on this project with my lab team and two other U.S. Companies for a couple of years. It is now ready to be built and made public, but it must be done in a way that doesn't threaten other nations. We have developed a propulsion system that combines electric energy and solar energy, enabling us to achieve speeds surpassing those of any known rocket. The reason we need to involve partners is to prevent anyone from weaponizing this technology."

John proceeded to explain the measures in place to safeguard the technology's secrets, emphasizing the requirement of top-secret clearance for those involved in the project.

Jim instructed Natalie to schedule a meeting with the President, Congress, and Senate as soon as possible. John informed everyone that he and Kate would be resuming work at the office since the doctor confirmed Katelin's recovery. Kate's sister, Susie, who bore a striking resemblance to Kate, would be taking care of Katelin when they were at work.

"Tomorrow, we'll be back at the office, and if there are any meetings you need us to attend, make sure to arrange them. Kate and I are fully prepared to tackle this. As I mentioned earlier, the reason we're initiating this new project is that the other three are progressing well and showing remarkable growth with our current team," John said.

He then turned to Jim and continued, "By the way, Jim, we will be compiling a new list of individuals we'll need for this project."

Jim responded, "Understood. We will gather experts from various projects worldwide and assign them to this endeavor. Both of you are the most exceptional inventors I've ever encountered, constantly reshaping our world. And now, you're about to make an impact beyond our planet. It's a genuine honor to collaborate with both of you. See you tomorrow to commence this exciting new project."

The Forty-Eighth Day

West Wing Meeting

J ohn and Kate had a tradition of starting their day with a breakfast discussion, so they quickly got ready and headed to the diner. It was their way of combining a meal with project brainstorming as they sat across from each other. They enjoyed the nostalgic tunes of old country music, gazing into each other's eyes. Ever since their teenage years, they had maintained this breakfast ritual in every city they lived in, nurturing their growing love.

After finishing their breakfast, they hurried back home to prepare for work. Within thirty minutes, they were out the door, entering the limo that would take them to the West Wing. Jim and several members of Congress and the Senate were already assembled, prompting John and Kate to join the meeting immediately. John took charge and began by asking a question that caught everyone off guard: "Before we proceed, let me inquire: Does anyone in this room lack Top-Secret Security Clearance?"

Jim, adopting a serious tone, picked up his phone to contact the President. "John, in light of the gravity you emphasized for this meeting, we double-checked everyone's security clearance, and I can confirm that everyone here possesses Top Secret Security Clearance. The President will be joining us shortly."

The unexpected arrival of the President left everyone, including John and Kate, surprised. He made it clear that he hadn't scheduled the meeting to ensure absolute confidentiality. The President addressed John and Kate directly, saying, "Based on what Jim has briefed me, we need to maintain the utmost secrecy regarding the new projects discussed today. No one outside this room should be aware of them until we decide which other countries we want to involve in this endeavor. Can you inform me about the companies or universities collaborating with you on this project and what they know?"

Kate stood up and began her explanation: "All individuals involved in this project possess Top Secret Clearance. The project is divided into numerous segments, and only John, myself, and the presidents of the two companies we are collaborating with comprehend how all the pieces fit together. Additionally, approximately twenty government employees working under John and me are conducting simulations and tests, all of whom also possess Top Secret Clearance."

She continued, "If you were to ask an engineer from one of the collaborating companies about their work, they might be able to discuss a chip on a circuit board and the testing to ensure it remains cool. They may be aware that the testing simulates conditions in space, devoid of air. However, that is the extent of their knowledge. Therefore, Mr. President, the only people who will possess a comprehensive understanding of the entire project and its purpose are those present in this room and the presidents of the collaborating companies."

The President smiled and responded, "Excellent! Let's proceed. If the individuals in this room believe this is a project the U.S. should fund and complete, then we will entrust you and John with its execution."

John rose to his feet and elaborated on the development of their revolutionary propulsion system, capable of propelling spacecraft in space faster and farther than any other known technology. Given the absence of friction in space, their innovation had the potential to enable the propulsion of large spacecraft. The room erupted in applause when John concluded, marking their approval to proceed.

Their next task was to identify the partners who could be brought into the project, ensuring that other countries did not perceive the U.S. efforts as a threat. John and Kate collaborated to devise a strategy leveraging their connections in Russia and China—specifically, their rapport with Andrei in Russia and the trust they had established with individuals in China. Success in securing Russia's and China's agreement would be a momentous achievement for both humanity and interplanetary travel.

Around 6 p.m., after returning home, they consulted Katelin about dinner preferences. John suggested barbecued salmon and steak, with a side of vegetables specially prepared for Kate. Katelin expressed her desire for a bit of both. Aware that the following day held significant importance, John and Kate decided to turn in early after dinner. They all moved to the den, where two beds were situated, and peacefully drifted off to sleep.

In the middle of the night, John woke up briefly, sipping some alkaline water before setting the alarm for 6 a.m. The diner beckoned; it was their custom to discuss important matters, particularly before significant meetings.

The Forty-Ninth Day

Breakfast and West Wing Meeting

T he alarm sounded, jolting John and Kate awake. They quickly
dressed and approached Katelin's bed, informing her that they
were heading to the diner and would likely return around 7:30
a.m. With a sleepy nod, Katelin settled back to sleep. John and Kate
set off with two security officers following them in a car.

Upon reaching the diner, the security guards who had run with them
took a table near the entrance, ensuring a clear view of the establishment.
John and Kate settled into a booth by the window, inserting a quarter
into the jukebox to select a playlist of country songs. They ordered
their usual breakfast, while the guards in the car outside grabbed some
coffee and maintained watch over the surrounding area. The increased
security was evident, with guards stationed both inside and outside
their home, protecting Katelin.

Seated across from each other, John and Kate engaged in conversation
about the topics they intended to discuss in the upcoming meeting.
They also touched upon Katelin's progress in recovering from the
attempt on her life. Deeply in love and appreciative of their bond
with Katelin, they felt fortunate to have each other and cherished their
unique family dynamic.

When they arrived home, the young doctor was there, ensuring
Katelin's well-being. He wore a smile on his face as he said, "I think
we can take away the wheelchair today. Katelin can walk around the
house, and if she feels OK tomorrow, she can venture outside."

John and Kate were initially surprised to see the doctor inside the house, but the guards recognized him and allowed his entry. Kate responded with a smile: "That's great news. I suppose Katelin will want to sleep in her own room soon."

The doctor, still smiling, added, "Let's see how she progresses over the next couple of days. Katelin, I'm proud of you. You're healing quickly, and you've been an excellent patient."

After bidding farewell, the doctor left the house. John and Kate began preparing for work. Just as they were about to leave, Kate approached Katelin and whispered in her ear, "I think this guy really likes you. He calls on you every day and says he's proud of you."

Katelin smiled and squeezed her mother's hand. The bond between a mother and a daughter is strong. John looked at the two beautiful ladies and felt grateful for his luck. He then called Kate and said, "Come on, beautiful. We have a big day ahead. Let's not be late for our own meeting."

John and Kate exited the house, accompanied by two security guards who joined them in the limo, while another car led the way to the West Wing. Two security guards remained at the house—one inside with Katelin and another patrolling outside. Jim had bolstered security, knowing that with new projects proposed and ongoing endeavors, there could be potential risks.

Upon reaching their conference room in the West Wing, people began gathering for the meeting. It was the same group as the previous day. John and Kate made a quick stop at Jim's office to provide him with a brief overview of their intended discussion, which pleased him. They then entered the conference room, where the President and Jim joined them, and everyone took their seats.

Kate stood beside John, and in her serious tone, she began, "John and I believe it's necessary to call Andrei, who has a close relationship with the President of Russia and was instrumental in persuading the President of Russia to withdraw from Ukraine. Within the same hour, we will reach out to China and hold discussions with their heads of state and President, proposing the same partnership. Once we secure agreements on how to collaborate regarding the new propulsion system, we can announce it to the press. People trust both John and me, so we will initiate the discussion, and then, Mr. President, you can follow up."

Kate paused, nodding to John, who took over the discussion. In a serious tone, John spoke about their vision for the first space journey: "We plan to expand our current space station, modifying it to accommodate more people and increase storage capacity for food. Additionally, we will incorporate the new propulsion system into our existing spacecraft, enabling travel between the space station, the moon, and back to Earth. The key component of this system is a rocket powered by solar energy, with batteries made of a groundbreaking material that allows for swift movement of the entire space station through space."

John continued, "However, once we enter the moon's or Earth's atmosphere, we'll require a different type of propulsion system, the second part of our project. Without it, we would have to rely solely on our standard spacecraft and their propulsion systems, significantly extending the time required to construct the necessary space station for interplanetary travel. This second propulsion system employs anti-gravity technology, enabling us to assemble the space station entirely on Earth and subsequently launch it into space. We have thoroughly simulated and tested these innovations in our labs and at the company sites responsible for their development."

Confident in their preparations, John emphasized, "Rest assured, all necessary tests and simulations have been conducted. We will request two astronauts from each country for this inaugural flight—two Russians, two Chinese, and three from the United States. One of the American astronauts, being most familiar with the new propulsion systems, will serve as the mission's captain. Upon lunar landing, one representative from each country will remain on the spacecraft, while the other half of the space station will orbit the moon. To err on the side of caution, we will return all astronauts to Earth, leaving only three individuals on the space station circling our planet—one from each country. The remaining four will return home. If this mission proves successful, we have simulated plans for future journeys to other planets. However, we will assess the outcome of this initial trip before proceeding."

Upon the conclusion of John and Kate's presentation, the room erupted in applause. When the applause subsided, Kate expressed her gratitude with a smile, saying, "Thank you for your applause. We have a substantial amount of work ahead and will provide weekly updates on the progress. As previously mentioned, refrain from disclosing the overarching plan until we give you the green light, which will occur after securing agreements with the Russians and Chinese. For now, if anyone asks about our gathering here, simply mention that we are discussing a future project for which we will share more details in a few weeks. Please refrain from divulging any further information outside this room."

As John and Kate exited the room, conversations buzzed among the attendees, impressed by the Medical, Storm, and Climate Projects and now eager about the Space Project. They marveled at the Leadership Program and contemplated ways to reward John and Kate for their groundbreaking endeavors. The couple's ability to continuously generate new ideas and rally global recognition for the United States as a leading force, ultimately changing the world, left everyone in awe. While the details of the forthcoming project remained exclusive to those present in the meeting, the anticipation of sharing the revelations in the coming weeks permeated the room.

John and Kate, accompanied by their team and the two presidents spearheading the Space Program, headed toward John's office, with Kate leading the way. Upon arriving, John assumed a serious demeanor and addressed the two presidents, saying, "I want to keep your respective teams in the dark regarding the overall project. Let them focus on their assigned tasks, and perhaps, in ten years, they will comprehend the grand scale of our endeavor."

Aware of the potential rewards, John continued, "Other countries will realize that in the U.S., individuals who conceive and construct groundbreaking advancements often amass wealth. You and your teams will be no exception, benefiting greatly once this project concludes. Keep this knowledge confidential to prevent ideas from being stolen. Kate and I will hold discussions with the Russians and Chinese, exploring possibilities for collaboration without divulging the secrets of our new propulsion systems. All astronauts and personnel involved in the project will only know that we have developed two new propulsion systems. One system can propel cities through space, while the other can transport large space stations out of Earth's atmosphere. The details and patents will remain ours, undisclosed to others."

The individuals reporting directly to John and Kate took great pride in their involvement with the project. Like their counterparts in the Medical, Storm, and Climate Projects, they understood they were part of a global effort to change the world for the better. Kate, adopting a serious tone, added, "I understand that you may want to share your work with your spouses, friends, or family, but refrain from doing so until John and I have secured the necessary agreements. Furthermore, if word gets out that you possess confidential information, it could jeopardize the safety of your loved ones. We will inform you when the time is right to reveal your involvement in the Space Program."

Kate turned to Valerie and instructed her, "Valerie, please schedule two meetings tomorrow—one with Andrei in Russia and the other with the relevant representatives from China. Determine a suitable timing for the meetings, even if it requires some compromises. Notify them that it pertains to a new project we wish to discuss and that only individuals with top-secret clearance should attend. If we need to meet before 9 a.m., inform us."

On their way home, John and Kate received a message stating that the meeting with China would be at 8 a.m. local time, while the meeting with Russia would take place at 10 a.m.

The Fiftieth Day

Russia and China Meetings

J ohn and Kate woke up at 5 a.m. to go for a run to the diner for breakfast before heading to the West Wing for their meeting with China at 8 a.m. They were still sleeping in the den with their daughter, Katelin, so they informed her about their early morning plans. As the alarm went off, the three of them got up. Katelin, with a smile, jokingly asked, "Are you sure you don't want me to run with you to the diner? I guess someday you will let me know what is so important that would make you get up when it is still dark outside."

John and Kate smiled and kissed their daughter, ensuring she was alright, before telling her to go back to sleep. Kate reassured her, "In a couple of weeks, if everything goes well, you'll read about it in the newspaper or see it on the news. Get some rest and go back to sleep. We'll see you around 6:30 a.m. when we return."

Accompanied by two security guards and a trailing car, John and Kate ran to the diner. Upon arrival, they found only two other patrons already having breakfast. They played some old country music, and the server, familiar with their routine, brought them their usual order of decaf and regular coffee. The security personnel joined them for breakfast.

During their run back home, John and Kate informed the security team about the 8 a.m. meeting at the West Wing. They quickly showered and got dressed, and by 7 a.m., they were outside and headed to the conference room in the West Wing, reaching it around 7:45 a.m.

In the conference room, Valerie was already present, working on setting up a Zoom call with the participants in Beijing. Alongside John and Kate were the leader of the Space Project, Jean Meadows, and two of his direct reports. John began the meeting by introducing everyone from the United States, and then the individuals from China were introduced. He emphasized the top-secret nature of the discussion, stressing that no one outside the room, except the Presidents, should be briefed on the details. Translators were present to ensure effective communication between the two groups.

John reiterated the information he had shared during the previous meeting in the United States. He then proceeded to explain that they wanted China to build a specific part of the space station, while Russia and the United States would contribute to its construction as well. After describing the completed space station, including the involvement of all three countries, John was about to discuss the two new propulsion systems. However, he noticed the puzzled expressions on the faces of the Chinese representatives, indicating their confusion regarding how such a large space station would be launched into space and transported to the moon.

Kate stood up and provided an explanation, discussing how they had simulated and used their antigravity device to put significant portions of their section of the space station into space. She explained that after the construction was complete, a second propulsion system would transport the entire space station to the moon.

The room in China was already filled with trust and admiration for John and Kate, so when they finished their presentation and invited China to be their partner, the entire room stood up and applauded. The highest-ranking official in the room in China addressed them, saying, "We will seek the final approval from our President to proceed with the plan you outlined. However, judging by the sentiments in this room, we wholeheartedly wish to become your partners in the Space Project."

Referring to the successes of the Medical, Storm, and Climate projects, the speaker continued, "Our President holds great respect for you and John due to the significant cost savings and countless lives saved through these three initiatives. He has explicitly stated that if you and Kate seek our partnership, we will provide it. While we will confirm with our President, I am confident he will embrace this project as well. We will inform you today or tomorrow and provide you with the contact person who will coordinate with your team leader."

Jim and the President were briefed by John and Kate after the call. After approximately an hour, John and Kate received a call from the President of China. He informed them that he had already spoken with their President and wanted to personally convey his commitment to being their partner. He disclosed the name of the individual standing beside him, who would serve as their leader on the Space Project.

Expressing their gratitude, John and Kate informed the President of China that they planned to hold a joint press conference once they received confirmation from Russia on Monday. The President of China encouraged them to reach out to him directly if they required any assistance, emphasizing his ongoing interest in and satisfaction with their projects. With the call concluded, preparations began for the upcoming call with Russia, and Valerie was tasked with making the necessary arrangements.

Upon entering the room for the call with Russia, John and Kate noticed that Andrei and his team, along with the U.S. team, were already prepared. Following introductions similar to those in the China meeting, John inquired, "How would you prefer we announce this project? Kate and I can make the announcement and introduce the leaders, one representative from each country. Alternatively, we could involve the Presidents or have the leaders, such as yourself, say a few words."

Taking a moment to reflect, Andrei responded, "I prefer the approach of having you and Kate discuss the project as you did with the other three countries, followed by the leaders addressing how the projects will be executed in their respective nations. Let's aim for a live news broadcast to maximize visibility. Additionally, emphasize the novel aspects of the project, including the participation of astronauts from each country and the planned updates for the world. Our Presidents would appreciate receiving monthly updates on the four projects, while the media only requires biannual updates until we approach the launch phase."

Kate expressed her appreciation, saying, "Thank you, Andrei. That's the approach we will take, and we will share a copy of the speech with you today."

Following the call, both Kate and John were exhausted. They sent copies of their speech to the three Presidents and coordinated a suitable time with Valerie. Finally, they returned home to relax. However, upon their arrival, they discovered a note left by Katelin, explaining that she had gone out for dinner with the young doctor and that they had just missed her. Delighted by the day's successes and remembering their tradition of celebrating at Deanne's Place, they quickly freshened up and informed the security guards of their plans to dine at the restaurant. Accompanied by lights and sirens, the guards escorted them to Deanne's Place, where they were reunited with Katelin and the young doctor.

John mentioned to Kate, "I'm not sure if I mentioned it, but he expressed interest in taking Katelin on a date. His name is Jim Asher, and he worked as a surgeon at the hospital for two years."

Smiling, Kate responded. "Should we address him as Jim or Dr. Asher?"

John grinned and replied, "We'll see what he prefers and go with the flow."

As Katelin and Jim Asher approached, they noticed the flashing lights and sirens and paused before realizing it was John and Kate. After exchanging greetings, they entered the restaurant together, and the owner promptly seated them at a table for four.

With a smile, Jim Asher remarked, "Boy, this is excellent service!"

John and Kate just smiled in response, and John shared, "We're well-known here because we always come to celebrate special occasions."

Katelin then asked, "So, what's the special occasion this time? Or is it something you can't reveal?"

Kate smiled and replied, "For now, let's just say it's the first time our daughter has been out in several weeks, and things are looking positive. How is she doing, doctor?"

Jim Asher smiled warmly and reassured them, "She's doing well, which is why I agreed to her evening out. By the way, feel free to call me Jim."

John expressed his happiness, saying, "It's wonderful to see Katelin out and about. She's our one and only daughter. Dinner is on Kate and me. It has been a fantastic day, and it only got better when we saw Katelin."

Jim Asher added, "Katelin still needs to take it easy. Short walks are fine, but no running and plenty of rest."

Being driven and ambitious like her parents, Katelin asked, "When do you think I can return to work? I just received a double promotion, and I'm sure they want to see me back at the office soon."

In a serious tone, Jim Ashen replied, "I believe you need to stay with your parents for at least another week, and maybe in two weeks, you can consider going back to work. But I'd like to see you before you return."

They then enjoyed a delightful dinner together. Kate tried to extract information from her parents about the cause for celebration, but they simply said she would read about it next week. Kate felt proud of her parents, and they were equally proud of her. It was heartwarming to see them together, and Jim Ashen was attentive to Katelin throughout the evening.

When they arrived home, Jim Ashen gave Katelin a warm hug and a kiss before Kate and John entered the house. Katelin joined them shortly after and remarked, "I think this will be the last time we will all sleep in the den. Tomorrow, I'll be sleeping in my own room. I bet you have your alarm set for 5 a.m. again. Are you going to work on Saturday?"

John smiled and replied, "We plan on waking up early, but we don't have to go to work. You need your rest, so how about I set up your room tonight, and you can sleep without us interrupting you?"

Katelin smiled back and said, "Thank you, Daddy. I'll be okay, and I won't lock my door so you can check on me."

Kate and John headed to their respective bedrooms as well as Katelin's, making all the necessary arrangements. They also informed the security team that they would be sleeping in their own bedrooms from now on. The guards expressed gratitude for the update, and they continued to assign one guard inside the house and another outside.

Looking forward to a leisurely Saturday, John and Kate hoped to sleep in and perhaps invite Katelin to join them for breakfast. However, if they woke up early, they planned to go for a run and wake up Katelin upon their return.

Early Run and Breakfast with Katelin

I t was a pleasant change for Kate and John to sleep in their own room, but their ingrained habit of waking up early persisted, and they found themselves rousing at around 7 a.m. Hastily donning their running attire, they informed the security team that they intended to jog for approximately three miles in the neighborhood before returning home. By 9 a.m., they had completed their run and entered Katelin's room to wake her up. Kate suggested, "How about getting some more sleep until around 11 a.m., and then we can head to the mall? We'll grab a bite at The Cheesecake Factory and do some shopping. Are you up for it?"

Katelin beamed with excitement and replied, "Yes! It's been a whole month since I last went shopping, so I'm definitely ready. As for breakfast at that place, I'm not sure, but I'm hungry, so let's do it. I bet Dad also wants to catch a movie, so maybe we can fit that in too."

Katelin dozed off for a little while longer while Kate and John leisurely prepared for the day. John informed the security team about their plans, and by 11 a.m., they were all in the limousine with four guards accompanying them, en route to the mall.

Upon arriving at the entrance of The Cheesecake Factory, the manager hurriedly approached them, expressing his apologies for their previous unpleasant experience and his gratitude for giving them another chance. He warmly stated, "Everyone here adores the three of you, and we'd like to make amends. Please allow us to treat you to this meal. We already know your preferences, so there's no need for you to place an order."

The Columbos family exchanged smiles, and John replied, "Thank you for the generous offer, but we insist on paying."

The owner smiled in return and insisted, "Just leave a generous tip, and that will suffice."

John nodded in agreement, and the owner escorted them to their usual table. The waiter promptly arrived, already aware of their preferences, and simply confirmed their orders before heading to the kitchen. Within five minutes, a regular coffee, a decaf coffee, and a glass of orange juice were placed on the table.

Kate, sitting beside Katelin in the booth and facing John, remarked with a smile, "They really know us well. I guess we always order the same things for breakfast."

Kate's gaze was filled with love as she spoke to John. "Katelin already knows this, but when we were dating back when I was a senior in high school and you were a freshman in college, we used to go out for breakfast every Saturday. We were young and poor, and we always ordered the same thing. Eventually, the waiter knew our order as soon as we walked in. John, my love for you hasn't changed."

She reached across the table, holding John's hand, while Katelin's hand rested beside hers. They shared a heartfelt smile.

Katelin joined in and her smile filled with affection: "I remember when we lived in Tokyo, and you two would explore different restaurants every Saturday. You had weekends off, and you'd always try to convince me to join you. One time, I gave in. We walked for miles to a hotel, where we enjoyed a buffet on the top floor while a lady played the harp. It seemed like you both always made breakfast outings a special tradition. We went to a different restaurant every weekend in Tokyo."

John and Kate listened attentively, exchanging smiles between themselves and Katelin. Finally, Katelin playfully interjected, "Okay, we're falling behind. We should stop talking and start eating."

As they finished their breakfast, a commotion near the restaurant entrance caught their attention, and they saw Jim walking over to their table. Jim greeted them with a smile and said, "I apologize for disturbing your weekend. It seems like I always manage to do that whenever you're trying to relax."

He took a seat next to John and glanced at Katelin, who playfully responded, "I know my dad tells me this sometimes. I can't repeat anything I hear at this table."

Jim chuckled and replied, "You're just like your parents. You can read minds."

Then, in a hushed tone, despite no one else being around, he continued, "Both the Russian and Chinese Presidents contracted our President and expressed their belief that the announcement is too significant for just the two of you and the Space Project Leaders. The Presidents want to be involved in this announcement, so both of you will have to come in today and tomorrow to finalize and obtain approval for their speeches. On Monday morning, we'll have a rehearsal for all the speeches to be delivered later."

John and Kate simply nodded, and Kate said, "We'll meet you in the West Wing in about two hours."

Jim smiled and nodded back, saying, "You both are remarkable. I'm sorry to have disrupted your weekend."

He then left the restaurant, leaving everyone wondering why the Secretary of State had been conversing with John and Kate.

Katelin smiled at her parents, gripping their hands, and jokingly remarked, "Well, I thought you were in trouble when one president wanted you to stay at the White House. Now, it seems you must be in real trouble if three presidents are actively seeking you out. I'm so proud of you both. Have fun this weekend, and I guess I'll find out more on Monday along with the rest of the world."

John and Kate exchanged glances and then focused their gaze on Katelin. Kate said, "Just so you know, we feel incredibly fortunate to be your parents. We're going home now, and we want you to get some rest. You've had enough excitement and exercise for today. We'll be home late tonight, so don't wait for us. We'll probably be ordering some West Wing pizza tonight."

As they left the restaurant, John informed the security team that their plans for the movie and shopping had been canceled. Instead, they would all be heading home, and he and Kate would be heading to the West Wing in approximately an hour. This change worked well for Katelin, as it was evident she was already growing tired due to her recent operation and limited outdoor activities.

Once they informed Jim of their arrival, John and Kate entered the conference room in the West Wing. They had already contacted Valerie and the Space Project teams in the United States, Russia, and China, who were waiting for them on a Zoom call. Kate expressed her gratitude to Valerie for gathering everyone together, explaining that they were having breakfast with their daughter when they received the news that the president wished to be part of the announcement.

John then addressed the group, saying, "Kate and I have discussed what needs to be accomplished today and tomorrow. Today, we must finalize the presidents' speeches, and each of you will need to deliver your respective speech to them, making any modifications they desire to feel comfortable with their part in the presentation. Everyone will have copies of each other's speeches, including ours. We also need their approval for our speeches. We have a lot of work ahead of us today. Here is the initial draft of all the speeches that Kate and I have prepared, but you must modify them to ensure your own comfort before presenting them to your presidents."

Kate promptly shared the materials John and she had prepared during their one-to-two-hour limo ride, including the speeches they planned to deliver on Monday, with some adjustments to accommodate the presidents' desires.

Kate continued, "John and I still need to work on our speeches, and we want each of the Space Project leaders to have a part in the overall program. So, please work on your respective sections. We'll allocate two hours for each of you to make the necessary changes, and then we'll reconvene for a rehearsal."

Over the course of four additional rehearsals, everyone gradually became comfortable with their parts. Due to the time zone differences, some individuals worked through the night and morning, while the U.S. team stayed engaged until 10 p.m. Eventually, they agreed to collaborate with their presidents on Sunday, making any final adjustments and reconvening early on Monday morning.

John and Kate forwarded all the speeches to Jim and instructed him to review them with the president, making any necessary changes by Sunday noon. The other two presidents were given the same instructions. The plan was to finalize everything by Sunday night for a press conference at 9 a.m. on Monday. Additionally, press conferences were scheduled for 9 p.m. on Tuesday in China and 4 p.m. in Russia. This would mark the first time that the presidents would address the world simultaneously from their respective countries.

The Fifty-Second Day

Early Run, Breakfast, and Work

A ll the speeches were carefully crafted to ensure they captivated their respective presidents' countries, avoiding any repetition. Each president had the opportunity to review their speech, and by the time John and Kate arrived on Sunday, the only speech they needed to work on was their own. All the leaders from different nations attended the event and made their revisions and updates, which were then passed on to the two presidents. Jim, too, received the changes so that he could review them with the U.S. President.

The Leaders informed Kate and John that their President had made no further revisions to the speeches they had written. John and Kate were also responsible for introducing the leaders of the Medical, Storm, Climate, and Space Projects, who would each deliver a brief address. Consequently, John and Kate worked on these speeches as well.

Upon returning home that Sunday night, John and Kate felt a tinge of concern, apprehensive about any unforeseen surprises that might arise during the conference. They went to bed with these worries in mind but made plans to wake up early. They intended to quickly visit the diner for breakfast before rushing home to begin their day's work promptly at 8 a.m. They wanted to ensure they were fully prepared for one of the most significant press conferences, scheduled to commence at 9 a.m.

During dinner that evening, they discussed the content of their speeches with Katelin. However, they assured her that she could listen to the entire conference from home and update them on the commentators' feedback after each speaker. They instructed Katelin not to speak to anyone until the event had concluded.

Katelin expressed her immense pride in John and Kate, and in turn, they conveyed their deep admiration for her. Like any close-knit family, they had great love and respect for one another.

They were aware of the sacrifices Katelin had made to remain close to them. They cherished their time together, and Katelin, too, relished every moment with them. As they retired to bed that night, they couldn't help but feel a sense of apprehension for the day ahead.

Early Run, Breakfast, and Press Conference

They woke up very early, while it was still dark outside, and checked on Katelin, who was still asleep. They decided not to wake her until they left for work so she could get some rest and allow her body to heal.

As they ran to the diner, they noticed that Jim had increased the security. Three people would be staying at the house, and three Security Guards would run with them to the diner, with three more following in a car. Since it was early, no one else was at the diner, so John and Kate sat at their usual booth. The six security guards took separate tables near the door, keeping an eye out for anyone suspicious who might walk in.

They all ordered breakfast, and John and Kate discussed the speeches and how they would organize everything. They played some old country music on the jukebox. It was a crucial story they had to convey, but they knew that one wrong word from any President or Leader could be disastrous.

John went home feeling worried and went to work with a sense of concern. However, he and Kate were known for excelling under pressure. They didn't want that to change. Little did they know, this meeting wouldn't go as planned. The one thing that did go according to plan was the Presidents, Jim, and themselves walking together to the press room, accompanied by the Leaders of the four projects.

John and Kate stood up and began the meeting by introducing everyone. The President of China and his four leaders were in a room in Beijing, while the President of Russia was in Moscow with his four leaders. They all joined the Zoom call, visible on camera in the U.S. press room. The U.S. President would appear on a Zoom call with the President of China, while in Beijing, the China President would meet with his four leaders in person, with the U.S. and Russian Presidents joining the meeting via camera.

It was a breathtaking sight. John and Kate expressed their gratitude to Valerie and Natalie for making the technology work seamlessly. Kate began by discussing the successes of the Medical, Storm, and Climate Projects, inviting each leader to talk about their country's accomplishments. After each President and leader spoke, there was thunderous applause around the world.

Feeling relieved that everything had gone as planned so far, John delved into the details of the Space Project. The expressions on people's faces during each press conference revealed their sheer amazement.

Once John finished, it was the U.S. President's turn to discuss the Space Project in their country and their plans. However, John and Kate realized that something was about to change when the President of Russia started speaking instead of the U.S. President.

The President of Russia began with a smile, saying, "If you look at John and Kate now, you'll notice a worried look on their faces because I am deviating from the script and will be saying something they were not aware of."

With a bigger smile, he continued, "What they don't know is that the three Presidents decided to focus on one thing—John, Kate, and their leaders."

The President of Russia praised the Medical, Storm, Climate, and Space Projects, stating that they were making the Earth a better place to live and expanding into space. He commended John, Kate, and the leaders as exceptional individuals who excelled even in the most challenging projects, stating that he would present each of them with the highest award and honor for their contributions to Russia. Then he passed the baton to the President of China, who expressed similar sentiments and bestowed the highest honor upon John, Kate, and the leaders of their respective countries. Finally, he turned the meeting over to the U.S. President.

The U.S. President reviewed the successes of each project and then announced that John and Kate had already received the highest award for a government employee and U.S. citizen. However, after discussions with Congress and the Senate, a new award was created—the Leadership Award. John and Kate would be the inaugural recipients.

After each President spoke, there was a round of applause. But when the U.S. President concluded the meeting, the applause reverberated around the world. John and Kate were once again taken by surprise, just as they were with the North and South Korean Presidents. They embraced each other and expressed their gratitude to Jim and the U.S. President.

It was a day that John and Kate would never forget, and they couldn't wait to return home and share the news with Katelin. When they arrived home, they found Katelin still watching the news on TV. Every channel was praising John, Kate, and the United States. They felt proud to be Americans.

The reactions in China and Russia were also evident. The people there admired their leaders and held John and Kate in high regard. They, too, expressed their pride in being Russian or Chinese.

Of course, Katelin insisted, "I don't care what the doctor says; we are going to Deanne's Place."

Kate immediately dialed Katelin's doctor, Dr. Jim Ashen, on his cell phone. Recognizing Kate's number, Jim Ashen answered promptly. Kate asked, "Is it okay for Katelin to join us for dinner tonight at Deanne's Place if we bring the wheelchair?"

Dr. Ashen replied, "It's alright if I accompany her. In fact, she won't need the wheelchair if I'm there since she can hold onto my arm for support."

Kate smiled and said, "That's a deal! You can stop by our place in one hour, and we can all go together in a limo."

Then she turned to John and Katelin, who were wondering why she made that arrangement, as John wanted it to be a family-only occasion. Kate explained with a mischievous smile, "It's good to change things up a little. We'll have some different conversations with him at the table. And you both know how much you mean to me. I love you both, and we have so many cherished memories together. Let's invite someone in and see if he and Katelin are a good match."

John shook his head, smiling, and said, "Well, at least we know the doctor said it's okay for Katelin to be with us tonight, and she won't even need a wheelchair."

They all changed their clothes, made reservations for four, informed security about their plans, and settled down to wait for Dr. Ashen. While waiting, Katelin amusingly recounted their surprise when the Russian President expressed his gratitude and presented them with an award. Being private individuals who preferred to avoid the spotlight, their reaction was understandable, but it was also the reason why people admired them so much. Katelin shared her concerns about the increased visibility and potential risks of individuals seeking attention. They discussed Jim's foresight in increasing security measures, which had proven crucial.

Just as the doorbell rang, Dr. Ashen stood between two security guards. "Thank you all for allowing me to join you," Dr. Ashen said, addressing the group.

He continued, "I understand this is a special time. Katelin seems to be almost fully recovered. I can tell by the way she stands and walks. Before we leave, if you don't mind, I would like to examine her bullet wound to ensure there is no infection and that it is healing properly."

Dr. Ashen inspected Katelin's wound and smiled, saying, "I believe Katelin can return to work next Monday. I recommend light exercise for her this week."

Katelin smiled eagerly, gesturing towards the door. "Can we all go to dinner? I'm starving."

Everyone piled into the waiting limo, and when they arrived at Deanne's Place, the owner gave them a warm welcome. "It is an honor to see you all again," the owner said, greeted them. "Please, let the dinner be on me this time," he offered.

John's expression turned stern as he replied, "Okay, this time only. But if you're giving us dinner for free, the waiter should expect a very generous tip."

The owner smiled and replied, "When people know you dine here, it brings in so much business. You are now more famous than anyone in the world."

John and Kate exchanged smiles, and Kate added, "We come here to celebrate not only because of your exceptional food but also because we love the story of your daughter on the back of the menu. She was beautiful, intelligent, and accomplished so much. She was on the verge of achieving even more when she tragically succumbed to cancer—a cancer that was cured the year after her passing. Her story has inspired John, Katelin, and me to be even more vigilant in looking after Katelin's health. It has truly touched our hearts."

Suddenly, a graceful older lady approached their table, wrapping her arms around Kate. It was the wife of the owner and she said, "You know our story so well."

"The work you're doing with The Medical Project will help alleviate the pain we endure every day. I can understand why the President and people around the world love you so much. Thank you for dining with us on your special occasions. It means a lot to see you here," the older lady said, expressing her gratitude to the couple.

At that moment, tears welled up in the eyes of everyone at the table. John met the lady's gaze directly and said with a somber tone, "Thank you for sharing your story with us. It's a precious gift we will never forget."

They had a delightful meal and interesting conversations, just as they always did at Deanne's Place. When it came time to settle the bill, they left a tip twice the size of the total amount. Witnessing the challenges faced by Deanne's parents, they realized that they, too, could have experienced similar hardships with Katelin and even themselves.

As John and Kate rose to leave for the limo, they embraced Katelin tightly, reluctant to let go. However, Katelin gave them a look that conveyed that it was time to move on. Hand in hand, John and Kate made their way to the waiting limo, with Katelin following closely behind.

Unexpectedly, a person approached John and started to ask a question, but the two security guards quickly intervened and removed him from the area. Upon searching him after the limo had departed, they discovered a gun in his pocket. It reminded them of the tragic fate of John Lennon, who had been killed at a young age under similar circumstances. Later, they recounted the incident to John, Kate, and Katelin, warning them of the need for increased caution.

John Lennon's unfortunate incident made them realize that they couldn't engage in conversations with just anyone who approached them. They understood that, until their popularity subsided, security measures would be necessary. That night, they contacted Jim, expressing their gratitude for the additional security and for saving their lives. Jim assured them that they were exceptional individuals who deserved protection.

During their conversation with Jim, John and Kate noticed that Katelin and the doctor were engaged in a serious discussion outside, culminating in a goodnight kiss. Observing this, John and Kate purposefully averted their gaze, feigning obliviousness. However, Katelin, aware of their intentions, approached them from behind and, with a mischievous smile, asked, "Do you like this guy? Should I consider dating him?"

John and Kate exchanged knowing glances, and John gestured towards Kate, indicating that she should respond. Having been together since high school and college days, they had a deep understanding of each other. With a serious tone, Kate replied, "We highly value your judgment in all matters, and we trust that you will make the right decision regarding people. We will support whatever you choose."

Katelin sighed and expressed her concerns: "Well, that doesn't help much. The thing that worries me the most is that we're both incredibly busy people, and finding time to be together will be challenging."

John, although he typically didn't involve himself in Katelin's dating life, felt compelled to offer some advice. Speaking with a serious tone, he said, "You know, Mom and Dad weren't always working on the same projects. When we first met, she had her own commitments, and I had mine. But we were so deeply in love that we figured it out. If he's the right guy, both of you will find a way to make it work. It might require some compromises from both sides."

Katelin smiled warmly, appreciating her parents' support and the confidence they had in her judgment. After enduring the trauma of being shot and now undergoing recovery, this day held great significance for her. She bid her parents goodnight and headed to bed, joined by John and Kate.

Aware that tomorrow would be an ordinary day, John and Kate decided to have breakfast at home with Katelin around 8 a.m. John set his alarm for 6 a.m. to fit in a morning run.

Scheduling Meetings on All Projects

John and Kate both woke up when the alarm went off at 6 a.m. Kate informed John that she would join him for their morning run, so he informed the security team that both of them would be running on the street today. They quickly got dressed in their running attire, and Kate took a quick peek into Katelin's room to ensure she was alright.

Katelin was awake and informed her mom that she would take care of breakfast and have it ready by 7:30 a.m. She got up at around 6:45 a.m. and started preparing coffee, bacon, eggs, and toast.

After John and Kate finished their run, they showered and dressed for work, then headed down for breakfast. Katelin invited the security guards to join them, so she was busy cooking for everyone. John always found it amusing that when he invited the guards in, they rarely accepted, even for just a cup of coffee. However, when Katelin invited them, they all came in for breakfast.

Observing this, both Kate and John were thinking the same thing. Katelin was going to ask if she could go back to work. Anticipating the question, Kate spoke to Katelin with a serious tone: "Do I need to call the doctor, or can you handle it? We need to obtain clearance from him stating that you're ready to return to work. You should also contact your workplace to inquire about the return procedure and

265

when they can accommodate your return."

Katelin and Kate were always on the same page, which is why they rarely argued. John cherished their interactions, whether it was an argument or a conversation. Seeing them together brought him joy. Since Katelin's birth, Kate knew she had gained a friend, a shopping buddy, and a daughter.

After everyone finished breakfast, the security team, John, and Kate proceeded to the limo. The limo followed a security car that led the way to the West Wing. Three security guards remained with Katelin, guarding the house.

Kate and John immediately met with Valerie to arrange meetings with the Project Leaders. They needed to discuss ongoing projects that were in a maintenance phase and those that were just beginning, such as the Space Project. The projects in maintenance required monthly meetings unless an emergency arose, while the Space Project necessitated meetings with John and Kate once or twice a week.

Valerie managed to schedule everything accordingly, and the Space Project meeting was set to take place in two hours. During the press conference, they received an update on the Storm Project, which was effectively tracking and neutralizing two storms. They also learned that the Medical Project had been deployed worldwide and was widely utilized. The manufacturing issues with the Climate Project devices had been resolved, and they were even considering adapting the device for use on the space station to produce clean oxygen.

Now, John and Kate's primary focus shifted to the Space Project, as it had yet to undergo extensive testing outside the lab environment. China, Russia, and the U.S. had already started manufacturing their respective components for the space station. This meant that assembly would commence soon, culminating in the launch of the complete space station into outer space.

Critical decisions lay ahead, such as whether the space station would include astronauts, provisions, and a new propulsion system for space travel. Each country had to utilize the materials provided to construct their portion of the space station. Once completed, everything would need to be transported to the U.S. for final assembly before being launched from a specialized pad into space. Numerous decisions needed to be made, and comprehensive testing was imperative, demanding John and Kate's undivided attention. As a result, they would temporarily sideline the other projects unless any issues arose.

John and Kate intended to meet directly with each Project Leader and the individuals involved in the Space Program. People began to gather in the conference room, and Valerie arranged for representatives from China and Russia to join the Zoom call.

To commence the meeting, John inquired with the Leader of the U.S. Space Program about the completion and testing of the launch pad. The Leader confirmed that the launch pad had been constructed and successfully tested, rendering it ready for the delivery and assembly of the space stations.

Kate then posed similar questions to the other leaders, inquiring about the completion dates for their respective portions of the space station and the arrival of the two astronauts from each country who would be launching with the space station from the U.S.

All the leaders, including the representative from the U.S., confirmed that everything, including the astronauts, would be ready within a week. Kate concluded the call by stating, "This means that the leaders from Russia and China, the astronauts, and the space station should all be here within the next two weeks. We will have a similar call next week, and after that call and in two weeks, we will all gather in this conference room."

John then said, "Before we conclude this meeting, I think it would be beneficial to schedule another meeting for tomorrow. It should last approximately two hours, starting at 9 a.m. our time. This way, we can accommodate China's time zone and ensure that Russia can participate as well. During this meeting, I would like to discuss the testing progress and the status of the completed launch pad. As this involves a new antigravity system, we need to conduct comprehensive tests. While I am aware of the results from the lab simulation, I would like to see the planned testing and its outcomes."

Once the meeting concluded, John, Kate, and the leader of the Space Program engaged in further discussions. They aimed to ensure that they could discuss the testing process without divulging any sensitive information. After careful consideration, they reached the conclusion that it would indeed be feasible.

That night, as John and Kate returned home, they had concerns about the upcoming testing. However, upon arrival, work was momentarily forgotten as they shifted their focus to Katelin. She appeared to be in good spirits and even prepared dinner. She informed her parents that she planned to move out the following day and mentioned a nearby house she was considering purchasing. However, she expressed the possibility of needing assistance with the down payment. They collectively decided to visit the house over the weekend. Additionally, Kate and John planned to go for a run to the diner the next morning, with Katelin joining them in the limo.

The Fifty-Fifth Day

Security Problem and Meeting

J ohn and Kate always preferred to review how they wanted an important meeting to work out, so jogging to the diner was the only way John and Kate could get some exercise, eat breakfast, and discuss some key issues for the day. Early in the morning, the diner was generally empty, and the guards routinely checked for bugs to ensure no one was recording their conversations.

Katelin will be joining them, so they will have to discuss things at a high level. Still, they got up at the crack of dawn, roused Katelin up, and put on their running outfits. By 5:30 a.m., the three of them were out the door. Two guards stayed at the house, three ran with John and Kate, and two followed in the car with Katelin.

When they arrived at the diner's entrance, John and Kate observed that Katelin was breathing heavily from the short distance from the car. John said, "We were worried that this was going to be too much for you. You just had surgery and almost died a few days ago, and now you are waking up early to be with us."

Kate replied, "Leave her alone. I want her here, and the doctor said she was getting better."

Katelin just smiled because she knew they both loved her and said, "Don't worry about me. Next week I will be running to the diner with both of you."

Kate chuckled, and then they walked to their booth at the restaurant, inserted some money into the jukebox, and started listening to some

269

classic country. The waiter took Katelin's order. He already knew John and Kate's order, and they both started talking about the upcoming meeting. After they were done, Katelin said, "You guys are the smartest guys in the world. How did this happen?"

John smiled and shook his head, saying, "Listen, honey, when I was in high school, I would listen to the teacher talk about extra credit in order to raise my grades up to an A or B. My GPA in the class was a B because I gave my friend an A for no reason other than the fact that he built a little rocket. I did this in almost every class. The smart students did not have to do extra credit work because they got A's on their tests. I just had to work harder to improve my grades. Your mom always did well academically during college; everyone in her class wanted to study with her or copy her notes. Now, I don't know if part of that was because she was pretty, but she was exceptionally smart. In college, she got almost all A's. During high school, she had to balance employment and school, so she did not devote much time to studying."

Kate smiled and said, "So now, Katelin, you have our secret. We are not geniuses. We just work harder than others and surround ourselves with genius people and companies."

Katelin just laughed, and as she did, so did everyone around her. "That is why people like you both," she added.

Katelin added, "Despite your success and all these awards, you remain humble. Thanks for the teaching moment. The three of us need to be extra careful. I'm going to have some rest; I have to go to work. I'll see you when you get home, whenever that will be. It seems like you will have a busy day."

As they were all going out the door to the diner, the press got word they were there, so they were asking questions as they all left the diner. John, Kate, and Katelin all decided that they may have to cross the diner run off their list for a while. John and Kate had to ride in the limo with Katelin and a police escort because security was worried about the number of people surrounding them. One of the officers saw a person with a gun, so they arrested him.

When they got home, the police surrounded the house because someone had tried to break into it. A security guard was shot, and the person who tried to break in was killed. John and Kate talked to the police and security for a while but knew they had a worldwide conference call at nine, so they had to get ready quickly. Several security guards stayed at the house with Katelin, and John and Kate had a police escort to the West Wing. When they got there, it was about 8:15 a.m., so Jim wanted to see both of them in his office.

John and Kate went into Jim's office; he looked upset and told them to have a seat. Then, with a solemn tone, Jim said, "We need to change some things about your living arrangements. I did not want to do this because I know both of you like your freedom, but you have become more popular than the President and Vice President. Also, no actor in the movies, singer on stage, or even Company President has your popularity."

Jim added, "In the government, the President and Vice President are given a house to live in, and it is very secure. I am talking to some leaders in Congress and the Senate, and we may have to do something similar with both of you and Katelin. No decision has been made yet, but in the present environment, two security guards have been injured, and it is very important that we keep you safe and make it impossible for anyone to injure either of you or Katelin. Do you understand what I am saying and what needs to be done?"

John and Kate have never seen Jim so upset and concerned about anything like he is now, so trying to calm him down, Kate expressed, "Jim, we will do anything you say because we know you have our back all the time. Also, John and I would like to see the two security guards that got injured right after our 9 a.m. meeting, which is due to start in about fifteen minutes."

Jim just shook his head and said, "Let's meet after your 9 a.m. meeting is over."

John and Kate saw people gathering for the 9 a.m. meeting, and Valerie was connecting with the China and Russian Space Project

Leaders. From the expressions on the faces of the meeting participants, it appeared that this morning's events had already made headlines. The Russian and Chinese spoke up first, asking, "Are you both alright?"

Kate responded seriously, "We just discussed security for us, and I think whatever we do here in the U.S., your countries should consider doing the same thing."

The U.S. Leader expressed the sentiments of his country when he remarked, "We are just happy you are both safe."

"You already know the reason for this meeting. We want to know if the space launch platform to launch the space station is built and tested to send things into space and bring them back safely," John added.

"The Launch Platform is built, and we have launched since several things into space. We are still in the process of bringing them back, so we have some work to do," expressed the U.S. Leader with concern.

"There will be controls in the Space Station to aid in the takeoff and landing. Have you been able to operate those controls remotely? We need to thoroughly test everything before the astronauts go into space and come back," Kate explained.

"That implies something as large as the space station has to be transported to the moon and back to Earth. Therefore, we must launch an object that is as heavy as our space station and, once outside of Earth's atmosphere, will accelerate rapidly toward the moon. Half of it will orbit the moon, and I will have the latest propulsion technology onboard to make the trip even quicker. Half of the space station will remain in orbit around the Earth, while the other half will return to the launch site utilizing our new propulsion technology. When will all that be tested?" Kate asked.

"I plan to have all that tested this week and will let you know if something goes wrong, which would delay the launch of the space station," The U.S. Space Project Leader said with apprehension.

John then turned his attention to the U.S., Russia, and China, saying somberly, "This question is for China, Russia, and the U.S. Leaders. When will your portion of the Space Station be built, and when will the two astronauts be ready for space travel?"

On Monday, all of the leaders, together with the astronauts, will convene at the launch pad to begin assembling the space station. John and Kate were pleased with the responses, so he called the meeting to a close.

After the meeting, John and Kate went to Jim's office to give an update and discuss security. Two security guards were sitting in Jim's office, each with bandages around their shoulders. They both stood up when John and Kate walked into the room. John and Kate hugged and thanked them warmly, asking if there was anything else they could do. Both men humbly declined and then went on to detail what had transpired.

"We executed two men who were attempting to steal information on Medical, Storm, Climate, and Space Projects. We tried to explain that there was nothing of the sort in the house, and then they threatened to kidnap both of you. We warned them that it would end badly for them if they didn't give up. They fired shots in an attempt to escape, but ultimately decided to rather die than get arrested," one of the security guards said in detail.

It was at that point that Jim chimed in, saying, "This is only going to get worse. Unless people realize that capturing or killing either of you is physically impossible, protecting Katelin and the two of you will be next to impossible when you launch the Space Station. We need to keep you and Katelin safe. The only way to do that in Washington is to keep you in a secure facility, which is something only billionaires and business presidents have."

"All your security and support staff will live in the compound. The need for this level of protection for the other leaders is up to you to determine. So far, they haven't attracted nearly as much attention as you have, which means that most people probably don't know who they are," Jim added.

John and Kate looked apologetic. "We don't like to lose our freedom, but we both know this is the right thing to do. We understand that this is not a singular case like the Medical Research Project. People are approaching us from all directions. When do you want us to start using the new facility?" Kate continued.

"Thank you for doing this. Tomorrow, helpers will arrive to pack up your home in preparation for the relocation, but there is already enough in the complex for you and Katelin to move in tonight. What occurred this morning must not happen again tonight," Jim responded with a heavy heart.

After the meeting, John and Kate were driven to the compound, and Katelin was picked up at her home and brought there as well. It took them three or four hours to get used to the new house, but it seemed like a hotel with room service. The complex featured jogging trails, a restaurant, a fitness center, and a sauna. John, Kate, and Katelin all felt safer here than where they had been.

John had an early morning alarm set since he knew the daily Space Project meetings were important and would begin promptly at 9 a.m.

The Fifty-Sixth Day

Testing of Antigravity Devices

W hen John woke up, he decided to try and get Kate to go with him running, but she declined and said she would go tomorrow and he should scout out the running trails and gym. John got on all his running clothes, looked in to ensure Katelin was OK, and opened the door. A guard was there, but he said he would be safe within the compound but not go outside.

John took advantage of the facility's sauna. He began with a forty-minute run, during which he switched on the sauna at the gym, ran for another forty minutes, and finally completed his workout by doing some yoga. After a quick swim in the pool by the sauna, which some people call *"hot yoga,"* he ran back inside the house. The whole exercise routine took about 2.5 hours. John thought it was great since he could now eat almost anything without gaining too much weight.

He shared the exercise with Kate, but she said it was too strenuous and suggested cutting it down. She never liked to see John gone that long. The good thing about living in the compound is that it is closer to work and the West Wing. The luxuries of the compound included room service in the morning, so they ordered breakfast, ate it with Katelin, and then headed over to the West Wing.

When they arrived, the Space Project Leader was not present, but some of his managers were, and they had already set up the TV to broadcast the antigravity equipment's testing. The leader was there at the launch site. The Space Project Leader had an audio system ready

275

so he could give a rundown of events as they unfolded.

He started by telling everyone that everything was simulated in the lab and built to John and Kate's specifications. The launchpad was solid metal, so current could run through it, and it was one square mile. The saucer on it duplicated the weight of the space lab they would be sending into space. Additionally, it was circular and the size of a football field.

There was a countdown, and when the count got to zero, the big round saucer started slowly lifting off the launch pad. The crowd of about a thousand people and the press were amazed because they were used to hearing rockets and loud noises.

When the saucer got about a hundred feet off the ground, the Space Leader ordered the saucer's speed to be increased so that it could reach the moon as quickly as possible once it had left Earth's atmosphere. When they increased the saucer's speed, it took off precisely like witnesses claim to have seen flying saucers.

In a few seconds, it was out of sight to the human eye. It traveled through space at a speed that no rocket had ever before achieved. The saucer was on automatic pilot. In a few hours, its solar-powered propulsion system will slow it down so it can orbit the moon. After that, it will separate in half. One piece will continue to circle the moon, while the other piece will return to orbit the Earth.

John and Kate told the Space Project Leader to let them know when it reached the moon, and they would return to the conference room. Everyone throughout the globe was amazed as this unfolded on the news. John and Kate were happy that Jim was looking after them and had them move to the compound. John and Kate were happy to learn that Jim was looking after them and had relocated them to the compound.

John and Kate returned to the conference room a few hours later and saw the saucer circling the room before it split into two. One kept circling the moon, and the other, using the new propulsion system, was heading back to Earth.

John and Kate left the conference room again. A few hours later, they were summoned to the conference room, where John announced, "This is an important part of this test because we need to line up the saucer with the launch pad and bring it to a soft landing."

It all happened according to the simulation done days earlier on the computer. This was done live and with real equipment. There was a worldwide roar of applause when the saucer landed. John, the Space Project Leader, and Kate, his assistant, conferred for a few hours after it landed to discuss how they could improve future operations.

While they were talking, the President and Jim came into the conference room, and the President stated, "I am getting calls from other Presidents, Prime Ministers, and Kings from all over the world congratulating the U.S. and you guys."

With a broad smile on his face, Jim stated, "The Senate and Congress are delighted right now."

Everybody shook hands and hugged. You could hear everyone in the West Wing let out a cheer when the saucer landed. Kate said with a smile, "We may do this test one more time before we send the China, Russia, and U.S. astronauts up with the new space station."

The President stated, "I will be calling a press conference for 9 a.m. tomorrow because the press and people around the world want to learn more details on what they witnessed. I believe we need to stress the partnership with Russia and China. It may be good to have them at the press conference via video. Let your Space Project Leaders know about it, and I will call the Presidents and brief them on our plans."

John and Kate thought that was enough for one day, so they made plans with Katelin to celebrate at Deanne's Place. They told security, and they said it would be fine, so they met Katelin for dinner at Deanne's Place.

Katelin was at the table when they arrived. When they walked in, Katelin smiled and said, "Well, now I know why they put us in the compound. I like the compound, but what was on TV was unbelievable. That thing going up into space without any rockets and coming back from the moon was unbelievable."

She looked at her mother and said, "You are a great lady, and I am proud to be your daughter. You have done so much for women. I can see why all the professors and students liked you in college."

Then she looked at her dad and said, "You are a lucky guy! Mom is smart and beautiful."

John just smiled and said, "I say that to myself every day. She is just like you. I am a lucky guy because I have two of you."

Security people had tables all around John and Kate. They arrived before they showed up to ensure no one could get to their table without being stopped. The owner of Deanne's Place came over with his wife, hugged them, and said, "I know you won't let us pay for the meal, but we made something very special for you tonight when we knew you were coming: for Mr. Colombo, we know you like salmon and shrimp, so we have a special dish of that with a sauce; for Mrs. Colombo, we know you like vegetables, so we will have a big plate of different types of vegetables; for your daughter, we know she lived in Japan and liked miso soup and different types of vegetables and meat in the soup."

The three of them just smiled and shook their heads yes, and Kate said with a smile, "You know us well!"

When they all finished their meal, they skipped dessert. John and Kate then held hands as they walked out of Deanne's Place. Katelin was just walking behind them, and there were two guards in front of them and another two guards behind them. Everyone in the restaurant knew who they were, and you could see them talking and waving to them, showing their appreciation for all they had done for the world. John and Kate just nodded in gratitude to each person who said something or waved.

When the three of them got into the limo, John and Kate just looked at each other and started talking about when they could go places without being noticed. Katelin stopped them after about fifteen minutes and said with a smile, "It will never stop for both of you because you will never stop inventing things that help the world. Get used to it!"

When they all went to the house in the compound, John and Kate decided to run together tomorrow morning, while Katelin still needs to rest until the doctor informs her that she can return to work.

The Fifty-Seventh Day

Press Conference with Russia, China, and the United States

J ohn and Kate knew they had an important press conference at 9 a.m., so they woke up at 6 a.m. to get on their run and have breakfast with Katelin before going to work. Before they left for their run, they peeked in on Katelin, and she woke up and told them to have a good run and that she would have breakfast ready for them at 7:30 a.m. This would allow them to get to the West Wing well ahead of the press conference.

When they returned from their run, they noticed the young doctor was there making a home visit to ensure Katelin was healing well. They walked in the door, and both sat at the table, having coffee. The household staff was serving them.

Both Kate and John looked surprised, and John said, "Well, you guys know how to relax and order room service."

Both Katelin and the doctor just smiled, and Katelin said, "Hurry up and get dressed for work so you can sit down with us and have some breakfast."

John and Kate rushed to their room, showered, and dressed for the press conference. When they got to the breakfast table, the breakfast was all set up for them since Katelin knew what they always had for breakfast.

The doctor had left because he had surgery early in the morning. He merely stopped by to check on Katelin and let her know she could return to work on Monday if she wanted to. He even gave her a letter in case her superior needed one.

She was going to call work when they left to see if her job was being held for her or if she would be doing something new. When John and Kate left for the press conference, Katelin wished them well, and they wished her well on her call.

When John and Kate arrived at work, the President was in Jim's office, and they both pointed to the conference room. John and Kate headed straight there after stopping by their office to tidy up and get their materials for the press conference.

When they got to the conference room, the President said with a serious look on his face, "When I talked with both the Russians and Chinese, they both expressed their concerns about all the things that could go wrong, and also when things were talked about in the press, it was just a U.S. thing and not a partnership."

With a serious tone, Kate said, "The launch was in the U.S. and also the landing because we need to keep some things a secret, but we will mention again the partnership with them and how important this is to everyone in the world."

Jim smiled and said, "Let's give the leaders of Russia and China a chance to speak. The President will start the conference by talking about the seven astronauts and the size of the space station."

"We like the change in plan you had. You are going to leave six astronauts in space. There would be three circling the moon and three circling the earth. You could bring them home at any time, so that is safe, but that meant we could leave the astronauts from U.S., China, and Russia circling the moon while another set of astronauts from each these countries orbit the earth. Just one U.S. astronaut would be coming home after this trip."

John then said with a serious tone, "We discussed this with each of the leaders after the test launch, and we decided since we could bring them home at any time with the new propulsion system and the space station was so big, they had big hallways, enough food to last a lifetime, a gym, real toilets, and all the modern things a home would have; they all decided it would be good to stay there for at least a month or two."

After the discussion, they all went to the press conference. When the President entered the room, both TVs were turned on, and the Russian and Chinese presidents were on screen. The U.S. President stopped at the podium and said, "This is a great partnership we have here."

The U.S. President then introduced the other two presidents, a loud cheer was heard around the world. John and Kate both got up and presented the details of the mission. The leaders of the U.S., China, and Russia each described their parts in the mission. There were multiple rounds of applause during their speeches.

Everyone could see how amazing the mission was and how many new inventions went into making it happen. On top of that, there was a closeness between nations that no one had ever seen. It was the best press conference they had ever had anywhere in the world.

When Kate and John left to go home, they contacted Katelin and said, "Guess where we are going to eat tonight?"

Katelin said with a happy tone, "I have something to celebrate too. I will meet you at Deanne's Place in one hour."

Unwinding and Yet Another Weekend Interrupted

J ohn had incorporated additional exercises into his routine since they moved to the compound, taking advantage of the safe running area, gym with a sauna, and pool. His exercise regimen now spanned 2.5 hours, including running, hot yoga, and swimming. This Saturday morning, Kate and Katelin went for their first walk around the compound since Katelin's recovery from the gunshot wound.

By 11 a.m., they were ready to head to the mall for breakfast. Security felt a bit nervous, but they believed everything would be safe. Shopping was a shared love for Kate and Katelin, while John preferred going to the movies. Eating together was always a delight, which is why they engaged in rigorous exercise routines.

Upon their arrival at the restaurant, the security team had already secured the area, ensuring that nobody could approach them without being intercepted. As the restaurant attracted visitors from various places, some people waved at them upon their entrance, although most individuals remained oblivious to their presence.

Everything went smoothly, and they enjoyed a delightful brunch before heading out to do some shopping. Unfortunately, there were not many appealing movies playing, and Kate expressed her reluctance to spend two hours sitting in a theater. Thus, John was outvoted, and he decided to visit a bookstore while the girls continued shopping.

While John was perusing the bookstore, he received a call from Jim. Informed of John's location, Jim suggested they talk face-to-face, as the matter he needed to discuss was of important.

Jim arrived quickly, just as John was exiting the mall. With the limo's lights and sirens on, Jim pulled up beside him, rolled down the window, and suggested they converse in the car for privacy. John instructed his security detail to inform Kate of his whereabouts.

With a serious tone, Jim smiled and began, "The President received a call from the Prime Minister of Japan regarding your work on the Earthquake Project. They have a team working on a similar initiative and have expressed an interest in partnering with you and Kate. While the President does not consider it an emergency, he is slightly concerned about our allies seeing us collaborate with China and Russia while wondering about their own involvement."

John chuckled and responded jokingly, "Are there no secrets left? It seems that whenever we embark on a project, someone on the other side of the world is doing the same thing. I suppose they say great minds think alike, even in different places."

He continued, "Anyway, Kate and I discussed this as part of our next set of projects. We wanted to wait a little longer until we had done more work, but we both agree that partnering with Japan on this one is a good idea. They construct their buildings on big springs, so when an earthquake hits, the buildings sway from side to side without cracking or collapsing."

Just as they were about to conclude their discussion, Kate approached the limo and knocked on the window. They briefed her, and Kate said, "Tell the President that John and I will be on a plane to Tokyo on Sunday, and we'll meet with them on Tuesday morning. I'll get in touch with Natalie to arrange the plane tickets and have the U.S. Embassy car pick us up Monday afternoon. We'll also need tickets for the company working with us on this project, the Project Leader, and Jane Meadows, who has been assisting us with security."

Jim responded, "Kate, let me handle all the security and logistics for this trip. I'll provide the plane, and you can invite whoever you think is appropriate. I don't believe it's safe for you to fly on a commercial airline at this time."

After approximately half an hour, John, Kate, and Katelin were on their way to the compound when John received a call on his cell phone. It was Jim. With a confident voice, Jim informed John, "You will be flying on Air Force One for this trip. The President has decided to join you and your team. You'll be staying at the Prince's Palace, which is reputedly very secure, and all the meetings can be held there. The U.S. Ambassador would like to take you and Kate out one night, and his car and security will be available to you and the President."

Kate said, "You did well, Jim. I already feel safe. I'll provide you with the list of the people from the company working on this project: the Earthquake Project Leader and his staff, and Natalie."

As soon as she hung up with Jim, she called Natalie and instructed her to compile the list, while John called the Earthquake Project Leader to ensure that his staff was ready for the trip, which would likely last one week. John also contacted Bill Collins, who was in charge of their security, and asked him to coordinate with the President's security for this trip.

This was one of the reasons everyone loved working for Kate and John. They knew that whatever they were working on would change the world, receive significant visibility, and allow them to visit remarkable places and meet influential people. This trip had the potential to be a game-changer, as predicting earthquakes had never been accomplished before. With the computing power available today, John and Kate believed it was possible, and the trip to Tokyo, Japan, could be the first step towards making it a reality.

Accurate earthquake predictions could save billions of dollars, but false alarms could also result in significant costs. To develop nowcasting models, they turned to machine learning techniques, leveraging vast amounts of data, including seismology readings and surface deformation information.

Once the trip planning was completed and they were pulling into the compound, John called Jim and said, "As you recall from the climate devices, we had to map the Earth, and we're utilizing some of that information. We're also mapping what lies beneath the surface. Japan has done an excellent job of constructing buildings that can withstand earthquakes, but being able to predict earthquakes could benefit other countries that are not as advanced as Japan. I suggest you reach out to the leaders in Congress and the Senate to brief them on the upcoming project, ensuring that they are not caught off guard and have given their approval for the Earthquake Project. I will personally brief the President on the plane."

John and Kate were aware that the next day would involve a long plane ride, so they wanted to fit in a good exercise session in the morning. They set their alarm for 6 a.m. Katelin expressed her wish to join them, and both Kate and John wanted her to come along as well. However, considering that she had just returned to work in her new job, they assured her that they would call her every day and planned to have breakfast together around 8 a.m.

The Fifty-Ninth Day

Travel to Tokyo on Air Force One

J ohn woke up promptly as the alarm went off, and Kate said, "I'm not going to do your 2.5-hour routine. I'll just run for about an hour, so I'll meet you back here at 8 a.m. with a coffee."

John wished he didn't eat so much on days like this. He began his exercise routine with an hour-long run, followed by turning on the sauna, another hour of running, Yoga in the sauna, a short swim, and then a run back home.

Kate was already home, sitting with Katelin and enjoying their coffee. They had a cup ready for John when he showered and got dressed. As soon as he was ready, he joined his two favorite ladies for a cup of coffee. They were all excited—John and Kate had a new project to work on, and Katelin had a new job with new colleagues.

This would be John and Kate's first time traveling on Air Force One, adding to their excitement. Even their security detail was thrilled, as it was their first time traveling on the prestigious aircraft as well.

Upon reaching the airport, they saw the President boarding the plane. They caught up to him just as he was getting on. The President said, "When we take off, let's plan to meet in my conference room so you can bring me up to speed on the Earthquake Project."

Kate responded eagerly, "John and I have been focused on this issue since our time in Tokyo. We'll be joined by the Earthquake Project Leader and the President of the company that has been working on the software modeling."

After the plane took off, everyone gathered in the conference room. John stood up and began, "With our powerful computers, we've utilized vast amounts of data, including seismology readings and information on Earth's surface deformation. Using this data, we have successfully predicted the occurrence and location of earthquakes."

He continued, "Earthquakes account for nearly half of all deaths from natural disasters in recent decades. Failure to provide warnings about strong quakes is costly in terms of lives lost and the expenses incurred in post-earthquake repairs. False warnings can also be costly due to unnecessary emergency responses."

John expressed his curiosity: "It will be interesting to see how the Japanese software system compares with ours. If they are similar, then we know we have a reliable system. If they differ, we'll need to determine the best software for accurate earthquake prediction. Valerie has arranged a meeting with the Japanese team on Tuesday morning."

The President responded, "I have other meetings scheduled with the Prime Minister and others, but I'll try to join your meeting toward the end."

During the remainder of the trip, most of the people rested and prepared their presentations for their Japanese counterparts.

Travel to the Prince's Palace and Dinner

T he plane landed in the afternoon, and a limo was ready to transport everyone to the Prince's Palace. The journey from Narita Airport to the palace took about an hour. Upon arrival, John informed the security team that he intended to run to the Emperor's Palace and then to Ginza for some shopping. Kate preferred to relax, so John embarked on a five-mile run accompanied by four security guards. Tokyo is generally a safe city, so they didn't anticipate any problems.

When John returned, everyone was ready for dinner. They debated whether to visit one of the department stores in Ginza, as many of them had several restaurants in their basements. Alternatively, there were several upscale hotels with excellent dining establishments.

Kate suggested going to the Capitol Hotel Tokyu and dining at one of their restaurants. She had always wanted to try the coffee diablo at their main restaurant, so they made reservations. The dinner was exceptional, as expected from that restaurant. However, the coffee diablo didn't live up to their expectations. Nevertheless, the showmanship involved in preparing the coffee was outstanding. The coffee was poured from one pot to another, and as it was poured into the cup, it was lit on fire. The captivating performance lasted approximately thirty minutes. It was a unique experience that would undoubtedly be a topic of conversation upon their return home, as the coffee diablo is an unparalleled spectacle.

After dinner, they were taken on a short sightseeing tour around Tokyo. The city was breathtaking, especially when illuminated at night. The driver took them to Shinjuku, where numerous nightclubs were bustling. They didn't stop at any of them, but it was intriguing to witness the vibrant nightlife. Following the sightseeing tour, the limo returned to the Prince's Palace.

John and Kate had never stayed at the Prince's before, but it was an esteemed honor to do so, given that many princes, kings, presidents, and prime ministers had occupied the same rooms. They had an early start the next day for their meeting with the Japanese Earthquake Leader, scheduled for 9 a.m. John, Kate, and their accompanying team wanted to retire early to ensure they had enough time for exercise and to be prepared for the morning meeting.

Before going to sleep, they decided to give Katelin a call, as she would probably be waking up. They managed to reach their daughter, and Katelin asked, "Did you see where we stayed and ate most of the time when we were there?"

Kate replied, "We're planning to run there tomorrow. We did have a fantastic meal at the hotel where we stayed during our visit. Tomorrow, the work begins. How are you feeling?"

Katelin was in a hurry and said, "I took a walk around the compound and went to the gym. I'm regaining some strength after my surgery. Someone tried to break into the compound, but the guards caught him. We'll hold him for Jane."

John, with a serious tone, said, "Be careful; you're our only daughter. Have fun in your new job."

After ending the call, Kate contacted Jane with a very serious tone, saying, "Jane, we need you to make an example of the person who attempted to break into the compound. People need to understand that they will face lengthy prison sentences if they try to cause harm to a government employee or their children."

Following that call, John and Kate settled into bed, turning on the television to catch up on the news. Most of the coverage revolved around the President's presence in Japan and their own presence accompanying him.

Leaders Discussing the Earthquake Project

J ohn and Kate woke up around 6 a.m., eager to take a run through their old neighborhood before the 9 a.m. meeting. In the past, John used to run around the Prince's and Emperor's Palaces every day with a coworker who had graduated from Annapolis. Although John's running abilities had slightly declined over the years, he still enjoyed the challenge of running with Kate and their four security guards at a slower pace and shorter distance.

Despite the passing years, everything remained the same—the familiar neighbor, the unchanged buildings, and the quiet streets that would soon be bustling with people.

The run flew by, and John and Kate quickly prepared for their meeting. At 8:45 a.m., they were out the door trying to find the conference room. As they walked down the hall, they noticed a gathering of people in a large room. When they arrived, the doors opened, and everyone filed in, finding their seats.

John initiated the meeting by pointing out the presence of the American attendees, saying, "I notice that everyone from the U.S. is here. We have the U.S. leader, one of his team members, the president of a company supporting our project, and one of their representatives. Of course, you already know Kate and me."

The Japanese Earthquake Project Leader then introduced himself and his team of five members. He looked towards John, signaling for him to begin the discussion.

John recognized that it was his responsibility to initiate the discussion. Adopting a serious tone, he spoke, "Kate, our team, and I have taken the work we conducted on the Climate Project, which involved mapping the Earth's surface for hotspots, and expanded it to explore the depths below the surface. We have developed sophisticated mathematical models based on the movements of known tectonic plates and utilized extensive data, such as seismology readings and surface deformation, to predict earthquakes. It would be valuable to compare our models with yours to determine if they align. If they differ, we can collaborate to refine and develop the best software."

Everyone agreed with John's proposal, and they proceeded to run multiple tests with their respective software to evaluate the consistency of the results. After several hours of testing, they glanced at the clock and realized it was already midnight—an expected occurrence when analyzing and debugging software. John suggested, "Why don't we pause here? We have made significant progress, and we should be able to conclude our analysis tomorrow. Let's reconvene at 9 a.m."

As it was too late to go out the U.S. team decided to order room service. John and Kate returned to their room and placed an order, planning to wake up early the following day for another run through Tokyo. They informed the security team of their plans and went straight to bed.

Leaders Discuss the Earthquake Project

J ohn and Kate awoke around 6 a.m. and decided to take a run through their former neighborhood in Tokyo. Afterwards, they stopped for breakfast at a familiar spot, a local joint called Anna Millers, which they used to frequent during their time in the city. While the breakfast wasn't as extravagant as those found in hotels, it satisfied their simple cravings—two eggs, potatoes, toast, and coffee—for a mere $2.00. Anna Millers, an unusual chain throughout Tokyo, served as a nostalgic reminder of their past.

The morning air in Tokyo was always refreshingly cool, unlike the humid runs they endured elsewhere. It brought back memories of their routine: running to the diner, enjoying breakfast, and running back home. Unrecognized by the locals, John and Kate savored a quiet breakfast in the company of four security guards, relishing a rare moment of tranquility before their jog back to the hotel.

There was always something distinct about the taste of eggs in Tokyo, a topic that John and Kate couldn't help but discuss. They also noticed the prevalence of male participants in the meetings, a consistent trend they had observed during their previous stay. Despite Kate's superior knowledge on certain subjects, she willingly took a back seat in the discussions, recognizing the cultural dynamics of Tokyo. They adapted effortlessly to the customs of each country they worked in, unfazed by the need to adjust their roles. Today, however, marked an important day, and over breakfast, John and Kate planned the desired outcomes and prioritized the key issues they wanted to address.

Both the United States and Japan boasted intelligent Earthquake Project Leaders who shared a mutual desire for accurate results. John and Kate decided it would be prudent to let them lead the upcoming meeting. After breakfast, they rushed back to the hotel and arrived just as everyone else was filing into the room. John, as usual, initiated the meeting by asking the Earthquake Project Leaders from both countries about their preferred course of action after the extensive discussions held the previous day.

Both teams agreed that the United States had the most reliable data mapping of Earth, thanks to their involvement in the Climate Project. Therefore, they decided to utilize the American database for the software. However, when it came to the software's functionality and drawing conclusions, Japan's approach appeared to be more favorable. The programmers in the meeting collaborated and successfully developed an excellent earthquake prediction tool.

As the meeting drew to a close, the President of the United States and the Prime Minister of Japan entered the room. The attendees stood up and turned to John, awaiting his update. It amazed John and Kate how their past endeavors, including the Medical Project, Storm Project, Climate Project, and now the Earthquake Project, had instilled trust and respect in people from all corners of the world. Regardless of their location, John and Kate were regarded as capable leaders.

John expressed his appreciation for the collaborative efforts of both the teams in the U.S. and Japan in creating an outstanding Earthquake Prediction tool. He then turned his attention to the President and the Prime Minister, asserting, "We believe we possess the most exceptional software and data mapping system for predicting earthquakes. However, before making a formal announcement, we need to conduct extensive testing. Earthquakes account for nearly half of all deaths caused by natural disasters. While the instinct may be to warn people in advance, we must exercise caution. If our calculations are slightly off and the earthquake doesn't occur when predicted, it could result in unnecessary emergency costs and, worse, a loss of credibility for future warnings."

John suggested their recommendation moving forward: running their prediction tool to identify the next two or three earthquakes and sending teams for evacuation purposes. However, they should not publicize it at this point, as modifications to the software were necessary to improve accuracy. Once these modifications were made and three more earthquakes were correctly predicted, they would make a comprehensive announcement about their partnership and achievements. Until then, if the press or anyone else inquired about their activities, they were to be informed that they were working on a joint project and conducting further testing before making any formal announcements.

The President and Prime Minister were pondering the same issue when the Prime Minister spoke up, saying, "What if you predict an earthquake somewhere in the world but choose not to inform the people, resulting in 10,000 deaths and millions of dollars lost?"

The leader of Japan chimed in, having asked the question himself and knowing that Kate and John would agree with him, given their previous discussions. He politely responded, "That is an excellent question, and we have deliberated on it. We would ensure that we dispatch a significant number of personnel to the locations of the next two predicted earthquakes to do everything necessary to prevent casualties and mitigate damages. As we anticipate two forthcoming earthquakes, we must prepare our teams, and either you or the President need to contact the leaders of those countries to warn them about the upcoming earthquakes. Additionally, we should inform them that this is still a testing phase, so we should aim to limit the press coverage as much as possible."

Both the President and the Prime Minister agreed with this approach, prompting the President to ask in a serious tone, "So, where will these next earthquakes occur?"

John's voice carried a somber tone as he responded, "We predict that within the next month, there will be five earthquakes: California, China, Indonesia, Iran, and Turkey. We have precise information regarding the exact locations, dates, times, and potential magnitudes. Our team needs permission to enter these countries to adjust our software model and improve its accuracy. We also need teams to assist in possible evacuation efforts."

The revelation astounded both the President and the Prime Minister. The Prime Minister remarked, "You have done an exceptional job. What you have accomplished will save millions of lives and billions of dollars. When we publicize this, people around the world will be as amazed as the President and I are. I hope we can make the announcement next month, so we can avoid the additional burden of secrecy."

The President then instructed John and Kate, "I want both of you to collaborate with your respective U.S. and Japan Earthquake Leaders to devise a strategy for the announcement. Additionally, we need a plan for supplying early warnings of earthquakes and determining which earthquakes we should alert the public about. The Prime Minister will contact the Presidents of the countries involved and inform you of their preferences. He will also inquire about securing permission for your entry into their countries."

Reflecting on recent events, the President mentioned an incident where he observed a painting moving on his wall and then noticed that all the paintings had shifted in some way. Although he was unsure if it warranted an alarm, he emphasized the need to establish ground rules for warning people.

Everyone in the room looked at the President and agreed with his remarks, committing to provide a comprehensive update in one month after completing thorough testing. As the President and the Prime Minister exited the room, the President leaned over to John and asked if he and Kate would be ready to depart later that day, receiving an affirmative response from both of them.

John asked everyone to remain seated after the President and the Prime Minister left, saying, "The U.S. team will be heading back today, but I want the Earthquake Leaders and their teams to meet on a daily basis. Make any necessary modifications to the software to enhance its accuracy. Kate and I would like you to arrange a weekly call with us for the next couple of months, where we can discuss problems and find solutions. This project has become one of the most important endeavors for both our countries."

Addressing the Earthquake Team Leaders, John requested that they provide information on who would be sent to the five countries and the software changes being made to improve accuracy. After a lively discussion among the attendees, John expressed his admiration for everyone's contributions, concluding the meeting. As people filed out of the room, they were aware that they were part of something that would save lives and change the world. They were ready to put in any amount of work necessary to bring it to fruition.

Just like all of John and Kate's projects, the teams were invigorated and delighted to work with two of the brightest minds in the world. It was yet another successful trip for John and Kate.

Limos were waiting to transport everyone to Air Force One. The President invited John and Kate to ride with him to the airport. Overwhelmed with pride, the President turned to them in the limo, a tear in his eye, and said, "Both of you make us Americans proud to be Americans. Every time I hear about and witness the results of one of your projects, you amaze me. I can tell people enjoy working with you because I receive constant requests to be part of your projects. As I observed the people in that room while you described the project, all I could think was, 'Wow, this is something extraordinary.' People from different parts of the world are working together to make it happen. I can sense that the Prime Minister feels the same way. Our leaders in Congress, the Senate, China, Russia, and the rest of the world share this sentiment."

The President continued to express his admiration, particularly addressing Kate. He acknowledged her expertise and leadership in the climate project and earth mapping, praising both her and John for their ability to discern the appropriate leaders for discussions based on cultural dynamics. He marveled at their capacity to understand who should lead each conversation, concluding with another resounding "Wow!"

With smiles and tears of joy, everyone in the car, including John, Kate, the driver, and some of the security personnel, relished the uplifting atmosphere. Even the President, who had experienced moments of pressure and distress, couldn't help but feel good when he was around them. Their presence had an extraordinary effect.

John and Kate silently acknowledged that it was the most extraordinary limo ride they had ever experienced. As they boarded the plane, they asked the team to gather in the conference room after takeoff. There, John and Kate expressed their heartfelt appreciation for the team's hard work, mentioning how proud the President and the Prime Minister were of their achievements. They also reminded the team of their assignments and the work that needed to be accomplished. Kate concluded the meeting, stating, "Now the real work begins. We must make all of this happen, and we have only one month to test and optimize everything, ensuring our earthquake predictions are accurate."

Everyone rested, with Kate and John instructing the team not to return until Thursday. They advised them to take a day to adjust their bodies to the U.S. time zone and rejuvenate.

Rest Day, Dinner with Katelin, and the Unexpected Guests

John and Kate woke up several times throughout the night, struggling to adjust their sleep habits back to normal. Sometimes their bodies still thought they were in Japan, and it usually took a day to regain synchronization. That's why they decided to give everyone the day off.

With little sleep, John and Kate decided to go for their morning run around the compound when they woke up at 7 a.m. Katelin, already in the kitchen, was having her usual low-carb breakfast of coffee, eggs, and bacon. Though Katelin wasn't overweight, she always had to watch her figure.

While Kate engaged in a conversation with Katelin, John stayed in the bedroom, getting dressed for the run. Kate tried to convince Katelin to take the day off and spend time together, something they had done since Katelin was in first grade. Sometimes Katelin would give in, but most of the time, she valued her education too much to skip school.

This time, Katelin told her mother that she had to go to work, but she would try to leave early. John admired the unique relationship between Kate and Katelin. It seemed like they were friends who enjoyed the same things and had a parent-child bond.

John believed that the mother-daughter relationship was something he could never fully comprehend, attributing it to the dynamics of their connection. He would often say, *"That's just the way it is between mothers and daughters, and it's beautiful to see."*

John appreciated the happiness it brought Kate to have Katelin around. When Katelin's picture appeared on magazine covers and billboards in Tokyo, John felt immense pride as her father. He would jokingly say, *"Now I know how a famous model's dad feels."*

Kate had always believed that something like that would happen for Katelin because she recognized her daughter's beauty. The same intuition extended to her work as well. Kate knew that Katelin would continue to thrive in her career because of her interpersonal skills and ability to make things happen. People from headquarters were now coming down to observe Katelin's work and determine if her success could be replicated throughout the company. Her stores were outperforming all others in the United States.

As John listened to the conversation in the kitchen while getting dressed for the run, he decided to join in, breaking his habit of quietly listening. He entered the kitchen, looked at Katelin with a tear in his eye, and said, "Katelin, my lovely daughter, you have a relationship with your parents that your mother and I never had with ours. Since the day you were born until now, we have always cherished having you around. Even when we go on vacation, you want to come with us, and we want you there. That's special! I suppose we can blame ourselves for instilling the work ethic you have, which always leads you to excel."

John's expression became serious as he continued, "Now I'm concerned that they keep piling more work and responsibilities on you. You need to find a way to either treat work as a game, so you can enjoy it and it doesn't feel like work, or take some time off with your mom to have fun."

He emphasized the importance of managing stress and work. If Katelin found joy in her work, that was great, but if it caused her significant pain, they needed to make changes. John assured her that he and Kate were looking out for her, just as she had looked out for him when she noticed how down he was during Kate's absence in Tokyo.

He appreciated how she encouraged them to go out for dinner together during that difficult time.

John concluded, "I want you to be very cautious about stress and work. If treating it as a game works for you, then that's wonderful. But if it becomes too much, we need to change something. Mom and Dad are here for you, and you need to recognize for yourself when it stops being fun."

Both Kate and Katelin had tears in their eyes. Katelin responded, "Wow, Daddy, I love you both, and I know you love me. I will be very careful. Today is an exciting day for me because people from headquarters are coming down. I need to be there, but I promise I will meet you both for dinner at Deanne's Place. I'll let you know the time once I'm at work. You guys are amazing, and enjoy your day off."

John looked at Kate and said, "Well, we'll have to wait until dinner to be with Katelin. It's just you and me, my love. How about breakfast and a 2.5-hour exercise?"

Kate smiled back at John, her eyes still tearing up from his heartfelt words. She replied, "That's exactly what I want. Just you and me. Let's do this exercise so we can enjoy tonight's celebration."

As John and Kate stepped out the door of the house, they were greeted by four security guards, one of whom was Bill Collins. John recognized Bill from previous occasions and greeted him, "Bill, it's good to see you again. Why so much security when we're in the compound?"

Bill quickly responded, "Since that intruder incident the other day, we've been concerned. Jane will take care of him, and he'll be going to prison for a long time. You'll hear about it soon. But until then, we've doubled the security to ensure nothing like that happens again. Two guards will accompany you on your exercise, while two others will remain at the house. We've also received your message about tonight at Deanne's Place with Katelin. We'll have extra security there as well. The President and his wife asked if they could join you. Their daughter is still in college, so it will only be the two of them."

Kate and John exchanged smiles as they began their run. Kate commented, "It would be an honor for Katelin, you, and me to have dinner with them. Once Katelin gives us her work schedule, we'll inform the President about the additional guests."

After their run, John and Kate usually spent time sitting in chairs in their yard, enjoying the scenery. They liked to be close to each other and talk about everything. Having known each other since high school and college, they always had something to discuss, and their love for each other was strong.

Sitting in the yard while holding hands and talking, Kate's phone suddenly rang. Seeing that it was Katelin calling, Kate answered, "How's my beautiful girl? Your dad and I just finished our exercise, and we were sitting in a couple of chairs, relaxing. We have a couple of guests who will be joining us for dinner. Did you find out when you can leave work and meet us at Deanne's Place?"

Katelin replied with a hint of concern in her voice, "Well, I was surprised to find out that the people who came down to observe our business were the President of our company and some members of the board. So the day has been a bit hectic, but everything went well. They asked me to join them for dinner tonight since they'd be staying overnight. I told them I'd love to, but I already promised to have dinner with my mom and dad, and I said they were welcome to join us. There will be about three of them, so it'll be a total of six at the table. Is that okay?"

John and Kate smiled and almost laughed at the situation. John said, "Actually, there will be eight of us because the President and his wife will also be joining us at Deanne's Place. We agreed to their request. We were just about to call them back once we knew your work schedule. If your bosses are comfortable meeting with the President of the United States and his wife, then we'll proceed, but we'll need to go through a security check."

Katelin smiled and said, "When did we become so popular? I guess we should check with the President and his wife before making any final decisions."

After hanging up the phone, John and Kate called Bill, the head of security, and informed him about the situation. Bill assured them that the President and his security team were on board with the dinner plans. John and Kate were accustomed to celebrating their achievements with just the two of them and Katelin, so having additional guests made it more exciting yet different. They were the first to arrive at Deanne's Place, and the increased security presence indicated the imminent arrival of the President.

The owner of the restaurant greeted them warmly and led them to a round table that could accommodate eight people. With the President's security already in place for a couple of hours, it seemed evident that the President was indeed coming. John and Kate took their seats and ordered drinks, engaging in conversation about the earthquake project and brainstorming ways to improve its accuracy. Soon, they spotted Katelin entering the restaurant with two men and a woman from her executive team. John and Kate stood up to greet them, sharing stories about the restaurant and their tradition of celebrating success there.

Then the President and his wife arrived, and everyone stood up to welcome them. After a brief exchange about the weather and jet lag from the trip to Japan, the President addressed the group with a serious tone, emphasizing the need for discretion. They were there to discuss some business matters with John, Kate, and Katelin, and they wanted to ensure that nothing about the dinner would be leaked to the press.

Everyone agreed, and the President of Katelin's company chimed in, "Everyone in my company understands these rules. We recently had to dismiss someone from our board because they leaked information to the press and our competitors while we were discussing new products and a change in direction for our company."

John, with a smile on his face, attempted to ease the tension. However, Katelin seemed uneasy, as she, like her parents, felt uncomfortable when people talked about her. She interjected, "We understand that you came down here to assess Katelin's performance. Kate and I knew she was special when we were having a conversation at our dinner table. She was making a list of pros and cons to make a decision about something happening in high school. We thought that was excellent. Then she said something we had never heard before, and we don't know where she got it from. She mentioned that creating the list of pros and cons was easy, but assigning weights to each item was the challenging part. Kate and I exchanged looks, trying to anticipate what she would say next. She stated that there could be one pro or con on the list that outweighed everything else. She has always possessed common sense that helps her come up with fantastic ideas, and I'm sure that's happening at work too."

Kate interrupted John with a smile and a slight chuckle, saying, "Don't ever ask her to tell a joke. When she was in grade school and junior high, we used to try to have dinner at a set time. One day, we decided to go around the table and tell jokes that we thought were funny. When it was Katelin's turn, she asked, 'How do you turn off a light switch?' John and I pondered it for a while but couldn't come up with the answer, so we gave up and asked her to enlighten us. With a big smile on her face, she replied, 'With a peanut butter and jelly sandwich.' Then she burst into laughter, and whenever Katelin laughs, it's contagious. But we realized we had to tell her it wasn't a good joke; otherwise, she'd keep telling it to people. We spent about twenty minutes trying to explain why it wasn't funny, while Katelin persisted in explaining why it was. She's always good at making her point, so we just agreed to disagree. It may not be a great joke, but I can tell you it's the one I remember the most."

John chimed in, "As you can tell, we love her dearly. One day, when we were in Tokyo—I don't know if she mentioned it to you—she was a model. She appeared on the front covers of magazines and on TV, and she even had her face on large subway advertisements. Well, she was sitting on the couch with one of her girlfriends, watching TV. Kate was back in the States, and I was home alone with her and our dog. Suddenly, the dog peed on the floor, and I didn't see it. I came home wearing my three-piece suit, slipped on the pee, went flying into the air, and landed flat on my back in the puddle. I was furious and on the verge of grounding her for life because she wasn't taking care of the dog. But as I sat there in the puddle, Katelin burst into laughter at the whole situation. And when she starts laughing, you can't stay mad at her. So, I started laughing too, but I'll never forget that moment. We have so many crazy memories. She truly is the love of our lives."

Katelin, still smiling, expressed her gratitude, saying, "Thank you both, and I love you! Is it time to order dinner?"

Laughter filled the room as everyone shared stories about their children. Everyone enjoyed the delightful dinner. As the President prepared to leave, he caught up with John and Kate, requesting that they schedule a meeting on his calendar the following day to discuss the Space and Earthquake Projects.

As soon as Kate and John got into the limo, they contacted Valerie and informed her about the President's request regarding the Space and Earthquake Projects. They wanted to meet with the project leads an hour before the President's meeting to receive an updated status and inquire whether the President wanted additional attendees. They also asked Valerie to check if Katelin could join them for dinner at Deanne's Place, just the three of them, at 7 p.m.

Upon their arrival at the compound, Valerie returned their call and confirmed that they were on Jim's, the President's, calendar at 11 a.m. for a meeting with only the two of them. They instructed Valerie to schedule the two project leaders for 9 a.m.

John and Kate went to bed, pondering the purpose of the President's meeting regarding the two projects. They set their alarm for 6 a.m., ensuring they would have enough time for their 2.5-hour exercise routine.

Meeting with the President

J ohn and Kate woke up at 6 a.m. when the alarm went off. They quickly changed into their running clothes and checked if Katelin was asleep. As they opened the door, Katelin spoke up, "I don't want to go running with you. I didn't get in until late, so I'll give you an update tonight at Deanne's Place. Everything is good, so don't worry. I don't have to be in until noon since the meeting we had went on until 4 a.m."

They completed their entire exercise routine, showered, got dressed, and were in the limo heading to work for their 9 a.m. meeting at 8:30 a.m. When they arrived, about ten people—five from each project— were waiting in the conference room.

Kate started the meeting with a serious tone: "Why do you think the President wants to meet with us regarding these two projects? You know John and I don't like surprises. We want a status update on both projects."

The Earthquake Project Leader stood up, a little embarrassed, and said, "I should have mentioned this earlier, but when we went to China to warn them about an upcoming earthquake, they expressed their desire to be contacted and made a partner, considering they experience numerous earthquakes."

John, wearing an upset expression, replied, "We partnered with Japan because they added value to the work we had already done. Do you know if China has anything to offer that would enhance our predictions? If they can add value, we can consider partnering with them as well."

The Earthquake Leader looked embarrassed and responded, "I'm not sure, John. I'll get back to them and explain the reasons for our partnership with Japan. If they believe they can contribute something valuable, we can consider partnering with them too. I'll let you know as soon as I have an answer."

Kate remained calm and said, "It might be too late for that since we have to meet with the President in a couple of hours. You should have approached us sooner with this request. Let's get your China Earthquake Leader on the phone now."

Valerie got the Earthquake China Leader on the phone, and John had a discussion with him. Based on their conversation, China agreed to manufacture all the equipment needed for the Earthquake Project. John, Kate, and the Earthquake Leader then agreed that China would be one of the partners alongside Japan and the U.S. when the announcement was made.

Kate then turned her attention to the U.S. Space Project Leader and asked, "Your turn! What issues do we have with the Space Project?"

The Space Project Leader looked embarrassed, kept their head down, and said, "I'm sorry. I should have approached you earlier with this problem, but I thought I could resolve it. The Russians would like to land on the moon before returning to Earth. I've been running computer models to see if we can make that happen. It seems feasible, and I was about to reach out to the Russians to develop a plan and present it to you."

Kate exchanged a glance with John, and they nodded in agreement. Kate, with a smile, responded, "I like the idea of putting an astronaut on the moon and returning them to the space station before coming home."

John then spoke up with a serious tone, "Team, we want you all to make decisions and take action without needing to check in with Kate and me constantly. Just send us a message or email outlining your plans. Please don't delay things to the point where one country's

President has to call another."

The meeting concluded, and John and Kate prepared to meet with the President and Jim. They proceeded to the Oval Office, where they sat opposite the President and Jim. The President initiated the conversation with a smile, stating, "My three favorite people. I've said it many times—you three are the best of the best. I wouldn't be receiving requests from other countries to collaborate if you guys weren't doing something remarkable. The Russians want to land on the moon while we're there, and the Chinese want to be partners in the Earthquake Project. Do you have answers to these questions, and what do you suggest I tell the Presidents of Russia and China?"

Jim and the President looked at John and Kate, waiting for a response. Kate spoke up and said, "We just spoke with the two project leaders, and we're assessing the feasibility of a moon landing during this mission. If it's safe and viable, we'll include it in the mission. Regarding the China partnership in the Earthquake Project, if they can provide all the required equipment as they've promised, they will be a partner alongside Japan and the U.S.A."

The President smiled and replied, "I'll inform the respective Presidents that our teams are working to address their requests. Let me know if anything might hinder these two developments."

The President then turned to Jim with a concerned expression and said, "I heard there was an attempt on your life, and we caught the person responsible. Is there anything we can do to prevent further attempts on your lives?"

John and Kate appeared surprised, and Jim saw their expressions. He grabbed their hands and said, "We were already in the process of prosecuting the person who broke into the compound when the attempt on my life occurred. Jane Meadows is working on changing federal laws so that any attempts made against individuals working for the federal government or their families will be severely punished. This has been a problem across all branches of government. Jane is scheduled to go on TV as soon as we pass some laws and prosecute the people we've caught.

Potential criminals will think twice before making another attempt."

The President appeared somewhat satisfied but spoke sternly, "Until all of that is done, I want security for all three of you increased. Additionally, consider the people who report to you. If they possess information that others may want, they could be potential targets for abduction. I'll be sending a letter today to the head of our security to enhance protection and meet with the three of you."

All three of them smiled and nodded in agreement. Jim then expressed his gratitude, saying, "Thank you, Mr. President. Right now, it seems that people or groups are attempting to steal what the U.S.A has invented. If your letter can extend security measures to companies and subcontractors working for the government, it would be beneficial, as we collaborate with several companies on all our projects."

The President, with some disappointment, replied, "Jim, you've done an excellent job with security, so I'll put you in charge of this matter. I expect companies to handle their own security, but if we hire subcontractors, I'll extend the same level of security to them. Keep in mind that my primary concern is for the safety of you three and your families. I'll leave it up to Congress and Jane to pass the necessary laws and ensure appropriate punishment for the criminals. We need to show them we mean business."

All three of them nodded in agreement, and Kate expressed her appreciation, saying, "Thank you, Mr. President. Jim has done an outstanding job of keeping John, Katelin, and me safe."

The meeting ended with everyone shaking hands. As John and Kate made their way back to their offices, Kate suggested that they arrange a meeting with Jane Meadows through Valerie. They all agreed, and Kate called Valerie to set it up for 4 p.m. in the conference room.

At 4 p.m., John, Kate, Jim, Jane, and Valerie convened in the conference room. Jane, a former prosecutor, possessed excellent speaking skills and took the lead, outlining her efforts regarding existing laws, recent attempts made over the past year, the resulting punishments, and plans for stricter penalties to ensure that offenders never leave federal prison. She also provided updates on pending matters, such as the attempt on Jim's life. After listening to her for about two hours, they all shared the same sentiment. Kate expressed it on behalf of Jim and John, saying, "I'm so happy that we put you in this position. The individuals who were caught will deeply regret ever attempting to kill us. Great job!"

Jim, in a stern voice, added, "If anyone obstructs your progress or hinders your efforts, let us know. We need to accomplish everything you're planning as soon as possible."

The meeting concluded with everyone shaking hands, and Jane expressed her appreciation for the opportunity she had been given. She could see the significant impact she was making, but she also knew that this job would eventually come to an end if she performed it well. What she didn't realize was that John and Kate already had her next role planned once she had successfully put all these criminals behind bars.

John and Kate were ready to head home but thought it would be a good idea to have dinner with Katelin and Jane at Deanne's Place. They always enjoyed introducing Katelin to accomplished, strong women who exemplified the kind of woman they wanted Katelin to see.

Unbeknownst to John and Kate, Katelin already looked up to Jane as someone she aspired to emulate. Jane possessed beauty, intelligence, and kindness—the best mother a daughter could ever want. If Katelin wanted to know what a good husband was like, she needed to look no further than her own dad, who was nice, caring, strong, and good-looking. However, John and Kate never saw themselves in such a light, which is why they continually introduced Katelin to strong women. Nevertheless, Katelin always understood what was happening and firmly believed that no one could surpass her parents. It was this belief that propelled Katelin to strive to never disappoint them. She knew exactly how they would handle any situation and aimed to do the same. She was the love of both their lives. When she was little, they never had to spank her, and as she grew older, she never required much discipline. She was the perfect friend and daughter to Kate, always ready to assist her dad whenever he needed help.

Everything was set up for dinner with Jane and Kate at Deanne's Place, scheduled for 7 p.m. John and Kate arrived first, ensuring that Jane and Katelin were seated together at a small, round table. Jane arrived next, followed by Katelin. Kate began by describing Jane's background as a lawyer and a District Attorney, as well as her new government position. Jane felt a bit embarrassed but was eager to learn more about Katelin. She asked, "What have you been up to lately? I'm aware of your triumph over cancer and the attempt on your life, but what are you doing at work?"

Katelin smiled and replied, "This is something my parents and I haven't discussed yet because it just happened. The other day, I thought I was being interviewed for a new position at our company, which was supposed to take about an hour. Little did I know, it would turn into a comprehensive review of everything happening in my area of the company. The meeting was with the board and CEO, and it started at 7 p.m. and went on until 4 a.m. in the morning. That's why I was still in bed when you went for your run the other day. I didn't realize it at the time, but they were considering me for board membership, and they offered me the position. They asked me what salary I wanted, and I initially gave myself a ten-percent increase. They chuckled and suggested doubling my current salary, along with other benefits. So, it's a good thing we're dining at Deanne's Place tonight. I have some good news."

John and Kate's eyes welled up with tears, and Kate struggled to express her words as she said, "Honey, we're so proud of you. We always knew this day would come for you, and we believe you'll rise even higher. We see you every day and know what you're made of. You've been astonishing us every single day."

John added, "Ever since you were in high school, I could see how hard you worked and the uncommon common sense you possessed. When you set your mind on something, you poured your heart and soul into it until you achieved your goal. Your mom recognized all of this the day you were born. I thoroughly enjoyed watching you accomplish every milestone. I'm ecstatic that your company saw the same potential in you that we see every day."

Katelin and Jane both had tears in their eyes, and Katelin said with a smile, "Jane, you know they're biased because I'm their daughter."

Jane simply smiled, gave her a hug, and then, as the waiter approached the table, remarked, "Well, this will certainly be a dinner I'll never forget. I suppose we should order."

After placing their orders, the dinner turned out to be exceptional. When everyone finished their meal and dessert, they stood up to leave. As John, Kate, and Jane rose from their seats, applause filled the room. The presence of the press and the awareness of their important work resulted in an appreciative response. Katelin smiled and leaned over to Jane, whispering, "Isn't this fun? People are truly proud of everything you guys are doing for the world. Please keep them safe."

As John and Kate prepared to enter the limo, they turned to Katelin and asked if she would be joining them. She wore a big grin and replied, "I told you about my new job, and one of the benefits is having a limo, driver, and security."

John, Kate, and Jane smiled and shook their heads. Jane then chimed in, "I'll gladly take you up on your offer for a limo ride. I took an Uber to get here today."

Kate added, "Hop in; we can give you a lift to your house."

When Kate and John arrived home, it was very late, so they decided not to set the alarm and simply sleep as long as possible. They peeked into Katelin's room, and she raised her head, saying, "Your favorite daughter is home. I don't have anything to do tomorrow, so don't wake me up."

The Sixty-Fifth Day

Quality Time with Katelin and Addressing a Serious Matter

J ohn and Kate woke up at 7 a.m. but decided to stay in bed and sleep a little longer. The moon landing and the seven astronauts' arrival weren't scheduled until the end of the week, so they had some time before needing to focus on that. They also expected to announce the earthquake partnership soon, but they knew those discussions could wait until Monday. They had asked Valerie to schedule meetings for 9 a.m. to discuss the space launch and the earthquake partnership.

They also decided to review the Medical, Storm, and Climate projects since they hadn't received updates on them in a while. Kate and John grew slightly concerned about their weekend being interrupted if there were any issues with these projects. However, just as they were about to go back to sleep, the phone rang. It was the Space Project Leader, and his tone sounded grave. He informed them that four of the astronauts had fallen ill and were unlikely to recover before the planned launch on Friday. While they had two backup astronauts available, none of them had the expertise in propulsion systems required to guide the large space station.

Kate immediately suggested, "All of the astronauts were supposed to be in town on Sunday. We need to schedule a meeting on Sunday night after they all arrive. Please ask Valerie to set everything up. We will proceed with the Space Launch on Tuesday as planned. Keep the two astronauts isolated and monitor everyone who had contact with them."

The U.S. Space Leader responded. "Thank you, Kate. Everyone was counting on making this happen. I will work with Valerie to arrange the meeting and inform you of the time and location."

After hanging up, Kate turned to John and said, "It looks like we might be going into space ourselves. We're not going to let a couple of people catching colds stop us."

John smiled and patted Kate on the back, saying, "We can do it. We keep ourselves in good shape, and I know you've been craving some excitement. We know how to operate all the equipment since we were involved in the design process. I can already imagine how disappointed those four astronauts will be. We just need to get Jim's approval."

Kate smiled back at John and said, "That's why I love you so much. You're just as crazy as I am. I think we'll tell Jim about this after our Sunday meeting. I believed he had plans with his whole family today. Let's not disturb his weekend until Sunday night, when we have all the facts."

John looked at Kate, returning her smile, and said, "I can't go back to sleep. Should we get up and do our 2.5 hours of exercise, or try something different?"

Kate suggested doing something different, and they made love that morning, savoring their time together. They stayed in bed, cuddling, until around noon, when they finally decided to get up. John started preparing breakfast, and Kate went into Katelin's room, waking her up with the news, "It's already noon! Dad is making your favorite breakfast—potatoes, eggs, toast, and coffee."

Katelin always woke up with a smile on her face, and today was no different. She responded, "Great! My favorite breakfast with my favorite people—what's going on? The phone has been ringing. What's up?"

Kate looked at her daughter with a smile and said, "You'll be the first to hear both the good and bad news. We'll tell you over breakfast."

John saw his two favorite ladies entering the kitchen and couldn't help but exclaim, "Wow! I'm a lucky guy. Two of my favorite people; if you guys get the coffee, I'll finish breakfast."

During breakfast, John and Kate shared their idea with Katelin, who responded in the same manner they had when discussing it with each other—she thought they were crazy, but that's why she loved them so much.

After finishing breakfast, John and Kate asked Katelin if she would join them for exercise, assuring her they would go at a slow pace. She agreed, and they all changed into their running clothes. Two security guards who would follow them in a car around the compound greeted them as they opened the front door. While running, Katelin informed her parents that the doctor had been calling her and asking for a date. Kate then suggested, "Tell him you'll agree if it's a double date at Deanne's Place tonight."

John grumbled a bit, but Katelin said, "I'll call him now since I'm running with my cell phone to keep track of my running parameters on my smartwatch."

She looked up Dr. Jim Asher's number in her contacts; she knew he would answer as it was his private cell phone number. Dr. Asher picked her up, recognizing Katelin's name on his screen, and greeted her, "Hello, Katelin. How's my favorite patient? How are you feeling?"

Katelin replied, "How's my favorite doctor? I'm doing fine; I'm actually exercising with my parents. Don't worry! They're going slow with me. The reason I called is to ask if you'd like to be my date on a double date with my parents at Deanne's Place tonight around 7 p.m."

He responded quickly, "Absolutely, I'm in. Should I pick you up, or should we just meet there?"

Katelin chuckled slightly but quickly replied, "We'll meet you there."

Kate had a big smile on her face and clapped. John was not as happy as his wife, but he loved his daughter so much that he smiled and put his arm around Katelin and Jim.

John glanced at his watch, realizing that their exercise routine had taken three hours, and gestured back towards the house, indicating that they needed to head back home. They always enjoyed sitting in a couple of chairs after their run to discuss whatever was on their minds. Upon arriving home, they informed the security personnel of their plans for the evening so they could inform Katelin's security detail and contact Deanne's Place.

By the time they had showered and gotten ready for dinner, it was almost 6 p.m. John took only a few minutes to prepare, as he always wore the same casual outfit. Kate and Katelin, on the other hand, took their time selecting the right dresses and applying their makeup. John was sitting and watching TV when they entered his room, and he immediately stood up. Kate smiled and gave him a hug, sensing his joy at going out with two beautiful people who took his breath away. He was incredibly happy.

John remembered numerous occasions when they would go out together, and heads would turn to catch a second glimpse of them—tonight would be no different. It was amusing how women would approach Kate, complimenting her on something—a fact he would always bring up during their outings. There was never a time when she didn't receive a compliment. He would always express gratitude and tell the ladies that they had made Kate's day because her happiness brought him immense joy, and he could see that those compliments truly made her happy.

When they arrived at the restaurant, they discovered Jim Asher already seated at the table and surrounded by security personnel. As soon as he saw Katelin, Jim stood up and put his arm around her, telling her she looked beautiful and expressing his gratitude for her call. She simply smiled, and the four of them took their seats at the table.

Jim Asher initiated the conversation, saying, "I can always tell when you're coming because your security always arrives before you. But this time, I noticed security in different uniforms as well."

Katelin smiled and replied, "That's my fault. I got a promotion at work and now serve on the board, which comes with certain benefits, including additional security. I suppose one of the board members was kidnapped, and they don't want a repeat of that incident."

Jim Asher chuckled and jokingly remarked, "I feel very safe."

John, in a slightly upset tone, interjected to show his discontent with the comment, "We're very proud of our daughter."

"Okay, guys, we're here to have a good time. Please be nice to each other," Katelin said with a hint of irritation.

Kate, trying to calm the situation, added, "Both of you are incredibly successful individuals, and John and I are proud of both of you. Jim, these are challenging times, and while things may improve, there have been attempts on our lives. So we have to be cautious."

Jim Asher shook his head and said, "I'm so happy to see that Katelin is recovering faster than most people who have been shot. She was in good shape to begin with, which explains the quicker recovery. Given her new responsibilities, I want to review her schedule and ensure she doesn't rush into her new job too quickly."

John and Kate both smiled appreciatively, and John thanked Jim, saying, "Thank you, Jim. It's something I worry about every day because I know my daughter. If you let her, she'll work twenty-four hours a day, seven days a week."

"I won't allow that. She'll be in my office once a week until she's fully healed. By the way, Katelin, I received a call from the doctor at your company asking about your health, and I gave you a clean bill of health. I need you to maintain that," Jim Asher replied sternly.

Kate then said, her eyes welling up with tears, "Thank you, Jim. We're counting on you and Katelin to ensure she stays healthy. She can handle any job. That's who Katelin is. Whatever she sets her mind to, she accomplishes. Not many people can say that about someone. We've seen her move to Tokyo with us. She joined a rifle team in the U.S. and asked the American School in Japan (ASIJ) if they had a rifle team. They said no, but she insisted on forming one. Within a month, ASIJ had a rifle team, and Katelin had girls performing at games. Then she expressed her desire to model while in Tokyo, and within a month, her picture was on magazine covers and subway banners. Whatever she wants to do, she makes it happen. That's why John and I always say she can do anything she wants. We've witnessed it firsthand. You know you're a lucky guy."

Katelin chimed in, "You know, they're biased because I'm their daughter."

John, his eyes moistened with tears, responded, "She always says that, but what Kate said is true. She's the youngest person on her board because they see what we see every day. It's our joy to be around her. She's special, and we need to keep her safe."

"You can count on me, sir. You guys have done a good job, and I can see that whenever I see her," Jim said, reassuring Katelin's parents.

Katelin, tears glistening in her eyes, added, "Okay, guys, I know you love me. And Jim, just so I can get you back, I want a double date with your parents so I can experience what you're going through."

Laughter filled the air as Katelin had a knack for making things happen. Her smile was contagious, and when she laughed, everyone couldn't help but join in. They all enjoyed a fantastic dinner, and when the bill arrived, the doctor offered to pay. However, John insisted on covering the expenses as long as they dined together. It was something he had become accustomed to whenever he took Katelin and her friends out, and he would continue doing it for the rest of his life.

Jim understood, thanked him and Kate, and reassured them once again that Katelin would be safe with him because he genuinely cared for her. Kate smiled at his words, while John wore a look that said, "I'll believe it when I see it," yet he smiled at Jim and shook his head.

Katelin informed John and Kate that she would have Jim take her back to the compound, and they agreed. John knew her security detail would be following them.

On the way home, Kate and John discussed Jim, both expressing their positive opinions of him. They believed he was a great guy, and John always trusted Katelin's judgment on everything. Kate had a particular fondness for him, not only because he was nice but also because he resembled Ryan Gosling.

John and Kate knew they had a significant day ahead of them. Checking their calendars, they noticed a meeting scheduled for 9 a.m. on Sunday with all the astronauts, the Space Leadership Team, and the other Space Leaders from different countries. They understood that the timing had been arranged to accommodate Russia and China, ensuring they wouldn't have to stay up all night for the call.

They also left a brief message with Valerie, asking her to schedule a meeting with Jim on Monday morning to address an issue that had arisen over the weekend and needed resolution. They advised her to deliver the message late on Sunday, so as not to interrupt his weekend.

As they settled into bed, aware they needed to be at work by 9 a.m., they set their alarm for 6 a.m. and planned to go for a short run to ensure they made it in time for the meeting. They also confirmed with Katelin that she was home so they could inform her of their plans.

Morning Relaxation and a Big Meeting Ahead

J ohn and Kate woke up at 6 a.m., went for a quick run, got dressed, and arrived at the West Wing by 9 a.m., where Valerie was getting into the process of setting up the meeting. All the astronauts and the U.S. Space Leadership Team, along with the other Space Leaders from various countries, are joining via video conference.

John commenced the meeting by explaining the purpose of the gathering and inviting suggestions on how to handle the situation with the four ill astronauts. The Russian and Chinese representatives brought up the fact that Kate and John were the only ones capable of taking the astronauts' place, as they had the necessary expertise to operate the controls.

John and Kate were prepared for this discussion and informed everyone that they would check with their respective bosses to see if they could fulfill the mission. If given the green light, they would be honored to be part of the first flight using the new propulsion system. The room erupted in cheers, and a few more topics were discussed before they decided to reconvene at 10 a.m. on Monday. This would provide an opportunity for everyone to confirm with their superiors and ensure that they were on board with the plan. They shared that they had already received approval and that everyone believed the mission would be safer with them at the controls.

John and Kate instructed Valerie to schedule a meeting with Jim at 9 a.m. and inform him that they needed his approval for something important. They also suggested reserving some time for Jim to speak with the President, estimating that about fifteen minutes would suffice.

Valerie efficiently arranged everything, never encountering any difficulty in getting John and Kate on anyone's calendar. People always wanted to meet with them, and the interactions were always positive.

After the meeting, John and Kate returned to the compound to continue their exercise routine. When they reached Katelin's room, they found her still in bed. They asked if she wanted to join them in their activities, just like on Saturday. She agreed to have potatoes and eggs for breakfast and exercise with them, but declined another fancy dinner like the previous night. Instead, she suggested having a cozy pizza night at home. They all agreed, and John started preparing the potatoes and eggs while Kate brewed the coffee.

John couldn't help but notice Katelin's constant smiling and admiring gaze directed towards Kate. He decided to capture the moment on camera this time, as it was something he would cherish throughout his life. Witnessing the love between a mother and daughter was a beautiful sight to behold.

In public, Kate used to get too close to Katelin, prompting Katelin to playfully say, "Stop it; everyone will think we're gay!" Kate would often wrap her arm around her or hold her hand.

John knew he was a fortunate man, and while lost in his thoughts, Kate interrupted, saying, "John, finish the potatoes and eggs; we're hungry. The coffee and toast are ready. Sit down and join us."

John looked at Katelin and, with a smile, said, "I don't say this about many guys you're dating, but Dr. Jim Asher isn't too bad."

Kate glanced at John and chuckled, "You don't say, John. Do you think he would be suitable for your daughter? Can you trust him with her? Is there anyone you trust?"

John, with a smile but a serious tone, responded, "Yes, there are two people I trust wholeheartedly, and that's you and Katelin!"

Kate and Katelin felt immense pride upon hearing those words, as they knew he truly meant them. Kate had saved his life numerous times, and he knew Katelin would do the same.

After breakfast, they stepped outside, and this time the guards were aware they would be running. Four guards joined them as they jogged around the compound, eventually making their way to the gym for some yoga and sauna time. After about 2.5 hours of exercise, John announced, "Okay, now the fun begins. Let's refuel by ordering pizza for an early dinner. We have a big day tomorrow and important meetings ahead."

They informed the guards that they would be running at 6 a.m. and needed to be at work by 9 a.m. for their meeting with Jim. Katelin had to communicate the same to her guards and arrange for the limo service, although she would skip the exercise this time.

John and Kate wanted to stay in shape in case they received approval to go to the moon. They wanted to be prepared for any upcoming missions.

Big Meetings and... What's Next?

J ohn and Kate woke up at 6 a.m., went for a quick run, got dressed, and arrived at the West Wing at 9 a.m. It felt like Groundhog Day. They were scheduled to meet with Jim in his office, feeling a sense of déjà vu. They explained the problem to him and shared the suggestions made by the Russians and Chinese regarding their potential involvement in the space mission.

Jim chuckled and said, "Instead of you two, can I go? I've always wanted to go into space. I can't afford to lose both of you."

Kate spoke up and replied, "Jim, the astronauts who are sick are the ones we trained on the controls. We are the only ones who know how to operate them. One of us will be responsible for the controls on the moon, while the other will handle the controls while orbiting the Earth."

Jim responded, "I don't want one of you circling the moon for a month, and I don't want one of you landing on the moon's surface. Both of you can fly to the moon and back, and then return to Earth together. If you can guarantee that neither of you will be the one landing on the moon and that both of you will fly back while the two space stations continue circling the moon and Earth, I think I can convince the President. Let's call him now."

They made the call, and the President agreed with Jim's approach, recognizing that John and Kate were the only individuals who understood how to work the controls, apart from the sick astronauts. The President granted approval pending agreement from the Russians and Chinese.

During the 10 a.m. meeting, John announced, "We have received the green light to join you all on this mission."

A resounding cheer erupted in the conference room as everyone acknowledged the increased safety that John and Kate's presence would bring. They had trained the astronauts on the controls and now planned to accompany them on the mission. Jim could hear the cheer and knew he had made the right decision. However, he couldn't shake his worry, aware that missions often presented unexpected challenges. With numerous components and new parts involved, there was always the potential for things to go awry.

John and Kate canceled all the meetings they had scheduled for the day and the rest of the week. They needed to be fitted for space uniforms and wanted to review all the details with the ground crew and their fellow astronauts.

As the sun set, everyone knew precisely what their roles would be on this mission. John and Kate put the entire team through one of the most rigorous reviews they had ever experienced. The crew respected the thoroughness of the process, understanding that it could save their lives if any problems arose.

John and Kate realized they would have to stay with the other astronauts at the base that night, so they called Katelin to update her on the situation. She informed them that she had already heard everything on the news. Katelin expressed her pride in them and wished them well. She reassured them not to worry about her, as she would be staying at the compound. However, she had been invited by the President to attend the launch, and he had made transportation and security arrangements for her.

John and Kate found it difficult to sleep but managed to get a few hours of rest. They headed to the gym at the site for a little exercise before joining the other astronauts for breakfast. The launch was scheduled for 9 a.m., ensuring it could be broadcast at a suitable hour in China and Russia.

Departure from Earth to Landing on the Moon

S eeing the massive Space Station all packed up and ready to be sent into space was a breathtaking sight. Jim and Katelin, together with the President and the leaders of Congress and the Senate, visited the astronauts in their hotel room the night before launch.

They asked to speak with John and Kate. When they arrived, they had to wait a few feet away from the door. With an earnest look, the President said, "It takes a couple of remarkable people like the both of you to inspire all of this. People are aware of your struggles to revive the Medical Project and the Storm and Climate Project, both of which occurred at a time when there were attempts on your life. What you have done has earned the admiration of people worldwide. Have a safe journey."

People clapped and applauded from a safe distance, aware that they could not approach them due to the risk of bacteria.

John and Kate smiled at each other and said in unison, "Thank you, Mr. President, and all of you for supporting us."

When they looked back, they saw the other astronauts standing not far behind them; they exchanged pleasant nods and smiles.

The eight astronauts arrived at the Space Station a few minutes later. Everyone on the space station settled into their designated seats and fastened their seat belts. John and Kate were operating onboard and chatting with the launch crew.

The ground crew and John and Kate were on the same page about how things functioned. When applying electromagnetic force, it was like two magnets repelling each other. In order for the Space Station to take off and soar straight up, John, communicating with the ground crew, had to apply this force in exactly the proper way.

A gigantic space station began to rise from the ground as John and the ground crew began to power it, but no rockets could be seen. A universal sense of awe and wonderment was all that could be heard. The space station had already begun to depart Earth's atmosphere and was rapidly disappearing from view. With the help of the personnel on the ground, John cranked up the Space Station's engines to their utmost, and it began its direct course for the moon at a rate of speed unprecedented among rockets.

There was plenty of room for everyone on the Space Station to stand up and take a stroll. It had spacious common areas, six private bedrooms, and two fully stocked kitchens with sufficient food, depending on the astronauts' regular diets back on Earth. It would be possible to divide the space stations in half. Both parts would have three bedrooms and a kitchen.

The air purification and oxygen levels were easily customizable through climatic devices. In addition, a warning light would activate if anything approached the Space Station, and if the crew deemed it necessary, they might destroy the object.

Solar and stellar energy provided all of the electricity for the Space Station. In order to complete a circumlunar orbit around the moon, the Space Station would use its jets to slow down as it approached the satellite. Everyone got a thirty-minute notice to buckle up in case John had to assume manual control and a warning light went on. Everything went off without a hitch, and John didn't even have to take the helm. The Space Station resumed its predetermined course around the Moon.

On the Space Station, there was a spacecraft that could hold three astronauts. It would work similarly to the Space Station but also have its own propulsion system if needed. It was already agreed that the U.S. government did not want John or Kate to land on the moon. However, everyone agreed that one person from each country would land on the moon. Hence, a Russian, a Chinese, and a U.S. astronaut boarded the spacecraft. John and the U.S. pilot had been trained to slowly eject the spacecraft from the Space Station. As the spacecraft approached the moon's surface, the magnet power was reversed to slow it down. Everyone, including the astronauts, rejoiced when the spacecraft touched down safely.

Each astronaut then planted their national flag in addition to the unified flag, gathered samples from the moon's surface, snapped photographs, and returned to the spacecraft. At the precise instant that the Space Station was closest to the spacecraft, power was applied. The Space Station in the spacecraft was drawn like metal is drawn to a magnet. As the spacecraft approached the Space Station, its speed was reduced in preparation for docking.

They did not need to employ the spacecraft's new propulsion system because the takeoff worked similarly to the liftoff on Earth, only in reverse. Once more, the world erupted in joy.

The plan now is to split the Space Station into two parts. One would continue circling the moon and have two astronauts stay on that Space Station. The primary objective was to test the new propulsion technology and return home. The three astronauts who landed on the moon would be stationed on that Space Station indefinitely.

After completing their experiments, the three astronauts from each country would return to the launch site in the United States, where John and Kate would land in the other spacecraft. Then the Space Station would be brought down to the launch pad.

The Sixty-Ninth Day

John and Kate's Return to Earth

Everything worked as planned when the Space Station returned to Earth. John and Kate hugged the Chinese, Russian, and American astronauts orbiting the Earth. Then they got into the spacecraft attached to this Space Station. Over the U.S. launch site, the spacecraft began to get sucked into the launch pad's magnets, bringing it into Earth's atmosphere. John and the ground crew adjusted the power so the spacecraft landed softly.

Once again, everyone observed the landing with amazement since they were used to hearing rocket parachutes. Everyone rejoiced when they landed, even the astronauts orbiting the moon and Earth. It was a tremendous success. John and Kate could now add *"astronauts"* to their résumés.

The President, the heads of Congress and the Senate, and Katelin were there to greet them. Even though they had to spend the night on the base to ensure their safety, they were in continuous touch with Katelin, planning for dinner at Deanne's Place after they could get off quarantine.

While in quarantine, John and Kate stayed in contact with the three astronauts circling the moon and the three astronauts circling the Earth. They discussed their plans for coming home.

The plan was for the three astronauts circling the moon to stay there for one month, land the 4000-square-foot Space Station on the moon, and take the spacecraft home, or maintain the Space Station in orbit around the moon and return home.

There was enough food, beverage, and oxygen to last for half a century, which is a lifetime for each astronaut. The goal of establishing a Space Station community on the moon is to eventually grow to include many outposts.

Since landing the Space Station on the moon remotely was possible at any moment and did not require these three astronauts, they would be returning to Earth in one month. The crew of six would first return to Earth by docking with the orbiting space station before returning home in the spacecraft.

John and Kate used all the time in quarantine to help the six astronauts. They also had Zoom calls with the World Leaders of the Space, Storm, Climate, Earthquake, and Medical Projects. They were astonished when they were told they would have dinner with the President and Jim. While in quarantine, they pondered how this would play out.

Right around 7:30 a.m., a cart with Kate's vegetables and John's steak and salmon was wheeled into their dining room. There were two TVs wheeled into the room. When the TVs were turned on, there were the President and Jim in the White House dining room with Valerie and Natalie, who set everything up. The President told Kate and John to pour themselves a glass of wine. Then the President made a toast, thanking John and Kate for another successful mission. There was some discussion about the trip they made in space, but the President and Jim wanted to save some serious discussion for after the meal was over. The President did bring up the need for a Press Conference on Friday since everyone wants to hear about the Space Project.

The President then spoke gravely about a serious issue, saying, "We are being warned that countries are trying to duplicate what we are doing on the Space Project. They know we are using magnetism. What should we do about that?"

Kate, equally in a solemn tone, continued, "Mr. President, we just had a meeting with the Worldwide Space Leadership Team. They won't try to steal or replicate what we have since they know we're making it available to them, and it would be too expensive for them to make duplicates. More than half of the controls currently used on the spacecraft and Stations are programmed. It is impossible to duplicate and steal that software because it is heavily guarded. We've made it clear that we'll launch whatever they want into space for a reasonable price, so there's no point in them spending money trying to duplicate it. Also, they know we are not using anything we have for war. The Space Leader will explain this to their country leaders. If there is a specific country that you'd like John and I to speak with, we'll explain to them why it's impossible to replicate what we have done. As the Space Project has progressed, so has the intelligence of our computer software. All the Projects share a similar backstory."

The President remarked in a somber tone, "We also have countries that are trying to duplicate the solution in the Storm Project and stop storms."

John said, "Again, the solution is patented, but even if they steal the patent, why would they want to do this? All they have to do is tell us which storm they wish to stop, and we can do it for less money than it would cost them to halt the storm themselves and steal the solution."

Jim said, "I think I am seeing a trend happening here for both the earthquake and the remaining Medical Projects. We provide the lowest prices in the industry while using more advanced and sophisticated tools. Not only that, but we are not hiding anything. We're letting everyone use the Medical Project Application and letting them know when and where the next earthquake will hit. As the number of people using the application grows, its intelligence improves, so everyone who agrees to use it will reap benefits."

"You got it, Jim. We are sharing what we have, so it doesn't make sense for someone to duplicate it. In all cases, they will not be able to duplicate it. We are open to working with them like China has if they can add anything of value to our partnership. Much like how Russia and China collaborated to construct the 8,000-square-foot Space Station,"

Kate said in a humorous tone.

The President said appreciatively, "This is why you are our leaders. I usually feel better after finishing a conversation with you three. Thank you both for having dinner with me. How is the quarantine going? After you're released from quarantine, please schedule a press conference. Take tomorrow off and hold it on Friday. Everyone wants to see you both."

Kate responded gratefully, "Thank you for asking about our health. We are both doing fine. At the press conference on Friday, Valerie and Natalie will have the astronauts circling the moon and Earth present. In addition, we need global leaders to discuss each initiative and spread the word that we are giving back to the community by sharing our resources. Also, if you can, try to have it around 9 a.m. so that China and Russia may broadcast it to their respective populations and everyone can see it."

Jim and the President nodded their agreement to Valerie and Natalie, signaling that they should move forward with making it happen.

The meeting ended, the TV turned off, and John and Kate high-fived each other. The two then decided to grab an early night so they could rush home to meet Katelin first thing in the morning.

Rest Day and a Surprise Dinner Invitation

F irst thing in the morning, Kate and John were driven back to their compound home in a guarded vehicle. Katelin had already left for work and left a note saying that she would be happy to join them for supper at 7:30 p.m. that night at Deanne's Place.

John and Kate decided to go on a long walk since they both felt the urge to work up a good sweat. They donned sauna gear and went for a run, stopping after an hour to sweat it out and then continuing for another hour. They performed some yoga in the sauna, did a little swimming, and then headed back home. They really needed it, despite their exhaustion.

They got into the shower together and made love. Day by day, John and Kate's affection for one another grew. They feel great and have each other's backs, so they are never afraid, even though they risk their lives every day to make the world a better place.

Since they were anticipating a hearty meal for supper, they instead brewed some cold coffee when they first got home. Anything cold after a strenuous workout always tastes better.

Just as they were about to relax in bed and watch some TV, the phone rang. It was Jim. They always pick up when Jim calls, since it is usually something terrible.

Jim was in a great mood and positively said, "Hey guys, I know when

I call in, it is usually a crisis that needs to be solved, but this time, it is just about having dinner. The President and I had nothing planned for the day, and both our wives were attending a ladies' event, so we both thought it would be great to have dinner with a couple of astronauts. Can you both come to the White House for dinner at 7:30 p.m.?"

Kate looked at John, and they both smiled and nodded. Kate answered the phone cheerfully: "We had planned to have dinner with Katelin. Can we bring her along?"

With a smile on his face, Jim responded, "Yes, bring her. All of you have top-secret clearance, and she knows the rules about not sharing anything we discuss. Why don't you try to make it here by 7:30 p.m.?"

John replied positively, "She knows the rules, and I will remind her. We appreciate the invitation and your consideration. It should be fun."

John and Kate were so proud of Katelin that they couldn't wait to tell her. Whenever they could get her to meet influential people, it made her grow. Kate took up the phone and enthusiastically told Katelin, "We are all going to the White House for dinner. The President and Jim wanted to have dinner with two astronauts and their daughters, and you're invited if you promise not to tell anybody about what you will hear tonight. You can come straight from work in your work clothes. Tonight will be a lot of fun, and we promise not to embarrass you or brag about how great you are. Everyone will be talking about their daughters if we do that."

Katelin said, "Thank you for thinking of me. It will be exciting. I believe they really wanted to talk with both of you. You two have a way of making people feel at ease, and that's a skill that some people in high positions need."

John sarcastically stated, "Now that you are on the board of your company, you would know these things."

Katelin knew what he was doing, so she said, "Daddy, stop, please! See you at 7:30 p.m."

John and Kate marveled at their daughter's resemblance to both of them in the sense that Katelin also dislikes it when people discuss her.

John questioned Kate in a grave tone, "What do you think we will be asked at this dinner? Do you think they'll be interested in hearing about the news conference we'll be holding the next day, or perhaps the progress being made on our other projects?"

Kate speculated, "It can be any or all of that, but we are both good at responding to any question, so I am not worried."

John just looked at Kate, nodded his head, and smiled, saying, "You're right!"

Kate and John unwind for the rest of the day. The two then began preparing for the White House dinner, and as John watched Kate put on a beautiful black skirt with some pearls, he couldn't help but be amazed at how beautiful she looked and how lucky he was to have her. Kate saw his gaze and turned to him, saying, "Put your eyes back in your head. We don't have time for that. Hurry up and get dressed."

They were parked outside the White House and decided to call Katelin to see if she could get off work in time to make the dinner. When Katelin answered the phone, Kate said, "We are at the gate to the White House, and the dinner is supposed to start in about fifteen minutes. Where are you?"

Katelin chuckled and said, "Turn around. We're in the car behind you with my security. By the way, my security and driver are very impressed."

John and Kate both laughed when she hung up the phone. The President and Jim were informed that John and Kate had arrived, and they went out to welcome them, saying, "Welcome; it is not often we get to greet a husband-and-wife team that not only traveled on the biggest Space Station ever but were in on the design of it."

From that moment on, John and Kate exchanged puzzled looks, then smiled at each other, knowing they were in for an unexpected surprise. Katelin arrived in the dining room after Jim and the President. They were greeted with cheers and applause as they entered the dining room, which was full of their former professors, friends, and current coworkers, like all the Jane Meadows and some of the U.S. Project Leaders, as well as members of the press.

The President told everyone to grab a drink and said with a big smile, "We know we could not surprise you unless you were in space or quarantine, but everyone wanted to do something special for both of you. We must turn in your daughter because she helped us with this surprise. You both have helped many people from all across the world, but these are just a few that are so proud of what you have accomplished together. They also knew you'd be happy with the role you played in their accomplishment. Because you and your partner care deeply about doing good for others and the world."

"You might want to catch up with some of these people you haven't seen since grade school," the President suggested.

John and Kate's youth was captured beautifully in several stunning photographs. It is impressive to see how close they were before they actually met.

"You will both have fun looking at some of these photos and talking with your friends," the President commented.

He added, "You will also recognize some of these people since they are working on Space, Earthquake, Climate, Storm, and Medical Projects. I know some of the people you brought over to work on these projects with you. In some cases, you went to college with them, and in other cases, you worked with them on numerous projects in the past. It is an incredible privilege to be around such brilliant individuals who invent and make things happen. I'm sure there have been instances where both of your lives have been saved by the other. There is one thing that never fails to occur. Whenever someone's project ends, Jim and I get calls from them because they want to be transferred to your group. It comes as no surprise that John and Kate rank first in the country in our latest opinion poll. People clearly like working for you.

"Since you have received many awards from the United States, we thought it would be nice to provide you with a keepsake that you can display proudly in your home. This vase was painted by a famous artist, and I hope you will remember this special day every time you look at it. Well, enough of me talking; let's raise a glass to John and Kate and give them the floor for the rest of this conference."

There was a lot of rejoicing and applause. Even the President gave a round of applause before taking a seat. After thanking the President, Jim, and their daughter for the wonderful surprise, John and Kate got up. They began introducing themselves to everyone at the table by pointing to them and giving their names, where they had met them previously, and a few words about how they had benefited them. Because maintaining contact required so much effort, they made sure to get everyone's contact information before the conference ended. For John and Kate, this will go down as one of the happiest days of their lives.

Everyone had a great dinner once the conversation had died down. It was a late night filled with hearty toasts and stimulating conversation. When the celebration ended and everyone went home, Katelin told her driver and security detail to come get her the next morning at 8 a.m. because she was going to stay the night at her parents' house.

Fitness Routine and a Major Press Conference

J ohn and Kate knew they had one of their biggest press conferences today. The Space Project, along with the other projects, would be discussed. It would be broadcast at 9 a.m. to ensure maximum global coverage. On days like this, they liked to run to dinner, discuss the press conference, have breakfast, and then run back home. Since they were now residing on the compound and there was no dinner, they got up early to get in approximately 2.5 hours of jogging and sauna.

Every morning at 5 a.m., they would get out of bed and sprint to the gym, where they would then turn on the sauna, run for a while, and finally return to the sauna to do yoga. Today, nothing went according to plan. When they arrived at the gym at around 6 a.m., they found Katelin at a table they had set up there. Five or so booths near the windows featured jukeboxes. It even had the same menu as their diner. After hearing that the gym planned to open a restaurant and the diner had expansion plans, Katelin stepped in and put the two businesses together.

When they entered, Katelin rose to greet them and urged them to sit down, adding that she had already turned on some of their favorite country music. John and Kate could not believe what they were seeing. Looking at Katelin, they both nearly said simultaneously, "We love you! We are really lucky to have you as our daughter."

John responded, smirking, "You are certainly something. First, the dinner last night and then today's breakfast; you have done well!"

Kate said, "No wonder you are on the board at your company. You like to make people happy, and you are doing a good job."

After John and Kate sat down with Katelin, he stated, "Same rules apply. You cannot talk to anyone about what we discuss at this table. Kate, I suppose we should start by asking the Russian astronaut currently circling the moon to say a few words about the mission. Next, we will have the Chinese astronaut orbiting the Earth share his thoughts with us. We must have Valerie warn them of our impending action. Then we can ask if anyone else has any other comments or questions."

John added, "Once they are done, we can switch to the Climate Project and see if Russia can give an update on Ukraine. Then we may switch to the Earthquake Project and get up-to-date information from Japan and China. I have not heard any updates on the Storm Project since we ended the cyclone in Taiwan. We can also request updates on that matter. They are now using barges rather than rockets. The oldest Project should have some good statistics. Let's alert whoever keeps track of the data that we're interested in knowing which country has had the greatest reduction in its medical problems."

After the discussion, John, Kate, and Katelin were ready to head home. When they finished showering and getting dressed, the two automobiles with security took them off to work. Around 8:30 a.m. in the morning, John and Kate arrived at the office and proceeded straight to the conference room. Jim and the President were also present, and they were given a rundown of the evening's events.

All agreed on how the press conference would be organized, and the President said, "Let me know when you are ready to announce the next project you want to work on. For this, a simple update would be appreciated; nevertheless, I am frequently asked who poses the biggest threat regarding war and the bombing of any city in the world. I have no doubt that you are diligently trying to solve the issue."

John and Kate just smiled, and John said, "We will give you and

Jim an update on that after this press conference."

When John and Kate entered the press room, the TVs were switched on, revealing the astronauts orbiting the moon and Earth. All the leaders and their presidents became visible. It was indeed a worldwide press conference. Members of the press from all around the world were present, and the others were in their respective countries' press rooms.

The applause lasted for a couple of minutes, and then the U.S. President thanked all the leaders and presidents worldwide. He then turned the meeting over to John and Kate.

John got the other astronauts to talk as planned, then described when the other astronauts would be coming home. A loud cheer went up when the Space Leaders finished.

When the Storm Project Leader reported that no major storms had occurred since the project's inception, another round of applause erupted. After properly anticipating five earthquakes, they made the announcement that they could now anticipate when the next earthquake would occur.

The remainder of the press conference proceeded without a hitch, and when the Medical Project figures were shown later, showing a decrease in both fatalities and the emergence of new diseases, another round of applause erupted.

After the press conference, when the President, Jim, Kate, and John were returning to the conference room, there were cheers and applause all through the West Wing. No one else was invited to this meeting because of how sensitive it was. The President tasked John and Kate with investigating whether or not it was possible to ensure no one could ever set off a nuclear bomb capable of obliterating a major city like Chicago, New York, etc.

The President's main concern was not winning the war but preventing fatalities. At the outset of the meeting, Kate reiterated the mission once more. Then, in a serious tone, she said, "With all the earthquake sensors and climatic devices, along with our current radar around the world, it has helped us detect when any rockets with nuclear devices are being fired or being transported. Our computers can identify objects with the help of sensors and programs, but the trickier part is defusing the bomb without injuring anyone. If a rocket is fired and our current defense system detects it, we'll retaliate with twice as many, destroying both nations and killing billions of people in the process."

Kate turned to the Presided and continued, "Mr. President, you are familiar with our space stations, and we have a method of repelling any asteroids headed in their direction, much like an invisible screen that will not allow anything near it. We have developed a technique to detect incoming rockets, capture them, and then disable them in a safe location. If a country fires a thousand rockets, we need a location to store them, a way to disarm them, evidence of what that country was attempting to achieve, and an international agreement on punishment. That would also apply to the United States. We're close to running our final tests on the software and hardware that can accomplish this. However, we can't always wait for that because sometimes we need all the leaders of the world to agree on the punishment for the country that would try to launch a war. No one will shoot rockets or even carry them if they know they will be caught, so long as nations agree on the punishment and all countries know we have a method of preventing all nuclear weapons.

"In a week's time, everything will be tested and working. It is important that as soon as we confirm that everything works, we get an agreement on the punishment. We can't talk to anyone about this until it is tested, so people don't fire their rockets. Before we know it, everything, including figuring out who launched the rockets, is up and running. They may think they can destroy us, but in the long run, it will be impossible."

The President and Jim's eyes widened at the news, and the President exclaimed, "WOW! Let me know when everything is tested, and Jim and I will start making calls to all the country's leaders. Also, we will devise possible punishments for countries that try to start our next war. You two never fail to amaze me with the incredible ideas you come up with.

When all this is tested and we get our agreements, everyone concerned about war and the many deaths will feel much better. All of humanity's hopes and dreams for a peaceful world will finally be achieved."

John explained, "We are working with a small group of people around the world, and each person has top-secret clearance and does not know what they are working on. Kate and I, and now the both of you, are the only people who know the total picture. I will update you and let you know when everything can go live."

The President expressed, "Thank you, thank you, thank you!"

The President and Jim left the meeting room beaming, planning how they would tell the country's leaders about the good news as soon as they obtained approval from John and Kate.

John and Kate just stayed in the conference room, saying, "I guess we need to call Katelin and see if she can meet us at Deanne's Place for dinner. We need to celebrate something else, but we will not be able to disclose it to Katelin for a while. We will just tell her to wish for world peace."

www.ingramcontent.com/pod-product-compliance
Lightning Source LLC
Jackson TN
JSHW020012130125
77002JS00002B/5